Nineteen-year-old Yemisi Adeniji is a breathtakingly beautiful Nigerian woman who is attending San Jose State University when she meets Edukoya Adekunle, a widowed attorney who coincidentally also grew up in the Orissa Kingdom. Even though Yemisi is eventually headed back home to reside permanently with the man she married in a traditional ceremony prior to her departure, she and Edukoya fall in love. But what Yemisi does not realize is that Edukoya is harboring a secret.

After they eventually marry and have five children, Edukoya reveals that he is the crown prince of the Orissa Kingdom with vast real estate holdings under his control. When the death of his father brings him back home to ascend the throne, Edukoya designates Yemisi as the crown princess. As he transforms into a symbol of hope that his people can count on at a moment's notice, Princess Yemisi raises her five boys while caring for an entire kingdom. But when love pushes her to make a monumental mistake, she sets out down an unexpected path where many more challenges await.

In this fascinating tale, a beautiful Nigerian princess must overcome seemingly insurmountable obstacles as she struggles to balance the duties of her crown with her family responsibilities.

PRINCESS YEMISI ADEKUNLE

IJEOMA ONONUJU

BALBOA.PRESS
A DIVISION OF HAY HOUSE

Balboa Press books may be ordered through booksellers or by contacting:

Balboa Press
A Division of Hay House
1663 Liberty Drive
Bloomington, IN 47403
www.balboapress.com
844-682-1282

Because of the dynamic nature of the Internet, any web addresses or
links contained in this book may have changed since publication and
may no longer be valid. The views expressed in this work are solely those
of the author and do not necessarily reflect the views of the publisher,
and the publisher hereby disclaims any responsibility for them.

The author of this book does not dispense medical advice or prescribe the use
of any technique as a form of treatment for physical, emotional, or medical
problems without the advice of a physician, either directly or indirectly. The
intent of the author is only to offer information of a general nature to help
you in your quest for emotional and spiritual well-being. In the event you use
any of the information in this book for yourself, which is your constitutional
right, the author and the publisher assume no responsibility for your actions.

Any people depicted in stock imagery provided by Getty Images are
models, and such images are being used for illustrative purposes only.
Certain stock imagery © Getty Images.

Print information available on the last page.

ISBN: 978-1-9822-7380-4 (sc)
ISBN: 978-1-9822-7381-1 (hc)
ISBN: 978-1-9822-7379-8 (e)

Library of Congress Control Number: 2021918190

Balboa Press rev. date: 09/03/2021

CONTENTS

PART 5: AN INNOCENT FLIRTATION

PART 6: THE HONORABLE MADAM

PART 7: THE MIXED FRUIT BASKET

PART 8: DR. FELICIA ADEKUNLE, PHD

PART 9: THE LOVE LETTER

PART 10: GENEVA GETAWAY

PART 11: FUN WITH CHIKA

PART 12: LOVE AND THE INCREDIBLE SACRIFICE

PART 13: DEAR SISTER IYA IYABO

PART 14: HOPE AND OPTIMISM

PART 15: THE DEATH OF A KING

PART 16: THE KING'S WILL

ACKNOWLEDGEMENTS

I conceived writing this book in the summer of 1978, when a newly employed young girl, Ms. Yemisi, walked up to my desk and introduced herself to me. I was twenty-three years old. She said, "My name is Yemisi, and what about yours?" She extended both of her hands for a handshake, simultaneously. Arrogantly, I didn't respond to her inquisition with an answer. I just looked at her from head to toe, and briefly nodded my head. When she walked out, I ate myself alive. She was only being friendly, and the least I could do was politely accord her the same appreciation. She was friendly with everybody in the office except me. She stayed away from me, but with our eyes constantly crossing each other's path. She was beautiful and humble.

I reminisced about this Yoruba girl a great deal. Not to befriend her, but to conjoin her with another humble personality, then working at the same company, Edukoya. I married both personalities in my mind, just wonderful people. I wasn't their friend, a choice I gladly made, because it gave me an opportunity to observe them from a distance, these remarkable individuals was the birth of this novel.

The search began in earnest, in search of a girl from the Yoruba tribe who will more than adequately fulfill my vision of an exceptionally attractive Yoruba Princess, all in one, physically built, morally, and emotional attributes. She has to be extraordinarily pretty and humble. Years passed, about thirty-eight years in the making, until FaceBook presented to me, Ms. Ebisanmi Omolewa. This young lady made my dream come true. I could visualize her as a symbol, something extraordinary, and out of this world but real. I could write my book. She also agreed to be on the cover of this book.

Special thanks go to her. I will also seize this opportunity to thank my other friends, Cynthia Obodo, who represent Chika, Kelechi Emehara, who represent Felicia Adekunle, Chidimma Ononuju Ndubusi, who represent Ahunnaya Anumnachi, Ann Ononuju, who represent Iyabo, and Charity JBrown, who represents Charity.

PART 1

THE NIGERIAN LANDSCAPE

CHAPTER 1

In Lagos, Nigeria, the wealth of the handful of extremely rich families was amazing. All the lucrative landed properties at Ikoyi and Victoria Island were in the hands of a few wealthy families. They'd bought the land parcels about two hundred years earlier. The owners didn't sell the parcels of land outright; instead, they leased them. Each lease lasted between thirty and a hundred years. Their well-documented deeds said the land parcels and their developments would revert back to the original owners or to their next of kin upon the leases' expiration. However, the land parcels were developed, exchanged hands, and were released to third parties without due respect to the details in the original agreements. With massive developments, the land parcels bloomed in value and eventually were estimated to be worth more than $200 billion. The original landowners had assumed the developed lands would have relatively short leases and exchange hands multiple times, thereby earning the lessees enough to cover rent. The manifold returns on their original investments would discourage the lessees from holding on to the land parcels when the original leases expired, thereby allowing the lease agreements to be naturally terminated. There was no final payoff in growth value included in the enormous structures that later continued to improve the lands' values. Their growth values were talked about, but some of the original landowners were talked out of deals by relatively educated real estate agents who intentionally undervalued their foresight.

Most of the original owners of the land parcels were not educated. Few had attended elementary school, and most of them could barely read and write. Almost none of the original landowners were academically sophisticated enough to understand complicated long-term lease agreements, and they did not have the foresight to anticipate the huge surge in the future growth of the land parcels. To compound the landowners' mistakes further, most of the deeds were made out of handshakes and neighborly trust. Most of the agreements were not immediately written down and documented. Some of the handshake agreements were written after years had passed. This was a huge mistake, and it was left to the courts to sort out fair settlements and compensations for the original lessees who'd pioneered the growth of the land parcels as well as the original landowners.

The land parcels were largely leased in the nineteenth century. There was no country called Nigeria at that time. There were small kingdoms headed by kings called *kabiyesies*, which continued to exist later in modern-day Nigeria, when most of the agreements started expiring.

Kabiyesi Lawansin Adekunle I, being an educated man, used his education to his advantage. He had his own deeds written by a lawyer, Justice Johnson Adenipe, and approved by a high-court judge, Justice Edward Ogbolowomere. Justice Adenipe had not been called to the bench yet and was still a single lawyer working alone in his law chamber when he wrote the agreements for Kabiyesi Adekunle I. Lawyers were scarce in those days. There were no law firms, but there were law chambers. There were no typewriters then, but his handwriting was uniform.

The Lagos Mainland Courts had their hands full with the deed cases. They had their work cut out for them, especially because none of the original signers of the agreements were still alive, and the deeds hadn't addressed the anticipated future growth values of the structures on the land. The claimants were the grandchildren and great-grandchildren of the original signers of the deeds. To ease the problem, about a dozen lawyers put agreements together. Though the original lawyers had passed away and some of their law chambers had vanished as a result of their deaths, their uniform handwriting gave the court a sigh of relief in putting the pieces together.

Kabiyesi Adekunle I's grandson was Kabiyesi Edukoya Lawansin Adekunle III. Kabiyesi Adekunle I withheld 22 to 32 percent of the land development from the developers by making himself a copartner in the land developments. He came with the land, and his partners came with all the monies and managements to improve the land. He took a huge percentage cut in leasing his land parcels to the developers. In some cases, he leased the parcels for barely 5 percent of their worth. He leased some parcels for nothing and positioned himself as one of the controlling interests in the development. The land, and all the improvements thereon, reverted back to him upon the lease's expiration. That was how his grandchildren, especially Edukoya, who was willed 72 percent of the properties, became extremely rich. Edukoya was a handsome and well-groomed young man. He was married to Bola Abiola Adinikpe.

Bola Adinikpe was a gloriously pretty young lady with dark skin that was inviting to all men. Every man wanted to date her. She was early on her feet. She attended the prestigious Queen's College, Lagos, and the Cambridge University campus in Ibadan, where she earned a degree in biological sciences. All the boys lusted after Bola Adinikpe, but she was interested in only an Igbo boy, the naturally handsome and brilliant John Okorocha, until she met Edukoya. Edukoya was equally brilliant, extremely good looking, and a desirable young man. Edukoya was a Yoruba boy and also the son of a wealthy king. He met her at her school's get-together dance party. He and John Okorocha were attending King's College, a sister school. Little did Bola know initially that they were best friends and twins from different mothers. After graduating from secondary school and marrying Bola Adinikpe, Edukoya later went to the London School of Economics, where he earned degrees in economics and law.

Bola had seven children for him, all girls. After she birthed Bunmi, Dr. Henry Yardley, her physician, advised her to stop having babies. The only reason she was constantly getting pregnant was for her husband to have a male child. At that time, it was unheard of to have an executive queen in Yoruba land. Bola sought a baby boy who could take over the kingship from her husband, who was expected to ascend the throne when his father, Kabiyesi Lawansin Adekunle II, died. She hoped for a male child out of the enormous love she had for her husband. Bola didn't mind the risk in getting pregnant an eighth time, thereby putting her life in enormous medical danger. She lost a lot of blood after she miscarried twin baby boys. She never recovered from the miscarriage. The excessive loss of blood compounded by her emotional defeat from losing the twin boys overwhelmed her. On Bunmi's second birthday, Bola Abiola Adekunle died. The love of Edukoya had left him. It was a hard-felt spiritual and emotional defeat for him. He packed his bags, came to America with his seven children, and settled in San Jose, California, where he met Ms. Yemisi Adeniji.

Yemisi Adeniji was on her way back home to Nigeria to reside permanently with her husband. Yemisi was practically a married woman, having completed her traditional wedding ceremony before she left for her studies in America. She was

4

nineteen years old, wise, and breathtakingly beautiful. She was attending San Jose State University, getting a degree as a nurse practitioner. She was an attractive young woman with a beauty that brought lust to the consciences of men. Edukoya and Yemisi met at a marriage ceremony, where a mutual friend, Alexander Alahije, introduced them. The conversation ended on a high note. However, there was no exchange of phone numbers.

They ran into each other again in Antioch, California, at a party hosted by another mutual friend, Ms. Scholar Adede. A call came in from Edukoya's babysitter that his four-year-old daughter, his last baby, had developed a high fever. Unfortunately, he'd shared a ride with a friend, who had left to buy additional drinks for the party when the call came in. Since Yemisi was a nurse, lived in San Jose, and was about to depart from the party to prepare for her final exams the next Monday morning, she offered to give him a ride and also take a look at the baby. Yemisi was passionate about children.

There was a high degree of pure innocence initially, as Yemisi was far younger than he. Edukoya was a forty-year-old man. Besides, he was consumed with the thought of his daughter falling sick with a high fever. San Jose was a long drive from Antioch, about eighty-five miles away. The newly built, beautiful Highway 680 offered them time to size each other up. They told each other the sad and the uplifting stories of their lives. It turned out they had many things in common, including their local government area in Ondo State, Nigeria, where both had been born, and they both had grown up in the Orissa Kingdom. She knew of his father, Kabiyesi Adekunle II of Orissa Kingdom, but she had never met him before. Edukoya was a lawyer practicing in Lagos. A remarkable thing happened on their journey to San Jose: they fell in love. She wound up spending the night with the family, monitoring the baby's fever. She had her final examination on Monday morning. That sacrifice fueled a must-have-her thought on the mind of Edukoya Adekunle.

They were later married and had five children together, all boys. Later, he revealed to her that he was the crown prince of Orissa Kingdom, with vast real estate holdings under his control. The death of his father, Kabiyesi Lawansin Adekunle II, brought him back home to ascend the throne. The sacrifice Yemisi had made for his little daughter Bunmi continued to fuel his appetite for love for her. His last three daughters, Helen, Kayinde, and Bunmi, called her Mama Yemisi, and his oldest four daughters, Kenmiejo, Elisha, Bola, and Alewun, addressed her by her first name. Kenmiejo was practically Yemisi's age. Edukoya once told Princess Yemisi she was his best friend. He made her the crown princess of Orissa Kingdom.

CHAPTER 2

As an economist, Edukoya approached discussions with numbers and graphs. As a lawyer, he set legal precedents. He found out the hard way that none of those approaches worked. He then turned to his crown princess, Princess Yemisi, for help.

Princess Yemisi was quite comfortable in her new role as the crown princess of Orissa Kingdom. She captivated the audience she touched. The vast real estate accumulations were hers now to bear. Her extraordinary physical attraction conveyed a presence that made others feel they must stand and listen. She took extraordinary steps to get the lease owners and the land parcel owners to agree on a road map of compensations. She called it a win-win. She proposed releasing the properties back to them at the current lease price for fifty years, as long as they were willing to take care of the management and the upkeep of the properties. She also proposed a fixed cap on the interest rate, also for fifty years, and then the properties would revert back to the original owners of the land parcels when the leases expired. The new lease would naturally terminate on the expiration date.

There were some bottlenecks to be sorted out, such as the banks' guarantee on a fixed interest rate for that long period of time. It was to be worked out before everyone signed the new deeds. Her respectable integrity assured the courts she would bring much-needed peace, so the courts gave her free hands to settle the dispute. The assignment was as risky as it could get. It was a must-win for her husband's kingship, because the win would guarantee that 30 percent of the proceeds from all his assets went to Orissa Kingdom. As he had promised his kingdom, 30 percent of the annual proceeds from all his assets would keep rolling in forever to keep up with the needed developments in Orissa Kingdom. After all, her husband, His Lordship Kabiyesi Edukoya Adekunle III, was relatively inexperienced in his new role of leadership as the newly anointed king of Orissa Kingdom.

The first execution of her duty as the crown princess of Orissa Kingdom was to kiss her husband in public among his cabinet of executive chiefs. Kabiyesies did not kiss their wives in public or show any romantic emotion toward them in public. Kabiyesies were supposed to have tough skin, without relaying the slightest weak emotion when passing judgments. They were supposed to be strong and have no softness in their bones. To kiss their wives in public betrayed their strength, as it resonated an acute sign of weakness in their leadership. Kabiyesies' wives were a mere touch from a distance. Their wives came to them only when they were needed. Even going to bed together was channeled through a gofer, and their wives were invited to go to bed with them. Princess Yemisi wanted to make a statement. The point she was conveying by her action was "You can't touch this." She was not invited to go to bed with Edukoya; she went to bed with her husband, and five boys she gave him were the evidence.

Her second duty as crown princess was to be a mom first. She took good care of those dear to her husband's heart, the children from her husband's deceased wife, Bola Abiola Adekunle, their seven daughters. The well-cared-for kids chose on their own to call her Mom. However, after a happily fought, painstaking battle with the girls, she managed to stop the older four daughters, Kenmiejo, Elasha, Bola, and Ilewon, from addressing her as Mom. The girls reluctantly settled for her first name. Every once in a while, Bola and Ilewon addressed her as Mom. Old habits died hard. Yemisi was tired of fighting a losing battle, so she let them have a ball with their choice in addressing her.

She put the kids on the front burner, and sometimes it seemed she was neglecting her own biological children. She tutored and prepared them for higher education. Her achievements were what Bunmi always remembered: "Mom used small rocks and sticks to teach me numbers." Every Friday evening, she assembled the girls to go over their homework. She corrected them where they went wrong, without insult. She pathologically drummed home the importance of good manners, good behavior, respect, and, above all, love. They were her twelve children. She talked her husband out of buying her a luxury car; instead, she opted for a converted Mercedes-Benz luxury minibus with enough room to contain a family of fourteen.

In the third execution of her duty, she convinced her husband to build modern medical clinics around the village of Orissa Kingdom in order to make medical care easily accessible to the villagers. Four modern satellite medical clinics were built and staffed with doctors and nurses. Each local government area got one clinic. The clinics fed into the main hospital at Agbala, the capital city of Orissa Kingdom. She rebuilt the main hospital from head to toe, quadrupling its size. Kabiyesi Edukoya Adekunle III designated it as Orissa Polytechnic Teaching Hospital after the Orissa Polytechnic Institute was elevated from an advanced technical school to a full university, thanks to another undertaking by Princess Yemisi. The move made Orissa Polytechnic and Orissa Kingdom as a whole more visible in the eyes of the federal government as well as the

Federal Department of Education and Health. That meant more federal nairas flowing into the school and into Orissa Kingdom. Yemisi worked with the state governments to fund a new highway leading to the school. The highway cut across Orissa's main avenue, thereby benefitting the whole kingdom. Since she had a medical degree and was an experienced nurse practitioner, she owned the satellite medical facilities as her husband's greatest achievement on the throne as Kabiyesi of Orissa Kingdom. A woman held her as her greatest hero after Yemisi made sure her grandson was delivered safely. The child was the woman's only grandson.

Meanwhile, the battle of the land was raging, and everybody was anticipating what Princess Yemisi would do next. She set up a committee to study the entire layout of the land parcels. Ikoyi was about 136 square miles and was reserved for key government and corporate officials as residents. Victoria Island was about 170 square miles, including the recovered lands from the lagoon. Both islands, in the colonial years, had been known as European quarters. Recently, a slum island, Morroco, had been added to Victoria Island, which made the island much bigger. The residents of Morroco were evacuated to miserable project apartments with considerable neglect by Governor Jakunde to make room for a more modern luxury expansion. The island added an additional 195 square miles to Victoria Island. Victoria Island had been viewed as the financial capital of West Africa, with marble high-rise buildings.

Ikoyi eventually could not be distinguished from the rest of Lagos State anymore. Street hocking of merchandises was everywhere, including Victoria Island. There were small mom-and-pop food stores everywhere and street hockings too. There was no street cleaning, and the once attractive and well-groomed flower beds, the envy of the rest of Lagos City, turned into wild forest. These issues were unheard of on Ikoyi and Victoria Island, where, in the height of colonialism, the Europeans had exercised segregation and racism to their premium. Their racist and segregationist quarters were established in all major cities throughout Nigeria. The areas' latest segregational name was GRA, which stood for "government reserved area." There were a handful of luxury hotels in Ikoyi and Victoria Island corridors. Even Ikoyi Hotel and the Federal Palace Hotel, which used to be the premium hotels, were replaced by five-star hotels due to poor maintenance. The newly built hotels had their rooms priced out of the world.

The national capital's move to Abuja initially did a lot of disservice to Lagos State, Nigeria, especially Ikoyi and Victoria Island, where the pricy real estate was. Real estate took an unusual initial big hit and plunged rapidly. Eventually, things stabilized, and real estate values were on the rise again. In fact, residential complex rent quadrupled in value. Rent for a two-bedroom flat was extremely pricy. That led to unorganized and unruly satellite townships springing up in the middle of nowhere near Ikeja, the capital city, in the northern part of Lagos State. The townships were within Lagos State's limits. Ikeja did a profound job of accommodating the townships by providing them with half-baked running water, electricity that wouldn't light, and poorly maintained paved roads with boreholes as big as lakes. Indeed, the federal capital's relocation to Abuja did Lagos a world of good.

The rapid devaluation of the naira, the national currency of Nigeria, aided the rapid rise in the real estate values overall in the country. Real estate was staged as the safest haven to protect one's wealth against runaway man-made inflation. In the early 1970s, the value of the naira surpassed that of the dollar and the British pound. At one point, one naira was worth $2.25.

Eventually, the value drastically reversed course, and one dollar was worth 380 nairas per the official market bank rate. People would get more nairas for a dollar if they had their dollar at hand and were willing to chase after the street foreign exchange vendors, where it was relatively easier to get foreign exchange than from the banks. Fifty- and hundred-dollar bills were worth more in value for the street vendors due to the notes' high demand by merchants. The fifty- and hundred-dollar notes provided convenience for merchants carrying large amounts of money. The merchants traded only in cash to get a better wholesale deal for their goods. Plus, the foreign merchants did not trust any Nigerian bank drafts or traveler's checks. Verification of those monetary instruments took about thirty days before the foreign banks would honor them.

Why didn't most of the merchants do their business with the banks? The Nigerian banks' protocols wasted merchants' time. The foreign currencies' allocation, especially the dollar, the pound sterling, and the euro, caused the delay. Often, one didn't get foreign exchange currency on demand the same day unless one bribed his or her way out. Further, most of the merchants, although smart, bright, and sharp, were relatively undereducated, with secondary school education or less, which limited their ability to understand the protocols and the bureaucracy on paper. Lack of adequate education brought complexity, and they didn't want to embarrass themselves by asking too many questions that the banks assumed, by their being international businesspersons, they should have already known.

Most of the college-educated business personalities who joined the road merchants were more likely to go to the banks and wait out the time. The banks would give them an ongoing fair market rate if they were buying the foreign currency. It was safe and relatively cheaper than a street vendor's rate. However, if the banks were buying from a person as an individual, it would be considerably below the rate the street vendor would fetch for the customer's hard currency. Counterfeit foreign dollars, euros, and pounds sterling were more likely to be found on the streets. Most street foreign exchange vendors were honest, and they staked their reputation on the line. They had permanent locations with proudly visible street addresses displayed boldly on their business cards. The real incentive for taking the risk of exchanging foreign currency on the street was time. The transaction was quick and easy. There was no paperwork to be filled out, and there was no appearance of intimidation for the undereducated merchants. The only paperwork involved was the currency exchanging hands. First Bank of Nigeria eventually drastically cut down on bureaucracies and protocols. Customers just signed the paper for the exchange, and the money was theirs. However, First Bank's convenience could be short-lived when their allocations by the central bank ran out. Then one had to bribe his or her way to get hold of the hidden stash of high-flying foreign currencies.

Most times, bank employees bought up the high-flying currencies and resold them at a higher rate to make their ill-gotten fast additional monies. It usually cost them nothing to obtain the foreign currencies as long as they replaced the currencies in due time. Giving further incentive to trade currencies on the street were large bills: fifty-dollar notes and, better yet, hundred-dollar notes. Street traders had them in abundance because they paid a little better rate to buy them from people returning from abroad. Banks would give whatever was available at the counter. The price the banks paid to buy a dollar note was the same price as in fifty- or hundred-dollar notes from the central bank of Nigeria. Unless one was a premium client and willing to give bribe to get the larger denominations, the banks would give whatever was on the counter in the exchange transactions. The bribes, when added to the official cost of buying the currency from the banks, amounted to the same price as buying the currency from the street's foreign exchange vendors. Most times, the added bribery and tips to the banks' employees made the currency exchange from the banks even more expensive. The most important advantage to buying from the street's foreign exchange vendors was time, which was of the essence.

The devaluation of the naira had started a long time ago. It didn't go unnoticed. The economists sounded warnings, but to the deaf ears of government officials, who were mostly satisfied with their own self-aggrandizement. An economist named Udoji laid the foundation for the rapid devaluation's ultimate catastrophe. General Yakubu Gowon, the head of state of Nigeria, gave him a mandate to increase and adjust wages fourfold to sevenfold. Such a move was reckless, and it doomed the country later. Yakubu Gowon asserted in a United Nations speech that Nigeria had too much money and needed no financial help from the rest of the world. "We can take care of ourselves" was the message. His speech compounded and fueled foreign-made superfinished goods being dumped on Nigerian shores. The country was relatively underdeveloped, and locally finished manufactured goods suffered because they could not compete in the international market. Because all eyes were on the superfinished foreign products, and with the high-powered overvalued currency, there was no incentive to manufacture locally or improve locally made goods. Foreign-made goods became key and further enhanced the devaluation of the naira. President Olusegu Obasanjo further enhanced the devaluation of the naira. Born out of his softheartedness and overall moral empathy, he raised the minimum wage again by about 350 percent.

Raising the minimum wage concerned the folks in the hierarchy. They wanted their wages to be increased too. The higher-percentage marginal increase in the wages fueled the same nonsense that had doomed Udoji's catastrophe: unprepared-for and unplanned inflation. There was no cushion to pad the enormous cash outlays by the private sector. They had to raise the prices of goods and services in order to meet up with the enormous cash outlays. Furthermore, President Obasanjo, under his administration, watched the central bank create fifty-, hundred-, and two-hundred-naira notes. Johnathan Goodluck added five-hundred- and thousand-naira notes. That was madness due to the roundups. What did it do? It added more inflationary pressure. Also, the doing away with the kobo was the last straw that finally broke the camel's back. President Buhari had enormous responsibility to bear too. He allowed the Nigerian audience to spend money like drunken sailors with an unheard-of appetite for foreign-made goods. The issue was compounded by Buhari's naive incapacity to lead a great nation. Whether it was true or not, however, foreign parties underestimated his leadership of Africa's biggest economic power by gross domestic product (GDP). The lack of trust in his leadership put enormous economic pressure on the devaluation of the currency. It shot up the devaluation of the naira from 110 nairas to one dollar during the Obasanjo and Goodluck regimes to about four hundred nairas to a dollar in on-the-street devaluation under President Buhari's watch. One subsequent problem was a factual rumor that some of the old notes slated for shredding were reintroduced back to the street by disgruntled, greedy central bank employees who wanted to make fast money. The notes were largely exchanged for the high-flying foreign currencies at a relatively higher rate. The rumors were unsubstantiated; however, they raised adequate concern.

The rapid downfall of the currency was a result of irresponsible, thoughtless, and crazy fiscal policies. Rapid increase in the wages on Yakubu Gowon's watch enhanced the appetite for foreign superfinished products. To compound the issue, the implementation was done at once and fast. The size of the wage increase was unheard of in the world's history. Wages quadrupled in size, about a 400 to 700 percent increase. A high school certificate holder had his salary jump from 28.85 to 130.00 nairas in 1974 after the thoughtless endeavor began. This stupidity flooded cash onto the streets of Nigeria. The merchants, who ultimately bore the enormous brunt of paying their employees the mandated wage increase, matched the increase with higher prices for their goods and services. The goods' and services' prices significantly went up immediately after the increased wages were introduced. The increase took effect at once when the head of state signed it into law. Udoji, to his credit, wanted the wages to be gradually phased in. His advice was to have the increased wages phased in over five to ten years to allow the economy to gradually absorb the shock and adjust to such a surge in the wages. His argument was to provide mild shock to the economy.

Private enterprises, especially large corporations, were to be given tax incentives and provided with government loan guarantees over time to cushion the enormous cash outlays. It didn't happen. They were to phase it in when they felt comfortable doing so. The private sector was to obey the government's mandate. The private-sector employees pressured their employers to institute the federal government's mandate immediately. The delay in the implementation by the corporations caused many problems for their employees. The prices of goods and services were increasing at an alarming rate, while the corporate employees were still earning their old salaries. Their counterparts in the government sector had already received their increased salaries, plus enormous bonuses. The government employees' monies flooded the streets of Nigeria. Talk about a bonanza for the merchants— one had to see it to believe it. Although most corporations honored the mandate later, the delayed implementation by virtually all corporations in the country came too late. Even the bonuses and wage increases could not offset the cost of the delay for most private-sector employees. Udoji's team was given a specific mandate for the implementation and the time of completion. It was quick and rushed through, with nobody anticipating the huge negative outcome, which bankrupted the nation in just a few years. Compounding the issue further was the insistence for hasty, rushed implementation by Yakubu Gowon's administration. They wanted to take credit for empty success without anticipating the enormous shortfall that soon came later.

Princess Yemisi had her work cut out for her. The rapid devaluation of the naira persuaded her to stash cash abroad in foreign banks and keep a wait-and-see outlook. They brought in only the monies absolutely needed to run the palace and Orissa Kingdom. She had foresight, and any cash not intended to be used was converted into dollars and British pounds sterling at any cost on the street and in the banks. The notes were stashed at foreign banks. She heavily invested in real estate holdings, stocks, and bonds. At one point, Edukoya's stock holdings, with multiple stock splits, reached, in the United States, about 550 million shares combined. The value was estimated at the time of his death to be worth $10.5 billion. John Okorocha advised and arranged for Princess Yemisi to invest heavily in start-up companies, such as Apple, Microsoft, Intel, and Dell, and, later, the dot-com companies, such as Amazon, Yahoo, AOL, Google, and a whole host of others. They were relatively cheap investments with enormous risk. Few failed; most succeeded. The ones that succeeded enormously offset those that failed and turned the family's relatively small investment into a multibillion-dollar gain. At some moments, she wondered if she was doing the right thing and if she had bitten off more than she could chew. By her side was her beloved husband, Kabiyesi Edukoya Adekunle III, who kept fueling her with encouragement.

CHAPTER 3

The land deals overwhelmed Princess Yemisi a great deal. Once she thought she was making headway, it turned out the deals had much more needed work to be done. A twist came: the Lagos Mainland Court, though it had given her a free hand, now imposed new guidelines and restrictions. The initial deeds had been filed at four different regional courts: Eko, Apapa, Ikeja, and Yaba. Those courts imposed their rules and restrictions. The Lagos Mainland Court, commonly known as Eko Court, thought it was wise to join them. The money was huge, with derivatives in the hundreds of millions of dollars. That meant the local government areas where the original deals were filed stood to get millions of dollars in refiling fees. Corrupt entities wanted their cut in the deals too, and that compounded the problem. They dug in with uncountable lawyers representing both sides.

Before Lagos became Nigeria's capital city, it was made up of isolated islands: Eko, Ikoyi and Victoria Island, Apapa and Ajegunle, Surulere and Lawansin, Ijora, Ebutemeta and Yaba, and Ikeja and Ikorodu, with each island ruled by a kabiyesi. They were independent kingdoms. The islands were close in proximity and were separated by narrow ocean pathways called lagoons. As events unfolded, the islands collectively were slated as one large metropolis city by the British and baptized with a borrowed foreign name: Lagos City. Lagos was designated as the headquarters of British colonial territories in West Africa, with a British-appointed high commissioner to govern the territories. Then came the partitioning of Africa by the European nations. Nigeria derived its name from the River Niger. The British, in order to create a dominant colonial power in Africa, decided to combine the individual key tribes, Hausa, Yoruba, and Igbo, which were individual nations with tribal, ethnic, and kingdom governing bodies. They were convinced that bigger was better for them in order to allow pounds sterling to flow into the regions in abundance, which would help with the badly needed economic and social developments. The move later turned out to be a huge mistake, depending on individual perspective. With guns to their heads, naiveness, complexity, and lack of better-educated representations, the key tribes agreed to be bunched together to create the United Nations of West Africa, later known as Nigeria.

The land parcels were originally controlled by the tribal kings in Lagos, who allocated the land parcels the way they saw fit. Victoria Island was largely a wasteland and of no use to the tribal kings. Most of those land parcels were exchanged for favors or sold at almost giveaway prices, and most of the deeds were not documented until years later. When Nigeria became a nation independent from the United Kingdom, Lagos, the territorial headquarter of West Africa, became the capital city of Nigeria. Lagos was the capital city of the new nation, Republic of Nigeria, from October 1, 1960, the day Nigeria became an independent nation, to the late 1970s, when Abuja was finally designated as the official capital city of Nigeria. Abuja was a tiny pathway town near Lokoja, where the two biggest rivers, River Niger and River Benue, met. The country actually moved to Abuja in the late 1980s due to the infrastructural developments: housing, roads, water, a central sewage system, an airport, and more. River Benue was expanded into a man-made lake to provide fresh water for the millions of people anticipated to reside there. A city in the middle of nowhere was created, and it was going to be a planned city with beautiful landscapes.

The conception of a permanent location for the Nigerian capital city was in the works from the beginning. In fact, it was conceived during the negotiation of the independence to have the capital city of Nigeria located in a more central location, with the territory designated as a no-person's-land. Lokoja was chosen because it was a more central location where the two biggest rivers in Nigeria, fairly equal in distance from both ends, the Niger and the Benue, met. The city of Lokoja was also chosen because the journey to the capital city from the far corners of the nation provided fairly equal distances. Abuja was the most centrally located national capital city in the world. It was the key incentive that got the Hausas as well as the Igbos aboard in joining to create the union. However, the idea of a more centrally located capital city was delayed because the new nation didn't have the means to fund the most expensive undertaking in modern world history. Just the cost of converting River Benue into a man-made lake that supplied fresh water to the city hovered around the tune of $11 billion and counting. It was built by Bethel Corporation, an American company headquartered in San Francisco, California. Oil revenues, the benchmark of the Nigerian economy, renewed the appetite for the capital city's stay, and to the crude oil's credit, it made the impossible dream possible. Oil revenues, which had their mainstay from mainly the delta regions, sponsored 96 percent of the projects undertaken by the federal government of Nigeria, including the money wasted on the World Black and African Festival of Art and Culture, which became a faded memory.

Nigeria had three major regions, with each capable of sustaining a nation on its own. The Hausa settled in the north;

the Yoruba settled in the west; and the Igbo, the Efik, and the Abolima settled in the east. Hausa, Yoruba, and Igbo were the three major tribes of Nigeria. On the whole, Nigeria had about sixteen tribes. Most of the tribes resided in the southeastern block of the country. Because of easy migration architected by the Atlantic Ocean, River Niger, the Cross River, River Benue, and the Imo River, the southeastern region had migrants from all over the world. Each tribe came with their own language, traditions, and culture. The pocket cultures and traditions made it difficult for the southeastern block of the country to have a common voice in anything. That was why the concept of a breakaway of the southeastern migrants from Nigeria was doomed to fail on arrival. The Igbos were the dominant tribe in the southeastern region. They usually had one voice. The minor tribes surrounding the Igbos were easily persuaded to side with the union for their own best interest. They simply did not trust the Igbos to lead them. They also provided easy access to the Atlantic Ocean, which was a must for the Igbos to succeed as a nation. The Niger basin alone had 60 percent of the tribes in Nigeria.

The Yoruba were the mainstay tribe in Nigeria and, in fact, in West Africa. They stretched from Nigeria, which was their main port of call, to Senegal, with the Atlantic Ocean providing them with a navigable international route. Ninety percent of slavery took place in the Yoruba lands. Almost 100 percent of African Americans who initially migrated to America as slaves were Yoruba. In the middle belt of the Atlantic Ocean settled the slaves who came at the tail end of slavery. They were largely from the far eastern block of West Africa. They were dumped on the islands when the persuasive need to end slavery by the British and the French, which were the leading world powers then, took a dangerous turn for the slave traders.

The dumped slaves settled in the North Atlantic islands and became known as the Caribbean islanders. Late slaves, a huge number of West African slaves, mainly from the eastern block of West Africa, settled in Brazil and the South Atlantic islands. However, cross-migration and trade between both sides of the Atlantic Ocean had existed before slavery. The America Indians and African blacks who resided along the stretch of the equator intermarried in huge numbers, which gave way to mostly brown skin colors, a mixture of red Indian blood with red black African blood.

The Hausas in the northern portions of Nigeria were mainly migrants from Sudan, Mali, the vast majority of Niger, and Chad. The Igbos were descendants of the Hebrews. The Efik were mainly from South Cameroon. A tiny island bordering Nigeria and Cameroon, Bight of Biafra, rich in crude oil, on the west coast of the Atlantic Ocean, had recently opened up a two-century-old wound between Nigeria and Cameroon. The Efik, mainly the Calaba, who claimed the island to be theirs, were not going anywhere. They were happy to settle on the Nigerian soil. The population of the tiny island was divided into three groups: the Igbo with 55 percent of the population, the Efik with 35 percent of the population, and the Cameroonians with 10 percent of the population. Because the Nigerians were the dominant population on the island, Nigeria had clear claim of the island.

Lagos State was a metropolis with a population nearing fifteen million people. It was made up of parcels of islands. The capital city was Ikeja. Ikeja became the headquarters of Lagos State by default. Since the federal headquarters was housed on the Lagos mainland in Eko City, as well as numerous local government areas' headquarters, the crowd left Ikeja as a welcome alternative choice. Ikeja was located in the north of

Lagos State. It had extensive dry and relatively undeveloped land compared to the rest of Lagos State. Ikeja harbored the three major airports in the state: domestic and international airports named after slain head of state Murtala Mohammed and the military airport. Murtala Mohammed led the nation for only six short months. The changes he brought to bear within those short-lived six months and their impacts would be forever felt in the heart and soul of the nation. When the announcement came that he had been killed, elders, youths, and children stood still and wept with tears visibly gushing down their cheeks. They'd felt he was Nigeria's last hope. So far, they had been right. Lagos State was comprised of Ikeja in the north; Surulere and Lawanson in the east; Yaba and Ebutemeta in the west; and Apapa, Ajagunle, Ijora, Eko, Ikoyi, and Victoria Island in the south.

The bones of contention for Princess Yemisi were her land deals on Ikoyi and Victoria Island. In those days, the whole of Lagos's territorial headquarters was in one place, with satellite regional offices located in other key areas. The headquarters had been segmented and paired up with their local government area, which was a good thing. It distributed governing close to the people. Unfortunately for Princess Yemisi, it also segmented the land cases, which called for more time and money devoted to each case. Though that should not have had any bearing on the cases' results, where money was involved so was the evil that followed it—in this case, billions of dollars. To compound the issue further, the Lagos mainland, which was called Eko City, had multiple local government areas. In fact, Ikoyi and Victoria Island had separate jurisdictions of local government areas. It made the seemingly open-and-shut case more open, more complicated, and more complex. The legal precedent His

Lordship Kabiyesi Edukoya Adekunle III had been trying to avoid set in big-time.

It was taking a big toll on Princess Yemisi Adekunle. She realized that because of it, she was neglecting her fundamental moral duties as a wife and as a mother. Lovemaking, which was a must for her and her husband, took a backseat. She remembered that sometimes they'd had sex four or five times a day. It was beginning to fade into distant memories. The cooks and the stewards now oversaw what they ate for breakfast, lunch, dinner, and even snacks. Her physical exercises were all but abandoned. Her physique was beginning to sag. She began to see minor wrinkles creep up on her face. She gained a little weight, and that was a no-no for her. Finally, she took a look in the mirror and saw herself again. She said to herself, "I can do this."

PART 2

THE CUTE COUPLE

CHAPTER 4

Princess Yemisi realized her health was far more important than the land-ownership bickering. What about her family's well-being? What about her physical and mental health and that of her family? The kids were now grown, five men and seven women. They had two additional lawyers in the family besides Kabiyesi Adekunle III, Amibo and Babayade; two software engineers, Malcolm and Ilewon; and a college associate professor with a PhD in mathematics, Dr. Ephram Adekunle. Ephram was a Harvard University mathematics professor. There also were four medical doctors, Kenmiejo, Elisha, Bunmi, and Tunde, and a registered nurse, Kayode. Kayode lived with her husband in America, an Africa American, who was also a physician. The family also had a politician, Senator Helen Adekunle. She had just won a federal senatorial seat representing her state. Yemisi's last-born as a recent college graduate, Oyodele. He was presently serving in the Nigerian Youth Service Corps. Oyodele had a seat awaiting him at MIT to do his doctorate in structural engineering. He'd graduated with first-class honors with a perfect GPA of 4.0 from Orissa Polytechnic Institute.

Princess Yemisi took another look in the mirror, naked. Glancing at herself, she thought about all her achievements and accomplishments so far as crown princess. She breathed a sigh of relief and spoke out loud. "We have done something right." Princess Yemisi was still intact, including her breathtaking attractiveness. She had managed to keep her figure intact.

After sensing she'd gained a little weight, she had reduced her food consumption. She ate a small portion of food at a time and seldom indulged in fast foods and snacks. She ate mostly vegetables and grains, but she didn't claim to be a vegetarian either. She did not drink any form of alcoholic beverage, including wine, or sugary beverages. She did not smoke cigarettes or anything smokeable. She bore no anger toward anyone; she was full of life and had a positive outlook on life. Yemisi was satisfied with her life. She treated people she met with love and respect. She had grown used to strict exercise and diet regimens. She did not want to let herself give in to rich food temptations and indulgences just because she could afford them. What had happened to Iyabo Adeniji, her elder sister, scared the hell out of her. Yemisi attributed that to overindulgence, because Iyabo could afford to have the finest things in life. Iyabo Adeniji, in her day, had been the most physically attractive woman in Nigeria and perhaps the world.

Princess Yemisi jogged at least three miles three times weekly. She played basketball, soccer, and baseball at least once a week, alternating the sports. She coached basketball at Orissa Girls' Secondary School. She ran on the treadmill daily and indulged in a handful of her indoor gym equipment. She played long tennis and Ping-Pong games with her guests and with her husband whenever he was available. Dr. Everest Oluomolewa in Lagos adequately made up for her lost time in the Orissa Kingdom. He played with her in all games whenever she visited Lagos, which she did frequently, mostly on business trips. She stuck to her diet and exercise regimens. At the age of fifty-three, there was not a single thing an eighteen-year-old did that she wouldn't do. She danced old, in-between, and modern dances. Her favorite music genres were hip-hop, Yoruba jams, and Yoruba *riddim* hip-hop. She was slim and fit, with her stomach as flat as if she'd never carried a baby. She had no stretch marks at all. People wondered where she had carried the five boys. Upon her feet, she was nicknamed Immaculate Goddess.

As she walked through her hallway, into the kitchen, and finally into the bar corner to sit down and relax, as always, the male helpers stood still, looking at the extravagant beauty of this goddess. They, of course, muted their astonishment, as did most people she came in contact with. Most people estimated her age to be around forty-two years old, and that was a conservative estimate. She detested being addressed as Princess Yemisi, but seeing that it was too much a waste of her time to fight it, she learned to live with it. With such attractiveness, people expected her to be rude, a snob, and arrogant; however, she was not. She had a heart and was polite and distinguished. She was not mean, was not boastful, and did not look down on people.

Usually, a typical kabiyesi had the tendency to be polygamous. In fact, Princess Yemisi gave her husband the green light and even sincerely prepared for another woman's accommodation. His Lordship Kabiyesi Edukoya Adekunle III would have none of that. He called it immoral and a betrayal. He had never cheated on Princess Yemisi. He hadn't cheated on his deceased wife, Bola Abiola Adekunle, and he had not cheated on Princess Yemisi.

Princess Yemisi was in love with her husband, Kabiyesi Edukoya Adekunle III. It was a match made in heaven. Indeed, both of them were in love with each other. Whenever Kabiyesi Adekunle III saw her in her transparent nightgown or naked, he acted like a high school kid who wanted to get something, at least a goodbye kiss, on his first date. Whenever they were in bed, even after all those years of repeatedly seeing her naked, along with her unbelievable sexual activities and sleeping together, he would always marvel at her beauty and her smooth, rich, firm body. With goose bumps all over his skin, he made the bed for her and even washed her underwear. He just couldn't get enough of her. Whenever she traveled, he had restless nights. They did romantic things that were unusual for a kabiyesi to do. They kissed and held hands in public. Kabiyesi Edukoya Adekunle III was a much older man, in his midseventies, about twenty-one years older than Yemisi. Seeing them together, a stranger would have thought they were father and daughter. Princess Yemisi didn't help the gap and outlook on their ages either, and Edukoya would not have had it any other way.

Her nature made Immaculate Goddess have a lifestyle that kept her looking young year after year. Earlier, in her early fifties, she had fallen down while playing basketball and broken her wrist. Her wrist had strengthened and healed so fast and so well that the orthopedic team had performed further tests, saying that her rapid recovery raised concerns of a larger issue. On further examination, the doctors had identified her as having a rare genetic defect. She had naturally active growth hormones. Her bone structures were still growing, which caused her to age at a relatively slow speed. Thus, at the age of fifty-three, she could comfortably pass for a thirty-three- to forty-year-old woman. Her youthfulness was compounded by her strict lifestyle regimen.

Her body rejuvenated, causing her to look much younger than her age. Even her hairs all over her body looked perfect in their natural black color, with zero artificial colorization. One would have had to fish hard to find any gray hairs. She used mild touch-ups to hide them further. With such an active lifestyle, strict diet, and strict exercise regimen, she aided her youthful appearance enormously.

One day, at Central Park in New York, where they were vacationing, a stranger bought ice cream for both of them. He was about thirty-six years old. He thought Kabiyesi Adekunle III was Yemisi's father. In a smooth-talking conversation, the young man asked her out for a date. Princess Yemisi glanced at her husband with a smile. Kabiyesi Adekunle III interrupted the conversation. He politely told the young man, "Our time is very limited here; we're vacationing from Nigeria. Some other time." Similar situations happened all the time. Once, on a walk with her children, all grown, in Abuja, while she was vacationing with Bunmi, Tunde, Kenmiejo, and her two boys, a stranger identified Tunde as Princess Yemisi's husband and Kenmiejo as her elder sister. They laughed for a long time. She responded, "Yeah, I'm married to my first son, my first daughter is my elder sister, and her children are my biological children." The stranger apologized.

Kabiyesi Edukoya Adekunle III was the type of man who always promoted equality among persons. One of his cooks, Evans Eleyenmi, played chess with him. He came to realize the cook let him win all the time. One day he invited a professional chess player to play chess with his cook. The cook beat him five times in a row. It prompted Kabiyesi Edukoya III to convince the young man to enter the upcoming national tournament for chess players. The cook won the cup. Evans Eleyenmi then became a feature in local commercials around the country. A celebrity, he still kept his old job as Edukoya's chef as a way to show his appreciation for Kabiyesi's kindness to him. He was promoted to chief helper at Kabiyesi's palace. He ate with Kabiyesi at the same dining table. Evans Eleyenmi went to adult night school, where he brushed up academically with a bachelor's degree in culinary management at Orissa Polytechnic Institute. His Lordship Kabiyesi Edukoya Adekunle III put people on equal footing with him always. In every aspect of life, Princess Yemisi was his true soul mate.

Kabiyesi Edukoya Adekunle III discovered hidden talents in people and shined them to make each person prosper. He was also a great communicator. Local disputes were settled without violence time after time. People trusted His Lordship Kabiyesi Edukoya Adekunle III's judgments. He never took sides and never took his popularity for granted. He never abused his popularity. He listened to his chiefs for advice. Sometimes they got it wrong, but most times, they got it right. However, in his wisdom, he never discredited his advisers or criticized them in public. His worst days were like his best days. Edukoya was always searching for solutions to make the lives of his people better. Though there were limited resources, he managed to put in needed infrastructure, such as drivable paved roads, water, electricity, a hospital, and satellite clinics in the Orissa Kingdom. Under his leadership, three major open-air markets were built with rooftops, paved streets, electricity, and running water. The markets had a water system and public toilets immaculately cleaned. The grandest achievements of his reign were the expansion and conversion of Orissa Polytechnic into a university with all the academic facilities that came with a university and also the expansion and designation of Orissa General Hospital as Orissa Polytechnic Teaching Hospital, which enabled the hospital to have nationally recognized research centers.

He encouraged the building of twenty additional gas stations in the kingdom, and he encouraged multiple local business investments in Orissa. He orchestrated incentives to attract local investments from all over Nigeria in the Orissa

Kingdom. A cooperative bank was established with largely his own funds to aid Orissa farmers and businesses. Such funds made Orissa grain growers an export community. They exported yams, potatoes, cassavas, rice, wheat, and varieties of vegetables. Most of the yams, cassavas, rice, and wheat were processed into flour. The processed cassava flour, called *gari*, was a key staple food in Nigeria and in West Africa. A solid 60 percent of gari was marketed abroad to earn hard currencies. The conversion of the currencies to naira enabled the employees to earn above-average wages locally. It made living bearable for the employees of the farms.

CHAPTER 5

They went to church every Sunday, and that was an exception to the rule. Kabiyesies seldom went to church services, unless for an important occasion, such as the church's key festivities. Kabiyesi got ready for countless meetings with his kingsmen, and Sundays were no exception. Kabiyesi Edukoya Adekunle III was a religious man and a true Christian. He was unconventional. He even kissed Princess Yemisi at the church and held her hands.

All the members of his household, including his house helpers, went to church on Sundays. They went with five vehicles: a pleasure car carrying Princess Yemisi and Edukoya, two SUVs carrying all his children, and two luxury Honda minivans carrying his helpers. The only animals that stayed home were Bunmi's dog and their livestock. For the family of His Lordship Edukoya Adekunle III, it was a religious routine. Nobody forced each other to go to church, even Ephram when he visited home from Harvard University, where he was a mathematics professor. Sitting at home inventing and creating excuses why one was not in attendance in church that Sunday looked miserably stupid. Edukoya would say in such cases, for example, "I didn't see Bunmi in the church today."

Princess Yemisi would go on the defense, interrupting him before he put a full stop in his sentence. "She is here. Look at her chatting with Alademabo, her best friend, in the corner. You know she likes to sit with her friends."

His reply would be "Very well, my love."

Sometimes Bunmi would not come to church, especially when she spent Saturday night at a friend's house and they stayed up all night chatting with their boyfriends. Princess Yemisi knew her husband trusted her judgment and wouldn't go any further.

At Saint Mathew's Anglican Cathedral Church in Agbala, where the bishop Reverend John Ashimolu presided, the seating was made up of an arrangement of pews. They were neatly arranged in precise order. The building had four sub-buildings attached to the main dome, where the bishop and other clergymen resided. The church was well decorated to the point that some of the faithful swore they saw angels there. One woman, Mary Shakunde, came early every morning to pray. She claimed she saw an angel sitting at the center of the church, precisely at the center of the dome. She was so religious about her prayers and beliefs that Kabiyesi Adekunle III, being the life patron of the diocese, intervened, and the church granted her an exclusive key to the cathedral so she could come pray at will. His assertion was "You don't play with people's faith."

His Lordship Kabiyesi Edukoya Adekunle III and his family had a designated royal seating arrangement at the cathedral. It was arranged with fourteen seats. There were two pews to sit six each and two royal seats in the middle of the two pews to seat His Lordship Kabiyesi Adekunle III and Princess Yemisi Adekunle. The two pews were for his twelve children. Kabiyesi did not ask for the seating arrangement. In fact, he fought bitterly against it, but in the end, the elders of the village and the elders of the church urged him to accept it. They said, "It will be insulting for the young men and women who contributed to make it happen. It was their way of showing appreciation for all your good works in the village to make life bearable for our people." They cited drinkable running water and drivable roads, among many other things he had accomplished.

The bishop liked to have a word with Kabiyesi Adekunle III after the service. The bishop usually came to the palace. He brought Lady Anna Perfecter Ashimolu, his wife, with him. The couples paired up: Princess Yemisi with Perfecter and Kabiyesi Adekunle III with Bishop John Ashimolu. Before they knew it, key elders of the village and the church streamed into the palace. Usually, the topic was from where they'd left off the previous Sunday get-together. There would be the introduction of a new topic as well, and both would be hashed out that Sunday evening. Whatever remained of the issues would be left for the next Sunday after service. For Princess Yemisi, a similar subcommittee took place with her. The group included Lady Anna Perfecter Ashimolu and three or four influential women from the kingdom. It was a small group, usually handpicked by Princess Yemisi. Unlike with Kabiyesi's gathering, the women were invited. The get-together was rotatory, given the large number of women of influence, substance, and progressiveness concentrated in the small community.

Serious topics were discussed, and sometimes it turned into a full-blown meeting. Princess Yemisi excused her audience to see that lunch was coming along well. In the small converted dining hall in the palace, where Kabiyesi usually received countless guests, four tables were set. The tables were of equal proportion in size, set in a square format. The women's small group would be served at one table; the elders of the church and the kingdom elders were at two tables; and Kabiyesi Adekunle III, Bishop John Ashimolu, Lady Anna Perfecter Ashimolu, and Princess Yemisi were at one table. The bishop prayed, thanking God for the food they were about to eat and finishing with "In Jesus's name. Amen." Anglican bishops were trained to invite topics in prayers when it was necessary to do so. They seldom stayed too long in prayer in those types of settings.

Reverend John Ashimolu had a PhD in theology, and Lady Anna Perfecter Ashimolu had a PhD in physics from UC Berkeley. She was a physics professor at Orissa Polytechnic. From time to time, she taught mathematics and physics at the prestigious Comprehensive Technical Coeducation Secondary School Academy in Orissa. They sacrificed a lot to be in Orissa Kingdom for the love of God.

While dining, there was silence. One could have heard a pin drop, until Kabiyesi Edukoya Adekunle III broke the silence, ordering wine. They had assorted types of hot drinks, both foreign and domestically brewed, and assorted types of locally made beer and wine were available too. Kabiyesi's favorite was a day-old palm wine. He took a glass, sat quietly, and drank it to the last drop. Reverend John Ashimolu took about two shots of brandy, and that was enough for him. The women were influential, progressive, substantive, well enlightened, educated, defiant, and liberated. They drank alongside the men. Princess Yemisi would have one glass of club soda mixed with freshly squeezed orange juice. Her regular guest was Professor Kenmi Tunde, who was also her closest friend. In fact, they had been teenage friends. Both of them had gone to the University of Nigeria, Ile Ife. Kenmi had finished at the college, while Princess Yemisi had completed her bachelor's degree at San Jose State University, where she also had completed her doctorate degree as a nurse practitioner. Professor Kenmi Tunde later went to Ohio State University to complete her doctorate in education.

Princess Yemisi Adekunle missed the Sunday get-togethers a lot while chasing the land deals. She always dreamed that her sole calling in life was to build a community to make life bearable for the people of the kingdom, whom she loved so much. She fronted her husband as the sole achiever, while in the background, she was busy with constructive engagements for the well-being of Orissa Kingdom. Kabiyesi Adekunle III called her his best friend. She gave her heart, spirit, soul, and body to everything she did. She respected herself and respected others, big and small. At fifty-three, she even played basketball with her teenage friends as she saw them. Full of life and breathtakingly romantic, at age seventy-four, Kabiyesi Edukoya Adekunle III had an erection that was astonishing and needed no medical intervention or enhancement. Princess Yemisi's all-around attractiveness could have made dead men wake up. She certainly did it for that seventy-four-year-old man, her beloved husband.

CHAPTER 6

Yemisi's birthday was an occasion dear to Kabiyesi Edukoya Adekunle III's heart. It was always an exciting event for His Lordship to reflect back on the pleasant past and to show his appreciation for a wonderful woman. It was an occasion when his dreams permitted him to revisit the past. He recalled when they'd met on the short eighty-five-mile drive from Antioch to San Jose and the breathtaking beauty holding Bunmi, monitoring her fever all night. It was time for him to reflect on this love who made family life the epic of her moral priority. This woman, Princess Yemisi, consciously removed all impediments in order to focus on her most important obligation: her twelve children and her husband. Kabiyesi Adekunle III held love as the ultimate culprit and the motivating fuel enabling his best friend to care. She was relentless in getting her husband never to back away from his moral obligations and promises to their people.

His dream took him to their winter jackets on a cold evening in San Francisco when unprepared guests got the surprise of the harsh, unpredictable weather conditions in San Francisco. San Francisco was only about forty miles away from the city of San Jose; however, he had only visited the city twice.

The first time Edukoya visited San Francisco was the day he arrived in America with his seven children. His friend John Okorocha, who aided in his relocation to America, picked them up in his converted 1969 Chevy minivan. John Okorocha was living in San Francisco, in the newly developed Victorian houses in the Stone Town Village, facing the Pacific Ocean. He was one of the first to buy a four-bedroom Victorian house, at a cost of $16,850 in 1968. The day was sunny, with the temperature above normal, about 92 degrees Fahrenheit. It was July 21, 1970. The good weather went on for about two weeks. Within that period, Adekunle moved his family to San Jose, where he resided for six years before moving back to Nigeria following his father's death to ascend the throne.

Although they had seen eye-to-eye on almost every issue, neither he nor Yemisi had had the guts to mention love to each other. The mystery of falling in love in that special instance was like a chick in an incubator. In fact, Yemisi interjected her suitor in Nigeria into their conversation from time to time. Princess Yemisi later admitted her interjection, though it made him mildly uncomfortable, was a throw-off. She also admitted the first day of their introduction at the wedding was the day she fell in love with him; hence, she kept every man she met, including her husband in Nigeria, at a distance. Yemisi admitted she bet against all odds, hoping they would run into each other again. Understandably, she volunteered immediately to give him a ride, cutting her visit to a dear friend short. Nevertheless, Kabiyesi Edukoya Adekunle III was a gentleman all the way.

Yemisi had visited the city of San Francisco several times. As a matter of fact, she'd roomed there with her sister Iyabo and a friend for three months in 1968, when she first arrived in America at the age of sixteen. She arrived at San Francisco International Airport, where Edukoya anchored as well. Having lived in the city for a while and made frequent visits to the city to see her sister Iyabo, she was used to the unsettled weather patterns. Adekunle's second visit to San Francisco was with the whole family, including Ms. Yemisi Adeniji, after an invitation from her sister, who still resided in the city with her husband

and children, and an invitation from John Okorocha, Edukoya's childhood friend. Unfortunately, the weather turned sour. Iyabo Adeniji, Yemisi's elder sister, wanted to see Prince Edukoya Adekunle and his seven daughters. John Okorocha wanted to see Yemisi, the young woman who had consumed Edukoya's heart.

Yemisi warned Edukoya that San Francisco's weather was unpredictable. Her personality was such that she wouldn't press him on any issue. Instead, she took an extra pair of coats and the kids' winter jackets along with them as a precaution. John Okorocha suggested a visit to San Francisco's waterfront and Golden Gate Park. Golden Gate Park had a world-famous planetarium. John suggested the kids would love it. Yemisi and Edukoya were still dating, and both were on their best behavior, as they were learning each other's temperament. Sometimes an experience could teach each other a valuable lesson. Though Yemisi was bothered by his laid-back attitude, she dared not mention it to him and show it on her face. *Suppose it is sunny*, she thought. *Then those hassles will be in vain.*

It was a big family. They came in John's converted minivan, which seated sixteen adults. First was the waterfront at Fisherman's Wharf. That year, the month of August was unusually cold in the city. Within a few minutes of their being outside, the winter coats she'd thoughtfully brought along with them came in handy. It was the first time Prince Edukoya Adekunle had seen a sign that she wanted to settle down with him. It was welcome news for him. He'd thought too late about bringing his own jacket, and it was a great surprise to see Yemisi had ignored his stubbornness and brought a pair of winter jackets for him and herself. He was speechless.

He took a big risk. He went to Iyabo and borrowed one of her rings. He proposed to Yemisi on the spot, in the presence of the tourist crowd, with his children chanting, "Yes, yes."

She said, "Yes, I will marry you." At that instant, both of them forgot Yemisi was already a married woman. They hugged and kissed passionately in the presence of the tourists, the whole family, and, more importantly, her future children.

A wandering mind needed the heart to settle down. On this birthday, he decided to write her a poem.

A Wandering Mind Needed
the Heart to Settle Down

What I wished for was to have you stay in my heart, and that is where you came to permanently reside. Glory be to God the day I found you. With the honor I hold so dear, I cannot cherish this life another day without you. You know me better than anyone knows me, even my own mother, the woman who bore me. You are my best friend. You never make me get mad at you. You tolerate my idiosyncrasies and make wisdom out of my ignorance. With our age difference, I thought it would be a onetime party. But you stayed. You've made my priorities your own priorities.

My interest is on your front burner. My children are your children. You are remarkable, always watching my back. Always affectionate and always romantic, even on our harshest down days, and there have been quite a few of those sad days. You have never denied me the pleasure that comes with love. You say repeatedly, "I love you." It makes me feel good when I hear you say that. They say love is the affair of the heart, and you certainly show it. I've always counted on you because you are my best-trusted friend. I know you will never hurt me. You've made satisfying me and our children your highest priority. No complaint and no criticism, to the point I have wondered if you are at all a human being.

You are a human being all right, because I've felt your soul, and I've felt your flesh. Even when I make a mistake, you think about it as a lesson, an asset to be learned from. I believe God sent you.

CHAPTER 7

Princess Yemisi, while walking alongside Kabiyesi Adekunle III with Bunmi and Oyodele on the streets of Ikoyi and Victoria Island, remembered the good old days and laughed out loud and said, "Amazing!"

Edukoya asked her why was she laughing, and she said, "The amazing stories about our family."

Bunmi was the last of the girls, and Oyo was the last of the boys. Though grown, Bunmi, a pediatrician, and Oyo, on his way to MIT to acquire his doctorate in structural engineering, always tagged alongside their parents on casual events, this time strolling along the streets of Ikoyi and Victoria Island. Oyo was being escorted off to America for further studies. After a week's stay in Lagos at the villa, Oyo's flight was on Thursday at 10:30 p.m. They thought about killing multiple birds with one stone while there in Lagos, so they went for a walk on the third day, Wednesday, visiting the neighborhoods of Ikoyi and Victoria Island, where they co-owned multiple land developments worth billions of dollars.

Ondo was quite a distance from Lagos. As always, they flew from Akure Airport to Lagos's Murtala Mohammed International Airport in their Boeing 737 jet. The grandfather of Kabiyesi Edukoya Adekunle III, Kabiyesi Lawansin Adekunle I, was the man who had started the ball rolling. He had been a visionary. After graduating from high school, he was among the first set of students to be admitted to the Cambridge University campus of Ibadan, Nigeria. It was quite a select few, with

Cambridge University insisting on only the best and brightest. The Cambridge University campus of Ibadan, later known as the University of Nigeria, Ibadan, was the first and only institute of higher learning in Nigeria at the time. The second was the University of Nigeria, Kano, in the north, which was mainly geared toward advanced Islamic studies for the Muslim community and was equally difficult to get into. Then came the University of Nigeria, Nsuka, in Enugu State; the University of Nigeria, Lagos, in Lagos State; and the University of Nigeria, Ile Ife, in Osun State. They were the pathfinder institutions of higher learning in Nigeria in the early 1960s. Ultimately, there were about 170 universities in Nigeria, federal, state, and private combined.

There were about that many professional management and technological institutions in the country. Every state in Nigeria had about half a dozen institutions of higher learning. Most had even more. For instance, Enugu State, which harbored the University of Nigeria at Nsuka, had about a dozen institutions of higher learning. The qualifying standards for admission into the institutions remained tough. Amazingly, the institutions were not competing for students as to lower the standards for admission to their institutions. Nigeria had a reservoir of academically distinguished students. All the institutions of higher learning demanded excellence from their students. Just because Ibadan was the pathfinder did not excuse it to be an exclusive club. Unlike with their counterpart foreign institutions of higher learning, the diplomas from virtually all institutions of higher learning in Nigeria carried largely equal weight. A graduate with a higher national diploma (HND) from Auchi Polytechnic was just as qualified as a graduate from the University of Nigeria, Ibadan, for a managerial position.

Kabiyesi Lawansin Adekunle I had a BS in physics with a minor in mathematics from the Cambridge University campus in Ibadan. He was employed after graduation by King's College in Lagos to teach mathematics and physics. This employment gave him the opportunity to discover a new and bigger township than the one he came from in Orissa Kingdom in Ondo State. It also afforded him the opportunity to discover new places along the way to Lagos. Lagos was relatively rural but quickly developing. Streets were being portioned, and street names were given. The British Nigerian colony was starting a territorial mail-delivering system, which meant street names with numbers identifying the houses were needed. The city of Lagos was mainly concentrated on the Lagos mainland, known as Eko City. The cluster townships, such as Yaba, Ebumeta, Ijora, Surulere, Ajagunle, Apapa, Ikeja, and others, were isolated from Eko City by the lagoon. To make matters worse, Eko City was surrounded by water. Indeed, it was practically an island. The way to get to Eko City was by boat across the lagoon. Ikoyi was a patch town to Eko City. It was also an island. Its location was naturally positioned as a wage town for sailors and pirates to get drunk. Victoria Island was practically a ghost village.

The monthly teaching salary of a highly qualified secondary schoolteacher like Lawansin Adekunle I was about nine pounds and seventy pennies at the time. That amount of money had enormous value and buying power. It allowed Lawansin to maintain two wives, live in a six-bedroom house in Eko City, pay his cook and maid, maintain his horses, acquire enormous land properties in Orissa and Ikoyi, and contest and win the kingship of his village, Orissa Kingdom. He also saved up enough money to acquire land parcels in God's forgotten places, the wasteland parcels later known as Victoria Island. A long way from Ondo, about two hundred miles away, he now owned the biggest parcels of land in Lagos, worth more than $2.5 billion, including their developments. That was why the court apportioned Kabiyesi Edukoya Adekunle III, his grandson, to supervise the equitable settlement of the land deal, and that was why Kabiyesi Adekunle III let his most trusted friend, his wife, Princess Yemisi Adekunle, handle this assignment.

CHAPTER 8

John Okorocha talked Prince Edukoya into going on a weekend getaway trip to Reno, Nevada. Reno was famous for gambling. In fact, almost all aspects of gambling were legal in the cities in the state of Nevada. The state of Nevada had had legal gambling laws before Nevada joined the Union. In fact, a gambling bill was one of the oldest bills signed into law in the state of Nevada. One of the state's provisions in joining the Union had been that the federal government would not meddle in that aspect of the state's law and business. Casinos provided the city of Reno and Nevada with huge revenues. The casino businesses were well regulated. Forty percent of Reno's revenue came from casinos, and they contributed about 32 percent of the state's revenue. The casino owners were required to make all the rules of the games public to all the gamblers. One had to have a license to operate a casino and had to display full disclosure of the rules of the game transparently. That way, everything was on the table. The licensee had to display full disclosure about the rules of each game played in the casino or anywhere in the state of Nevada where gambling was played. That included all retail outlets and service operatives. It made the introductions of new games seldom.

Nevada also had legal prostitution. It was among the oldest bills signed into law in the state. At first, they used to stay in drinking parlors called saloons. The prostitutes were organized to chase after men mining gold and other precious metals. Later, all prostitutes were required to carry legal identification cards given to them when they were registered, with their pictures conspicuously and boldly displayed on their ID cards. Group prostitution parlors were allowed, and the parlors were licensed to operate too. They gave the prostitutes maximum protection, and they were highly regulated by the cities and the state government. They also were an important revenue contributor to the cities and the state of Nevada. However, the law did not require the prostitutes to operate exclusively within the parlors. The law required the prostitutes to be licensed and registered, and they had to be roomed to engage in the act of servicing sex.

That was one reason out-of-town prostitutes joined the parlors, in addition to security and health reasons. The parlors had strict rules set by themselves and by the governments. They required the prostitutes to undergo regular medical checkups and wear protective gear at all times when engaging in any type of sexual activity. The prostitutes who joined the parlors charged more for their sex services, about $200 per engagement, excluding tips, depending on the sexual services the woman was to perform. Straight intercourse was usually underrated. The sex acts also enjoyed the parlor's maximum-security protection. The parlors also provided escort services for their clients. However, the escorts were advised not to engage in any form of sexual activity with their clients. Most clients insisted it came with the package, which it rarely did. However, most escorts made private arrangements to make their clients happy.

Prince Edukoya Adekunle was not a fan of these sexual acts; however, it was interesting to hear John detail the matter. John Okorocha had never engaged in the sexual services either. Mama Akudo, though she appeared naive at times, adequately fed him with all romantic activities as if they were going out of business. John had gathered the information in a sociology class at Stanford University when a classmate of his presented the discussion for his term paper. Yemisi was a persuading beauty, and she was more than enough for Prince Edukoya to chew on. Any man overlooking such a challenging beauty must have been out of his mind.

When Edukoya proposed, though his proposal was well received by Yemisi, they had not engaged in sexual intercourse. In fact, he always excused himself whenever he accidentally saw Yemisi half dressed or naked. It always bothered her when he did that.

With the few romantic hugs and kisses displayed, Yemisi wondered if she was not attractive enough for this son of a king. After their engagement, Yemisi assumed those respects of delayed sexual activities would jump out the window, but they didn't. She wondered if she was the right sexual partner for the prince. She wondered if their relationship was a way for him to hide his true sexual preference. She began to assume that after seeing him in the company of a couple of gay friends. Perhaps Bola's death had been so devastating to him that his choice for another sexual preference emerged. All the men in her past she had engaged in a romantic relationship had wanted to eat her alive before she pulled down her panties. Her ex-suitor had ejaculated in his underwear during a romantic engagement with her the first time they made love. Edukoya often highlighted how attractive she was and was honored to have her accept his proposal. She wondered if her agreeing to marry him was too soon and too quick of a response. She should have made him beg to the point that his manhood was sticking out of his pants, ready to have sex the moment she said yes, she thought.

It had been more than nine months since they were introduced at the wedding. It had been more than three months since their engagement. Overall, they had known each other for about twelve months since they entered into a romantic engagement; however, no sexual activity occurred. The hugging, kissing, and overall romantic engagements without sexual intercourse were beginning to bore her. She thought he was looking for a virgin. Bola, his deceased wife, had been a virgin when they met. Bola's few months' crush on John Okorocha had led to repeated pecks on his cheek. There had been no kisses plastered on their lips and no sexual intercourse involved. Edukoya was the only man Bola had kissed on his lips and the only man she'd had sexual intercourse with. The first time Bola had had sexual intercourse with Edukoya had been the first time they kissed, after their engagement ceremony. By the traditional engagement in Yoruba land, all the rituals about marriage had been completed. The lady had become a married woman. Edukoya had been a virgin too. Bola and Edukoya had gone to a self-taught sex school together. Maybe he was expecting the same situation from Yemisi, she agonized. She couldn't remake herself again. Being a thoughtful and respectable woman, she kept her agonies to herself. She refused to seek her sister's or anyone else's advice.

Yemisi had numerous sexual engagements with three men before her marriage to Edukoya. She was lucky to dodge pregnancy, even though she had no protection of any kind during her repeated sexual engagements with those men. Yemisi loved to have sexual intercourse, but she loved to have it with a particular man she was in love and romantically involved with at the time. The first time she had sex was in high school. He was her first love and the boy who broke her virginity. His name was Olufemi, and she nicknamed him Femi. How could she forget? The first time they had sex, Femi was struggling to put his penis into her vagina, when his father walked in on them. It was embarrassing. They were fourteen then, finishing class four in secondary, and they were both virgins. After that awful encounter with Femi's father, they went on having sex repeatedly now that Femi knew where to put his penis.

Then she met Kanyonde at the University of Nigeria, Ile Ife. She thought Kanyonde was the One. Kanyonde was exceptionally brilliant, a talent made for the Supreme Court. He was studying law, and he was good at all the subjects leading to his graduation. He was headed for first-class honors. She was a freshman, and at fifteen, she was a big girl, slim, fit, and exceptionally pretty. Kanyonde was tall and breathtakingly handsome. She saw him kissing another girl in the library. After that incident, things turned cold between them.

She met Dele at his graduation ceremony. He was a medical doctor graduating from the University of Nigeria, Lagos. Her close girlfriend Dodie at Ile Ife was Dele's younger sister. Yemisi joined her for her elder brother's graduation ceremony. Dele was so taken by her exceptional attractiveness and intelligence that he proposed to her after one month of dating. With his persistence, Yemisi agreed to marry him under one condition: that she utilize her federal government scholarship to study abroad as a nurse practitioner at San Jose State University. She then would come back and have an official church wedding ceremony. Both were Christians. The traditional ceremonies were performed in their village in Ondo State, and she moved in with him before taking off to America in 1968. She was technically a married woman when she met Edukoya.

She didn't think she had committed any offense to hurt him; after all, he was not in the picture by then. She had heard about Kabiyesi Lawansin Adekunle II as their king; however, the furthest thing from her mind was his son, the crown prince of Orissa Kingdom, proposing to her in wedlock. She couldn't dismiss her past. She enjoyed sexual intercourse very much by then, and there was nothing to be ashamed of. It threw her off when letters came from Agbala and Epele with the traditional wedding fully and successfully executed in their village in Ondo State. Edukoya's father, Kabiyesi Adekunle II, extended more than a full refund of all the monies spent in Yemisi's previous traditional marriage. She partially moved in to live with him, with her remaining belongings stored in Iyabo's garage in San Francisco. She thought they'd share his room and his bed, but he warmed her up to another room. That was a week before John Okorocha invited him on the Reno getaway weekend trip.

To her surprise, he invited Iyabo, who was married and had three kids of her own, to San Jose to stay with the kids while they took off to Reno. Iyabo was an industrial management professor at UC Berkeley. Patrick, her firstborn, born out of wedlock, was off to UC Santa Cruz, studying industrial chemistry. Reno was about 180 miles from the Bay Area. John worked the graveyard shift as a structural engineer and dozed off the moment they crossed the Bay Bridge, heading northbound on Highway 80 to Reno. John had comfortably gone to sleep. They were riding on the Greyhound bus service.

Prince Edukoya said, "I notice you are unhappy lately. Are you having second thoughts about moving in with me?"

After a moment, Yemisi replied with the same question: "Are you having second thoughts about me moving in with you?"

Edukoya, realizing that such an answer with the same question would not make any headway, stopped talking. Instead, he concentrated on taking pictures along the way.

They went into one of the casinos straight from the bus. Edukoya was excited to play the jackpots. He won twenty-five dollars in his first round of play. He'd invested twenty-five cents. He was carried away by his winnings, so he stayed on.

Seeing him so joyful and carried away, Yemisi pulled John aside, narrating her concerns. John knew him well and had the answer to her confusion ready for her before she could finish her sentence.

John and Edukoya had known each other since they were four years old. They had been neighbors. John's father had been the principal of Saint Gregory Secondary School in Yaba, while Prince Lawansin Adekunle had been a judge of the high court at Yaba. They also had been neighbors living adjacent to each other in Ikoyi. John and Edukoya had attended the same preschool, the same primary school, and the same prestigious secondary school, King's College, Lagos. They had been classmates when they met Bola. Bola had met John first, but due to default in tribalism, she'd chosen Edukoya over John. Edukoya had been torn apart when he learned the reason Bola chose him, and he'd refused initially to marry Bola. John had had to make peace between them by delaying his travel to America to begin his studies at Stanford University for one more weekend. He'd traveled on July 23, 1943. He had been Edukoya's best man. Edukoya and John were like brothers from different mothers.

John coached Yemisi on how to seduce Edukoya. Edukoya had narrated his own version to John earlier. John had reminded him how it had been with Bola, with Edukoya wanting a woman to make all the moves. John told both of them separately to grab what was theirs.

They settled in the hotel room for the night, sleeping in the same bed together. John excused himself, went outside, and claimed he needed a breath of fresh air. He came back with a justice of the peace. They were stunned and surprised. John Okorocha again was his best man. The girlfriend of the justice of the peace was the maid of honor. That night in Reno,

Nevada, was the first time they conjugated their relationship after they married. They agreed it was beautiful and worth the wait. From then onward, they brought out the tiger and the tigress in themselves. They made love countless times that night, and the result was the conception of Tunde, their first baby boy.

PART 3

AT THE COURT

CHAPTER 9

The Lagos mainland court set a date for the preliminary hearing of the land case. Meanwhile, an influential oil company had discovered a crude oil reserve in the area, along a 110-mile stretch of swampy land along Sepele Road. The fifty-mile stretch where the rich reserve was concentrated was within Lagos State's limits, and the land largely belonged to Kabiyesi Edukoya Adekunle III's family. The state and federal governments became involved in the land case big-time. They sent letters to the court outlining the first claim. Princess Yemisi got a copy of the letter and became outraged. She turned the letter over to her husband, His Lordship Kabiyesi Edukoya Adekunle III, for his review and to offer legal guidance. It was not what she had bargained for. The main rich crude oil reserve stretched out in a fifty-mile radius along Sepele Road.

A good portion of the wasteland, about a thirty-mile stretch, had been owned by the late Kabiyesi Lawansin Adekunle I. The land had been transferred to his offspring, with Kabiyesi Lawansin Adekunle II owning 70 percent of the land and his siblings owning 30 percent of the land. Lawansin II's 70 percent share had been willed to Edukoya and his siblings. Edukoya had gotten 70 percent of his father's share, and 30 percent had gone to his siblings. Edukoya was to donate 30 percent of the proceeds from his own share to the Orissa Kingdom if the land was to be sold or leased out. However, Lawansin Adekunle II had given Edukoya the greater controlling interest on all the lands he owned and their developed properties therein. Kabiyesi

Lawansin Adekunle I had bought the land for four pounds, six shillings, and two pence. The lands were attached wastelands with shallow water used mainly to cultivate rice when rice was introduced to the west coast of Africa. He'd bought it on December 14, 1858. At the time, he was a young man teaching at the prestigious King's College, Lagos, with ten years of teaching experience, making his same starting salary of nine pounds, eight shillings, and two pence monthly. He upgraded his father's mud house to a modern architectural design of the nineteenth century at a cost of twenty-seven pounds.

There was a serious debate about his taking in a second wife. Lawansin Adekunle's first wife could not carry a baby full term. They were married right after he graduated from high school, at the age of twenty, when he was attending the Cambridge University campus in Ibadan. They had been together for almost thirteen years. His own father had not had much luck either. He'd married two wives and had four children. Lawansin's mom had given his father him, her only child. After repeated infant mortality, they'd given up on her trying to have another child. The father's second wife, Alamo, had given him three more children, a boy and two girls.

There was a debate about concentrating on buying more landed properties with his savings, especially the forgotten wastelands south of Ikoyi and in the middle belt of Eko City. The latter undertakings were also persuasive. He had already developed a tiny parcel of land, his residence, near King's College, on the outskirts of Eko City, at a cost of twenty-eight pounds, including the cost of the land parcel. It was a six-bedroom one-floor house with outside plumbing. He also built three rooms, a boys' house, in his backyard with outdoor plumbing too.

The middle-belt Eko City land parcels were relatively small parcels costing a fortune at about five pounds for a plot of land. That was the cheapest land plot located on the outskirts of the city. The parcels also were scarce at that price. His father; his mother; and his wife, Rosalyn, pressured him to get a second wife. Being the first son of Olabanjo Adekunle, he reluctantly accommodated, taking on a second wife, Idowu Adekunle, because he needed children. Idowu was the mother of Lawansin Adekunle II. He invested his money in a certificate of deposit with the Standard Bank of Britain's operating branch in Eko City, with an annual yield of 24 percent compounded daily. That yield was able to help him accomplish both pressing issues. People rarely invested money in a bank at the time. The high yield became an attractive incentive to invest in CDs. The Standard Bank of Britain was renamed Standard Bank of Nigeria after Nigeria became an independent country on October 1, 1960. It was renamed again as First Bank of Nigeria in the mid-1970s.

During that time, King's College, Lagos, and other affluent secondary schools, which were few in number, were canvassing for the best and brightest kids around the relatively newly created territory to attend their schools. Nigeria's designation as a colonized territory came in 1914 after the amalgamation, when the Igbos, the largest southeastern tribe, reluctantly agreed to join the union. The schools were relatively rich, with few competing secondary schools to share whatever funds were available. They offered their best and brightest new incoming students free tuition. Most times, the scholarships extended to full room and board. The secondary schools were positioned as middle colleges. They offered A- and O-level diplomas. *O* stood for an ordinary certificate of education, which took a typical student five years to complete, while *A* stood for an advanced certificate of education, which took a typical student an additional two years to complete. The A-level certificate was almost equivalent to American associate's degrees offered at junior colleges. However, an associate's degree was basically a university-style degree program with almost unlimited professional career courses to choose from and might lead one to a professional career path, such as nursing and auto technician work, among many others. Conversely, an advanced certificate of education was structured like an upper-secondary-school extension classes. Students were exposed to limited classes and none geared toward professionalism. They were basically learning advanced English, mathematics, and more.

An exceptionally bright kid, Mathew Eleyenmi, took the entrance exam to enter King's College, Lagos, in 1864. Lo and behold, he scored 100 percent in English, arithmetic, geography, and Bible knowledge. Because the entrance examination took two days of intense writing and was far from where most of the students came from, they were housed, and all their boarding expenses were paid for by the school. A good number of them would get scholarships anyway when they were admitted into the school. The distance from home for most of the kids seeking admission to the prestigious secondary schools could top a one-hundred-mile radius. With travel made even more difficult by poor transportation and rough earth roads, it was prudent to house the kids for the duration of the entrance exam and interview. The result of the test was announced a day after the examination was over. The interviews were conducted on those who passed the entrance examination, and a handful of highly talented kids were chosen as the future form-one students for the following academic year. The students were prepared to spend about a week at the school's campus.

Mathew Eleyenmi of Ile Ife was a breathtaking, outstanding young man at the age of fourteen. His uncle Felix Eleyenmi, who was among the school's custodians, introduced him to the principal. His uncle was a partial housekeeper for the principal. Mathew was living with his uncle in Lagos, and Ile Ife was about 250 miles from Lagos. After Mathew scored a perfect 100 percent in all the subjects on the examination, King's College said he cheated on the examination, and the school was about to deny him a seat in form one the following academic year. Mr. Lawansin Adekunle intervened on his behalf by suggesting he retake the examination. This time, being the senior mathematics and physics teacher, he conducted the test himself with two teachers watching over him. Mathew Eleyenmi was a must-have student, even correcting a question he intentionally had worded wrongly. Mathew was instantly admitted, finished up the remaining term in form one, and was promoted to form two the next schoolyear. He took the first position on his final form-one examination.

Mathew had to go back to Ile Ife to his parents after that school year was over. He needed some stationeries for the next school year's first term. His family was poor, and it had taken them months, if not a year, to gather his provisions for the first school term. Although his school fees were paid for, as were room and board, by his scholarship funds, cash for other necessities and initial pocket money to begin the school term left his parents hard-pressed. After the initial cash outlay by him, King's College would extend eight shillings and ten pence monthly for his pocket money. He sent five shillings back home to Ile Ife to help pay for his siblings' primary school fees. His uncle had saved up some money and bought the stretch of thirty-five-mile-radius swampy wasteland on Sepele Road in Lagos in 1843. He bought the land for three pounds, twenty shillings, and four pence.

The wastelands had been used as a hideout for young men and women hiding from kidnappers for slave traders during slavery. Most of the slaves escaped from their owners. After the permanent abolition of slavery in the late 1700s, the swampy wastelands had become worthless. That was why the land was sold at a giveaway price, since it was no longer making money for the original owners of the land parcels. The swampy lands were sold for pennies or given away by the kabiyesi who had jurisdiction over the lands in exchange for favors done for him. The owners of the hideaways had made their ill-gotten money by collecting ransom from the highest bidder for the presumed lost slaves. Felix Eleyenmi was hand-greased and persuaded to buy the swampy lands after they were practically worthless to the landowners. He'd attended standard three in education and was knowledgeable enough to document the deed agreements in writing.

Money was needed badly for Mathew Eleyenmi's trip to and back from Ile Ife. It was a journey that would take him roughly eight days to accomplish. He was to come back to Lagos with Adetoye, his uncle's new bride. Mr. Adekunle rescued the kid again by fronting the funds. He bought the land for four pounds, six shillings, and two pence from Felix Eleyenmi in order to provide funds for Mathew Eleyenmi's trip. Among the fifty-mile stretch of the rich crude oil reserve, a thirty-five-mile stretch had millions of barrels of crude oil underneath the earth's crust. It was estimated to be worth more than $10 billion. The crude oil was near the surface of the earth. His Lordship Kabiyesi Edukoya Adekunle III and his family owned a thirty-mile stretch, and Felix Eleyenmi's descendants owned the remaining five-mile stretch of the land. Lawansin Adekunle I insisted Felix Eleyenmi reserve that five-mile stretch for his future generation. Felix Eleyenmi shared the land with his only brother, who'd raised him. He gave him two miles and kept three miles for himself.

CHAPTER 10

My husband,

All the years I have been with you have seemed so fast, likened to our journey from Antioch to San Jose that night. I made every effort to have you hold my hand, and you thought your hand was in my way of reaching the gear stick. You removed your hand quickly and said, "I'm sorry." Your hand was not in my way; I was reaching for your hand to hold mine. I fell in love then. You delivered gentleness in a profound manner—sometimes too profound. It bordered on thick-skinned. But there were corrections. You allowed your sincere actions that followed suit to explain. They were quick on the delivery. I thought you didn't want me anymore, having heard the tales of my past. You set no standard for me, and as a result, I didn't feel ashamed of my body. Initially, I thought you were avoiding me because I was not a virgin. You were very receptive to my little experience I carried along to the bed we shared for the first time. You measured me as the best. I watched you and assumed it was an exaggeration, but you meant it: "The best I ever had," you said. That enabled me to bring the firepower in me, and I went ballistic. You never stopped liking it, and you never stopped loving me. We held hands and kissed in public. Those hands that were short-lived during our trip to San Jose are now ours to hold forever.

The myth was over, and upon your ascending to the throne, you made me your crown princess. Me, the daughter of Lawrence Adeniji. It honestly caught me by surprise. Since Tunde was a baby, I assumed you would give the title to Ogunleye Adekunle, your immediate younger brother, at least to hold it temporarily until Tunde became of age. What were you thinking? You knew your death might automatically make me the queen of Orissa Kingdom. The first queen in Ondo State and perhaps in the entire Yoruba tribe. As if that were not enough, you trusted inexperienced me to handle the enormous land deals and your entire business empire. You gave me free hands to manage the resources of our people. You were proud of me, even when I thought I had let you down. I have found you, and I'll never let you go.

You are my life and my breath. I had thought I wasn't pleasing you enough. You have repeatedly assured me I was what you needed all this while. You constantly watched my back in case I fell, and you never let me hit the ground, not even once. You said to me, "I know you are a human being, because I felt your soul, and I felt your flesh." The same goes for me. I felt your soul, and I have continued to feel your flesh.

Each time I feel them, I wish it would never stop. You are an amazing man. You are a fine man. And you are my friend. I have been with a few men in my life. Sincerely, no man compared with you. You make me happy. I am the luckiest woman in the world because you made me feel so. I love you so much. I will never let you down. Thank you, my love.

Yemisi

After reading the documents from the court outlining the state and federal governments' first claim on the land, His Lordship Kabiyesi Adekunle III needed a trusted friend to handle the latest situation. The sincere letter from the heart of Princess Yemisi did the trick. He called her into their bedroom; carried her to bed; and gave her a long, tight hug and a long, drawn-out kiss. The kiss was satisfying to the extent that Princess Yemisi kept it a little longer. It was quite a kiss. Though their lips were plastered like glue, their saliva managed to leak out down their jaws. With the deepest penetration he'd ever had and her wetness likened to the ocean, their lovemaking set a new record.

At the end of the long, drawn-out romance, he said, "I trust you. Go get them, tiger."

Princess Yemisi came out of the bedroom smiling and full of rejuvenated vitality. She said, "The game is not over yet."

The state and federal governments appointed a three-judge panel to look into the cases. A portion of the rich oil reserve cases were transferred from state court to federal court. The landowners wanted to settle the cases individually, but Princess Yemisi wanted another approach. The governments would apply the divide-and-conquer strategy because they could afford the legal cost. However, Princess Yemisi saw it differently. She developed a plan of action. She summoned all the participants to visit the king's palace in Orissa. The strategy was to put up a united front. The union's four-day strategy meeting emerged with one voice. She opted for new leadership, but the union overwhelmingly chose Princess Yemisi to be their new leader. There were two torn cases before the courts. One of them involved the already developed areas on Ikoyi and Victoria Island, which was still handled by the state court. The other involved the swampy wasteland along the fifty-mile stretch of Sepele Road in Lagos, where millions of barrels of rich crude oil had been discovered. The cases were handled by the federal court of appeals. Princess Yemisi's team spent four days in their strategic mappings. Princess Yemisi Adekunle was now riding on new supreme horsepower.

CHAPTER 11

Good deeds were never forgotten. By coincidence, Mathew Eleyenmi's grandson, the Honorable Justice Sunday Eleyenmi, a federal appellate court judge, was appointed by the Justice Department of Nigeria to be the presiding chief judge of the three-judge panel reviewing the cases of Ikoyi's and Victoria Island's land deals. A thirty-mile stretch of the 110-mile swampy wasteland where the fertile crude oil field had been found belonged to Adekunle's family. A thirty-eight-mile stretch was in the center of the fifty-mile zone. The active crude oil was near the surface and ready to be tapped. That alone was estimated to fetch about forty million barrels of crude oil worth billions of dollars.

Those active land parcels belonged to Adekunle's family with a twist. The original agreements signed by Justice Anthony Ogbolowomiri in the mid-1800s stated that a five-mile stretch in the thirty-eight-mile area zoned by the government, where the active reserve was, still belonged to Felix Eleyenmi. Lawansin Adekunle I had persuaded him to keep the land parcels for his future great-grandchildren. Now the crude oil discovered there was estimated to amount to more than five million barrels and counting. The crucial document was buried among more than ten thousand documents to be analyzed. A twenty-three-year-old lawyer, Oliver Duruchi, fresh from the Nigerian Youth Service Corps and schooled at the University of Nigeria, Benin, uncovered the crucial revelation. It was a game-changer and a twist Princess Yemisi had not bargained for. She was of the belief the thirty-eight-mile stretch belonged to her family exclusively.

Coincidentally, the head chef of Kabiyesi Adekunle III, the chess player, Evans Eleyenmi, was the direct firstborn great-grandson of Felix Eleyenmi. Yemisi brought the new revelation and documents to her husband, Kabiyesi Edukoya Adekunle III, for his review. The brilliant lawyer went through the documents over and over and determined their authenticity. He concluded, "My chess friend is worth millions." The next step was to introduce Evans Eleyenmi as co-owner of a five-mile stretch of the land parcel adjacent to Kabiyesi Edukoya Adekunle III's land parcel to the entire Adekunle family.

Their hope that the cases would tilt their way had begun to fade. The Honorable Justice Sunday Eleyenmi, the presiding chief judge appointed by the federal Justice Department to oversee the cases, had a huge conflict of interest. Although he reassured the panel of his impartiality, the federal Justice Department boss did not buy it. His interest in the case was no longer simply in knowing the Adekunles; he owned the case as one of the coplaintiffs. His grand-uncle owned a sizable portion of the land deal, about a five-mile radius, worth millions of dollars. It would not have been much of a conflict of interest, if not for one little clause put in the original land deal: "All the land parcels located in the swampy wasteland of Victoria Island, about a thirty-eight-mile radius southeast of Victoria Island, shall be 60 percent belonging to Felix Eleyenmi and 40 percent belonging to Michael Eleyenmi." Felix Eleyenmi had put in the original clause before he sold the land to Mr. Lawansin Adekunle, out of love for his only brother. Michael Eleyenmi, the elder brother of Felix Eleyenmi, had put Felix Eleyenmi through school up to standard three. He'd paid for his brother's trip to Lagos and given him all the money he had saved for the seed money to establish his own business. The business had failed, and Felix Eleyenmi had landed a job as head custodian at King's College, making about one pound a month. He'd sent for Mathew, his nephew, to get him educated and paid his school fees up to standard six. Michael Eleyenmi was not lettered; he'd only learned how to read the Bible and write letters with questionable grammatical correctness. He'd stopped going to school at standard two when their father died, as there had been no funds left to finish his elementary school. He'd learned to read the Bible and was active in the church.

Michael Eleyenmi was the grandfather of the Honorable Justice Sunday Eleyenmi. Justice Sunday Eleyenmi was the cousin of Evans Eleyenmi, the great-grandson of Felix Eleyenmi. Although the land parcels were sold to Lawansin Adekunle I, the adjacent five-mile radius of the land, the epic center, was set aside for Felix Eleyenmi. Lawansin Adekunle I compelled Justice Anthony Ogbolowomiri to write in the clause before signing the documents. The five-mile-radius land parcel would be divided: 60 percent went to Felix Eleyenmi's descendants, and 40 percent went to Michael Eleyenmi's descendants. Because of his lettered high capacity in law, Justice Sunday Eleyenmi organized a legal team to represent the Eleyenmi family's interest in the land deal. The clause meant that Justice Sunday Eleyenmi was represented in the lawsuit against the federal government of Nigeria and the Lagos State government of Nigeria. The governments were sued separately. The lawsuit accused the governments of "willfully and wrongfully seizing land parcels, a fifty-mile radius southeast of Sepele Road in Lagos State in Nigeria, belonging to the stated parties, the united group of His Lordship Kabiyesi Edukoya Lawansin Adekunle III of Orissa Kingdom in Ondo State, Nigeria. Also, the represented parties are citizens of Nigeria and have chosen Princess Yemisi Adekunle, also a citizen of Nigeria, as the lead negotiator."

The governments were positioned as the defendants, and the landowners, headed by Princess Yemisi Adekunle, were the plaintiffs. The law chamber of Lawrence H. D. Obasanjo, Esquire, was assigned to represent the team of the landowners. The state of the case made it impossible for Justice Sunday Eleyenmi not to employ some degree of partiality. The state and federal governments concluded that his appointment to head the three-judge panel was shooting themselves in their feet, and for that reason, he had to be replaced. His petition to reinstate himself as the chief judge of the panel was denied.

To show transparency, the initial panel of judges was dissolved, and a new one was appointed. The new chief justice of the panel was the Honorable Justice Hillary Chukwunenyenwa Onyemerekwe. Justice Chukwu Onyemerekwe was a hard-nosed, no-nonsense judge. He had gone to school at the University of Nigeria, Nsuka, and graduated in the law class of 1976 with a perfect 4.0 and first-class honors. He had been the valedictorian of his graduating law class. In the speech he'd delivered to his law class of 1976, he'd said, "Ambition should be geared towards helping people, not to oppress people." Made for the Supreme Court, he was lettered as a Supreme Court law clerk for five years after his graduation.

He was quickly appointed to the federal bench as one of the appellate justices of the second district court of appeals in Lagos. He was later appointed as the presiding chief justice of the second district circuit court of appeals. He'd earned his LLD from the University of Nigeria, Ibadan and was an adjunct professor of law at the University of Nigeria, Lagos. He was also fair-minded. He'd married his secondary school sweetheart and had four children with her, all boys. They were grown now. Chike Onyemerekwe, the last of his sons, followed in his father's footsteps to the letter. He was his carbon copy.

PART 4

THE BROTHER I AM GLAD TO HAVE

CHAPTER 12

The graduation of Oyodele Fenmi Adekunle from the Massachusetts Institute of Technology (MIT) with a PhD in structural engineering was a big deal for the entire family of Adekunle, the kingdom of Orissa, and the state of Ondo. The news that he would be coming back upon graduation to take on a tutorial engagement with the Orissa Polytechnic department of engineering, his partial alma mater, and also open a civil engineering office at Akure was welcome to the entire region. His Lordship Kabiyesi Edukoya Adekunle III was featured as the keynote speaker of the doctoral engineering graduation at MIT. He was also featured as the keynote speaker at the general graduation ceremony, which was mainly for master's and undergraduate degrees. As a result, there were lots of activities his entourage would be engaged in that summer.

There were several engagement activities on the table for His Lordship Kabiyesi Adekunle III that summer in America. Top of it all was his coming home with his last born, Dr. Oyodele Adekunle, PhD. He would be traveling to Washington, DC, to meet with five US senators separately: two Republicans, two Democrats, and one Independent. He would address a joint session of the Congressional Black Caucus. While in Washington, DC, he was invited to the Howard University African Student Union graduation party. He also would be traveling to Houston, Texas, to address the Progressive Nigerian National Party, a political party that sponsored progressive presidential and senatorial candidates in Nigeria.

Kabiyesi Adekunle III was seen as a progressive leader. He then would be traveling to California to meet with his childhood friend John Okorocha. He would finish his American tour in California for about one week before heading back to Nigeria.

His entourage would disperse in Houston. That would leave him with Princess Yemisi and Dele to spend a quiet week at John Okorocha's villa, a ten-acre ranch in Yuba City, near Sacramento. Ephram, Lois, and their kids were back at Harvard, where he resided and taught mathematics at the university. Bunmi and Tunde flew back home to Nigeria from Washington, DC, after their father, Kabiyesi Adekunle III, addressed the Congressional Black Caucus. Both of them were medical doctors. They had taken time off for the all-important occasion of their youngest brother's graduation with a PhD from MIT. Dr. John Okorocha flew back to Sacramento to await the arrival of His Highness Kabiyesi Edukoya Adekunle III. John Okorocha helped start-up companies to reach their full maturity. He had made a fortune, with his wealth nearing $4.5 billion. The companies he'd nurtured to full maturity included Yahoo, Microsoft, Amazon, Intel, Dell, Apple, and more. He was seventy-eight years old. He frequented Nigeria but permanently resided in the United States. He recently had undergone open-heart bypass surgery. His friend Eduks, as he called Edukoya, would be spending the rest of his visit at his ranch with him.

On the second day of his visit with his oldest and dearest friend, John Okorocha, Edukoya started complaining of enormous fatigue and pressing pain in the upper center of his back. Having had similar symptoms, John quickly called his friend Dr. Franklin Omolewa, his cardiologist, to rush over and take a look at his friend Edukoya. The cardiologist said Edukoya was experiencing a mild heart attack and should be rushed to the hospital for further observation. Edukoya's experiences of pain and fatigue had started in Nigeria. It came, stayed for a relatively short period of time, and then went away. Sometimes he asked Princess Yemisi to administer to him some painkiller medicine, which he seldom took. During his speeches, he was sweating and needed constant drinking water. He didn't think it was a big health problem since he had experienced it before. On his way to the hospital, he was speechless, suffering a mild stroke. He was quickly rushed to the emergency room at UC Davis Medical Center in Sacramento. He had a heart attack and a mild stroke simultaneously. All those activities caught up with him. The occasional pain and fatigue became frequent and were indications of much larger health issues.

"Thank Jesus Christ it happened to him in America," said Princess Yemisi. That was the consolation. He underwent a series of tests at the hospital and was kept in the hospital for ten days. It was determined he had four full artery blockages that needed a bypass and two partial artery blockages that could be repaired through angioplasty. Thankfully, the heart attack and stroke eased up with no body impairment. The doctors advised him that with speech therapy, he would fully regain his voice and his faculties.

The next looming problem was cardiac arrest. A surgeon was assigned to him, and it was determined he would undergo open-heart surgery at the age of seventy-eight years. That was an enormous problem. What about the risk of surviving a six-bypass open-heart surgery at the age of seventy-eight years? What about his leadership role in the kingdom of Orissa? Who would be the temporary anointed kabiyesi of Orissa Kingdom? Princess Yemisi refused to step away out of his sight for the one month he waited for his surgery to take place. There was a secret arrangement made for Princess Yemisi to travel to Nigeria to hand over the reign of power to Dr. Tunde Adekunle, her first son.

Princess Yemisi, on hearing the plan, became visibly angry. Edukoya saw her anger for the first time after forty years of marriage. To her, nothing mattered anymore. She began to cry, for the first time imagining her life without the man she called her best friend. It was frightening. Consumed with this fear, she became sick and was hospitalized for three days for observation. There was a mountain of costs for all the hospitalizations. They were estimated to top $250,000 and counting. That was not a problem for His Highness. John Okorocha opted to absorb the total cost of their hospitalization. Edukoya was grateful. Dele; Tunde; Kenmiejo, his first daughter; and Kayide, a nurse who lived in Queens, New York, with her husband, Dr. Alex Johnson, a surgeon, waited throughout the surgery and were at his bedside after the surgery. The surgery went on for about ten and a half hours. The surgery took a little longer than normal because of the repair of the two partially blocked arteries.

On the suggestion of Dr. Alexander Johnson, a cardiological surgeon, UC Davis surgeons decided to do six bypasses. A video of the surgery was given to Princess Yemisi. John Okorocha was supportive of his dearest friend and was at his bedside the whole time he was in the hospital. John Okorocha and Princess Yemisi slept in the hospital with Edukoya throughout his stay. They showered and changed clothes there in the presidential lodge at the hospital. Mama Akudo made sure her husband, Edukoya, and Princess Yemisi were well fed while staying in the hospital.

The surgery was successful. Dr. Franklin Omolewa advised him that as soon as he felt better, Nigeria would be a good place to recover. There was scheduled physical therapy for three and a half months. After four months of his recovering from the surgery, he felt like a young man in his midtwenties, with increased and renewed energy and sexual appetite. Sometimes his appetite for sex bordered on uncontrollable.

Princess Yemisi welcomed the news after being sexually starved for a long time because of his frequent pain and fatigue before his surgery.

His two-week tour of the United States wound up becoming seven and a half months, nearly eight months. Dr. Okorocha, PhD, was a great host. He enjoyed the visit from his childhood friend. It gave them time to relive their childhood once again. Edukoya was a breathtaking guest. Goodbye was reserved for another day and another time; they embraced at the airport and said, "So long."

CHAPTER 13

John Okorocha was born in the village of Ife in Mbaise in Imo State, Nigeria. After his birth, his father, Godfrey Okorocha, took him and his mother to Lagos to live with him. His father was then the principal of Saint Gregory High School in Yaba. He had two more siblings, Mather, his only sister, and Andrew, the youngest sibling. Mather and Andrew were born in Lagos. Ife was a progressive and enlightened village of its time, with early developments rarely seen at that time. In fact, Ife was a relatively advanced village. The village eventually headquartered the diocese of the Anglican Church Missionary Society (CMS), with a presiding bishop resident at Saint Michael's Cathedral in Ife. Ife was a pioneer in education. The Anglican church built its first elementary school in Mbaise in the village of Ife. The school was named Ife Central School. The school was built in the mid-to-late 1800s.

Early pioneers of Mbaise owed their early education to Ife Central School. Although CMS built the school, it was nondenominational, to encourage all children to attend primary school education. Students traveled tens of miles to attend the elementary school. The remnants of its preserved old mud-house dormitories were visible for many years after. By the late 1930s, Ife became the first village in Mbaise to build a secondary school. The school was named Ife Grammar School. Again, the school was nondenominational, to encourage all students to attend a secondary school education. The secondary school was an early start-up for many talented people. The secondary school was also built by CMS. To attend a secondary school education was seen as attending a university in those days. Entrance examinations and consequent interviews were conducted to find the best to attend the school.

The students mostly came from thirty or so miles out of town. Dormitories were necessary for the out-of-town students. During those days, the government, out of lack of financial resources, had a passive interest in education. As a result, the churches, mainly Christian, Catholic, and Anglican dioceses, adequately picked up the slack. Indeed, the churches did an outstanding job of getting Nigerians ready to meet the challenges of the future. They set a high standard of education. Most students capped their education there in secondary school. Therefore, thorough preparedness was a must-have for many of the students. Although school fees were paid, church contributions made an enormous impact in aiding the schools. The teachers were directly paid by the dioceses, which in turn freed up funds for the schools' management.

One of the students of Ife Central School was Godfrey Okorocha, the father of John Okorocha. Godfrey Okorocha was spotted by a group of missionaries. He was working on his mother's farm, plowing ridges for her corn and cassava plants. He was fifteen years old and woefully uneducated. The missionaries were negotiating with the heads of the kinsmen of Ife to build a church, an elementary school, and a college campus. *College* was what secondary school was called in those days. The missionaries painted an uplifting future for what Godfrey would amount to with the elementary school being built in Ife. His name before his baptism was Ngozichukwu Onyekwere Okorocha. He was an instant early convert to Christianity. The attractive feature of the remote village was water. The village sat on the widest bank of the Imo River. The river served as an important navigational route and location of fisheries for Mbaise. It also had served as an important slave turnover point during the slave trade. Ife had a lot of spring water underground, which made drinkable water available, an attractive feature to the white missionaries who relocated there.

Godfrey and about a dozen other older boys started at Ife Central School. They used palm leaves to build the first classroom at Ife Central School. Arithmetic, English, the Bible, and geography were richly taught at the school. When they mastered the letters of the alphabet and numbers, they spent an enormous amount of time studying arithmetic, writing, and verbal communications in the English language. The aim was to rapidly teach English language skills for the purpose of translation. Translating what the English missionaries said to the natives in the Igbo language was a necessity to communicate with their followers, none of whom spoke English. The missionaries could not speak Igbo either.

Godfrey was the smartest kid in the class. He was a tall, well-built man. He had a light skin color and was a desirable, handsome man with a pointed nose. A white missionary lady took a personal and particular interest in him, to the point she almost crossed the line with him. She showed no regret for her attempted misconduct; instead, she sent him off to Lagos, where he was trained as a missionary minister. The attractiveness of Godfrey was absorbing and persuasive at the mission in Lagos. He was breathtakingly intelligent. At the age of twenty-seven, he was given a scholarship to England for further studies in education. At Cambridge University, he met another Nigerian, Lawansin Adekunle, who later sat on the throne as Kabiyesi Lawansin Adekunle II of Orissa Kingdom in Ondo State.

Godfrey Ngozichukwu Okorocha was a tight friend of Lawansin Adekunle. Lawansin Adekunle earned a degree in law, and Godfrey earned a master's degree in education. Godfrey spent nine years in London. By that time, things had improved in Nigeria with the reluctant amalgamation uniting the three regions of Nigeria: north, east, and west. Upon Godfrey's return from London in the early 1910s, the diocese of Lagos, who'd sponsored his scholarship, had a job waiting for him as the principal of the newly built Saint Gregory High School in Yaba. Meanwhile, Lawansin Adekunle started his own law practice in Ondo City, Ondo State. Both married elementary school teachers. It was not planned. In those days, most women's education level stopped as elementary school teachers. The men and women went to a teachers' training college. Both men attended each other's wedding ceremony. First was Lawansin Adekunle in Agbala in Orissa Kingdom, and later that year was Godfrey Okorocha in Lagos. Each was the best man at the other's wedding.

Lawansin later moved to Lagos to team up with a law chamber. He had two sons. His first son was named Edukoya Lawansin Adekunle, and Edukoya's brother was named Ogunleye Debayo Adekunle. Lawansin's eloquence and persuasive style of presentation catapulted him to a seat on the bench as a high-court judge.

Godfrey Okorocha had two boys and a girl. The first boy was named John Ngozichukwu Okorocha, the girl was named Mather Amarachukwu Okorocha, and the baby boy was named Andrew Onyekwere Okorocha. Godfrey bought a big plot of land from Adekunle I on Ikoyi and built two four-plate houses with four large bedrooms each. He occupied a house with six large bedrooms.

Lawansin developed one of his father's big vacant lots on Ikoyi into a huge villa with sixteen large bedrooms and four seating areas. Coincidentally, they built their houses adjacent to each other. They refused to put up a divider fence, so their kids could play freely. The kids went to the same elementary school. As a result, John and Edukoya became tight friends at the age of two. They were classmates at the prestigious King's College in Lagos. They played together and got in trouble together.

The memories of those days were the high point of Edukoya's eight-month stay when he was recovering at John Okorocha's ranch in Yuba City after his bypass open-heart surgery.

CHAPTER 14

On the eve of November 23, 1932, Crown Prince Justice Lawansin Adekunle rushed home to Orissa Kingdom because his father, His Lordship Kabiyesi Lawansin Adekunle I, had seriously taken ill. Lawansin Adekunle I was by then the longest-ruling monarch in the history of Orissa Kingdom and perhaps the longest-ruling monarch in the history of the Yoruba tribe. He had ruled Orissa Kingdom for seventy-two years. Full of life and energy and breathtakingly handsome even at his age of 106 years, he was still tender and always at his best. Orissa's community loved him. He faced a serious health issue: heart disease coupled with rapid organ weakness. Modern medical interventions, at that time, were in their infant stage. Though Kabiyesi Adekunle I was educated, he relied on local herbalists to pick up the slack when modern medical interventions were not available. The nearest adequate medical facility was at the Cambridge University campus's Teaching Hospital in Ibadan, which was quite a distance from Orissa Kingdom. They too lacked adequate means of curing heart disease then.

The local herbalist and native doctor, Alamo, was an inadequate substitute to treat highly complex and complicated heart disease. Surgical intervention, as in open-heart surgery, was a myth and was nowhere practiced in the world then. With some luck, Alamo managed to do okay in general health treatments. Alamo searched for medicinal leaves and tree stems in the bush, knowledge mostly transferred to him from his father or close relatives. He cooked them and bathed his patient with the warm water. The herbalist also cut into pieces medicinal stems from trees, cooked them, and gave the mixture to his patients to drink. Sometimes the patient experienced minor relief, mostly out of luck due to the body's efficient self-healing mechanism, especially when warm liquid was introduced to it.

Often, the patient depended on a combination of the herbs and modern medicine, which the locals called "white man medicine," to get better. Sometimes it worked, but most times, it did not work. In fact, in most cases, the sickness got worse. The Alamo, was richly called a doctor. The villagers assumed he could see the future and could cure all diseases.

The practice of blind medicine endured, and like modern medical practitioners, the practitioners specialized. They specialized in heart disease, eye issues, gynecology and obstetrics, orthopedics, and more. Orthopedics seemed to draw the most curiosity.

Alamo meticulously aligned broken bones properly and then bandaged them together with hot spices used to coat the bones. He gave the break sufficient time to heal. The hot spices enabled all the liquids in the body to flow fast and with limited hindrance. As a result, the bones took a short period of time to heal properly. It was nothing short of a miracle. In fact, in most cases, they healed faster than with modern orthopedics. The bones healed with zero side effects and limited scars.

The luck-driven orthopedic successes of Alamo were inevitably persuasive. The compelling evidence had been told over and over again. The astonishing physical accomplishments reassured and reinforced faith in Alamo's power to heal all diseases, even the most profound, incurable diseases on earth, such as HIV, Parkinson's, Lou Gehrig's disease, cancer, and more. His Lordship Lawansin Adekunle I wholeheartedly believed in these medical practices. His indulgence proved to be fatal this time. The combination of the herbs with aspirin tablets was a killer medication. Aspirin could work well on its own. Aspirin was a medication commonly used to relieve headaches and heart disease in those days. Aspirin basically was a blood-thinner medicine used to relieve pain. It also was a muscle relaxer. In fact, aspirin later was proven to be effective in modern medical cures with a combination of surgical intervention.

There was a late last-minute rush to take him to Cambridge University Teaching Hospital in Ibadan. However, on the way to the hospital, the accompanying physician pronounced him dead. His son, Crown Prince Justice Lawansin Adekunle, was holding his hands with tears in his eyes when he passed away. They had to turn around and angrily headed back to Orissa Kingdom.

The burial of Yoruba kings was placed on record. There was no excuse to settle for less this time. His funeral spelled out his amazing credentials and accomplishments, one of which was the acquisition of the parcels of land on Ikoyi and Victoria Island in Lagos State, eventually worth billions of dollars, including the developments. In his will, 30 percent of the value from ongoing proceeds of the land was set aside for the progressive developments in Orissa Kingdom. He had ruled his kingdom without taking away a single kobo into his pocket. His key ambition had been to build a first-class medical facility for his kingdom. The land parcels were of little value by then; hence, he fell short of his ambition. That ambition was a burning wish for all Adekunles who ascended the throne. A makeshift medical facility was built to alleviate the medical needs of Orissa Kingdom during the reign of Kabiyesi Lawansin Adekunle II. The ambition was finally brought into reality by Princess Yemisi Adekunle, with the approval of her husband, His Lordship Kabiyesi Edukoya Adekunle III. Kabiyesi Edukoya Adekunle III built the state-of-the-art Orissa Polytechnic Medical Center.

CHAPTER 15

John Okorocha paid a visit to the palace. Those in the palace had never seen Kabiyesi Adekunle III as happy as when his childhood friend John Okorocha, whom he called his brother, made a phone call to him one afternoon to detail his itinerary for his upcoming visit to Nigeria. The call came when he was in an important meeting with the governor of Ondo State. All phone calls were to be withheld when Kabiyesi Edukoya Adekunle III was in a meeting, especially such an important one; however, when such phone calls were from John Okorocha, his dearest friend, he insisted on answering the call. Kabiyesi was somehow sad while listening to the governor's proposal, but when John Okorocha concluded his call by saying he would make a visit to the palace to spend quality time with him, his face lit up like fireworks on New Year's Eve. He sprang up and danced with the phone in his hand, in the presence of the governor and his entourage. He shouted aloud, "All right!" When John said he would be staying for a week or more, he danced even more. The governor of Ondo State, as crazy as he was, joined him in the dance. Edukoya, for a moment, took his mind back to their childhood days, when they'd shared a bucket of water to bathe; shared their food; shared their clothes, including their underwear; and shared their beds. For a moment, he remembered their days of innocence. They'd even shared one woman, Bola, though Edukoya had won by default due to tribalism. Bola's decision to be his girlfriend instead of

John Okorocha's never for a moment left a bitter taste between them. They were close.

Kabiyesi told him over the phone he had a big surprise for him. John tried in vain to learn the surprise during their phone conversation, but Edukoya wouldn't tell him. Thankfully, Princess Yemisi, during her recent three-week stay at his villa to undergo a medical checkup, do some badly needed shopping, and evaluate their enormous investment holdings in America, had not given Uncle John any hints. She was too ashamed to indulge in such grapevine conversation. She didn't want to shoot herself in both of her feet. Usually, Uncle John knew everything about his niece. However, Yemisi hid from Uncle John her lust for a forty-eight-year-old man, Dr. Everest "Eva" Oluomolewa, and she refused to hint to John about Felicia, because it would have opened up a chapter on Eva, a chapter she wanted kept to herself and Dr. Oluomolewa forever. She proved she was not stupid. She proved that the best-kept secret was the secret you kept to yourself.

Felicia and her pregnancy by the king were the news. Felicia's marriage to Edukoya had been the only wedding at which his surrogate brother was absent and wasn't his best man. He could hide his extramarital affair from John, but he couldn't hide the adorable twin babies Felicia was about to deliver for him. Owning up to his decision to take in a second wife without apportioning any blame on Princess Yemisi, he thought, was the best way to relay the message to John.

He intentionally had not invited Dr. Okorocha to his wedding to Felicia to avoid lengthy explanations. It was better explained in person.

However, Dr. Okorocha's visit to the palace was delayed to accommodate Felicia's rush to UC Davis Medical Center to have her twin babies delivered there. They resided at John's villa for the three-week stay in California. John had no idea the babies were his dearest friend's, though an odd feeling struck him. Dr. Felicia Adekunle was too young to be the king's wife. Since Kenmiejo accompanied her and did the delivery of the twins, John wrongly assumed Felicia was her sister-in-law. Kenmiejo positioned her that way to fool John. Kenmiejo knew her father well, and she kept his secret. It was better if the explanation came from the horse's mouth, she thought.

To the surprise of the governor and his entourage, the king instantly changed his tone with a smile. Credit went to John Okorocha's phone call as he began to see eye to eye with the governor's mounting agenda. They ended the meeting with a tour, a discussion of Felicia's pregnancy carrying the twins, and the new features Princess Yemisi had added to the palace. They ate *amala* with fresh fish pepper soup for lunch and drank the best champagne in the house to wash down the meal. The meeting was a success, with the governor agreeing to extend the express road to Orissa Polytechnic. Before the governor said goodbye, he whispered in Kabiyesi's ear that he would like to meet with John Okorocha during his upcoming visit to the palace. Edukoya nodded in agreement.

John Okorocha's visit was the news that dominated the king's mind for the entire week. In the beginning, Felicia was rather touched off because she couldn't get him to perform sexually in bed that night. Even when she took the extraordinary step of giving him a blow job at length, he still was a no-show. Felicia was not good at giving blow jobs or having any form of oral sex performed on her either. Though Felicia welcomed the frequent sexual engagements with the king, kissing, touching, and straight sex were where it ended with her. She had managed to avoid oral sex and, at the same time, seemed to satisfy the king and herself sexually. Dr. Felicia Adekunle was unbelievably pretty, with a huge intellectual capacity. Those qualities made up for her lack. John continued to dominate the king's mind throughout the night. John had met Felicia when she and Kenmiejo visited for her checkup during her pregnancy with the twins.

John was not the type to ask questions or probe into personal matters. He assumed Felicia was a sister-in-law from Kenmiejo husband's side. They stayed at his villa in Yuba City for a few days before departing to Nigeria. As a matter of fact, he later became the twins' godfather when they were born. Felicia's relationship with the king was not made clear to John Okorocha.

The king's erection crawled into its shell quickly because he was overjoyed by his dearest friend's upcoming visit. Felicia quickly found out, as Yemisi and Akudo had, that the best thing in such a situation was to take a cold shower and call it a night. That was what Felicia did. She was a little jealous of Edukoya's passion for John; however, she understood. It was a special friendship and a relationship that did not include any bit of sexual intimacy. Felicia anticipated seeing John Okorocha again. She couldn't wait to see him, the third person she called Daddy.

At the age of eighty-six and with his bypass operation, John Okorocha knew age had taken a serious toll on him. John waited too long before having the surgery, and as a result, he had multiple complications. Unlike Kabiyesi, who sprang up like a spring chicken three months after his surgery with uncontrollable sexual urges, John seldom had sex after three years of surgery. He also had a pacemaker installed near his heart to aid the heart in pumping blood. The doctors warned him that no matter his urges to engage in sexual intercourse, he should do it with enormous caution because of the pacemaker.

John Okorocha started regaining his interest in sports activities again late in his life. In secondary school, he had been good at every sporting event. At King's College, Lagos, he had been a flag bearer who, as the senior prefect of the school, perfected the art of humanity.

His full-blown heart attack necessitated open-heart surgery immediately. Before his surgery, John consumed beef in large quantities. Afterward, he ran away from beef and seldom ate chicken. He ate chicken well roasted without the skin. His nutritionist, Comfort Nwakowa, MS, highly experienced in the field of nutrition, put him on a permanent diet regimen to save his life.

The king was in Ikeja to welcome home his surrogate brother, John Okorocha. Kabiyesi Edukoya Adekunle III came with his jet to Murtala Mohammed International Airport in Ikeja to welcome his dearest friend.

The welcoming of John was remarkable. The plane landed at one o'clock in the afternoon from George Bush International Airport in Houston, Texas. He was seated in first class with his wife, Mama Akudo, and two of his younger kids, Chukwuemeka, forty-seven years old, and Chisomaga, forty-five years old. The two older kids, Nkemjika, sixty-two years old, and Chinyerenwa, sixty years old, had moved to Nigeria after their studies in America and had children and grandchildren. Nkemjika was a general surgeon, and Chinyerenwa, John's only daughter, was a high-court judge in Owerri, Justice Chinyere Ihenacho. The two older kids had been born in Nigeria, while Emeka and Chisom had been born in California. Both younger kids had followed in their father's footsteps. They'd attended Stanford University, majoring in software engineering, and each had a PhD. They were also married with children. The pregnancy with Chisom had been an enormous health cost to

Mama Akudo, as everybody called her. Her tubes had been tied after Chisom was born. However, it didn't affect her sexual desire one bit. Even at her age of seventy-six, she still lusted for sexual intercourse with her husband like a twenty-year-old kid. She was proud to say, "Only one man has kissed my lips and taken me to bed." She couldn't say the same about her husband, and she never bothered to ask him. She called John Daddy Me.

When John Okorocha arrived at Akure Metro Airport, the king's entourage, including the governor of Ondo State, were waiting for him. Cars stretched for miles, from Akure Metro Airport to Kabiyesi Adekunle III's palace at Agbala. John Okorocha's reception was beyond anticipation. A huge crowd of people came to visit him. The feast went on for two days. There was music, with four bands invited. Seven bands came on their own, and none of the bands were paid for their services. They worshipped their king because Edukoya was an extraordinary, heartful king. Kabiyesi Adekunle III's concerns were his people's concerns too. John stayed for nine days, with Kabiyesi's four kids who were doctors monitoring his health around the clock. Edukoya promised him he would return the visit to Ife in Mbaise when things settled down. Adekunle III's pilot used his jet to pilot him to Owerri in Imo State, where his entourage were waiting for his arrival. They included Nkemjika and Chinyerenwa.

Felicia Funmi Adekunle's case wasn't on the front burner after all throughout Dr. Okorocha's visit to his surrogate brother's palace. It was as if John had been informed of the situation. However, he wasn't informed. In Nigeria, taking on a second wife, especially for a king, happened a lot, so John took it in stride. Although Felicia's children had been born in America under his nose, John was not fully aware of the situation. John wore the pretense well, to the point Mama Akudo and his children assumed he knew about Edukoya's affair, the wedding, and his twins before they arrived at Kabiyesi's palace. Mama Akudo demanded to know why the secret now, after about three years of marriage, and he smiled. His smile told her he had not known beforehand.

Mama Akudo knew her husband well. John and Mama Akudo had married when she was just fourteen, and he had been twenty-six years old. After three years of marriage, he went off to America, living with his parents, the caretaker of Akudo, and his two babies, Nkemjika and Chinyere. Akudo was the sweetest and prettiest girl in Ikoyi, where his parents resided then.

Dr. Oluomolewa was invited to the occasion at the palace. In fact, he and his family were offered a free ride to Kabiyesi's palace at Agbala in Ondo State, but he declined the invitation, citing a series of life-threatening surgeries that week. There was truth to that, but the real reason was that he did not want to be a distraction and a spoiler. He knew Princess Yemisi well and knew not to take chances, because she would drag him to a blind corner and invade his body right under the nose of his wife, Charity, and the king.

CHAPTER 16

The visit to Nigeria by Dr. John Okorocha was his last homecoming. It ended on a sad note. John Okorocha died in his father's *obi* at the age of eighty-nine. He had anticipated his death and wouldn't go back to America till his death. He was survived by his wife of sixty-four years, four children, twenty grandchildren, and five great-grandchildren. He was a remarkable and loyal friend of Kabiyesi Edukoya Adekunle III. He was rushed to the hospital in Abbo, Mbaise, driven there by his son, Nkemjika, who was a medical doctor. When he got to the hospital, he asked his wife, Akudo, to call Edukoya to tell him his life was now in God's hands.

It was the first time Kabiyesi Edukoya Adekunle III had visited Ife in Mbaise. The king had found excuses to visit Imo State on numerous occasions. When he came, he always resided with Chika at her villa in Amaraku, Mbaino. The phone call came at around three o'clock on a fateful Sunday morning. Kabiyesi called his pilot to get air clearance and permission to take off from Akure Metro Airport and land his jet at Owerri Metro Airport. Within the hour, his pilot called him; the clearance was completed. He then made a dire phone call to Mama Akudo with tears gushing from his eyes, asking her to pick him up at the airport by seven o'clock that Sunday morning.

On the rough but manageable paved road, John Okorocha's chauffeur, accompanied by Chukwuemeka, his second son, drove them to Ife, where Mama Akudo was anxiously awaiting their arrival. Princess Yemisi joined him for the visit. The home in Ife was a simple, modern two-story house with state-of-the-art furnishings. John Okorocha had always been a simple man, so His Lordship expected nothing out of the ordinary from him. The house was tastefully built, with sixteen large bedrooms, two very large bedrooms for himself and Mama Akudo, seventeen full bathrooms, three half bathrooms, four large sitting areas, one executive parlor upstairs, and two large gourmet kitchens. Surrounding the main building were four two-story minimotel-style buildings with ten moderately furnished, sizable suites each. Most of the minimotel-style suites housed one- and two-bedroom apartments. The buildings housed his guests, close relatives, and his helpers. The compound was solidly paved, with lawns and flower beds positioned at sites. He'd put in a multipurpose play area that served as a playground for his grandchildren and great-grandchildren. His compound faced the bank of the Imo River, with a solidly paved lane to get from the village's street to his compound.

When it was certain his death was closing in on him, his son Nkemjika ordered him to be taken home, where he could die peacefully in the comfort of his own home, surrounded by his loved ones. Kabiyesi Edukoya Adekunle III met him in his bedroom. Immediately, John heard his voice, and he opened his eyes and sprang up from the bed. He called him Eduks for the last time. He assured Edukoya everything would be okay. They laughed and cried together. John comforted Edukoya the most because he was visibly crying and shaking at the inevitable loss of the only man he had ever loved dearly. John said, "One last thing. Take care of Mama Akudo and my family. Besides you, they are the persons who matter most in my life." Then he sent for Mama Akudo, and there was a rush in the huge bedroom by all his loved ones to say goodbye for the last time. John held

Edukoya's hand with his right hand and Akudo's hand with his left, and slowly, he gave up.

The death of the man shocked Princess Yemisi in the hardest way. She began to think about her own husband, Kabiyesi Edukoya Adekunle III, and his mortality. She had seen many dear deaths, including her father, Felix Adeniji; her mother, Comfort Adeniji; and her sister Iyabo, but none topped how she felt about the death of John Okorocha, the dearest friend of her husband and the man she gladly loved to call Uncle John.

Kabiyesi left that evening by four thirty. He drummed it into the ears of his children, especially Nkemjika and Chinyerenwa, John's oldest children, to inform him in every step of the funeral arrangements. He promised he would be there.

As Yemisi and Edukoya lay in bed that night, Princess Yemisi began to cry, with tears gushing down from her eyes. She thought about Mama Akudo and how lonely she would be in the future. John Okorocha was the only man Mama Akudo had known. She thought about her husband, Edukoya, and what would happen to her if she woke up one morning and found herself without him. She turned him to lie on his back. She went on top of him, moving delicately because of his surgery; laid her head adjacent to his right shoulder; and dozed off for the night. Edukoya gently laid her down in the bed when she comfortably slept. Sexual intercourse was on her mind that night, but she understood Edukoya was consumed with missing his dearest friend, so she muted her feelings.

The Anglican Diocese of Mbaise put John's burial three weeks after the date he passed away. Kabiyesi Edukoya Adekunle III was detailed on every arrangement for the burial. John Okorocha's children were summoned to Agbala to plan the funeral. It happened that Kabiyesi's other good friend, the president of Nigeria, was arriving in Owerri to begin a four-day tour of Imo and Abiam States. A funeral invitation was extended to him, and His Excellency accepted the invitation. His Excellency amended his tour to five days, as it would have been rude of him to leave in the middle of the funeral ceremony. Dr. John Okorocha had been an important man and had accomplished a lot for the people of Ife and Nigerians in America, regardless of tribal origin. He had made positions for tens of thousands of Nigerians in corporate America. The president also had been a schoolmate of John Okorocha, who'd introduced him to a girl he later married when he came back from England. Although the president had been John's junior at King's College, they had been teammates, playing soccer for King's College. The president's important assignments could wait. The president quickly realized it was one of those rare and coincidental opportunities for him to show leadership and statesmanship. Besides, he had known John Okorocha faintly at King's College and become his personal friend later when he had a brush with him in California. A friend had reintroduced John to him as a quiet billionaire.

His Excellency had made phone calls to him twice: once before his surgery after he had a heart attack and again after the surgery, while he was at his ranch in Yuba City, recovering. He had not been president then. John Okorocha was known to all Nigerians in Northern California as the man who went out of his way to help others, especially all Nigerians. He spoke Yoruba, Hausa, Efik, and Igbo fluently.

On hearing that His Excellency would be attending the funeral of John Okorocha, everybody wanted to be there. The magnitude of his death rose to the peak. His Lordship Kabiyesi Edukoya Lawansin Adekunle III and his entourage were featured prominently. His entourage from Orissa Kingdom chartered two Boeing 747 jumbo jets to attend the funeral. They came with music, food, drinks, toilet pots, makeshift bathrooms, water, toiletries, gas stoves, and tents. They sent seven buses and two eighteen-wheelers loaded with supplies, including four small electric generators, before their arrival. Orissa people brought so much food and livestock, from chickens to cows, that their leftovers were shared by the Ife community after they left the funeral. The funeral of Dr. John Okorocha lasted for four days.

Twenty governors came, including the Imo State governor, who was featured prominently and positioned himself as the chief guest of honor and host. The governor was remarkable, and so was the president of Nigeria, who went out of his way and joined the governor to receive the guests. The Bay Area and Sacramento wings of Nigerian foreign unions sent their delegates. The funeral procession included the Anglican bishops of Mbaise, Egbu; the archbishop of Owerri; bishops of Orlu, Nkwere, Mbaino, and Okigwe; and Reverend John Ashimolu, the Anglican bishop of Saint Mathew's Anglican Church, Agbala, Orissa Kingdom. Archbishops of Lagos and the archbishop of Owerri, Reverend Ben Nwankwo, led the procession. Reverend Michael Akim Adebanjo had been close to John Okorocha. Whenever he'd visited Northern California, he'd made it a point to lodge at John's villa in Yuba City. John had been his classmate, a fierce competitor, and the topmost student at King's College, Lagos, with a perfect A score on the London General Certificate of Education examination. Forty pastors were in attendance. The funeral service was at Saint Michael's Cathedral in Ife. Ife and Mbaise had never had an event like it before. Kabiyesi Adekunle III insisted on paying for everything, including John's dog's food.

The church funeral lasted for six hours. It started at 10:00 a.m. on the dot and ended at 4:00 p.m. on the dot. Several men and six women gave eulogies. Among the women was Princess Yemisi. The president of Nigeria spoke for about five minutes. The keynote speaker was his dearest friend, a man who knew him so well that he could tell his footsteps when he woke up in the middle of the night and walked to the bathroom: His Lordship Edukoya Adekunle III. He held his tears enough to finish his eulogy, and at the last paragraph, he walked up to John's coffin, finished reading the last paragraph of his eulogy, and burst into tears. The whole fellowship congregation stood up with him. The archbishops of Lagos led him to his seat.

When Princess Yemisi came to the altar to speak, all eyes were on her extraordinary attractiveness, even at the age of fifty-nine. The grapevine whisper "You know she is about sixty years old, but she doesn't look it at all" was widespread throughout the fellowship. In her black blouse with a Yoruba-style black wrap to match, which had taken her six hours to make for the occasion, she looked gorgeous. One man said, "The right man will know what to do with this woman in bed," and his surroundings laughed. He spoke in the Igbo language.

Kabiyesi and Yemisi were the only guests from Orissa Kingdom who slept in the main building. Others were comfortable in their tents. Key elders of Orissa Kingdom and the key guests from Saint Mathew's Cathedral, including Bishop John and Dr. Perfecter Ashimolu, were housed in the luxurious minimotel-style buildings. At last, water, stoves, toilet pots, bathrooms, and electricity were no problem. In the space of three weeks, John's children had nailed every service needed for the burial to the minutest detail. Orissa people didn't have to cook at all or even boil water. They were adequately fed, and the enormous amount of leftover food was shared among the Ife community.

On the third night, Princess Yemisi woke up Edukoya at one o'clock in the morning and demanded he make love to her. She thought it would be like pulling a tooth to get him to perform, but to her surprise, his penis was fully erect before she finished undressing him. It was a night to remember. They did it in Igbo land in Ife several times that morning.

PART 5

AN INNOCENT FLIRTATION

CHAPTER 17

Professor Everest Oluomolewa was a neighbor who recently had moved into his father's house next door to Kabiyesi Adekunle III's villa in Ikoyi. He was forty-three years old and an American-trained cardiothoracic surgeon. Eva, as he preferred to be called, had graduated from the University of Southern California (USC) with a BS in molecular biology. He later had earned his MD from Duke University. He'd come back to USC to do his residency and trained as an accomplished surgeon there. He taught surgical procedures at Lagos University Teaching Hospital (LUTH) for an untold, alarming salary partially paid in a foreign currency of his choice. Since he was a cardiothoracic surgeon, it was welcome news to have him as a neighbor. His father willed the house to him while he was still alive.

His father, Timothy Oluomolewa, was a businessman with landed properties throughout Lagos State. He was married to two wives, but his second marriage to a Yoruba lady was by default. In 1966, when the northern Nigerian riot began with the Hausa's genocide against the Igbos, the fear was that it would be widespread throughout Nigeria. However, it was not so in western Nigeria, especially Lagos, which was then the sitting capital city of Nigeria. The Igbos had always considered themselves to be marginal, and rightly so, based on the evidence on the ground. For fear of being killed, Harriet Oluomolewa, Everest's mother and the wife of Timothy Oluomolewa, took her two children, Eva and Esther, back to Oratta, Owerri, in Imo State. There the kids polished their Igbo grammar. Timothy had to marry another wife, Fumilayo, who gave him four more children, one boy and three girls. Two days after the civil war was announced to be over, Timothy came and took Harriet and the kids back to Lagos. However, the kids opted to finish up their secondary school in Owerri. Everest attended Holy Ghost College in Owerri, and Esther finished at Owerri Girls' Secondary School. The jump-over class in 1970 after the civil war enabled both of them to graduate at the same time. Eva scored distinction with nine aggregates, while his younger sister, Esther, scored grade one with thirteen aggregates on the West African School Certificate of Education examination. Esther went to the University of Nigeria, Lagos, and studied law, while Eva came to America and did medicine.

Professor Oluomolewa had a persuasive and tempting personality. He was active in a handful of sports, which was welcome news to Princess Yemisi. He was tall and midway-light-complexioned just like his mom, and for some unexplainable reason, he had a naturally gifted pointed nose. He was simply handsome, a carbon copy of his mother. His sister, Esther, did what intertribal and interracial children were meant to do: bring the ends of the earth together. She was gorgeous, with an intertribal blend that would awaken a man's sexual appetite. Their mother was Igbo, and their father was a Yoruba man. They had the best of both tribes. They spoke Yoruba and Igbo fluently. Dr. Everest Oluomolewa was married to Charity, an Asaba woman he'd met at USC when he was doing his residency there, which made him appear to align himself with the Igbos. Inevitably, Igbo was largely spoken in his household, but he had always identified himself as a Yoruba man. His wife, Charity, seldom indulged herself in physical exercises, though she looked gorgeous. Princess Yemisi, on the other hand, was a lover of sports. Charity Oluomolewa had been slim all her life. She was also extremely pretty and fit.

It seemed Princess Yemisi picked up a romantic interest in Professor Everest Oluomolewa. She repeatedly called him Eva. She developed a huge crush on him. She selectively invited him over to have lunch with her when her husband, Edukoya, and Dr. Oluomolewa's wife were absent. Princess Yemisi would cook the food herself. She created tennis tournaments so they could stay longer in the game during the competition. She frequented Lagos with every excuse she drummed up. When they played sports, a brush of a slight fall by him would invite the hands of Princess Yemisi to help him get up, and when she fell down, she would scream like a wounded lion, calling for his help to lift her up. At the age of fifty-two, Princess Yemisi Adekunle was still athletic. She was still an attractive, desirable, and beautiful woman. She looked like a twenty-eight-year-old woman who had a distinguishing taste for beauty. Princess Yemisi had no wrinkles on her face and had a body that tended to inspire lustful desire in the men she associated with, and Eva was a desirable culprit. She was slim and fit. She was tempting and adorable. She could have made a man in a coma wake up fast. The thought of making passionate love with Princess Yemisi increasingly crossed Dr. Oluomolewa's mind each time they got to play sports together. Those thoughts were better sealed off in perpetuity. The unthinkable notion that the kabiyesi of Orissa's wife was in love with another man while still married to him was suicidal. It was not a funny joke.

The climax was when she phoned him to pick her up at the airport in Ikeja. Princess Yemisi had never done that before. Usually, Kabiyesi Adekunle had two chauffeurs in Lagos and several others in Orissa Kingdom. One chauffeur was for him exclusively, and the other was for Princess Yemisi and general errands. Princess Yemisi could use whichever chauffeur was available too.

Dr. Oluomolewa was busy getting ready for surgery when she called. She never had called him at his job before. He sent one of LUTH's chauffeurs to pick her up on her arrival from Akure's Metro Airport. He told the chauffeur to drop her off at her residence.

Princess Yemisi was visibly angry when she saw the chauffeur without him. She'd wanted him to come alone to pick her up. She was hoping to open up a secret love affair with him. For his own part, his concentration was on a surgery to remove a fishbone fragment stuck in the throat of a patient who'd been eating *ewedu* soup with *amala fufu*.

The surgery took a little longer than expected. It was compounded by a blackout in the middle of the surgery. He used a flashlight to continue the surgery until the backup generator came on. Nigerians had learned their lessons well. All electrically operated equipment in the surgery room, including nonessential equipment, was connected to a battery charger in case there was a blackout in the middle of a surgery. Blackouts in Nigeria were frequent, up to 70 percent of the time. Most times, the blackouts lasted for days. Luckily, with their work-around tactics, the number of deaths as a result of the blackouts was nearly zero.

The surgery took five and a half hours to complete. It was successful. Dr. Oluomolewa came out of the theater looking exhausted. The last thing any surgeon wanted to hear after a complicated surgery, or any surgery, was someone yelling at him. But that was what Princess Yemisi did.

Instead of going home, she asked the chauffeur to drop her off at LUTH, at his office. Professor Oluomolewa was surprised to see her waiting for him in his office at the hospital late that night. When surgeries took that long, especially in an emergency situation, the surgery team were allowed to spend the night in the hospital. In Dr. Oluomolewa's office, his office couch turned into a bed.

Immediately, he asked, "What happened?" He began to rant. "I instructed the driver to take you straight to your place; instead, he brought you here." He wanted to continue, but Princess Yemisi interrupted him. She went off on him. She explained that she'd asked the chauffeur to drop her there. She said she wanted his company and had hoped he would come alone to pick her up. She expressed wasteful time and gross disappointment.

Professor Oluomolewa was stunned and quiet. After she finished talking, he said he did not know what to say. But he asked her, "Why my company?"

She told him what a wonderful husband she had, but she was lusting for a youth. She was disappointed in herself. Dr. Oluomolewa asked her permission to put his arms around her shoulders to comfort her. She welcomed his thoughtfulness. He too confessed his deep lust and burning desire to make love to her. It was the first time she'd told him to call her Yemisi only.

She cried, as she was about to waste thirty-six years of a beautiful and faithful marriage. Eva said he wouldn't let them cross that line, out of respect for his wife and her husband. He added that he'd sensed why she wanted him to pick her up when there were two chauffeurs doing nothing. Eva said he'd sent the LUTH chauffeur while hoping to distance himself from a big mistake. He confessed he'd had time to pick her up and still go in for the surgery.

Her tears and lipstick soaked his long-sleeved white shirt. She was sorry for the mess. He said it was all right; he would tell his wife a patient had done that to him while he was consoling her. They laughed and emerged as tight platonic friends. It was about two thirty in the morning, so Dr. Oluomolewa let her sleep on the sofa bed in his office, while he slept on the recliner seat and dozed off quickly.

Early in the morning, Dr. Oluomolewa went to check on his critically ill patients before departing with her to their residences in Ikoyi. They kept the close call as their little secret forever.

CHAPTER 18

Justice Onyemerekwe convened an informal session to resolve the case of the plaintiffs, the united team of Kabiyesi Edukoya Adekunle III, against the defendants, the federal government of Nigeria and the Lagos State government. The informal talks were to wet the ground and see if the soil could hold the wetness for a long time.

Meanwhile, Princess Yemisi's crush on Dr. Oluomolewa was not a mere taste of forbidden fruit; it was an all-out destiny.

The World Health Organization and Nigerian universities and colleges' faculties of medicine and biological sciences teamed up to address cardiac issues in Nigeria and the West Coast of Africa. The architect of the team was Professor Everest Oluomolewa. The endeavor had the blessings of the federal government of Nigeria, the United States, the European Union, the United Nations, and the Red Cross. Nigeria, because of its size, sophistication, and massive poverty, was used as a testing ground for the proposal. The solutions derived there would be used in the neighboring West African countries. The situation called for board members. As a friend, Dr. Oluomolewa relayed the ongoing issue to Princess Yemisi. She immediately offered to join the board. Dr. Oluomolewa said he would think about it; however, he hinted that the board would be largely made up of medical professionals and biological scientists. He forgot for a moment that Princess Yemisi had an ND degree from San Jose State University. She had also been deeply involved in the health-care issues of Orissa Kingdom.

In truth, she wanted to be around him all the time. She had a loving and adorable husband. She had twelve successful grown children, five of whom were hers biologically, and two adorable two-year-old twins. She was married to a king. She was the crown princess, which meant she was next in line to become the queen of Orissa Kingdom. Her husband was rich beyond anyone's wildest dreams. Yet she was sleepless at night, thinking about the young medical doctor she couldn't have. She was not willing to give up her marriage for him, but she wanted him for her own toy collection.

Dr. Oluomolewa thought their last encounter had put any interest she had in him and the lust they had for each other to rest. He believed he had moved on. He believed he had settled the score, and he was comfortable with his pretty wife, Charity. However, the saying was true: "Beauty provided those who had it, man or woman, the wings to fly, and they flew with audacity to their destination of choice." She wanted him, and she was going to have him with time.

Dr. Oluomolewa was caught between a rock and a hard place. He discussed the board situation with his wife without telling her the whole story. His wife, on face value, reminded him Princess Yemisi would have a significant positive impact, given her vast experience in the medical field. She blindly encouraged him to put her on the board and also to seek thoughtful, mature advice from her. It was like a welcome blessing to do evil. Although he'd thought he had moved on, sleeping with that breathtaking woman had not escaped his memory. He was just managing the thoughts. In fact, out of guilt, he happened to love his wife even more. In bed, he tended to go to extraordinary lengths to please her, including doing things he hadn't done for her in the past.

Dr. Oluomolewa wanted sexual intercourse with his wife more frequently than usual as he tried to substitute his feelings for Princess Yemisi for his wife. However, it was not working. Professor Everest Oluomolewa's new leave on his wife was attributed to her having called the project his "new extended purpose in life." Charity felt that Princess Yemisi, being a wonderful neighbor in his corner, would be a positive influence for his organization. Organizers of such nonprofit health initiatives were not paid; however, they stood to make tons of money from traveling allowances and consulting fees. The consulting fees were always negotiable. They might include a lump sum of money for the time period they were needed. They could also negotiate need-based consulting fees when the duty involved special contributions. On such a world stage, Dr. Oluomolewa stood to make about half a million dollars annually, excluding numerous speaking engagement fees.

He was excited about his new project and, in particular, for Princess Yemisi to join the board. But he had to play hard to get. He wanted Princess Yemisi to ask for the position again. He practically wanted her to beg for it. His wish came through. Yemisi sent for him to address the issue once again. This time, he asked a crucial question. He wanted to know what her husband thought about her joining the board. She thought for a moment and then said, "I have not discussed it with him yet." She asked him if he had discussed it with his wife. He said yes and told of her approval and encouragement of having her on board. Princess Yemisi didn't believe him, as she thought his audacity to discuss anything about her with Charity would have been curtailed by their flirtation. She asked to speak with his wife. To her surprise, he agreed. He picked up her house phone and beckoned Charity to come over. When she arrived, he excused himself to allow the two women to talk about the birds and the bees and also the grapevine gossip about their neighbors and mutual friends, including him.

He held his breath, hoping Princess Yemisi did not spill the beans or initiate a discussion Charity would interpret to mean a whole lot more. Charity was an intelligent woman and educator who did not allow anything to get past her.

Luckily, Princess Yemisi was smarter than that. She left the discussion flat and quickly turned the topic to her garden. She showed Charity her garden with a variety of rare fruits and vegetables grown mainly overseas. For the first time, they became instant friends. Both agreed they should be on a first-name basis. Princess Yemisi went first. "Call me Yemisi."

She replied, "Charity."

They got around to the subject of the board of directorship. Charity brought up the topic. She said, "Eva discussed with me the idea of bringing you on board as a member of the board of directors." Dr. Charity Oluomolewa was a smart woman; she framed the discussion as if Dr. Oluomolewa, her husband, had initiated the invitation to the board.

Princess Yemisi said there were ongoing discussions about it and added that she would discuss it further with her husband, Kabiyesi Edukoya Adekunle III, before giving him an answer.

The way Charity framed the question gave Princess Yemisi some dignity and class. It saved face and brought the conversation to life. It showed her that Dr. Oluomolewa and Charity had not forgotten her real worth as the crown princess of Orissa Kingdom. Charity also made it a brush-off topic by not dwelling on the subject matter for too long. They quickly moved on to other issues confronting their neighborhood, Ikoyi, and the nation. They discussed a variety of issues, and Princess Yemisi began to have her as a trusted close friend. Charity was clean, neat, and easy to talk to.

Their friendship mushroomed with time and grew larger than life. Princess Yemisi did not ask any questions or bring up any discussion that suggested things out of the ordinary. It calmed the nerves of Dr. Oluomolewa that Princess Yemisi listened more and let Charity do most of the talking. Before they left, Princess Yemisi introduced her to Chikanele and her two boys. Yemisi called Chika her closest, dearest, and most trusted friend. The name Chika rang a bell, which prompted Charity to greet Chika in the Igbo language: "Kedu ko di?" (How are you?). Charity killed two birds with one stone; she added another breathtaking friendship with Chika.

CHAPTER 19

Every Saturday and Sunday morning, Dr. Oluomolewa went jogging. He was good at it; he jogged four miles in about thirty-six minutes. He did it before going to church on Sundays. He jogged alone. His wife, Charity, didn't want anything to do with jogging. She would occasionally join him to jog, but she usually jogged at a slow pace. She jogged for about one and a half miles before returning home.

One day she joined him in a four-mile race. Competition, virtual or not, had a way of reinforcing energy. They did four miles in thirty-two minutes. She came back exhausted. Both of her ankles swelled. She couldn't walk all day. Thank God it was a Saturday. Being devoted Christians, the Oluomolewa family never missed Sunday services. Charity was a member of the Saint Gregory Anglican Church choir. The church was one of the things the Adekunle family had in common with the Oluomolewa family.

Charity gave up jogging altogether, preferring to walk to her destinations.

The Saturday morning after Charity's visit with Princess Yemisi on Friday, Dr. Oluomolewa went jogging as usual. He did not know Princess Yemisi had watched his routine and timed his exit from his house. Princess Yemisi dressed in tight-fitting sport shorts that arrogantly displayed her Brazilian butt without panties. She wore a tight-fitting sleeveless blouse that showed off her dazzling curved body and thirty-six-cup breast size. She was like a billboard showcasing her youth again.

Despite her five boys having been breastfed, her breasts were amazingly still standing at her age. One could see through her blouse to her amazing nipples, enlarged, ripped, and ready to be sucked. She wore comfortable, top-of-the-line Adidas footwear. She went a little early to the nearest bus stop, at the corner of their street, to stretch her legs at the bench, waiting for Everest's arrival.

Within moments, like clockwork, he arrived at the bus stop. She asked him if she could join him. He hesitated a bit, explaining what had happened to Charity. Finally, he said, "Why not? It will provide me much-needed company and competition."

Princess Yemisi kept quiet and her cool and joined him. All her basketball playing with her children and her house helpers paid off. The run was nothing to her. She raced him and won. They did the four-mile run in under twenty-six minutes. This time, he was exhausted, but his ankles did not swell up.

Charity was surprised to see him back so soon. Dr. Oluomolewa had met his match. He asked for a glass of cold water.

Princess Yemisi left later that afternoon to join her husband and family in Orissa Kingdom in Ondo State. Akure was about a twenty-minute flight from Ikeja.

It became their routine. She would come to stretch her legs at the bench at the bus stop and wait for him to arrive. The competition was good for him. They raced and took turns winning over each other. Princess Yemisi finally told him her husband had accepted the offer for her to join the board of directors after he raised concerns about her enormous workload. As crown princess, she had Orissa Kingdom to manage. As a lead negotiator in the land deal, she had the court and the lawyers to deal with, and as the chief executive officer of her husband's vast investment holdings, she had more than $10 billion of an investment portfolio to deal with. If the state and the federal governments had their way, the plaintiffs stood to get nothing. Now she had a board-of-director membership to contend with, which could involve a lot of traveling, and she would be in the company of her newfound friend, a relatively lustful younger man.

Dr. Oluomolewa asked for her stance on the issue of joining the board, and she said, "I accept."

He replied, "I'm going to take it to the rest of the present board members, and you will be invited to be sworn in at a later date."

Their conversations slowed down their pace. Sometimes they preferred walking. As a cardiothoracic surgeon, he always recommended brisk walks for his patients, especially after they underwent open-heart surgery. The walking bought them time to talk about everything, and they did. When she was sworn in as a board member, their prayers were answered. Now they would be working together, which meant seeing each other more often, including during lunch and meetings, and traveling together. Individually, they anticipated their path would one day cross into romance and ultimately lead to sexual engagements. Princess Yemisi and Everest were looking forward to that day.

Her husband, His Lordship Kabiyesi Adekunle III, was getting sicker every day. He had increasing pain in his chest and upper back. He was fatigued all the time and was beginning to encounter slow erections because his mind was consumed with the pain. Most of the time, there was no erection at all. Yemisi was about fifty-four years old, and he was about seventy-five. Sexual activities were no longer that fun for him with constant pain and fatigue. He adored her beauty and her breathtaking body, even at her age. He watched her naked without any erection, something that had been out of the question for him before his sickness. It pained him a great deal. His penis occasionally became erect by means of artificial medical enhancements, but he was not able to perform for long due to his enormous fatigue and increasing pain, especially at the tail end of the intercourse, during ejaculation. They tried to use medical enhancements on four occasions, but his blood pressure shot up through the roof, and he was on the brink of having a heart attack and stroke. Being a nurse practitioner, she was able to stabilize him in those instances. He also had enormous pain in his upper back when he woke up from deep sleep.

He had four doctors in the family. They ran a series of tests on him and determined he should see a cardiologist. He was able to recover a little bit to attend Oyodele's graduation ceremony in the United States.

Princess Yemisi Adekunle loved to have sex a lot. So far, she'd done so only with the man she was in love with, her husband of thirty-six years, Edukoya Adekunle III. For some time, she had been suffering from sexual starvation. It had been too long. She had held her loyalty to the brink. She remembered when they'd had sex at every chance they got and at every corner of the globe. They'd had sex in the backseat of their car; in the swimming pool; at the park; at the beach; in the parlor, on a couch, love seat, recliner seat, or single chair; in the bath together; in the middle of the road with traffic passing; in the bush; on the plane and bus; and at the airports—everywhere. She remembered having breakfast in bed at two o'clock in the afternoon because they were busy getting the best from each other. They were good to each other; they couldn't get enough of each other. Now all had been washed away to faded memory. They were borderline sex addicts with each other. It was only them and all about them. They were sex maniacs

130

only to themselves. Slowly, the erections of her beloved Eduks slowed to a crawl due to the constant intervals of acute chest pain and fatigue. Most times, he lay down on the floor with grueling back pain and fatigue or succumbed where he was seated and collapsed. It was torture, and the only relief came from a constant intake of potent painkillers with enormous side effects. He was continuously drowsy all the time. However, the pain didn't go away.

The only time he had a moderate erection on his own was with Chikanele, Princess Yemisi's administrative assistant, when they engaged in their secret romantic affairs. In such instances, his penis produced moderately weak erections that were able to penetrate Chika's vagina because she was soaking wet. Their sexual intercourse did not last long enough for him to even ejaculate or for Chika to reach a badly needed orgasm. The weak erections, when they occurred, did not satisfy either of them. Edukoya was madly in love with Chika, and his penis tended to harden at the tail end of their sexual encounters when he remembered how much he loved her. But when he ejaculated in those painful instances, the enormous pain came to the brink of his having a heart attack. Chika also endured the sex without reaching orgasm because she loved him so much with passion.

Edukoya was also patient with Princess Yemisi. Sometimes Princess Yemisi put his penis into her vagina without an erection, all the way in, to see if an erection would occur. They were just shallow penetrations with his penis coming out as soon as she put it in. They were unsatisfying experiences for both of them. She kissed him for the longest stretch of time, gave him long blow jobs, massaged him, and hugged him warmly with no erection result at all. His mind was on the pain.

Princess Yemisi was a classic romantic genius, but his erections seldom came in her sexual engagements with him.

After such a sexual encounter, he would be on the brink of collapsing. He would experience enormous pain in his upper back, fatigue, and tiredness. On three occasions, a local physician intervened and recommended a long rest with a heavy dosage of potent painkiller medications. However, the outcome of such a long rest was more painful. Sex without a full erection of the penis that stood up like a pine tree was never going to be the same. She began to think her attractiveness was fading from his eyes and mind, even though the trusted local physician labeled his fatigue and pain as panic attacks that came with age. She began to feel unattractive to him. The doctor made a huge error in his diagnosis. Such sexual encounters gave way to mild heart attacks that could have led to fatality.

He experienced pain and fatigue on his upcoming visit to America. Meanwhile, Princess Yemisi drummed up her last option, which backfired on her. She wanted him to sleep with another woman, a woman who was extremely attractive, athletically engaging, and much younger than she, to see if the erection would come back or at least improve. She overlooked Chika, a desirable, attractive, obedient friend who had all the qualities she was looking for and who had already mastered the act of making Eduks happy.

She tried to get him involved with an attractive lady who'd go to bed with him. It was her stupidest idea. The lady was a teacher at Orissa Polytechnic Institute, Dr. Felicia Funmi Adebayo, PhD. She was twenty-nine years old and a recent widow who'd recently miscarried upon hearing about her husband's sudden death. He'd died in a motorcycle accident. Felicia's husband had been getting a paid ride to the airport when the accident occurred. Both he and the motorcyclist had died at the scene. It was a kind gesture of empathy for Princess

Yemisi to give her a two-bedroom flat to reside in free of charge at the palace while she taught at Orissa Polytechnic Institute.

Orissa Polytechnic was a university-style polytechnic institution that awarded bachelor of arts and science degrees, master's degrees, and even doctorates. It was a huge campus, about twenty-five square miles. The campus land had been donated by the Adekunle family and Orissa Kingdom. Dr. Felicia Adebayo taught biological sciences at the institute. Felicia was a stunningly attractive woman. She was slim and fit. She was heavily into sports activities and coached Orissa Girls' Secondary School's basketball team. They won the Ondo State basketball competition that year after she volunteered for the coaching assignment, and consequently, she took over as their head coach.

Kabiyesi Edukoya Adekunle III was very fond of her. She always went to greet Princess Yemisi and the king every evening when she drove back from her engagements for the day. In such cases, Princess Yemisi would engage the two in an endless conversation. She would then excuse herself and vanish to do her chores, leaving the two alone. She encouraged her husband into misguided sexual encounters with Felicia. After he hesitated for a while, he decided to try Yemisi's way without knowing it was a setup by her. Princess Yemisi finally succeeded in getting them to engage in a series of sexual encounters, with no successful erections resulting.

After the sudden death of her husband and the miscarriage, Felicia was understandably vulnerable and lonely. She appreciated their help and comfort, especially from such a good-looking king. They thought they were having a secret affair, not knowing it was a setup by Princess Yemisi. However, in all of the king's sexual engagements with Felicia, his penis refused to become erect at all, not even once. They tried on many instances, but it was futile. Felicia was a little disappointed, but she had begun to fall in love with his remarkable personality. To her, a half loaf of bread was better than none. She anticipated that things would improve with time.

Things did improve after his open-heart surgery, with both Felicia and Chika begging for time out from this tiger, who suddenly became a sex maniac. The make-believe secret affair between the king and Dr. Felicia Adebayo was why Eduks agreed to let Princess Yemisi join the board. It was to get her out of the house more often in order to make room for Felicia. However, even with all the numerous sexual encounters with Felicia, his penis slowed to a crawl. It did not become erect even once. Chika had the best luck with him having a moderate erection without medical enhancements. The relationship between Edukoya and Felicia was getting serious. An innocent scheme was becoming a permanent stay as his second wife, one with a younger outlook on life, one whose future was ahead of her, and one he would have access to at a moment's notice.

Felicia began to fall in love with Kabiyesi Edukoya Adekunle III. Suddenly, Princess Yemisi felt betrayed by her, as she began to notice Edukoya's distance from her. She also began to feel jealous. The only consolation was his weak erection. Felicia was not getting it, and Princess Yemisi was not getting it from him either.

The ceremony for a traditional marriage to Felicia would wait until after they came back from the United States of America. Princess Yemisi didn't tell Dr. Oluomolewa this crucial news, for fear of his calling her a spoiler who was using him as a substitute and using him to clean up her mess. Having been starved for sex for too long, she just wanted Everest to make her feel like a woman again. Feeling like a complete woman would entail engaging in sexual intercourse, which came with the package.

CHAPTER 20

The preliminary hearing on the land case was postponed until Kabiyesi Edukoya Adekunle III was back from his tour of the United States. The Honorable Justice Chukwu Onyemerekwe was aware of his condition. The lead negotiator, Princess Yemisi, was not going to be present at the hearing. Justice Onyemerekwe had seen his father die from similar ill health. Before his elder brother, who was then in America, could finish the arrangements to bring him to America for further treatment, he'd died. Edukoya's issue reminded Justice Chukwu Onyemerekwe of his past and the never-forgotten, painful memories of those days. He was finishing up at Nigerian Law School by then. The case was postponed indefinitely till the king got better or died. Kabiyesi Edukoya Adekunle III was in the United States for almost eight months, receiving badly needed medical attention. John Okorocha telephoned Justice Onyemerekwe and thanked him for his understanding. They spoke in the Igbo language. Kabiyesi Edukoya Adekunle III was residing in his mansion on a ten-acre lot in Yuba City.

"The health of this stunning gentleman is more important," Justice Chukwu Onyemerekwe wrote in his ruling. That bought the team of His Lordship Edukoya Lawansin Adekunle III, led by Princess Yemisi, more time to lay out their strategies and tactics.

There were no complications with his surgery. Edukoya was an active man. He'd led King's College to three straight regional championship soccer matches during his time in that school.

He still played soccer on regular occasions. His grandfather had taught mathematics and physics at King's College, Lagos, for about twenty years before taking up the throne as kabiyesi of Orissa Kingdom. His father, Lawansin Adekunle II, had gone to school there too.

The late Kabiyesi Ifeoluwa VI of Orissa Kingdom had been damned wicked and unprogressive. People said he ate corruption for breakfast every morning before he went to work. Upon his death, Orissa's people revolted; either all his family members were banished from the kingship, or there would be no king at all in Orissa Kingdom. The youths of Orissa Kingdom, led by a charismatic, progressive young man in his midtwenties, Mr. Oyokadele Duruenmi, saw to the change in the kingdom's leadership. Finally, the will of the people prevailed. There was a context in more than two hundred years to seek another family for the throne. Lawansin Adekunle I was a natural. The people of Orissa saw the writing on the wall that things were changing rapidly. They wanted an intelligent and educated man for a change to lead them. Lawansin Adekunle I was begged by his people and his father to give up his lucrative vice principal assignment at King's College to lead his people. His mother, Iya Telima Adekunle, personally visited him in Lagos to plead her case. It took her four days to reach Lagos. He was positioned to take over as the principal of King's College, Lagos, that year upon the retirement of the present principal, Sir Henry Seward, who was moving back to England. The tears in his mother's eyes drowned his soul and emotion. He had never refused his mother anything, and this would not be a start. He packed his bags, and with his two wives, four children, and mother, he returned home to Orissa to ascend the throne with almost 97 percent of the vote. He was well qualified. Lawansin had been the first person in Orissa Kingdom to obtain a college degree. He was ahead of his time.

As Edukoya was recovering from the surgery, after five months of feeling pretty strong, he saw Princess Yemisi's breast and marveled at her naked body. Something caught his attention, and he focused on her with utmost interest and curiosity. She was changing into her see-through silk nightgown, as she did every night before going to bed. She always changed in the presence of her husband to draw his appeal for her remarkable body, and she never wore underwear of any kind when she went to bed with him, even when she was having her monthly period. Her period had never prevented her from satisfying her man. Unlike most women, she had never experienced stomach cramps during those instances. Her nightgown was made from soft silk, with absolute transparency. However, she wore a long overrobe on demand. Her aim was to remain as romantic and attractive as possible for her man. At age fifty-four, with five children all breastfed, this stunning beauty still had well-pointed, firm breasts with zero artificial support. Her body was still luscious. Edukoya couldn't do any better, even with Felicia and Chika stacked together. Yemisi had always won the match for overall exceptional beauty. He looked at her curves, and her butt was still perfect, like a Brazilian butt. Men paid a lot of money to travel to Brazil during Carnival to look at the black Brazilian ladies with well-fitted butts and roundish, pointed breasts, but Edukoya was fortunate that he didn't have to go to Brazil to find one; he was living with the perfect creation.

He said, "Oh my Lord! Lady, you're beautiful." He was himself again, appreciating his perfect gift from God. Amid his admiration, his penis began to show a sign of erection again after years of erectile dysfunction. His penis became erect slowly, and finally, it firmed up as hard as a rock. It was erect like a pine tree, with the cap well wrapped, ready for action. He beckoned the princess to lock the door and come to his bed to see what he saw.

When she arrived at his bedside, she saw his penis sticking out from his body as hard as a rock and with zero support. Her eyes lit up and were fixed on it. She held the penis in her palm. It was very firm, and she looked at it with intense admiration. She screamed with the loudest voice, "Wow!" He had been doing his routine exercise, which included walking on a treadmill. John Okorocha had all the exercise equipment money could buy, having suffered the same ill health. John also did his routine exercise. One thing Princess Yemisi loved about her frequent visits to John's villa was his exercise equipment. There was always an additional order of new machines each time she came for a visit.

She spent about an hour and a half on the machines daily. She was always ready and fit to make love with her husband, even when she was on her period. Most women wouldn't dare to let a man touch them when they were on their period. Most women abstained completely from sex due to the heavy and lengthy bleeding, which was of no fault of their own. Most women experienced pressing stomach cramps and headaches during that time of the month. Princess Yemisi was blessed. She was not an ordinary woman. She was remarkable, and she knew it.

She asked him, "Are you ready to do it?"

He replied, "Oh yes! I'll try it."

It wasn't difficult at all. Yemisi gave him a blow job to harden his penis even more, and in the process of rocking back and forth, she reached her own deserved orgasm. Because of his new surgery, he could only do it dog style from the back. It was wonderful. They took a needed breath of fresh air and fell asleep in the same bed.

What about Felicia and Chika, especially Felicia? Kabiyesi Edukoya Adekunle III contemplated. If only he could show Felicia the tiger he had become. Chika already knew this tiger. They had been having secret romantic affairs for a long time. The probability of Edukoya and Princess Yemisi being together as they used to be was showing signs of weakness and fading. If Princess Yemisi had not been unbelievably pretty, fit, romantic, and in love with him, he would have found enough excuses to absorb Felicia or Chikanele into his life. However, he still left the door open for a second marriage with either of them. Princess Yemisi would soon turn sixty, and she could not be at her best with age. His excuse was that they need a younger woman to fill in the vacuum Yemisi would soon create.

He was underestimating the resilience of this remarkable beauty. Princess Yemisi could give any woman, old or young, a run for her money. She was gifted and talented. Princess Yemisi had introduced Felicia to coach Orissa Girls' Secondary School basketball team. She had been a part-time coach there before assigning the duty to Felicia. Kabiyesi Adekunle III was wrong. The princess was not complaining or anticipating when she was going to get old. Edukoya was just lusting for a pretty younger woman. Men had their eyes on Princess Yemisi all the time. Even some pastors at their church, Saint Mathew's, turned their eyes whenever she passed them by. One of them in particular, Reverend Moses Osalewa, PhD, a good-looking young man in his late thirties, gave Princess Yemisi double Holy Communion—double bread and double wine—each time he served her. One day he nearly misstepped by looking at her breathtaking, attractive butt as she turned her back and walked toward her seat after the communion. The congregation nearly took notice.

However, Princess Yemisi Adekunle was lusting for another man, Dr. Everest Oluomolewa. Her sexual attraction to Eva was muted for now, as Edukoya regained back his erection and also found her once again appealing. Even with his difficult positioning during intercourse due to his surgery, she always reached a climax with him due to some creative interventions. For instance, he had to be in a certain position because of the surgery to have sex with her, mostly from her back. She preferred a little bit of this and that during their sexual intercourse, and he tried his best under the circumstances to meet her expectations. She concluded that a half loaf of bread was better than none and was willing to compromise because she loved him dearly.

Eva was not completely out of the picture. If she thought about him, given the distance from home, her feelings for him grew deeper. Compounded by her husband's open-heart surgery, she was afraid her attraction to the young man must be deeper than just a lust for one-night-stand sexual intercourse. She was in love with Dr. Everest Oluomolewa, even more than the love she had for her husband. To compound the issue further, Charity, Eva's wife, persuaded Eva to call Kabiyesi Adekunle III and offer them his empathy as a close neighbor and friend. Charity got the phone number of where they were staying in America from Dr. Tunde Adekunle, his first son, when he came by to check on the villa in Ikoyi. Charity reminded her husband that if surgery was needed in Nigeria, he would be the closest trusted cardiothoracic surgeon they would allow to operate on him. Dr. Oluomolewa didn't want to seem overreaching. He didn't want to give Yemisi the impression his call was more than a friendly, innocent gesture. He wanted to position his call as a cardiologist and a neighbor. He was also lying to himself.

Deep down in his mind, he welcomed calling her. He was also beginning to fall in love with her. Absence had the tendency to draw those in love closer. Their feelings for each other had passed lust. When she heard his voice over the telephone, she melted down and shed tears of joy. Thank God Edukoya had gone out for a walk in the neighborhood with John; otherwise, her excitement would have been noticeably seen as something out of the ordinary. John Okorocha's wife, Mama Akudo, gave them space to catch up on old times.

Yemisi was finishing her conversation with Charity when they walked in. Princess Yemisi gave the surprising phone call to him. His Lordship Kabiyesi Adekunle III was grateful for Dr. Oluomolewa's call.

CHAPTER 21

Sorting out the pieces was complicated for the Adekunles upon their return from the USA. The original plan had been to stay for a two-week tour of the United States, but it had been seven and a half months. Critical decisions in Orissa Kingdom had been delayed, suspended, or abandoned. The local government areas, which were the designated official government voices of the people, did nothing. Briberies and corruptions were wired in the officials' bloodstreams. They had always worked hand in glove with the king to get things done for the Orissa people. Orissa Kingdom covered four local government areas. Dr. Tunde Lawansin Adekunle IV did not step up to the plate. He was afraid of being criticized for overreaching before his time as the future king of Orissa Kingdom. Instead, a committee of chiefs from each kindred was assembled to run the government of Orissa Kingdom. In a committee of chiefs where there was no clear leadership, the vision that propelled bold events to occur would always be limited. As a result, even issues that needed quick responses, such as the makeshift health clinics around the Orissa communities, were met with weak enforcement that spelled disaster.

The first thing Edukoya did was review all the documented and undocumented decisions made in his absence. They were plenty of them. While he was reviewing them, he was also confronted with his ongoing relationship with Felicia. He was also perturbed at himself for not preparing his son Tunde to have a feeling for the throne, which he would one day occupy.

He blamed himself for all the things that had gone wrong in Orissa Kingdom when he was absent. Out of the disasters emerged a solution that guaranteed, at a minimum, such disasters would be curtailed: for the first time, he copied the setups in a typical American city. San Francisco and San Jose were his model cities. He saw himself as the mayor of a big city. The setup brought clashes between him and the chairmen of Orissa's local government areas. He bypassed the chairmen of the local government areas and dealt directly with the Ondo state governor and the president of Nigeria to get much-needed help to solve the collapsing and pressing infrastructural needs of his kingdom.

There was no accountability, from trash collection to road repairs, hospitals, clinics, and the maintenance of schools. Seeing that he could not meet all the obligations himself, he officially made Princess Yemisi, his most trusted friend, adviser, and wife, the official crown princess of Orissa Kingdom, next in line for the throne of his kingdom. He had two important reasons: first, she had demonstrated confidence in her ability to govern with the little power she had as a designated crown princess of Orissa Kingdom, and second, he wanted to free up enough time for him and Felicia to be together. Kabiyesi Lawansin III was bent on absorbing Felicia as his second wife. When Felicia tasted sexual intercourse with him after he regained his erection, she confided in her best friend, Adetoye, that the sex with Edukoya was as sweet as honey, and for the first time in her life, she reached orgasm with her vaginal fluid soaking wet like a sea. She said she had multiple orgasms with Edukoya, who had enough patience to allow her to reach her full potential. She was not going back from her promise to marry the king.

Meanwhile, Edukoya had no idea Princess Yemisi had fallen in love with Dr. Everest Oluomolewa, a man it seemed she couldn't have. The tension was on the increase. She dreamed of making love to him in Paris, in her hotel room, when both went for a World Health Organization conference, of which she was a board member.

It started with a common group dinner with Dr. Oluomolewa's entourage. After dinner, Yemisi and Eva went for a walk on the hotel premises. They walked for about twenty-five minutes before Princess Yemisi saw a toy snake, which looked like a real snake. Some kids, who were guests in the hotel too, were playing with their toy snake. The snake was battery-operated and moved like a real snake. At the first glance of the snake toy, Princess Yemisi shouted, "Snake!" and held Dr. Oluomolewa's right arm tightly. Yemisi was afraid of all reptiles, no matter how small, and topping the list were snakes.

She held him until they came back to her room on the twenty-second floor. He wanted to discharge her, go back to his room, and call it a night. He also wanted to call Charity to know if she and the kids were okay. However, Princess Yemisi asked him to stay for a while because the sight of the snake, although unreal, had upset her a great deal.

One thing led to another, and soon they were kissing and cuddling. Yemisi was romantically experienced. She melted him, and before he knew it, he was stripping her naked, and she was doing the same to him. She then gave him a blow job, one he had never experienced before: a desirable woman swallowed all of his seven-and-a-half-inch penis, pretended to bite it off from its attachment, and let him ejaculate in her mouth. He practically shot his sperm through the roof, pouring every bit into her mouth, which she gladly swallowed.

She did not reach orgasm with him that night. He did not penetrate her vagina either. He said he was sorry a dozen times before dozing off to sleep. Princess Yemisi was a little disappointed by how weak his erection soon became, but she was also understanding, pitying the poor man's inexperience. Then again, her body had always overwhelmed men. It had continued to overwhelm the king for many years.

Suddenly, she woke up and found that the sexual encounter with Dr. Oluomolewa had been a dream. She was still in Orissa Kingdom, in bed with the king, not with Dr. Oluomolewa in Paris.

Princess Yemisi had her work cut out for her. She had a lot on her plate to contend with, and she had to deal with it all. She had Felicia, the monster she'd created, to contain. After all, a king of such a large kingdom was supposed to marry multiple wives. She convinced herself she was lucky that it was just one woman coming in. Felicia was a woman she knew. However, she was blind about Chika, her administrative assistant, the king's favorite concubine, who had captivated his heart and soul as no other woman had. Chika was the woman the king was most in love with. Princess Yemisi would not shame the king yet, no matter how lustful and tempting the situation might have been with Dr. Oluomolewa. Yemisi was a strong woman. She thought about getting Eva off her mind by submerging herself in Orissa Kingdom's detailed management.

She organized and created a self-sustaining, functioning government with adequate oversight supervision. She asserted she would likely accomplish a lot that way while the king was still alive. Then she had to deal with another pressing issue by recognizing wholeheartedly and admitting to herself that she was madly in love with two men, perhaps equally. One lover had been with her through thick and thin, her husband of thirty-seven years, Edukoya Adekunle III, and the other lover was the one she could not have, Dr. Everest Oluomolewa. Dr. Everest Oluomolewa in particular drained her heart and emotions constantly. The emotional distance was increasingly making the temptation much closer. She thought about him constantly and continuously wet her panties just thinking about him or looking at him. It occurred multiple times and in multiple places, especially when she had a brush with him. Twice, at a board meeting, while looking at him, she felt her panties become wet. She had to excuse herself to the restroom to clean up. She used toilet paper as a substitute pad because she was still gushing vaginal fluid uncontrollably. She was not on her period, and there was no blood, just immense bodily fluid, though she still occasionally saw her period at the age of fifty-four.

She had gone as far as nearly shouting out Everest's name when having sexual intercourse with her husband. It had happened on more than a dozen occasions. She caught herself just in time before she uttered his name. She wondered how she could have such lust for a man she believed did not deeply feel the same way she felt about him.

On Everest's side, he was totally consumed with a love he dared not have. He wished it would all go away. Yemisi, regardless of her youthful appearance and breathtaking beauty, was still an older woman. If Yemisi had had babies earlier in life, she could have had a baby close to his age. He tried to convince himself with this constructive thoughtfulness; however, it did not hold water.

PART 6

THE HONORABLE MADAM

CHAPTER 22

"A woman of substance." That was the description used by Justice Chukwu Onyemerekwe to qualify Princess Yemisi Adekunle. It was unusual for people to stand up in the courtroom when a person other than the judge entered the courtroom. Maybe the head of state, but otherwise, it was unusual. However, they did for Princess Yemisi Adekunle. Whenever she entered the courtroom, all eyes turned to her. She weighed about 145 pounds, with relatively big bones, and was slimly built for her height. She had a flat stomach. She was five feet, eight and a half inches tall. Yemisi was sensitive to height, and as a result, she wore medium-high heeled shoes. She liked high boots because they accentuated her butt and hips. She was a billboard display, and she knew it. She had medium-light brown skin, which enhanced her overall skin texture and durability. She used simple over-the-counter lotions and over-the-counter makeup to texture her skin.

Princess Yemisi was so in favor of simplicity that she wore simple makeup and moderately priced, simple jewelry. She'd learned a lot from her mother. Her mother was a dressmaker, and she'd learned from her and from her elder sister, Iyabo, how to sew clothing, especially Yoruba women's garments and outfits. She sewed most of her traditional Yoruba women's outfits. Yemisi was always quick on her feet. She sewed most of her husband's traditional agbada outfits. She was stylish and up to date in her line of clothing. She designed and sewed most of her clothes for her personal consumption. A handful of designers suggested the outfits ought to be showcased.

Her disposition was nothing short of remarkable. Her curiosity and desire to know everything was mind-boggling. She absorbed like a sponge. Her intellectual confidence was breathtaking. Yemisi read and wrote well too. She read about 350 words per minute with flawless comprehension. Her spoken English had no Yoruba accent, and her grammatical writing was strong. Yemisi's managerial skills and her capacity to lead told her whole story. Her father, Mr. Lawrence Adeniji, was a regional area manager for the United Africa Company (UAC). Although he had only secondary school education, at UAC's corporate in-house managerial training, which offered potential managers profound cultural and comprehensive management training, he learned enviable, outstanding people skills. Yemisi was her father's special daughter. As a baby, she always sat on the floor next to her father's feet during meetings with people who visited their home. Maybe she didn't understand what the adults were talking about, but she learned an important skill from her father: to remain deadly quiet, listen, and choose your words properly before talking. This skill had made her second to none in people skills when interacting with others. She was a formidable leader.

On her entering Justice Chukwu Onyemerekwe's courtroom, everyone stood up, including all the judges and Justice Onyemerekwe. She was seated in a corner chair by the court attendant, and she remained quiet. Her lawyer moved to adjourn the hearing, citing His Lordship Kabiyesi Edukoya Lawansin Adekunle III's fragile health issues. Her lawyer cited his seven and a half months of sudden absence from his family and, most importantly, the kingdom he loved so much due to his open-heart surgery. The kingdom was practically in a mess, wired with bribery, corruption, and finger-pointing. The king needed an undefined time period to sort things out. Her lawyer said things were quickly moving in the right direction since he had put Princess Yemisi in charge. She had been implementing plans of action to curtail such derailment in the future.

Justice Felix Oluwayeye, one of the panel's justices, asked for a ballpark time frame. He said, "We will all die before this case is settled."

That statement drew laughter in the courtroom. The argument went back and forth, with her team of lawyers unable to come up with a time frame. Then Justice Chukwunanyenwa Onyemerekwe said, "Before I rule on this motion, I will give Orissa Kingdom's first lady, the lady of substance Princess Yemisi Adekunle, the floor to air her views on this matter. I duly trust you will be objective."

Princess Yemisi stood up, and the whole courtroom full of clients, lawyers, and judges stood up with her, and then they quietly sat down, leaving her standing to air her stance on the issue. The court remained deadly quiet. One could have heard a pin drop. She offered special thanks to her lawyers, the justices, and especially Justice Chukwu Onyemerekwe for giving her the floor. She called it unusual. She said, "The man who called me a lady of substance." The whole courtroom burst into laughter enthusiastically. They then remained quiet, listening to every word she spoke.

She spoke for under three and a half minutes. She said, "Progress is being made in Orissa Kingdom right now as we debate in this courtroom, as I have been made the official crown princess of Orissa Kingdom, next in line to the throne. I will indulge the court's mercy to allow us to come back in twelve calendar months to tell you about the progress made so far. A sooner settlement of this case is more to our best interest than the governmments'. The governments are here to stay, but we have a relatively short time period to live in this world. Therefore, we should sooner settle this case for our own benefit than the government of Lagos State and the federal government."

Justice Chukwu Onyemerekwe thanked her for her eloquence, consideration, objectivity, thoughtfulness, and sincerity. He adjourned the hearing for twelve calendar months. He expressed his deep sympathy for the king and wished him well. He also expressed good luck in all she was doing for the benefit of Orissa Kingdom.

On the way home that evening from the Lagos mainland to Ikoyi, with all the traffic, she felt tired and fell asleep in the back of her Range Rover. She was chauffeured. Many things came across her mind, including her husband's health. She had been telling him to go easy on sex, especially with the young Felicia. Edukoya had an enormously increased appetite for sexual intercourse after his surgery and after regaining his erection. At the age of eighty, he could only ejaculate about twice a day, though his erection still stood enviably. He constantly wanted to have sex. Felicia, Chika, and even Princess Yemisi were always ready to let him have it on demand. His erection, so far, had remained solid, tempting, and without artificial enhancement. Felicia appeared to like such attention a great deal, and she seemed to love more of his sexual advances. Immediately after she came back from work, she dragged him to the bedroom to have sexual intercourse. They would be in there for more than two hours, with her reaching climax and orgasm multiple times. The poor man could only ejaculate once, but his erection still stood solid to allow enough time for Felicia to have her way until she became exhausted. They would repeat the act at night when they went to bed. Felicia had mastered the technique for how to have sex with this man, despite his open-heart surgery, to her maximum satisfaction. She was monopolizing the king's sexual needs, leaving Princess Yemisi wanting.

As they were approaching Dr. Everest Oluomolewa's residence, her thoughts shifted to him. She wondered if they could ever be close to each other. She thought about her husband's increased sexual appetite, but at the same time, she was lusting for another man, with disturbing feelings of wondering when they would ever have a sexual relationship. Felicia's monopolizing the king's sexual needs made Yemisi's sexual attraction for Dr. Oluomolewa all the more persuasive and tempting.

The king invented and created excuses to visit Lagos frequently. He was actually going there to get it on with Chika. Chika, having starved for his affection all that while, could not wait to have him inside her. Yemisi could not see enough of the king even when they came to Lagos together. He was always involving Chika in everything they did and seeking her opinion, even on matters personal to both of them.

Princess Yemisi decided to come to Lagos alone. That way, she would be free to lust for Everest, the forbidden fruit. She was aware of the king's secret relationship with Chika, but she dared not bring it up for discussion, as she had created both monsters, Felicia and Chika. With her increasing lust for Dr. Everest Oluomolewa, she concluded that fighting those unwinnable wars would have been the height of hypocrisy.

CHAPTER 23

Princess Yemisi contemplated her many pressing issues. She thought about the people of Orissa Kingdom a great deal. She quickly put plans in place to have the palace's administrative staff align with the local government areas' administrative staff to get at least her main goals accomplished while her husband was still alive. She wanted more governing power. She was able to convince the people of Orissa Kingdom that the ultimate decision on how to run the land should rest with the king and not with the local government area administrators, whom she claimed were wired down with bribery, corruption, and finger-pointing. A vote was scheduled to uphold this notion. The argument was one of separation of power between the elected entity, who answered to the people, and a crown king, who did not answer to anyone. Princess Yemisi reminded the people about the late 1800s, when the reigning family of Kabiyesi Ifeoluwa VI was dethroned by the people of Orissa amid the same disgusting characteristics confronting them now. It had led to a new king from a different family being installed. She said, "Yes, the king will ultimately answer to all the people of Orissa Kingdom."

The local government area administrators struck a deal with the king. Both parties together set up a pilot program to see if Princess Yemisi would govern better than them for one year. A vote for the permanent concentration of power in the king's hand or the total elimination of the king's powers, which would make him a mere ceremonial king who showed up for important festival occasions, was scheduled in about a year. It was the biggest high-risk challenge undertaken by Princess Yemisi, putting every power they had on the line. She had the blessing of the king, which reinforced her confidence.

In the space of six months, Princess Yemisi was proven right. She concentrated on five key areas: health, roads, schools, electricity, and markets. Those five areas were visible issues the naked eye could see to evaluate them as wrong or right. She was impeccably brilliant. Princess Yemisi also instituted garbage collection.

With all the works in progress, a vote was scheduled sooner, before the one year came due, by the Progressive Radical Youths of Orissa Kingdom, to certify a permanent stay of the new deal. The concentration of power won by 95 percent of the vote. Three percent of the people voted against it, and there was a 2 percent margin of error. Kabiyesi Edukoya Adekunle III dedicated 30 percent of all his family's investment holdings worldwide permanently to the course of relentless developments in Orissa Kingdom. Enforcement of local tax collection was instituted and enforced with the strictest accountability ever seen in the history of Orissa Kingdom, the Yoruba tribe, or the nation. With the combination of funds, revenue was raised at an accelerating speed, which was used to accomplish large portions of the goals set up by His Lordship Edukoya Adekunle III in a relatively short period of time.

At age fifty-six, Princess Yemisi breathed a sigh of relief with her main goals adequately achieved. A university-style polytechnic school was established to offer bachelor of arts and science degrees, master of art and science degrees, and doctorate degrees in various academic fields. New professional colleges of medicine, law, social sciences, and business administration were added. Four satellite health clinics were expanded and improved into makeshift hospitals in each of the four local government areas to feed into the main hospital in Agbala, the kingdom's capital city, where the king resided. The main hospital was expanded, and the name was changed to Orissa Polytechnic Medical Center. It graduated about 30 physicians annually. The medical center supported sixty-five internships of health professionals annually from all over Nigeria. All the people of the kingdom never paid for basic medical care again. They received first-class medical care.

Ninety percent of the roads were either completed or nearing completion. Open markets were improved to accommodate basic necessities, such as paved streets, streetlights, running water, and clean bathrooms with marble floorings. Four coeducation secondary schools were built and added to the existing ones to guarantee that students never had to relocate to go to school, unless by choice. The elementary schools in each village were improved, and head-start basic elementary computer skills were taught to the students as early as first grade. Electricity and running water were made a household necessity for all the people of Orissa, though they had to pay to get them installed. Ninety-nine and a half percent of them did. The ongoing use of this utility was also paid for by the individuals who received the services. Life seemed to be improving for the people of the four local government areas that made up Orissa Kingdom.

There was another pressing issue: Kabiyesi Edukoya Adekunle III and Felicia were practically in a relationship. Felicia had moved to the main building adjacent to Princess Yemisi's lodge. However, Felicia had not yet become the official wife of the king. She was, in practicality, a concubine. The constant sexual intercourse paid off for her. Felicia became pregnant with twin babies, a boy and a girl. Kabiyesi Adekunle III, who thought he had a good thing going for him and thought he could eat his cake and have it too, found himself caught between a rock and a hard place. The music was forced to change tune with Felicia as the lead singer. Felicia was a breathtakingly attractive woman now in her midthirties. Her stomach was getting bigger on a daily basis and even more attractive and appealing to the king, because this slim, fit lady's weight gain during pregnancy added to her beauty. However, Edukoya had to approach her with enormous caution, though Felicia wanted sexual intercourse now even more from the king. His lust and desire for sexual intercourse now turned to old reliable Princess Yemisi, who did not mind being a substitute, having seldom seen sexual affection come her way recently because of Felicia and Chikanele's dominance.

Kabiyesi Edukoya Adekunle III broke his promise to Yemisi that he wouldn't take on a second wife. Edukoya was madly in love with Felicia, whom he saw as an intimate love partner, a dear friend, and a daughter. She called him Daddy, and she called the crown princess Mama Yemisi. Felicia was a loving, intelligent, and respectable woman. One couldn't resist her passionate personality. She was always charming, warm, and friendly. However, if her pregnancy was proven to be the king's doing, he would have two babies born out of wedlock, practically two bastard children. The king would have none of that. Princess Yemisi, seeing that she'd made the bed, reluctantly agreed for her husband to add on a second wife. In almost five years of constant sexual affairs between Felicia and the king, even when she was in her late period of the month, she hadn't gotten pregnant. Given the king's age, doubt hovered over Edukoya and Princess Yemisi; maybe there was another man. They wouldn't know if the babies were legitimate until the babies were born and a test could be administered to them.

To cause further doubt, twins did not run in Adekunle's and Felicia's families.

If they waited till the babies were born to claim legitimacy before marriage, they would be bastard children. Princess Yemisi, putting herself into the shoes of another woman, gave the green light wholeheartedly and welcomed her into the family. Felicia was by then seven months pregnant. The traditional marriage was rushed through, and Felicia at last owned her legitimate place in the palace as Felicia Funmi Adekunle, PhD.

The twins were born in America, as all the children of Yemisi had been. John Okorocha made all the arrangements, as usual, and he was their godfather. They stayed at his home. It was a natural childbirth, with Felicia displaying her athletic skill and ability. The babies came out effortlessly in much less time than usual, which prompted UC Davis's gynecology unit to throw them a party with enormous gifts to send them off. Kenmiejo escorted them to the hospital, and she was the attending physician who delivered the twins. Series of tests were performed there in America and at home in Nigeria by his four kids who were medical doctors. The overwhelming conclusion was that they were the thirteenth and fourteenth legitimate additions to Edukoya Adekunle III's family. Their nicknames were Promise and Miracle.

The other pressing problem was Professor Oluomolewa. Princess Yemisi was dying to have an ongoing sexual relationship with him. At the age of fifty-six, no matter how well people carried themselves, age began to show a perturbing trend. No matter the lotion she used, age was beginning to show traces of wrinkles. However, Princess Yemisi had faded the mild wrinkles with mild light brown lotion to the point that one could barely notice them. Because Princess Yemisi was sensitive to her body, she took painstaking steps to notice them. With the light makeup she always applied every morning before she set off for her daily activities, she would undo the damage caused by nature. She still comfortably passed for a beautiful black woman in her midforties. She still had dimples that made men look steadily till their manhood went crazy.

It turned out Dr. Everest Oluomolewa was not moving out of their neighborhood anytime soon, if at all. Princess Yemisi wished he would go away, and all her lust hopefully would disappear. He'd inherited the house after his father's death. She was just fooling herself. The king's villa was on a corner lot, in a huge compound. The villa was perfectly positioned where she could see movement in and out of Everest's front door from the master bedroom window of the king's villa. Because of this, Yemisi moved permanently to the master bedroom so she could see Dr. Oluomolewa's comings and goings. She always found excuses to come to Lagos, mostly on Thursdays through Saturdays. The real reason for her frequent visits to Lagos was to see him and accompany him on his Saturday jogging exercise.

She was still a fit, attractive, pretty woman. She dyed her hair lightly with a seemingly natural black-colored dye. The stainless permanent hair dye naturally wore off over time. The dye didn't stain her clothes and was moderately priced at Macy's department store in America.

Her constant uninvited and accidental brushing with Eva made her day. She looked forward to the tight hugging, which wet her panties. When such hugs took place, she kissed him tightly, plastering her lips on his, pretending it was a gesture of good neighborliness. However, underneath her clothes, she was soaking wet, and she wished it would turn out to be the real thing. She couldn't wait to go home to change her underwear.

Eva welcomed the whole deal. When his wife, Charity, was absent from the scene, he would return her hugs quite romantically, and they stayed longer than the norm. He kissed her with his tongue submerged into her mouth, with a noticeable lick from his penis onto his underwear too. They held and kissed much longer without saying a word. It was noticeable how his penis hardened, about to penetrate her vagina. The only thing preventing his penetration was her outerwear. She noticed it too on her upper leg, near her vagina. She then shifted his hardened penis with her hands in between her legs, at the center, pressing it hard on her. She pressed on him close, with both hands holding his butt tightly, rubbing her pubic hair against him to stimulate her climax. He too held her butt with both hands, pressing his hardened penis against her pubic hair too. On a few occasions, she reached her climax, and orgasm ensued with a sea of her vaginal fluid noticeably soaking her dress. Those few occasions were, in her mind, the greatest experience she had with sexual intercourse.

CHAPTER 24

Justice Chukwunanyenwa Onyemerekwe sent a motion to the team of Princess Yemisi to file a proceeding to resume the preliminary hearing. The federal government had allocated the parcels of land to the oil companies for drilling. However, the legal proceedings for a fair allocation of the proceeds were holding them back. The drillers were waiting patiently for the court's order to proceed with the drilling. Although the government had the upper hand in the case, Justice Onyemerekwe positioned Princess Yemisi's team as equal co-owners of the land and, with them as the plaintiffs, called the shot to please them. The new civilian regime called for government accountability and constitutional loyalty and obedience. The press, thus, held them to their words. Nigerians were testing freedom of the press for the first time and what that freedom looked like. News sensations always prevailed to humiliate the government, no matter the administration. Justice Onyemerekwe, by positioning the government as the underdog, hoped to persuade the press to be more sympathetic to the federal government and, as a result, show some objectivity in their writings. However, the government was not fooling anybody, especially Princess Yemisi.

A meeting was held at the palace, with the key actors invited to find common ground and a common plan of action. The team's plan called for Princess Yemisi to frequent Lagos as often as possible. That was welcome news to the crown princess, who would use the opportunity as the perfect excuse to see her boyfriend, Professor Everest Oluomolewa. To the surprise of the court, Princess Yemisi's team filed for the continuation of the preliminary hearing. A date was set for ninety calendar days. Princess Yemisi was eager to get to Lagos and begin work on the potential $10 billion of wealth sitting beneath the earth's surface. She wanted to get away from Kabiyesi Adekunle III, Felicia, and the newborn twin babies. She wanted to get away to meet with Dr. Everest Oluomolewa.

The last time they'd met to jog together, sexual intercourse nearly took place on the bus stop bench. Princess Yemisi sat on Eva's lap, facing him, with her legs spread wide apart, trapping both of his legs in the middle. That day, she wore tight-fitting black sport shorts with a zipper positioned from her front to her back. She wore no panties. His penis was fully erect and as hard as a rock. He was almost done unzipping her shorts open, with his penis ready to penetrate her vagina and their longest kiss ever, when they saw a familiar person drive by waving at them. Their compromising position was so embarrassing that they left in a hurry, laughing and fearing the worst.

Princess Yemisi was a romantic goddess. The next time they went jogging, they romantically stood facing each other. They hugged tightly, with their tongues submerged in each other's mouth. She stuck her right hand underneath his shorts, working up her feelings with his hardened penis. She asked him to stick his left hand underneath her shorts and work her clitoris simultaneously. The work paid off handsomely. She held him tightly and squeezed firmly his hardened erection until her orgasm ensued. Her vaginal fluids gushed out uncontrollably like a waterfall, soaking all over his left hand. In turn, he sent his sperm all over her right palm. They romantically wiped their bodily fluids on each other's sport shorts, squeezing each other's butt, with their mouths still plastered together.

Later that Saturday evening, she left in her jet for Akure to meet with her husband and the rest of her family, because the activities the following day, Sunday, were pressing and important to the king. The thought of having real sexual intercourse with Eva dominated her mind during the thirty-minute flight. Whenever she started thinking about having a sexual relationship with Everest, she became forgetful and restless because guilt had started to get the better part of her. But she always managed her emotions so well that people around her hardly noticed. She was perturbed by something she knew she dared not have. Whenever she thought about Dr. Everest Oluomolewa, which she frequently did, she became sexually aroused. If Edukoya was around at those times, she'd drag him away from Felicia into her bedroom to make passionate love with him. At the end of such an encounter, her husband would shake his head and say, "Lady, you've still got it. You are the best."

At the age of sixty-two, Princess Yemisi was still sexually active like an eighteen-year-old girl. As she got older, she became increasingly lustful for sexual intercourse and affection, and she could release vaginal fluids like a waterfall if she was sexually in the mood. She was not afraid to demand it from her husband, Edukoya, or from her boyfriend, Dr. Oluomolewa, whichever one was around at that time.

Kabiyesi Adekunle III, at his age of eighty-three, with three beautiful, sexually needy women lusting for his comfort, compounded with his health issues, wondered if he could hold on any longer. It was the subconscious main reason he agreed to let Princess Yemisi join the board. Maybe she could meet someone there who would provide her with some badly needed affection, and as long as he did not know about it, everything would be all right. He refused to tailgate his women; however, he did not encourage them to have a substitute either. Always polite and romantic, he did not allow them the urge to look for an alternative. Edukoya never asked Princess Yemisi about the presence of another man in her life. Even with her closeness to Dr. Oluomolewa, the king gave every indication he was satisfied with their relationship. However, the king repeatedly discussed Felicia's other sexual interest with Princess Yemisi, especially when Felicia confronted him with the twins' pregnancy.

Princess Yemisi got to wonder about Felicia's relationship with the king. Edukoya had broken all his rules. He went to bed with Felicia before he committed himself to marriage with her. If not for the pregnancy, the extramarital affair would still have been going on. Felicia was positioned as the king's concubine before they were married. Edukoya had sex with her all through her pregnancy, even up to the night her orgasm caused her water to break. Felicia was rushed to UC Davis Medical Center in Sacramento, California, on the king's Boeing 737 jet. Kenmiejo, his first daughter, an ob-gyn trained at Stanford School of Medicine, was the lead physician. She delivered the twins.

Two and a half months later, Felicia and Edukoya were back at it again, and they never stopped making love with each other, sometimes doing it three or four times a day, until he encountered another stroke that ultimately led to his death.

Edukoya's recent liberated sexual attitude was difficult for Princess Yemisi to get used to. All his golden rules, showing perfection in every aspect of his life, were now washed away. All of a sudden, the king changed his sexual attitudes when he started taking Felicia and Chika to bed. The question constantly on her mind was *Why not engage in an extramarital affair like my husband?* She suddenly realized she had already done that.

Princess Yemisi had been younger than Felicia when she got married to Edukoya, barely twenty years old. He'd kept her starved for sex for almost twelve months after their engagement when he was being the so-called perfect gentleman, which she hated. She never had strayed from their relationship, not once. At her age, now in her immediate sixties, she still could give any woman, young or old, a run for her money. She wondered what Felicia was doing right and what she was doing wrong. That thought bothered her a great deal. She began to feel unsure of herself, but she soon got back on her feet again. She realized she had made the bed, and she had to lie on it. She couldn't make herself the nineteen-year-old kid she once had been, and to demand that youthfulness from her, she felt, was a moral crime.

If virginity had been the reason he'd delayed intimacy with her before they got married, what about Felicia? And Chika, the other woman besides Felicia, whom Yemisi believed he was really in love with? Felicia had slept with six different men before she got married to her first husband. Chika had slept with three different men, and one of them had resulted in Princess Yemisi's adorable surrogate grandsons. Both were well-experienced sexual partners before getting involved with the king. Yemisi too had put all her past sexual experiences on the table before they got married. Felicia and the king had only a traditional wedding, but Yemisi had three wedding ceremonies with him: a traditional one, one in Reno by a justice of the peace, and the awesome church wedding ceremony in San Jose, California.

She recognized the hypocrisy. All of a sudden, she caught herself feeling sorry herself and jealous of Felicia. She then realized the king loved her the most, and that was the reason for her added responsibilities. Princess Yemisi was Edukoya's most trusted best friend and lover. The other woman her husband trusted was Chikanele, for reasons Princess Yemisi continued to wonder about. Edukoya had borrowed Chika from Princess Yemisi, traveling with her all over the globe.

As she was thinking those thoughts, the crown princess walked along the streets of Ikoyi alone, hoping to brush shoulders with Eva, the man she shouldn't have in her life.

PART 7

THE MIXED FRUIT BASKET

CHAPTER 25

The ninety days the court had set for the preliminary hearing passed, and the king was briefed about the proceedings. Kabiyesi Adekunle III, being an effective lawyer, initiated that the deposition should have one voice, and every question and every answer must have reference. That way, the government's lawyers would know Princess Yemisi's team came to settle in good faith. There was unanimous agreement to elect the lead attorney. Previously, Princess Yemisi had appointed the lead attorney, but they'd quickly found out it was not working. Lawyers, by nature or design, obeyed the rules of law and constructive democracy—that was, orderliness. Lawyers, by nature or design, respected authorities and leadership, especially when they were elected. That case must not be an exception to the rules, they agreed. So they elected Dr. Ayofenmi Ndubusi Kuye, LLD, to be their lead attorney.

Barista Ayofenmi Ndubusi Kuye was a challenging and effective lawyer. His home state was Ondo State. His father was from Okitipupa in Ondo State, and his mother was from Ikwere in Rivers State. His grandparents on his mother's side owned a small retail grocery store in Akure, a relatively old historic township in Ondo State, where his father, Joseph Kuye, met Alice Iheyinwa Ebele, his mother. Akure was the capital city of Ondo State and harbored the airport and a number of distinguished institutions of higher learning, including Ondo State University. They fell madly in love with each other. Despite huge opposition due to deep-rooted tribal concerns, both sets of parents finally reluctantly granted them their permission to get married. Akure became a modern city with a large population. During the civil war, his mother took her children—Ayofenmi and his sister, Sherrifatt—back to Ikwere, in fear of being killed.

Ayofenmi and Sherrifatt learned to speak Igbo in a hurry in Ikwere. They spoke Yoruba and Igbo fluently. Their mother made sure they never forgot how to understand and speak Yoruba, and she communicated with them mostly in the Yoruba language while in Ikwere. After the war, their father, Joseph Kuye, now a college graduate, having attended Yaba College of Technology with HND, working with Liver Brothers Nigerian as an engineer, came to pick them up.

Ndubusi, Ayofenmi's mother's favorite name for him, as a grown man, finished secondary school in the early 1970s. He was admitted to the University of Nigeria, Port Harcourt, where he earned a law degree, finishing with first-class honors in the late 1970s. He won a government scholarship and came to Ohio State University, where he earned his MBA. After his graduation, he got a work-on-contract job with AIG as a global adjuster and risk manager. He lived in San Francisco. While in San Francisco, he obtained an LLM and LLD from Golden Gate University.

He came back to Nigeria in the late 1980s and joined the law chamber of Wires and Wires, who had law offices in Abuja, Lagos, Port Harcourt, Aba, Ibadan, Akure, Benin, and Enugu. As an adjunct professor of law, he taught law management courses in various universities throughout Nigeria and abroad. He was the architect of his law chamber's expansion. He was not a good litigator; however, he positioned himself as an effective law manager, which he proved himself at handsomely. Ayofenmi was married, with seven children. The lead litigator positions were given to four lawyers: Barista Oluwoyeye, Barista Omah, Barista Tifenmi, and Barista Ododuwa. Barista Oluwoyeye, LLD, a graduate of the University of Nigeria, Benin, was elected as the chief litigator and spokesman for the team. Barista Oluwoyeye was a contract litigator and a law professor at the University of Nigeria, Lagos.

Justice Onyemerekwe finished reading his summaries and court rules with regard to Nigerian land tenure in general and as it pertained to Nigeria's and Lagos State's land guidance rules. He called on the opposition and the defense to submit their opposing motions. Barista Oluwoyeye handed the opposition documents to Barista Osondu Godfrey Omaa to submit. The chief justice of the panel, Justice Chukwu Onyemerekwe, received the motions from the plaintiff and the defendant. The court clerk entered them into the record. It took about three hours for that process to be completed. It was noontime, and Justice Onyemerekwe banged his gavel on his desk and adjourned the hearing until after the lunch break.

The court went on recess and then resumed at 1:15 p.m. After back-and-forth exchanges, the judges had heard enough of the arguments and counterarguments. Justice Onyemerekwe made eye contact with Princess Yemisi, who was sitting in the far right corner of the courtroom, and saw her yawning with a light brown handkerchief covering her mouth. He concluded everyone was tired after four and a half hours of deliberation. He whispered to the two other panel judges, and they nodded in agreement. He banged his gavel on the desk and adjourned the court till Monday.

It was Wednesday, and the Muslims were on the Ramadan public holiday, which took place on Thursday and Friday. Princess Yemisi, exhausted, fell asleep in the backseat of her Mercedes-Benz SUV. She had been chauffeured to the courthouse. She didn't see Dr. Oluomolewa waving at her at the junction, at a Mobile gas station. The driver woke her up, pointing at Dr. Oluomolewa waving at her. They had passed him already. She asked the chauffeur if the doctor was with his wife and children, and the driver said he did not know but added that he was standing alone adjacent to his car. She asked the chauffeur to turn back to meet with him, apologize for her nonresponsiveness, and also greet his family. When they got there, Yemisi looked for his kids and his wife.

Everest, sensing what she was looking for, said, "Charity and the children went to Surulere for the weekend to spend time with Rosalyn, her elder sister."

Not to raise any suspicion, she quickly discarded him and promised to keep him company that evening. They shook hands with a mild hug, and she departed. In the car, the chauffeur innocently raised Dr. Oluomolewa as a topic of conversation, but she mildly brushed the conversation aside. She didn't want the driver to know that she knew the doctor intimately.

That evening, Princess Yemisi walked over to Dr. Oluomolewa's house. He was waiting anxiously for her visit, wondering how that night would turn out. He was alone, with the house practically empty. Their maid, Victoria Aguroma, an attractive seventeen-year-old girl, had joined Charity on the visit. She was finishing up her secondary school education that year. There were a luxuriously built three-seat couch, a love seat, and two single recliners in the parlor. There was a guest room with a well-made bed. Before Charity had left to visit Rosalyn, their maid had made in the master bedroom a luxurious bed, without foreknowledge of the usefulness of her handiwork. It was the first time Princess Yemisi and Dr. Oluomolewa would be alone in his bedroom, the living room, or whichever room provided the easiest comfort. The mistake she made, which was not so much a mistake after all, was coming with her cell phone.

When she rang the doorbell, Everest opened the door for her. She wore a see-through silk blouse covered with a light black jacket. That evening, on purpose, she wore textured black silk leggings with no panties underneath, which coordinated with her tight Brazilian butt. She'd put on light brown lipstick and light makeup to match. She was simple, sexy, and attractive. Visible through her blouse, her large nipples stuck out like an eighteen-year-old girl's. Her body was still perfectly firm, even at the age of almost sixty. When Dr. Everest Oluomolewa glanced at her body, his erection stood up uncontrollably and was about to burst his shorts wide open.

They were kissing right from the door, when a phone call came in. Felicia's baby girl, Miracle, had a high fever and had been rushed to Orissa Polytechnic Medical Center. Right then, every bit of romance washed away. Yemisi headed to the airport in Ikeja to board her executive jet back to Agbala. The two chauffeurs had gone home for the day, so Eva had to drive her to the airport. She rested on his shoulder, crying and praying that nothing would happen to the little girl, whom the king had become attached to. She remembered Bunmi, who, almost forty-one years ago, had had a high fever when she was just two years old. When they got to the airport, they kissed inside his car before saying goodbye.

CHAPTER 26

That night was perturbing to Princess Yemisi, and she wasn't thinking about anything other than Blessing Jede Adekunle, the little girl nicknamed Miracle. She was completely consumed by her disposition. She remembered how pretty she was and how dramatic she could be. Princess Yemisi had nicknamed her Cinema because the little girl loved to entertain. At two, she could speak fluently so that the audience could understand. The younger of the twins, Jede was perceptive at her age. She loved to watch cartoons on television. She learned her numbers and alphabet in both English and Yoruba. Incredibly, she spoke English as well as Yoruba fairly well and correctly. Miracle reminded Princess Yemisi of Bunmi at age two when she came over to play with her. Blessing and Promise, the twin boy, and her biological grandchildren raced Princess Yemisi, chasing her all over the mansion, playing hide-and-seek games. They called her Grandma. As she remembered those little things during her thirty-minute flight to Akure, she began to cry and shake.

Princess Yemisi was terrified after watching her sibling die of high fever. Yemisi had been two years older than her sister. They had been playing in the sand, and all of a sudden, her little sister had developed a fever that kept increasing until her eyes turned blue. Her mother had gone to Akure to buy sewing supplies. Her father had been in Lagos, working as an area manager at UAC. Two of her older brothers had been off at boarding school, and her elder sister, Iyabo Adeniji, had been in form five, finishing up her secondary school education at

Orissa Girls' nearby. She had ridden a bicycle to school from home. Yemisi, her younger brother, and her sister had been left in the trusted hands of their elderly grandma to look after them.

One thing going for Felix Adeniji was his good looks, coupled with his marriage to a woman of extravagant beauty. They'd passed their good looks on to their children. Her little sister had been positioned to be the prettiest among her siblings. Her death had devastated Yemisi and, at the same time, firmed her up. Yemisi had vowed that it would never happen to her children, and that was why she'd chosen nursing as a profession. High fever among children led to seizures. Seizures, when not caught in time, could have a devastating effect and ultimately lead to death. It was good to periodically check children's body temperature. Princess Yemisi ordered the clinics in Orissa Kingdom to send nurses to every home to monitor children's body temperature and vital signs periodically. She ordered the clinics and Orissa Polytechnic Medical Center to give a once-a-year flu shot to every kid and every mother examined at the clinics.

Malaria and flu vaccinations had saved a lot of lives in Orissa Kingdom and drastically reduced the number of people admitted to the hospital due to those diseases. High fevers were mostly caught in time, which had reduced children's mortality rate by 95 percent. Whenever a case hit home, as in the case of Bunmi and Blessing, it always was keenly felt by Princess Yemisi. Therefore, no pleasure, even with Everest, could distract from the intensity of how she felt for the little girl. The fact that Felicia made the phone call elevated the seriousness of the matter. Felicia always addressed Princess Yemisi as Mom. She called her Mama.

The chauffeur was waiting at the airport with two police escorts. It was about eleven o'clock at night when they got to the hospital sixty-five miles away from Akure Metro Airport. By then, the baby had been stabilized. Felicia was in a corner of the baby's room, dozed off. The king was back at his palace. The doctors and nurses on duty that night quickly attended to the crown princess. They looked over the baby and hinted that she would be discharged in the morning when they finished checking her vital signs.

All the touching of the baby by the doctors, the nurses, and Princess Yemisi woke up the baby. She laughed when she saw Princess Yemisi and, in turn, woke up Felicia. Felicia, on glancing at Yemisi, started to cry. She said, "You are truly my mom."

Princess Yemisi phoned her husband to tell him she was back and in the hospital, visiting the baby. Edukoya was pleased and happy to know that, because it spoke volumes of the princess's character. She insisted on spending the night with the baby to relieve Felicia, who had been there with Jede all day. Felicia left with the chauffeur, and Yemisi stayed back. The hospital wheeled in a bed for her to sleep by Jede's corner.

Lying there in the relatively tiny bed the hospital offered, she had time to reflect on her past. She thought about her husband, His Lordship Kabiyesi Edukoya Adekunle III. She thought about her late father, Felix Adeniji, and saw similarities in them. She'd loved her father dearly. They had been close. Edukoya had become a substitute for her father. She had never called Edukoya by name from the first time they met at the wedding. In fact, she called him Sir, as he was much older than she. As a matter of fact, she never called him by any of his names. At first, she'd called him Baba Bunmi, and later on, she'd used the term *darling* or *love*. She had grown with this replacement of the man she'd cherished, her father. She counted her blessings and said, "I'm blessed." She then reflected on Felicia and said, "Face it. My husband is now married to two wives." Because of her breathtaking personality, Princess Yemisi wore the clothes well. She had completely absorbed Felicia into her bosom. It was hard to find equality with a person who called her Mama. However, she tried to do just that, such as letting her use one of the jets to go visit her brother living in Accra, Ghana. She reflected on Dr. Everest Oluomolewa, the lust and love of her life. She couldn't quite make out what she saw in that attractive and adorable man. Whether it was love or lust, he was always on her mind.

CHAPTER 27

Felicia Funmi Adekunle had captured Edukoya's deep feelings, just as Princess Yemisi and Chika had. Princess Yemisi was bothered by the intense warmness between the two. However, Princess Yemisi was not a spy and wasn't about to become one. Fortunately, a phone call came in from Frederick, Felicia's only brother, who lived in Accra, Ghana. Princess Yemisi picked up the call and transferred it to Felicia at her lodge. She was breastfeeding the babies alone with no interruption. The phone was central, with multiple landline links wired to outlets around the palace. One could listen to every conversation around the palace from any phone if the recipient forgot to press the control button. Felicia knew that well. She had used it countless times. This system had been vastly improved with advanced technology. Yemisi hung up the phone when Felicia picked up the phone on her end. However, in breastfeeding Teffi Promise Adekunle, her twin boy, who was restless, Felicia forgot to press the control button.

The control button also allowed multiple phone calls to be placed and received at the same time. But if the last user did not press the control button, the whole system would be tied up. Yemisi picked up the phone about thirty minutes later to call her chauffeur in Abuja to pick them up at the airport for a weekend getaway trip with her husband. It happened that Felicia was still talking to her brother, with an angry tone of voice. The high-pitched voice prompted Princess Yemisi to listen in on their conversation silently. The brother was begging her to cook up a scheme to extract money from the king. Felicia's brother said, "Princess Yemisi is so naive she will not be able to tell her left from her right when I get through with her." He said the king was so rich that the dupe would not make any difference to him. Felicia told her brother how nicely her new family had received her. She recounted her blessings to him, which was why she'd chosen the name Blessing for her baby girl. In the end, she banished her only brother from her life forever. She hung up the phone in tears.

The kids were fed, and they fell asleep. Kabiyesi walked into her lodge to say goodbye for the weekend without her. He saw her crying. He held her in his arms to ascertain what had happened. He thought she was crying about the weekend without him in her life, but that was not the case. Felicia asked Edukoya, "Do you trust me?"

He confidently replied, "Yes."

She told him that his money and power were not what attracted her to him. She told him Princess Yemisi had nothing to do with her initial lust for him. She said she was a grown woman who loved her profession as a teacher. She was attracted to him because, with all his power and money, he made ordinary persons feel good and positive about themselves. She said, "You are not a snob, and you make me laugh."

She said when the king asked her to bed for the first time, she was nervous but, at the same time, was ready because she'd loved him from the start. Unfortunately, he could not perform due to his erectile dysfunction. Then she realized Yemisi was setting her up to stimulate him to perform. Felicia said when he returned from America after his surgery and wanted to show her the sex tiger he had become, it made her fall in love with him even more. Felicia said ever since then, she had never stopped loving him. She said if he had refused to marry her with her pregnancy, she would have committed suicide. She showed him the pills and flushed them down the toilet. They were pills that induced massive heart attacks and were used in surgical rooms to resuscitate severe failing hearts. If taken in a large dosage and without a doctor's supervision, they could be fatal. Felicia told Kabiyesi she regarded him as an uncle, a dad, her husband, and a trusted friend, whom she never would betray, because she was madly in love with him.

Kabiyesi wiped away her tears with his hand and kissed her passionately. In the process, his penis became erect, and they made love in her lodge before he departed with Princess Yemisi to Abuja. However, before leaving her lodge, he said, "You made me laugh too."

On the way to Akure Metro Airport, Edukoya revisited what Felicia had told him, and the thoughts occupied his mind. That prompted Princess Yemisi to ask him what he'd discussed with Felicia, as the goodbye had taken unusually long. Kabiyesi never hid anything from Yemisi. "She was talking about trust," he said.

Princess Yemisi told her husband he should trust Felicia, saying, "Felicia is a genuine article, the one you must really trust." Princess Yemisi refused to discuss it further, lest she reveal her source. Felicia was not circumcised, as Princess Yemisi was, so it didn't take long for her and Edukoya to reach climax and orgasm. Yemisi was convinced sexual intercourse took place between the two; however, she dared not ask him about it. She realized when Edukoya finished having sex with Felicia, he would be totaled. She geared herself for another lonely night without sex from the man she loved most.

When they got to the villa in Abuja and entered their bedroom, Yemisi started slowly to undress in the presence of him. She wanted to take a bath before anything else, especially going to bed. *After all these years, she's still got it*, he thought. He looked at her breasts still standing ripe and firm, as if they were about to burst. He flashed back to the first time he had seen her naked, in their hotel room in Reno, Nevada, and she had not tarnished her nature one bit. He marveled at this perfect creation and shouted, "You are a goddess!" He could not help himself. He walked up to her and held her from behind, massaging her breasts. He sucked her breasts, and the salty sweat from her body added to the pleasure, and they wound up in bed.

Princess Yemisi was a genuine romantic goddess. She began by kissing him and then giving a blow job. He returned the favor in kind before he gently penetrated her with his rock-solid penis firmly erect. He didn't need any help, for her wetness equaled the Atlantic Ocean. Yemisi also needed no help, for his erection stood tall like a pine tree and as hard as a rock. Felicia's earlier intervention didn't matter at all. Yemisi had patience, realizing he'd just recently climbed the hill with Felicia. She constantly reminded herself of his age and his open-heart surgery. Edukoya was not a spring chicken anymore. Finally, he ejaculated, with her reaching orgasm at the same time. Taking a bath was for another day, in the morning. They went to bed. Gluing their bodies together, they slept like babies.

CHAPTER 28

Yemisi revisited her self-imposed alienation from Dr. Everest Oluomolewa. She couldn't help but wonder what her generosity had gotten her into. She often went to Lagos with flimsy excuses just to get away from the noise of the bed squeaking all night from Edukoya and Felicia having sex. Her lodge was adjacent to His Lordship's, and they shared a common entrance. She came to Lagos to get away from Felicia's cheerfulness. She came to Lagos for business, she came to Lagos to get the hell away from Felicia, and she came to Lagos to brush shoulders with the man she knew she shouldn't have anything to do with, Dr. Everest Oluomolewa. Ever since she'd met Dr. Oluomolewa, she had let him occupy a permanent residence in her heart and mind. She tried hard to remove his feelings from her mind; however, his feelings were on the increase and would not let up.

She wondered why an ordinary sight of him made her body behave like a runaway freight car. She vowed not to see a shrink but to deal with the situation on her own, all by herself. She concluded she had sold herself too short. She constantly asked herself what a PhD in psychology, sociology, or psychiatry could do for her that she hadn't already done for herself. Besides, getting a third person on board on the issue would have been like letting a cat out of a cage. It would wander away, and there would be no going back to that cage. If His Lordship Kabiyesi Edukoya Adekunle III heard about it, it would spell disaster for her marriage; herself; the love and respect from her fourteen children, which, as of now, she had taken for granted; the $11 billion investment portfolio; and, most importantly, everything she had been trying to do to make the people of Orissa Kingdom have a better life.

Unlike all the kings in the surrounding areas, especially in the Yoruba tribe, in which the kings had executive power and were profoundly paid for their duty, Kabiyesi Edukoya Adekunle III chose not to be paid like a king, and his expenses, personal and executive, were not subsidized by the people's funds either. It was their family's transferred tradition. His father, Adekunle II, had not been paid for his services as the king of Orissa, nor had his grandfather, Adekunle I. They got their money from their vast real estate holdings, and 30 percent of the proceeds were donated annually to Orissa Kingdom. They took the all-important assignment to help their people seriously. Princess Yemisi embraced the enormous undertaking and made it her second priority after her husband, the king, and her immediate family's well-being. Somebody would definitely see her going out of a shrink's office, and they would be bound to ask her to explain important personal questions that demanded sincere and honest answers. The thought of a potential broken marriage resulting from a lack of trust from Eduks, her husband, kept her feelings for the adorable Dr. Oluomolewa from surfacing.

The crown princess made up her mind. She might have had a darling lust and love for Everest, but letting his penis penetrate her vagina was a line she wouldn't dare cross. Holding her back from her crazy fascination of going to bed with handsome cardiothoracic surgeon Dr. Everest Oluomolewa were thoughts about how Charity would feel and the loss of the important respect she cherished from her. Charity called her Mama Yemisi, and she loved it. She had been trying in vain to get Felicia to stop addressing her as Princess Yemisi. She told Felicia she too was a princess. Charity addressed her as Mama, but behind her back, Yemisi was constantly making out with her husband. She felt low, guilty, and shameful. She believed if anything could stop her dirty fascination, it was Charity and her children.

Why did she have to feel guilty? What about a man with two wives and a dearly beloved concubine? She began to retreat from her guilt. She forgot momentarily that she was the one who'd made the beds, encouraged and persuaded Edukoya and Felicia to go on a romantic getaway vacation, and loaned her jet to the international observer team working with the World Health Organization, of which she was a board member. Dr. Oluomolewa, in fact, discouraged her from loaning the plane to them. She positioned it as a favor she was doing for him, and all she asked from him was to spend a little quality time with her and, in truth, have sexual intercourse with her—damn the consequences.

Meanwhile, Felicia and Edukoya were having the time of their lives on their getaway vacation. From Felicia's observation in Milan, Italy, she quickly learned that men and women, regardless of their ages, enjoyed sincere touching and feeling of their bodies by each other, both in private and in public. As the king and Princess Yemisi got older and their marriage increased on the calendar, Yemisi gradually stopped displaying those public affections she had been so good at. Business deals and accomplishments were more important to her than affection. The only time she showed affection was at night. The only place she showed affection was in bed with him. The king was present when Princess Yemisi gave Eva and many others so-called innocent hugs and kissed them on their cheeks. The hugs were displayed in public.

Kabiyesi would have liked her to revisit the old-time affections once in a while, regardless of where they occurred, in private or in public. To him, he was not asking for too much. Communication had been downright scarce between Princess Yemisi and Edukoya lately. They were on speaking terms; however, Princess Yemisi had a tendency to get into disturbing details when it came to every issue she was involved in. With her, everything seemed to be a big issue and important. She was an effective manager and a trusted partner who could get things done. However, her effectiveness robbed her sociological qualities, which Felicia and especially Chika had in abundance. His Lordship Adekunle III understood her well and would not have had it any other way. In fact, her detailed capacity was why he had fallen hopelessly in love with her in the first place. Her attention to detail was why they hadn't frozen in San Francisco.

Felicia understood the importance of Princess Yemisi to Edukoya, and she dared not speak ill against her. The king had made her his crown princess because he trusted her with his whole life.

Princess Yemisi could never betray Adekunle's family by going to bed with another man, regardless of how horny and lustful she might have been, at least not while the king was alive. She was not selfish.

One might have thought the crown princess had a conservative personality, but in reality, she was downright liberal. Dr. Everest Oluomolewa discovered that enviable personality about her. His feelings for her went from platonic lust for an attractive woman to a woman he wouldn't have minded marrying regardless of her age. He was definitely in love with her. But keeping the two lovers apart from each other was one thing they continued to hold dear in their hearts: the trust of their spouses. They could not and would not betray the trust of those equally important to them, Edukoya and Charity.

CHAPTER 29

The court resumed the hearing on the land case Monday morning at 9:00 a.m. on the dot. Princess Yemisi begged Dr. Oluomolewa to drop her off at the Lagos mainland historical federal courthouse, which once had housed the Supreme Court of Nigeria before it moved to Abuja, now the nation's capital city. One of her drivers was on vacation. He'd traveled to his village to celebrate the Yam Festival, which was a megaevent in those parts of the Igbo tribe. The chauffeur, Austin Ogboefi, was from Obosi in Anambra State. Obosi had naturally gifted soil that produced rich mixtures of fertilizers. Every crop seed cultivated in that soil grew a crop ten times the normal size. Even their livestock, such as chickens and goats, had their size doubled as a result of feeding off the rich crops produced from the land. The human offspring were larger than the average Igbo people also, and they spoke a well-understood Igbo dialect.

The other chauffeur was sick with a high fever. He was being treated at LUTH, with the crown princess paying his bills. The princess had gone to visit him four times. Each time she went there, the hospital staff only allowed her to stay by the glass window, and they positioned him so that both saw each other but with no bodily contact. The hospital had run some tests to determine the kind of disease. They were afraid such a high fever must have been triggered by HIV or Ebola. Those with such a high fever were usually isolated at LUTH in a kind of quarantine for serious observation and treatment even before the test results were known, based on past experiences with those types of diseases.

It turned out the chauffeur had none of those diseases when the test results came out. It was a high fever triggered by malaria and typhoid fever. He was given antibiotic medications, which overwhelmed the malaria virus; hence, there was a quick improvement in his health. They quickly removed him from the isolation room when the test results were negative and transferred him to a halfway room in the hospital to monitor him for a week and a half to see if the high fever came back again. He was kept in a private luxury room at the expense of the generous Princess Yemisi.

The World Health Organization was very involved with Ebola and HIV in West Africa, especially Nigeria, Africa's most populated country. They wanted to quickly contain the outbreaks there to avoid spilling the catastrophe over into neighboring countries and Africa as a whole. Because of their quick responses, Nigeria had statistically negligible casualties from Ebola and HIV. As a matter of fact, the World Health Organization declared Nigeria Ebola-free and statistically negligible in HIV count. Ephram, Yemisi's chauffeur, was lucky he was not a carrier of those diseases. At his point of death, Ephram confessed how many women he had slept with while married to his dearly beloved wife. His wife kept silent and listened to every detail of his confession. She used her head to count. In her overwhelming joy at his being alive, she forgave and forgot that silly indulgence of his.

Princess Yemisi and Dr. Oluomolewa kept their relationship purely professional in the presence of his wife, Charity, while he took her to the courthouse. Princess Yemisi sat in the backseat of the car, while Charity sat in the front passenger seat, with her husband driving the car. They dropped off Charity at

Saint Gregory Elementary School in Ikoyi. Saint Gregory was a rich people's private elementary school, and Charity was the headmistress of the school. Dr. Charity Oluomolewa had obtained her EdD in early childhood development from California State University, Long Beach, after graduating with her bachelor's and master's from USC, where Everest had met her while doing his residency there.

After Charity was dropped off, Princess Yemisi came to the front and sat in the front passenger seat. The moment Charity's eyes were out of sight, Princess Yemisi shifted and came closer to Dr. Oluomolewa. She leaned on his shoulder till they got to the courthouse. On their nearing the courthouse, she told him to pull over the car by the shoulder of the road and stop the engine. She then leaned closer to him and gave him a kiss he would never forget. She spoke softly into his ear: "This is a down payment. When you come back to pick me up, make sure you come alone this time."

Everest struggled to contain himself, but her charm was too much to bear. He drew her closer to him and responded with a bold kiss. The intense passion was nearly too much for her to bear too. Both laughed and smiled like two teenagers making out in hiding. She gave him four more kisses and then gently cleaned his lips with her tongue, her saliva, and tissues. She cleaned her lips too and put on more lipstick and makeup. This time, the lipstick was red. Her previous lipstick had been brown. She wore brown lipstick so it would not show when she kissed Eva. She touched her hair a little bit and glanced in the mirror and then at him. "How do I look?"

"You are nothing short of spectacular," he said. He drove her by the court entrance, she gently exited the car, and he drove off to the hospital.

It had been three weeks since Edukoya and Felicia left to vacation in Europe. It had also been three weeks since Princess Yemisi made love to a man, her husband. She was not used to going so long without having sex or affection, mostly from her husband. The temptation was raging like wildfire, and the only thing keeping her from the unfaithful indulgence was the absence of Everest in her bedroom.

Charity called her husband to pick her up first before picking up Princess Yemisi. Charity was having a late after-school board meeting with the school's committee. When Princess Yemisi saw her, she did well to conceal her disappointment. She was usually cheerful, but she entered the car and remained quiet. Her anger was boiling and was about to spill over. As they reached home, she tried one more trick to be alone with Dr. Oluomolewa. She remembered Ephram, her chauffer, at LUTH. She said she would be taking a taxi to LUTH to visit Ephram.

Charity immediately said, "No, Mama. Let Eva take you to LUTH."

Eva quickly agreed. However, Charity tagged along.

PART 8

DR. FELICIA ADEKUNLE, PHD

CHAPTER 30

His Lordship Kabiyesi Edukoya Lawansin Adekunle III had never taken Felicia on a getaway romantic trip before. He decided to take her to Milan, Italy, on a three-week vacation. Kabiyesi had had countless romantic getaway trips with Princess Yemisi and Chika. He had found excuses to get away with Chika on numerous trips around the world. There was no major city in an affluent country in the world he hadn't taken Chika to with him. In fact, on their first trip, to Ottawa, Canada, they first had engaged in a real romantic affair, which began in the hallway in the hotel near his lodge. Chika never slept in her hotel room again. Who could have resisted Chika, with her medium-sized brown eyes; pretty, tender-looking face; and smooth, slim, fit body perfectly polished by nature? Chika, with a bachelor's degree in business administration and working on an MBA at the University of Nigeria, Lagos, came in handy as an executive administrative assistant to the king. Chika was a speed reader and typist, typing more than 250 words per minute and reading about 350 words per minute with flawless comprehension.

Chika took shorthand too, and with that bundle of credentials, she positioned herself as the perfect excuse for the king to take her to most places he visited, even on some getaway trips with Princess Yemisi.

The city of Milan was not so romantic, but it was littered with high fashion in all types of wear. From Milan, one could get to any part of Europe with ease. Kabiyesi Edukoya Adekunle III carried a backpack. It left Felicia in shock. She too carried her own backpack. After they checked into their presidential lodge, they headed straight to the open-air market to buy some camping gear. That was another surprise for Felicia: Kabiyesi going to an open market to buy some gear. She watched him act like an eighteen-year-old freshman in college, and she loved that Kabiyesi of Orissa Kingdom came to her level. It was sunny and hot in Milan, with the temperature reaching thirty-two degrees centigrade.

They carried their backpacks on their backs, loaded with sporting gear, after they shopped at the open market. Felicia, like Yemisi and Chika, learned fast. They bought shorts and summer outfits for mountain hiking. Luckily for them, his pilot arrived in Milan by seven thirty in the morning, which gave them plenty of time to go do some shopping. They would leave to see the doctor early in the morning before heading to the Alps. They went to the open-air market's bathroom and changed their outfits so they could blend in with the crowd. Felicia, for the first time in her life, was a witness to the neatness of public bathrooms. Orissa public market toilets' neatness didn't measure up to the neatness of public toilets in most developed countries. Milan's public toilets were breathtaking.

At first, Felicia was scared to enter the public restroom, based on her experience with public bathrooms in Nigeria. Only recently had water-system bathrooms come to Orissa's open market, thanks to Princess Yemisi. Even with water-system toilets, Orissa's public toilets' neatness fell in sharp contrast with what she saw in most developed countries. She felt comfortable changing her clothes there. She could drop them on the floor to try on another outfit. The trip was an eye-opener for her. She saw couples holding hands, and every so often, the ladies wrapped themselves upon their men. Every so often, the couples clung to and kissed each other in public.

No one looked at the couples; everybody walked past them, minding his or her own business. They were not afraid to display their affection in the open.

She wondered if she could show affection in the open with Edukoya. The thought dominated her mind. For Edukoya's part, it was as if he and his granddaughter were walking the aisles and shopping together in the open market. He noticed that every time their bodies touched, it became an excuse for Felicia to grab him tightly. He thought she was afraid of the people and told her she could hold him if she liked. At that moment, her spirit lifted, and a smile appeared on her face. She thought he'd read her mind. She said, "Can I tell you something?" He obliged her request, and she said, "I love you so much," and she went ahead and kissed him in the open marketplace.

She held him tightly to the point the seventy-six-year-old man began to sweat all over his body. She too was sweating, but she did not mind. Being in the arms of the husband she loved and called Daddy was far more pleasurable than the drips of water coming from their bodies.

They went to the snack bar and ordered some food. Edukoya was a natural at these things. He ordered a sandwich for her and Diet Pepsi for the drink, which came automatically with the order. There were varieties of soda to choose from, and they were all included in the combo meal. She was not a big eater, and neither was Edukoya, so there were leftovers. The sandwich tasted good, but Felicia had disciplined herself not to have too much of a good thing. Even though she was slim and adorably light in complexion, her figure mattered a lot to her. She ate three-quarters of her sandwich and drank half the cup of Diet Pepsi. Edukoya, after being with Yemisi for nearly half a century, had changed his eating habits for good, and he welcomed it faithfully.

Wellness was the perpetual habit he loved most about Princess Yemisi. It had saved his life; thank God he was a good student. From the word *go*, since they met each other, Princess Yemisi had been monitoring his general health habits. She'd dragged him to the gym at least four times a week before they got a full gym in their home. She persuaded him to eat small portions of food at a time, with a regimen of quality foods on his plate. His heart problem was a result of high blood pressure. His erectile dysfunction was a result of acute chest pains, fatigue, and fear caused by worrying about his heart problems. As soon as the surgery was over, Edukoya sprang up like a spring chicken. He had a renewed vitality and a renewed hope. His stroke did not impair him in any way. He had his full body functions and activities. He resumed jogging, and in fact, he was featured in one of the Boston Marathons as a seventy-three-year-old man with a quadruple bypass who finished the race. Now he was set for mountain climbing, and he owed his renewed vigorous lifestyle to Princess Yemisi Adekunle.

When they got to their suite in the hotel, Felicia hung the Do Not Disturb sign on the doorknob. She lay down in bed, feeling exhausted. He opted for a shower, but Felicia begged him for a favor. He said, "Go on."

Felicia said, "Can you make love to me now before I explode?"

He said, "After we've taken a shower?"

She beckoned him with her fingers. "Now!"

He had never heard such a commanding tone of voice from Felicia before. It was wild and sexy. He said, "I'd better obey your command."

Felicia, in all practicality, exploded. She was wild in their sexual engagement. She screamed and touched him all over his body. It was as if she had been in prison or on an island, starved for a man's affection. She pushed him gently onto the bed, climbed on top of him at his lower waist, and started giving him a blow job, which was something she had never done with him or any man before. Felicia was indeed the real champion of her youth. Edukoya had never had sex like this with Felicia, with such intensity. Felicia was in equilibrium with Princess Yemisi and Chika. Felicia reached orgasm multiple times, and at one point, he stopped counting. He ejaculated twice. Anytime he touched her, he observed she reached a climax, and further penetration of his fully erect penis caused her to reach orgasm. He returned the oral sex in kind. The same thing happened with his tongue. Whenever he licked her clitoris, she would say repeatedly, "I love you so much," and each time she said it, her vagina gushed more fluids, as if they were flowing from a waterfall.

In the end, she was exhausted. She said before falling asleep, "Daddy, I love you so much. You have constantly made me feel like a woman. This vacation, with me and you alone at last. Thank you."

Edukoya realized the vacation in a different setting gave her a chance to bring out the animal in her, her sexual firepower, far away from the palace in Agbala. He saw the vitality in a young woman who was comfortable in her own identity and marriage with him, and she was not perturbed by being a second wife. Felicia had written her PhD dissertation on structural molecular identity. She was able to distinguish and isolate molecular structures as they related to human-borne diseases. With her high capacity in biological sciences, in the intellectual arena, she was in high demand in both universities and corporate environments around the globe.

She was a young woman full of energy, and she was a rare talent indeed. Felicia was an adorable, pretty lady and the envy of men. Her high intellectual capacity evoked in men a limitless ability to perform sexual intercourse with her. She was athletic and romantic. She earned a top salary as a professor of biological sciences, and Orissa Polytechnic was happy to have her, thanks to Princess Yemisi, who'd lured Felicia from the University of Nigeria, Lagos, to teach at the polytechnic school for her self-defeating purpose.

Meanwhile, Princess Yemisi flew to Lagos on a commercial jet. Her jet was leased to a group of international observers. Her chauffeur in Lagos picked her up. She frequented Lagos because the court issue was closing in on that portion of the land settlement where oil had been discovered. She also went to occasionally brush shoulders with Dr. Everest Oluomolewa, the fine man she knew she shouldn't have for any reason.

CHAPTER 31

Felicia and Edukoya were having the time of their lives in Europe. Edukoya was behaving like a kid again, playing hide-and-seek with Felicia in the lobby of the prestigious Redd Inn Hotel. When they found each other, they laughed loudly, hugged tightly, and kissed hard. The hotel attendants didn't mind. They were renting a presidential suite at a cost of 450 euros per night, and rumor had it they'd come to Milan in their private jet. In fact, all the guests in the hotel lobby were encouraged to join in the play. Almost all the guests in the hotel were retired persons who were loaded, were bored to death, and wanted to have a life on their vacation. Felicia accidentally spiced up such indulgence, and they were thrilled. When the game was over, they came one by one to thank her. Most of the guests in the hotel thought Edukoya and Felicia were father and daughter or grandfather and a granddaughter who was enabling him to relive his youth again. It was commonplace for parents to kiss children, even in public, among white folks, so they assumed the kissing and hugging between Felicia and Edukoya were normal.

Edukoya didn't mind; he loved it when people related to her as his daughter. Felicia, at the age of thirty-two, was a young-looking and attractive woman. She could comfortably pass as a nineteen-year-old girl. She welcomed the assertion as a compliment, and such welcoming often chopped away most stupid insinuations about their age difference. They sometimes made jokes about it when they were making love. "I'm having sex with my father," Felicia would tease. They laughed because it increased their sexual velocity, which resulted in the sweetness of their sexual engagements too. One more credit to Felicia was that she never took things too personally. Maybe her training as a scientist with a PhD from a world-renowned university, the University of Nigeria, Ibadan, gave her the clout to be bold in whatever activity she was engaged in. However, she seldom displayed her intellectual capacities, and Kabiyesi Edukoya Adekunle III loved that about her.

In a roomful of intellects, Felicia came in when she was invited, and she interjected her opinions only when she was invited to do so. In all aspects of her life, Felicia Adekunle carried that personality, and Edukoya loved it. When she touched and spoke to her husband, her commanding gentleness was also displayed. Edukoya once confided to his beloved friend John Okorocha during a two-week visit to the palace, "Her attitude encourages my continued sexual interest in her. It is like I want to have it with her more and more. Felicia has such a high managerial capacity that she finds solutions in every situation. That enables her to minimize her anger, and as a result, she hardly gets angry about anything, as if she was expecting it to happen. She is ready with adequate solutions. She is a genuine article and a true darling."

Felicia also made Edukoya laugh, and he loved it. Edukoya eventually realized that Felicia was right now in her life where she wanted to be.

He told John Okorocha, "With her high intellectual capacity, she'll do very well on her own. Money does not and will not faze Felicia at all. Her intellectual know-how was the key reason Princess Yemisi lured her from the University of Nigeria, Lagos, to a quadrupled salary to teach on Orissa Polytechnic's faculty of sciences. Her husband's death, compounded with her miscarriage, added to the incentive to get her away from Lagos and big cities altogether. She never in her wildest imagination dreamed her coming to a remote area called Orissa Kingdom in Ondo State would land her in bed with the king, let alone marrying him as his second wife. With her impeccable beauty and intellectual capacity, what man would not knock on her door to marry her?"

Princess Yemisi knew Felicia's worth in the family well. Princess Yemisi was caught between a rock and a hard place. She definitely needed her. Also, she came to the conclusion that the near death of Edukoya after the death of John Okorocha, his dearest friend, had been wiped out because of the presence of Felicia in his life. Edukoya fell sick immediately following John's death. To have Edukoya alive outweighed all the silver and gold in the world, because Yemisi loved Edukoya from the bottom of her heart. It was love that had brought her miscalculated medical solution, Felicia, to rescue his erectile dysfunction. Besides, Princess Yemisi had given birth to all boys. Her other older seven kids from Bola, Edukoya's deceased wife, were all girls, married, and off to different cities and countries with their families. Yemisi's sister Iyabo was older than she, near death, and off on her own with her family. Felicia was like her younger sister and her daughter and was the main friend she had right now besides Chika and Eduks.

Felicia was a remarkable personality; she fit in all shoes. Princess Yemisi concluded she'd better take this opportunity to be a positive role model for the twins and give Felicia all the respect and love due her. Princess Yemisi took steps to make Felicia a material and irreplaceable member of Adekunle's family, because it would matter to her children in the near future. Felicia had already referred to Princess Yemisi with the twins as "your grandmother," and she addressed Yemisi as Mama. The twins addressed Princess Yemisi as Grandma, and she loved it. She took them to most places she went to. They frequented Lagos and Abuja with her and their maid. They had also visited their country of birth, the United States of America, twice. Felicia was a natural at management. She let Yemisi have everything her way with the twins. She also found out, out of guilt and personality, Princess Yemisi let her into almost everything she did. The crown princess sought her advice on almost all pressing issues. Felicia also sought Princess Yemisi's advice on some pressing issues of her own. However, the most daring problem of Princess Yemisi, Dr. Oluomolewa, would forever remain concealed in her mind.

The thoughts of all those issues left mixed feelings on Princess Yemisi's mind. It was like mixed baggage. To compound things, Edukoya called to let her know they would be extending their romantic getaway vacation for another week and had gotten air and landing clearances to land his jet at Akure Metro Airport. For three weeks, since their absence, she'd had no sexual intercourse or romantic affection from any man, most importantly her husband. *A week's extension?* That did it for her. Princess Yemisi invited Eva for a snack. His wife, Charity, was away with the kids to visit her mother in Asaba in Delta State for a week.

When the snacking was halfway over, Princess Yemisi boldly invited Dr. Oluomolewa upstairs to her bedroom to listen to some classical music. Princess Yemisi could dance. She showed him the latest moves, and in the process, they started dancing close together, touching, feeling each other's body, and kissing the hell out of each other. Yemisi had sent Chika on a wild, fruitless errand with the hope she would be gone for hours.

Everything was set, and for the first time, Everest saw Princess Yemisi naked. It was far more than he'd dreamed of. Her body was impeccably built, with desirable legs and butt. Her smooth and firm yet soft body became an invitation to heaven. Yemisi was beautiful. Princess Yemisi, with the help of Everest, undressed first. She was slowly pulling down his pants, about to give him a blow job, when Blessing cried from her sleep.

The baby had had a nightmare, and her body temperature was running a little high. She was badly shaken. Every romantic feeling between the two came to a quick end, and Everest became the physician in attendance. She needed some calming with a warm bath. Yemisi gave her the bath and children's fever medicine, and she slept just fine.

CHAPTER 32

Justice Chukwunanyenwa Onyemerekwe ordered the court in session. There was bickering among the attorneys and the judges as they waited for the arrival of Princess Yemisi. She was always sporty and on top of things. Yemisi was respectful and would never have wasted the court's time. A lot was riding on the estimated $20 billion of crude oil underneath the earth in the portion of the land deal they owned. However, even such a deal would not take her away from attending to Blessing, her granddaughter. The fever was coming and going, and Dr. Oluomolewa suggested taking her to LUTH first thing in the morning for monitoring and observation. With respect, Princess Yemisi brought the cause of her delay, Blessing, to the courtroom before taking her to the hospital.

The plaintiffs' lawyers summoned Justice Onyemerekwe to his chamber to discuss the child's health matter. The Honorable Justice Onyemerekwe invited the other two judges on the panel and the defense attorneys to sit in.

The baby, meanwhile, was wrapped with light sheet cloth, as ordered by Dr. Oluomolewa. The doctor was giving them a ride to the hospital.

They waited on Justice Chukwu Onyemerekwe's courtroom floor with the rest of the attorneys. Barista Kuye, the lead attorney for the plaintiffs, spoke first. He explained that they were not aware of the situation. They and the court were witnessing it for the first time. The kid was technically her stepdaughter, but she called Princess Yemisi Grandma. It was a position in the kid's life that she gladly accepted. Their mother was in Milan, Italy, vacationing with the king. Princess Yemisi was up to the task of handling the kid's minor health problem. After he finished talking, Justice Onyemerekwe sent all the lawyers to the courtroom floor, leaving him and the panel judges to set the course of action.

Dr. Oluomolewa was busy with many surgeries lined up. Open-heart surgery took, from preparation to finish, about twelve hours. The actual surgery took about five to eight hours, depending on how many veins would be repaired or replaced. There was no rush. Critical care took about four hours, and that was the time when most patients made it or died. The surgeons were always mindful, handily monitoring the situation. The patient later would be transferred to the intensive care unit, with one nurse permanently assigned to the patient. That was the time when the doctors and nurses could release their breath. The surgeon, for the most part, was seldom needed further, and the cardiologist took over the patient. The surgeon would always stand by after the surgery to address any complication that ensued.

Princess Yemisi took LUTH's offer and returned home with Blessing with LUTH's chauffeur. After seeing Professor Oluomolewa's workload, she gave up on the candlelight dinner for two to thank him for Blessing's care. It was Dr. Oluomolewa who arranged for one of the hospital's chauffeurs to drop them at their residence in Ikoyi with his car. The weekend was approaching, and it was Wednesday evening. The twins were two and a half years old. Yemisi received a phone call from Edukoya asserting they would be arriving sooner: Thursday morning by seven thirty. Edukoya was a master of perception. Judging from his limited conversation with Princess Yemisi, he sensed they had been gone for too long. Felicia was listening in on the conversation between the two. Felicia sensed that too. For the remaining two nights, Felicia was on her menstrual cycle and was having mild stomach cramps. She suggested it was an opportunity for them to head back home, allowing Princess Yemisi to pick up where she'd left off.

The understanding Princess Yemisi was still in Lagos, so the call prompted the flight schedule to be changed. They would depart from Milan at midnight to arrive by seven thirty on Thursday morning. Instead of Akure Metro Airport, his jet would land at Murtala Mohammed International Airport in Ikeja, at the domestic terminal. Fortunately, LUTH made a turnaround decision to discharge Ephram earlier than expected. He was discharged on Monday night. Princess Yemisi gave him a few days off to recuperate after his deadly fever encounter. He lived in a self-contained two-bedroom help lodge on the compound. The grapevine alerted Ephram that Princess Yemisi desperately needed help to pick up Kabiyesi Adekunle III from the airport. He volunteered without giving it a second thought, though he was weak from the medications given to him at the hospital. Yemisi went with him in case he felt sleepy at the wheel from the medications. Princess Yemisi could drive well. She preferred to drive in California and Orissa Kingdom, where the traffic was orderly.

The twins came along with her and their babysitter. Kabiyesi whispered to Felicia that it would be better if she went straight home to Orissa with the twins while he stayed in Lagos with Princess Yemisi. Edukoya was understanding, and Felicia, with the children and their babysitter, flew back to Orissa on a 9:00 a.m. commercial flight to Akure, where their chauffeur was waiting for her arrival.

Princess Yemisi, seeing that the two of them were alone at last, was thrilled. They talked about the projects and town meetings in Orissa Kingdom. The king alerted Princess Yemisi that Felicia would be going back to teach at Polytechnic. He also hinted she'd be going back to coaching Orissa Girls' Secondary School's basketball team too. In her absence, which was nearing three years, Orissa Girls' had not won any championship match. Princess Yemisi spoke briefly about Blessing's fever. The king was happy all had gone well. Their friendly discussion was laying the groundwork for a romantic setting. She was desperately pressed for affection from him. She held Edukoya's left arm, gradually shifted, and rested on his shoulder.

He wanted no breakfast when they got home to the villa. He wanted to take a shower and go straight to bed. Edukoya never slept while in the air. Princess Yemisi was even more thrilled. He then asked about Ephram's health care. Ephram was happy to know His Lordship was concerned about his well-being. To compound the gratitude of seeing him alive, Edukoya said a little prayer and thanked God in the name of Jesus for sparing his life. He also advised him to stick to his wife from now on.

Ephram laughed and said, "So, Oga, you hear everything. Na, only my wifeoo," speaking in broken English.

When they entered the house, Edukoya went straight to take the shower he'd promised himself. Halfway into the shower, Yemisi asked if she could join him. She knew if she didn't get it there and now, she wouldn't get it, as he would be asleep. Sexual intercourse during the shower had many advantages. They didn't have to clean up after themselves.

PART 9

THE LOVE LETTER

CHAPTER 33

Princess Yemisi decided to write a letter to Professor Everest Oluomolewa. After thinking about her confused dual-love-affair situation thoroughly, she came to the conclusion she had better air her concerns to a trusted, friendly ear before she went crazy. Going to her female friends would have been a mistake, no matter how close they were as friends. It would have guaranteed the destruction of her marriage with Edukoya. She felt that no matter how close a female friend was, even a blood sister, unlike with men, there was a hidden, unspoken jealousy within females. She concluded that through the grapevine, there surely would be an intentional or accidental leak. She thought about going to Felicia but quickly dismantled such reasoning. No matter the promise Felicia made to her, at the bare minimum, she would hold it against her. Felicia was her biggest competitor and a formidable challenge too. Felicia had never sought meaningful advice of any kind from her. Besides, going to Felicia spelled a bigger disturbing factor: weakness. Felicia had always seen Princess Yemisi from a position of strength, and Yemisi was aware of it. Letting her guard down now, she was afraid, would remove the edge she held against her.

Unfortunately, that thought proved how little she knew about Dr. Felicia Adekunle. On the contrary, Felicia was where she wanted to be and wouldn't stain her relationship with Princess Yemisi, a woman she thought highly of and regarded as her own biological mother. Felicia was a remarkable woman whose kindest thoughts always were for the good and best interest of Adekunle's family as a whole. She loved Yemisi very much, and most importantly, Dr. Felicia Adekunle had the biggest crush on the husband they shared. Any attempt to sabotage Princess Yemisi had the potential of backfiring on her. By marrying the king, she was fundamentally happy being in second place as his second wife. Edukoya knew that; it was one reason he had been persuaded to fall in love with her.

Princess Yemisi decided to go to the only person riding the same horse: Dr. Everest Oluomolewa. She wrote him a letter first before discussing her difficult situation face-to-face.

My dear Everest,

The perturbing truth is, I have come to realize not too long ago that I love you so much. As a matter of fact, I am in love with you. I don't mean for you to panic. It is all about me—just me. I thought it was a mere crush and lust for a younger man, and I tried hard to shake it off but with a disappointing result. I have tried with little success to get you in bed with me, thinking that having sex with you would neutralize my feelings for you. These feelings have only increased. I love you very much. What can I say? I am stupid and foolish to fall in love with a happily married man. Also foolish to jeopardize a very good marriage with my husband, Edukoya. You have to conclude I am out of my mind, and you will be correct.

I think about you all the time. The mere sight of you makes my body move like a mad dog. When I think about you, making out with you dominates my mind the whole day, and I am confused and forgetful about any other thing. The sweating and wetting of my underwear has been a constant embarrassment, especially when we rub shoulders in public. My God, I want your affection, and I want you to make love to me. Damn it, is that too much to ask from you? Yes, it is too much to ask from both of us. We have two special people in our lives.

Poor Charity. I don't want her to stop addressing me as Mama Yemisi. It means a lot to me. I would be devastated if she stopped calling me Mom and if my relationship with her broke down. Your children have joined Charity, and they call me Grandma. It makes me feel I am part of your family. In fact, I am seriously part of your family. To throw all this away because of lust, love, or whatever you might call it is really disturbing to me.

If Edukoya hears about this, it will be the ultimate betrayal of his love and trust for me. God forbid. I will not hurt him in any way at all. I love this man. As a matter of fact, I am in love with this man. The only good news is, you are not asking me to choose between you and him. And I am not asking you to choose me over Charity either. You are a breathtaking, honorable man who will not entertain such a thought. I dream about you all the time. Sometimes it is so engaging I'll hear myself talking to you in my sleep. I have pressed Edukoya about my sleep-talking, and he's assured me I don't talk in my sleep.

Nowadays, I intensely concentrate on you when I am having sex with my husband, and I keep the focus on intercourse to extremity, getting unnecessarily engaged in the sex act. It is not fair to my husband. This intense concentration has robbed me of the excitement and joy of having sex with my husband. Most times, I quickly catch myself before I say your name in the middle of having sexual intercourse with him. If it ever happened, it would leave a permanent scar in my relationship with Edukoya. There would be no more trust coming from him forever. This is my biggest concern, and it frightens me. I love you so much. I can't see myself saying this, but it is the truth. I am very much in love with you. I just cannot help myself.

The amazing part of this is, I love my husband so much too, and I am very much in love with my husband too. I used to think it was a myth— falling in love with two men at the same time. Here I am, the real-life story. It is scary. May I ask you a tiny but important question? How do you feel about me? Are you in lust with me or in love with me? Spare me any "I like you very much" type of nonsense. Please be frank with me. I do want to hear you are in love with me too. I probably will be hurt if stated otherwise. But remember, I am not a baby. I am a big girl. I am a mature woman, the mother of twelve grown men and women and two twin babies. I can handle the truth. If you lie to me, I will never forgive you. Telling the truth will go a long way in dealing with my situation. Lying will definitely make the matter worse, and in the end, I will hate you.

Your dearest love,
Yemisi

When she went jogging with him, she handed the letter personally to Eva to avoid third-party contamination. He stood for a moment and asked, "Is it for us? The postmaster always sends our letters to the wrong address."

Princess Yemisi replied, "It is from me."

He saw there was no stamp attached to the envelope, and he nodded in acceptance and said, "From you?"

"From me, and I want you to read it alone," she replied.

Luckily, there was a back pocket on his shorts. He handed the letter to Princess Yemisi to put in his pocket while he continued jogging.

While Princess Yemisi was putting the mail in his back pocket, she couldn't help noticing the firmness of his butt. She asked him if she could touch it, and he said, "Go ahead." She grabbed both buttocks, with her two hands full, and started fondling them to the point his erection became uncontrollably hard, sticking out. By that time, she was also soaking wet. She was all over his neck, biting, kissing, and licking his sweat. She was out of control and invited him to put his hand down her shorts to massage her clitoris. Everest, now a pro, immediately screamed as climax overwhelmed with an intense orgasm. He didn't ejaculate, because her orgasm came too fast. Because she did not have her panties on while jogging, her shorts were visibly soaking wet with gushing vaginal fluid.

His whole left palm was covered with her vaginal fluid. His penis was fully erect and as hard as a rock. They waited quite some time for his penis to weaken. With such a beauty against him and her butt from time to time touching his penis, it took an extended time period to weaken. With love, for all its glories, patience overrode all, so they waited. He finally raced her home to take a badly needed shower. The question on his mind was *What can this letter be?* Maybe she wanted them to stop seeing each other. He contemplated the last time they'd met in her bedroom. It nearly had happened between them, and maybe he had gone too far. He contemplated he should have told her how much he felt about her—that he was in love with her—before going that far and seeing her naked in her bedroom. Maybe he was forcing himself upon her.

Yemisi said to him, "Are you watching where you're going? We have passed our houses. You have a lot on your mind. Is it the letter?"

Dr. Oluomolewa chose to confess before he opened the letter. He told Princess Yemisi that he was sorry for the other night, when it was about to happen between them but didn't, thanks to Blessing's fever.

Yemisi said, "Sorry for what? I wanted it so badly to happen between us."

Eva said before they could go any further, he wanted to make a confession. He confessed he was madly in love with her. He said he didn't know how she felt about him but presumed the letter would let him know where she stood, and he was sure that it was all a platonic relationship caught in a moment of weakness. They turned back and raced home.

Princess Yemisi raced him, and as they were approaching their homes, the overwhelming joy that she wasn't alone with her feelings led her to give him a bold kiss on his lips. She didn't care who was watching. She said, "Read the letter." She raced back to her mansion to take a badly needed bath.

CHAPTER 34

Dr. Everest Oluomolewa was ecstatic when he read Princess Yemisi's letter. He was overwhelmed with joy.

One evening, Charity was over at Mama Yemisi's mansion, drinking tea and eating some biscuits with her. She was looking at a photo album, and she came across three distinguished and impeccable-looking pictures of Princess Yemisi. The three pictures were among many that hung on the walls of their palace in Agbala and their villas throughout the world. Princess Yemisi was an astonishing, stunning, breathtaking, and elegant woman. One photo had been taken at the University of Nigeria, Ile Ife, during her matriculation event when she was sixteen. It was her first color picture. Color pictures were making their way to the market by the late 1960s, and it was expensive to acquire one. Iyabo, who by then was in the United States, had taken the picture when she came back on holiday to attend Yemisi's matriculation.

Princess Yemisi was practically Iyabo's daughter. Iyabo had raised Princess Yemisi from three years old, when her father died. Yemisi was Iyabo's only sister. Iyabo had taken courses in photography as a hobby at the University of San Francisco when she was doing her doctorate.

The second photo had been taken at San Jose State University in California at the age of twenty-six, when Yemisi graduated with her ND as a nurse practitioner. She'd already had three children, Tunde, Ephram, and Babayede. Malcolm had just been conceived, and she had been one and a half months pregnant with him. Edukoya had taken the picture. The king was a natural with a camera.

The last one had been taken at the mansion in Agbala at the age of forty-eight by a professional photographer during an event at the palace. All the photos looked very much the same, with slight variation given age. One had to look hard to tell their age difference. The last had been taken when Tunde, her firstborn, graduated with his MD at Northwestern University in Chicago. He had been twenty-seven years old.

She wore simple tailored dresses in all the pictures, unprepared for the poses. They turned out to be the most viewed photographs at the mansion, at their villas, and in their photo album. The pictures were simply brilliant. They portrayed the exact character of Princess Yemisi. Charity asked her for copies of the three pictures.

Yemisi gave them to her a week later, retouched, enhanced, and enlarged to thirty inches by twenty-four inches. Charity had no idea of the real reason Princess Yemisi brilliantly retouched, enhanced, and enlarged the copies. She framed them too, to be hung on their family parlor's wall. Charity was happy, thinking the pictures were for the entire family and their guests' consumption. Charity hung the pictures on the wall of their living room. Everest knew why Princess Yemisi had given the three pictures to her retouched and framed. Each time he saw the pictures, his body began to feel movements. If he continued looking at them, he would be aroused and ready to make love to his wife, Charity.

It had been three months, two weeks, and four days since he got Princess Yemisi's letter. He had read it twenty-seven times. He read it every chance he got. He read it while driving, eating in a restaurant, using the restroom, and more. He read it in hidden corners. The more he looked at her pictures, the more he said to himself, "I can't believe this. Princess Yemisi is actually in love with me." He kept saying it to himself over and over.

Princess Yemisi met Dr. Oluomolewa at Kingsway minisuperstore on Marina Way in Eko. She demanded his explanation for the avoidance and the delay in replying to her letter. He kept scratching his head like a hardened criminal who was brought in by the police to face justice. Being the remarkable woman she was, Yemisi quickly rescued him from his excuses and his lies.

She brought up a common familiar topic: the World Health Organization, of which they were both board members. She was beating about the bush, delaying him from leaving the store. She was able to talk him into coming for a small cocktail party she was having for the plaintiffs' lawyers the following weekend at her villa. She managed to create laughter that drew her nearer to him. She grabbed his shoulder and practically wrapped herself around his body. She didn't care who was looking. Her laughter frequently persuaded her to kiss him on his cheek. When they were about to depart, she pulled him into a corner and gave him a long kiss on his lips. Princess Yemisi wished he would initiate these romantic gestures from time to time, but she muted her concerns.

That afternoon, he made up his mind to swallow the bitter pill and reply to Princess Yemisi's letter. Dr. Oluomolewa wanted to stop hiding from her and from his self-imprisonment. He stopped playing basketball in their backyard, and he stopped coaching his children and the neighboring kids' basketball and tennis teams to avoid getting in contact with Princess Yemisi. He now jogged on Sundays, when the coast was clear, knowing Princess Yemisi was in Agbala, attending church service with her husband and the rest of their household. He was behaving like a seven-year-old boy who'd accidentally seen his female teacher naked. In his secondary school days, this tall and impeccably handsome lad had led Holy Ghost College in Owerri to win the national championship match in tennis. He'd played in East Central State's soccer final. He had been one of the ten top finishers at USC in basketball and had been recruited by the Lakers after he graduated. He'd played for one year while awaiting his medical school admission to Duke University. He'd also played on Duke's basketball team briefly as a graduate student studying medicine. He loved outdoor sports, and to deny himself this luxury perturbed him a great deal.

Starting the letter was a bit more agonizing than he'd thought. Yemisi had ended her letter with "dearest love," but he couldn't use those words, at least at the beginning, for fear of overreaching.

Dear Yemisi,

I was overwhelmed as well as surprised by your letter. It really got me thinking a whole lot about us. The pictures you gave us were my comforter, and they did add to the surprise. To have the crown princess of Orissa Kingdom fall in love with me was a very big deal. The excitement continued to be nearly unbearable. It took a while, about three weeks, to contain myself. I am still excited and happy to this day. Think of it for just a moment: you and I are in love with each other. I couldn't have dreamed this in a million years.

I don't have much to say. I never have much to say on anything. However, what I do know is this: I love you very much. In fact, I am in love with you and far more than you can imagine. The other day at the Kingsway store, you read my mind perfectly. I needed a kiss from you. Don't mind me if I seldom embrace you. I have to give you such respect out of fear of overreaching and out of the fear of rejection from you. Face it: you are an extraordinarily attractive lady. I was taught pleasurable romance is better initiated by the lady, at least at the initial stage. I still can't believe this astonishing woman liked me to the point of falling in love with me. I have waited for so long to hear you admit your feelings for me. As a matter of fact, we have waited for too long to admit our feelings for each other.

The next big question is, where do we go from here? How can we manage this situation to minimize hurting innocent parties around us? It definitely troubles me, and it was responsible for my delay in replying to you. I don't want to play hide-and-seek. I am afraid that is what it has boiled down to. Oh yes! I want to make love to you so badly. It is a matter of when, and if I get the opportunity to make love to you, I'll do it. I have loved you extraordinarily. I've thought a lot about Charity, and I've thought a lot about the king. The last thing I want to do is to hurt those breathtakingly beautiful people. On the other hand, I love you so much. It is like the forbidden fruits; eventually, Adam and Eve ate them, and afterward, they learned bad things. When we eat this fruit, I guess we will also learn bad things too. We have already learned bad things. I will always love you.

Your love,
Eva

He posted Princess Yemisi's reply. He wanted to surprise her, as she assumed his kiss with her at the Kingsway store had sufficed as his reply. But he did not know he made a huge and egregious mistake by posting the letter instead of hand-delivering it to her, as the princess had done with him. Again, it was a great opportunity missed for their romance. He didn't think through the consequences of posting a letter that could fall into the wrong hands.

CHAPTER 35

Princess Yemisi read Dr. Oluomolewa's reply, and she couldn't contain herself, but for a different reason. Dr. Oluomolewa had taken a big and unnecessary risk in mailing the letter to her. What if Chika had intercepted it and, if the king had been at his villa that week, handed all the mail to him, as he always demanded from her? The grapevine tale of the century would have doomed all the relationships: Princess Yemisi with Edukoya, Edukoya with Dr. Oluomolewa, Yemisi with Charity, Charity with her husband, and Everest with Princess Yemisi, the big one. It could have affected the trust of her family, including Felicia and, most importantly, her children, and the community of Orissa Kingdom. Although Chika was aware of Princess Yemisi's strong ties with Oluomolewa's family, the letter would have confirmed her suspicion all along, not that it mattered.

Everest was much younger than Princess Yemisi, and Chika's suspicion was clouded by that fact. It would have been the biggest surprise as well as the biggest disappointment of her life. Princess Yemisi had it made as the crown princess of Orissa Kingdom, with a palace, multiple villas, a jet plane, luxury cars, vast real estate holdings, and a vast amount of paper holdings, such as stocks and bonds, to the tune of billions of dollars. The inheritance of Kabiyesi Adekunle III had yielded a net worth of more than $11 billion and counting worldwide, thanks to Princess Yemisi's wise and lucky investment undertakings.

The investments were totally managed by her, Edukoya's most trusted friend, dearest love, and loving wife.

To think all those responsibilities would have been called into question was unbearable for Princess Yemisi. Thank God Princess Yemisi intercepted the letter from the postmaster on his arrival. She, having estimated the gravity of the mistake to her personally, decided to give the relationship a break for a while and perhaps forever. She felt it was thoughtless, foolish, childish, and a waste of her time to have indulged in such an expensive joke, as she now called their relationship. She would not call the relationship a total loss, and she would not talk to Everest to hear from him his side of the story as to why he'd sent the letter by mail. In truth, having rethought the whole relationship and having gotten what she wanted most— Everest's admission that he'd fallen in love with her—she now was talking from a position of strength, like a child who wanted a particular toy and then, when he got it, tossed it aside and wanted a different toy. Princess Yemisi felt she was making a fool of herself by falling in love with Dr. Oluomolewa. She was also lying to herself.

On Dr. Oluomolewa's side, after four months, one week, and two days without hearing from or seeing Princess Yemisi, he felt he had made the biggest mistake of his life by letting her know how he really felt about her. And he was almost right. He thought he was stupid and had made the biggest fool of himself.

Charity noticed his lack of cooperation, especially in bed. He seldom entertained romance with her. His erection quickly weakened. When he passed Yemisi's pictures that hung on their wall, his erection would go in reverse, crawling into its shell.

Princess Yemisi contemplated quitting her board membership, but her obvious love for Eva still lingered with her. She took a leave of absence from the board. Dr. Oluomolewa's thoughtlessness in posting his letter rather than hand-delivering it in person provoked her reevaluation of her feelings for him. But one thing he did right was to allow her to choose the battle when they would settle their differences. His patience gave him greater control to deal with the situation.

He ignored her completely and tried to concentrate on his wife, Charity, and his children. He coached the youth basketball team in order to get his mind off Yemisi. However, it was not working.

Princess Yemisi had a self-imposed exile on herself too. Unlike before, when she'd worked in her garden as often as her busy schedule permitted her, now she paid extra money to Chika to take care of the garden for her. Chika, her executive assistant, was good at farming the garden. Princess Yemisi increased her wage to accommodate her extra workload. Chika had a better yield from the garden, given her intense efforts, to the point some of the yields were taken to the palace in Orissa Kingdom. They grew corn, tomatoes, black-eyed peas of assorted types, and assorted types of vegetables, including *ewedu* leaves and *ogo*, two vegetable leaves mainly eaten in Yoruba and Igbo lands. Ewedu leaves were substituted for *okoro* vegetables, which were seasonal. When Princess Yemisi came to Lagos, she mainly stayed inside, but she watched every movement Dr. Oluomolewa made, from the window of her bedroom. She'd ask her chauffeur to drive through the basketball field on the pretense that she was just passing through, just to have a glance at Everest.

She used the land cases and their business holdings as excuses to frequent Lagos. Most times, she would depart from Agbala in the evening on Sunday after having Sunday lunch with the bishop and the small committee to get together a group to plan the week's itineraries. She was hoping to catch Dr.

Oluomolewa before he went to sleep. His thoughts dominated her mind.

As luck had it, one day Chika's sons, Dele and Jeje, came to her and asked if she could persuade Dr. Oluomolewa to let them join his basketball team. That was Yemisi's perfect excuse and a welcome face-saver to meet face-to-face with Dr. Oluomolewa again after almost five months of her arrogant self-detention. Instead of sending Chikanele to his house to ask him herself, inviting him to come over to her villa, or even calling him on the telephone, she took the two boys over there when she knew he was not at home. The maid of Charity knew her well and, like Charity, addressed her as Mama Yemisi. The maid invited them in to drop her message in writing. The real purpose of her coming into the house was to see if her photographs were still hanging on their walls. When she saw her pictures still hanging on their walls, she concluded that their bitter feud had not reached the bone. She looked around the living room and left with the boys after dropping the note.

It was welcome news for Dr. Oluomolewa to listen to her explanation for her arrogant, drawn-out silence. He came back by seven thirty, and Charity came back a little earlier, at about six. At that time, Professor Oluomolewa would not eat anything, even if he came home on an empty stomach. Charity excused herself from going over to Princess Yemisi's villa to know what her visit was for, because her kids' homework was due the following day. After a little persuasion from Charity, Everest went over to deal with Princess Yemisi's "important discussion," as the princess had put it. He contemplated the notion it could be a warning for them not to see each other again. That was why he wanted so badly for Charity to tag along. Yemisi couldn't possibly, in Charity's face, tell him off without adequate explanation other than their secret affair, and she wouldn't shoot herself in her foot in the presence of Charity either. He prayed God would keep their relationship going, at least as a platonic friendship. Dr. Oluomolewa adored Princess Yemisi. Sexual intercourse didn't come into play anymore. He honestly was in love with her and deeply committed to their relationship.

He was ready for the outcome, and he promised himself he would remain above it and would not beg for a second chance. He would conserve his dignity. Still, he did not know what had prompted her silence. He would go in, sit down, and listen to her grievances, and in the end, he would accept her verdict and exit her door without saying a word.

Princess Yemisi knew his routine, and she gave him a glass of cold water to drink. He drank a little, holding the cup in his left hand, practically sitting at the edge of his seat. She walked over to the kitchen. The crown princess did not like to shout at her housekeepers, especially her executive assistant, Chikanele, or call their names too loudly. She told Chikanele, who was relaxing in the kitchen with a novel, to send for the boys. Yemisi introduced the boys to him and told him their request.

He said in a loud voice, "Are you burning in your hearts with fire to play basketball?"

They shouted, "Yes!"

He said he would pick them up together with his kids to go for practice tomorrow and whenever there was a practice. It was an emotional relief for him. Chika and Yemisi couldn't thank him enough.

As he was about to depart, Yemisi sent the kids with Chika away and opened the front door herself for him to exit. Then she apologized for her silence. The discussion led them to sit down again, and this time, she invited him to her bedroom to avoid people listening in on her grievances.

Dr. Oluomolewa, weighing the magnitude of the consequences, knelt down and humbly apologized. He was deeply touched. In the end, he asked her how they should remain now. "Maybe as a platonic relationship?"

Yemisi said to him, "You said you were in love with me. When did you stop? I have not stopped being in love with you. Give me a kiss before going away."

The kiss was the longest kiss they'd ever shared. Their pants were down on the floor, when a phone call came in. It was Charity. Eva's mother was at his house. She'd been in the neighborhood, visiting a friend. He quickly rushed home to see his mother.

PART 10

GENEVA GETAWAY

CHAPTER 36

Princess Yemisi reconsidered leaving the board membership and decided she would stay for good. Dr. Everest Oluomolewa had begun to consume her thoughts a lot. She was fully in love with him and didn't care who noticed. Besides, she was too important of a board member to be missed. She loaned her jet plane to them at a moment's request, even though she shot herself in her foot by delaying her important chores whenever she loaned them her jet. Dr. Oluomolewa insisted she lease the airplane at a financial cost to the World Health Organization. Her intoxicated feelings for Everest were beginning to be noticed by some board members. The board members would go to Dr. Oluomolewa to ask for Princess Yemisi's help. The physician would quickly advise them to approach Princess Yemisi directly themselves. He succeeded in making his relationship with Princess Yemisi seem platonic, professional, and nothing more. The rest of the board members seemed to accept it.

In the absence of Princess Yemisi and Professor Oluomolewa, an emergency board meeting was convened to discuss the outbreak of babies dying from adulterated cough syrups sent by an Oriental economic power to developing countries. The concentration of infant mortalities was mainly in Ghana and Haiti. Nigerian shipments were delayed at Apapa Wharf in Lagos, due to some technically inadequate paperwork and the ongoing negotiation of a bribery amount to be paid to the customs agents before they would release the cargo to its owners. The cargo had been sitting at the dock for more than six months, awaiting clearance. The negotiated bribery amount, the customs duty, the freight, handling fees, insurance costs, and the cost of the products were too unbearable for the owners to afford. The owners just left the containers at the wharf. The delay saved innocent children from becoming victims of the economic power's greed. The news broke out that Ghanaian and Haitian babies were dying from the cough syrup. The World Health Organization's Nigerian branch quickly intervened. At two o'clock in the morning, Nigerian soldiers forced the customs agents to open the containers. What they saw was alarming. They quickly dumped the drums, about 278 fifty-five-gallon drums, into the ocean.

The team, with three board members, returned to their headquarters by five thirty in the morning. It was agreed to send two representatives from Nigeria to launch a complaint against the Oriental economic powerhouse at the headquarters of WHO in Geneva to hold the country accountable for the deaths of those children. They unanimously voted Dr. Everest Oluomolewa and Princess Yemisi to lead the team of science representatives from the Nigerian branch of the World Health Organization. They were going to stay for four days, ride on the same flight, and reside at the same hotel for their lodging. They were set to go with a team of scientists, technicians, physicians, social scientists, and historians. Dr. Oluomolewa was to deliver the WHO Nigerian branch's findings. He and Princess Yemisi were fully briefed about the meetings and the emergency situation. They discussed the matter with their spouses. Everest and Charity were in agreement, and so were Yemisi and Edukoya. Charity and Edukoya individually agreed that Yemisi and Everest could properly look after each other. They said, "Both of you are in good hands."

The team would board a commercial flight to Geneva. Yemisi's airplane was a significant target for sabotage, and the organization termed it an unnecessary risk that could be avoided. Also, they feared it would not be able to carry the team of fifty-two scientists, physicians, technicians, historians, and sociologists, including their technical gear and luggage. Edukoya and Felicia escorted Princess Yemisi to board the Air Swiss flight. Charity, their maid, and their children escorted Everest to board the same flight. The king and Professor Oluomolewa met at the airport. They embraced cheerfully, and Edukoya told him to take good care of his wife. Incidentally, Charity told Mama Yemisi to take good care of Eva. All the members of the team were seated in the upper-economy class. Yemisi and Everest opted to be seated in the upper-economy class with their teammates instead of in first class, so they could blend together. Because they traveled as a team, Air Swiss treated them as if they were in first class, with unlimited drinks and a choice of unlimited foods.

The flight arrangement was kept top secret to avoid acts of sabotage. The United States and the British air defenses secretly guided the airplane in the air to its destination. Even the pilots were kept in the dark. They got an Air France ticket but boarded Swiss Air. They took off at 10:55 p.m. to arrive in Geneva by about seven o'clock in the morning. Princess Yemisi and Professor Oluomolewa were seated together. As soon as the flight stabilized, Princess Yemisi went to sleep on the restful shoulder of Everest. Everest did not order any food or drinks, nor did Princess Yemisi. It was past meal time for him, and Yemisi joined him as well. To Princess Yemisi and Professor Oluomolewa, it was a whole new experience for them, deeply falling in love at that age. It was also their first time dating married people, and perhaps they prayed it would be their last. It was exciting for both of them. Midway into the flight, Everest fell asleep. They raised the armrest separating their seats and reclined the seats into a bed format. They faced each other, and their lips were about to touch, separated by a blade's wide. That was the first time Everest and Yemisi slept together. They enjoyed the night's rest and wished it would never end.

The plane touched down at seven fifteen. Prearranged shuttles took the entire team, including Princess Yemisi and Dr. Oluomolewa, to the Days Inn hotel complex, where the convention was taking place. Half the team were residing there, and the other half were residing at the Holiday Inn hotel complex. Kabiyesi Edukoya Adekunle III had already prearranged the accommodations for his wife, so Dr. Oluomolewa and Princess Yemisi would have adjacent rooms. The hotel CEO was a family friend of Edukoya's, and he took it upon himself to give the couple a desirable stay in the hotel. He linked their rooms together with a common door. The CEO, out of established customer courtesy and loyalty, upgraded Princess Yemisi's suite to a presidential suite at no extra cost to WHO. A quick cancellation was made to Dr. Oluomolewa's suite. He moved into Princess Yemisi's presidential suite because she had a lavishly furnished two-bedroom accommodation: a master bedroom and a guest room, with tastefully furnished living room settings. The WHO was refunded Dr. Oluomolewa's suite rent.

Princess Yemisi stayed in the master bedroom, while Dr. Oluomolewa stayed in the guest compartment. He had a busy schedule the morning of their arrival. The presidential suite came with two and a half bathrooms. One attached to each room, and the half bathroom attached to the living room. They went to their respective compartments, showered, and quickly dressed to meet with their team and guests in the hotel lobby. Princess Yemisi was no stranger to conventions, nor was Dr. Oluomolewa. Since they were leading the group, their punctuality was a matter of necessity. They came first to the lobby to receive their team. Dr. Oluomolewa urged Princess Yemisi to deliver a guardian's speech, which she did exceptionally well.

Before they came down to the hotel lobby, Princess Yemisi came into the living room and pleaded with Eva, who was already dressed, to zip up her dress in the back. The dress was wide open at her back, and he could see her underwear and her Brazilian butt perfectly. She wanted him to see it; it was the reason she'd searched thoroughly for that dress. He had to control himself. After the zip-up was done, she turned and embraced him tightly, giving him a kiss to remember. The convention began in earnest that evening.

CHAPTER 37

The first day of the convention was unusually hectic and lengthy. Princess Yemisi and Dr. Oluomolewa were exhausted. They went out with the team for dinner at about four thirty. They ordered vegetable salad, assorted fruits, and rice with stewed chicken for dinner. Dr. Oluomolewa overate his combo dinner because he had not eaten since last night. He then headed straight to the gym to burn the excess calories out on a treadmill. Princess Yemisi, though she had not overeaten, joined him in the workout for moral support. There were about fifteen team members already in the gym, working out. The hotel had complete gym equipment and a sports trainer round the clock seven days a week, including holidays. They had about thirty-five treadmills. It was a blessing to have the complete gym, and Yemisi and Everest had a ball. They came to their suite exhausted.

They went to their separate rooms, brushed their teeth, took quick showers, and went to bed tired. Princess Yemisi later came to Everest's room to say good night and possibly give him a good night kiss. However, Everest had mistakenly locked his door and dozed off. She could hear him snoring comfortably. Princess Yemisi took it angrily, as perhaps she was not invited to spend the night with him. She went back to her room, upset and perturbed. The one motivating factor of her accepting this trip was to be together with Everest at last. The condition was in the right setting, including the same flight and the same suite. Edukoya and Charity, blind to what the two were up to, had given them their unqualified blessings to do evil. Now she felt disappointed and wished she had never come. In fact, she contemplated going back to Nigeria the following day after the session.

Dr. Oluomolewa woke up in the morning, brushed his teeth, took a shower, and dressed for the heavy day's workload. He wanted to see how Princess Yemisi was doing and to demand an explanation for her denying him a good-night kiss. He went to his door, not knowing he'd mistakenly locked it. The door wouldn't open, so he shouted and banged on the door for someone to open it from the outside. He used the in-house telephone in his room to call the lobby, saying he was trapped and his door would not open. The management rushed their in-house technicians to Princess Yemisi's presidential suite.

Meanwhile, Princess Yemisi was on the phone with her husband, relaying their up-to-date experiences, when she heard banging. She rushed from her room to see what was going on. The technicians, with their master key, had already entered her suite.

The princess asked them what was going on, holding the phone in her left hand. They said Dr. Oluomolewa was trapped inside his room. She became concerned and excused herself from the conversation with Edukoya. The technicians asked Everest to turn the knob right to unlock the door, and he did. One technician said, "Now open the door," and the door opened. The technicians did not touch anything. Eva hadn't realized he locked the door before he called it a night by turning the knob to the left. He'd wanted to leave the door unlocked for Princess Yemisi to come in at will when she got ready to go to bed. The doorknobs in his house were turned left to unlock the door and right to lock the door. Seeing the identical knob in his hotel room, he'd turned it left, presuming it was unlocked, locking himself out of what was supposed to be a night to remember with a beauty queen. Everest laughed hard at his mistake. The technicians muted their laughter because they saw it as a common mistake by guests who did not frequent Holiday Inn in Geneva.

All the anger of Princess Yemisi washed away. She went to her room to finish her conversation with Edukoya. She told Edukoya the whole story, and he laughed hard as well. Princess Yemisi invited Everest to her room to help her zip up her skirt and blouse. When he got there, she was only wearing her bra and panties. Her beauty floored him; he was stunned by her body. He didn't see any wrinkles or signs of aging on her body. Her clothes were lying on the bed. He could not resist her attractiveness. He stood there speechless, watching her body in shock.

Princess Yemisi rescued him by asking him to make up for last night.

He said, "Now?"

She said, "Just a kiss."

It was an intense, passionate kiss, when the phone rang. The team was waiting for them in the lobby. He helped her put on first her skirt, slowly zipping it up with his erect penis intentionally pressed in between her buttocks. Then he gently helped her put on her blouse slowly, buttoning it up with his chest intentionally pressed against her nipples. While there, he massaged her stiff neck gently. She melted in his arms and asked him to make love to her right now, when a second call came from the team.

The minds of Everest and Princess Yemisi were on each other the whole day. They called the phone calls spoilers. They had been close that time to damning the consequences. Individually, they considered themselves madly and passionately in love with each other. They worried about the near misses, if nature was preventing them from making the biggest mistake of their lives. Once genital penetration happened in her vagina, there was no going back. The risk was at its magnitude. Princess Yemisi and Dr. Oluomolewa had been told by their spouses to take good care of each other. Those pleas were innocent. They didn't expect them to lust after each other. A dog never ate the bone that hung on his neck; it was the one to keep, and the dog was trusted to respect such bone. They had been able to keep the relationship secret, but nothing had happened yet. The trust had not been betrayed yet.

If something were to happen between them, it would be like letting a cat out of the cage, and there would be no going back to that cage. Princess Yemisi showered Everest as often as she had the opportunity with romantic and sexual affections. Any opportunity she got, she would go into romantic exercises with him. He welcomed the attention and affection a great deal. Charity, though pretty and sexually engaging most of the time, had a high moral personality that made her exercise limited open sexual affections. For instance, Charity seldom kissed in public or held hands in public. She dared not have sex in a parked car anywhere, including in their garage. She did not give a lasting kiss, just a peck on the lips or cheek, and she seldom engaged in oral sex. She let Eva have a ball sometimes with damning sensitivity. To her, such acts of romance were forbidden by God.

The only part of a man she would somehow comfortably allow to touch her vagina was his penis. No fingering either. Charity was not the type of girl to play with a man's penis to arouse his erection. Her grandmother had done a number on her during her circumcision when she was eight days old. Charity had been pretty as a baby; hence, her grandmother had feared the temptation of men lusting after her as a teenager would derail her from full maturity and opportunities, so she'd circumcised her by herself, flattening out her clitoris. Because Charity's circumcision had been done that way, she hardly reached orgasm without some kind of serious, lengthy, and creative intervention. That was frustrating for her. It made her hold in her sexual feelings, though she frequently pressed herself for sexual desire. She had no clitoris at all, which made it mostly impossible for her to attend climax to induce orgasm sooner. When she did reach a climax, it was trying and took a long time. The enormous massaging of the outer layer of her vagina to induce climax frequently scarred her vagina, making it overly sensitive, especially when she touched her vagina or urinated. The pain could last for hours. She also experienced near misses, which could be exhausting for her partner. Eva's patience often ran dry, but he dared not let her know about it.

Unlike Princess Yemisi, Charity hardly demanded sex from her husband, though she let him have it at his demand most of the time. She had never denied Everest sex, not even once, not even when they were having a serious dispute. She had not started off that way in the beginning of her relationship with Eva. She muted her difficulty with reaching orgasm with men. She did not tell Everest why half a dozen men she'd dated before had not worked out. She was too personal when it came to sexual intercourse. She could not make positive sexual movements in bed or show affection. Most of the time, she lay in bed like a log of wood and let her man have sex on a scheduled timetable. She didn't initiate romance, and most of the time, Everest's penis didn't become erect strongly, as he was riddled with guilt. Perhaps his demanding sex and affection from her seemed to be emotionally raping her.

She saw satisfying her husband sexually as a moral duty, when she actually did not want to have sex with him. Charity figured out a way to reach orgasm with Eva frequently when they were dating, because her marriage to him was a must. She was hopelessly in love with him. She was wild and giving to affections and sexual intercourse whenever he was around her, until she had her first child, Oreenmi Chijioke Oluomolewa. Charity became sensitive about her environment, and she dared not show affection at all in the presence of their kids. Hugging in private or in public was a rare thing for her to be engaged in. Her unresponsiveness and coldness to romance frustrated the hell out of Everest. Princess Yemisi, that romantic goddess, was what Dr. Everest Oluomolewa prescribed for himself. His manhood woke up uncontrollably whenever he was around Princess Yemisi.

He hoped that making love to an affectionate beauty like Princess Yemisi would relieve his tension and, hopefully, save his marriage with Charity. It might also increase the intense romance with Princess Yemisi, and somebody was bound to get hurt. The thought of two innocent loved ones hurting enormously impacted their romantic lust for each other. Subconsciously, they hoped something would foil their intended sex act when it was about to happen. So far, by sheer luck, it had been frequently foiled. But it wouldn't be long before there were no holds barred. What would happen from then onward? Approximately thirty minutes of intense satisfaction might cause a lifetime of pain and disappointment. Anger sometimes raged as they expressed these thoughts aloud. However, the bottom line was, they were deeply committed to each other and very much in love. As far as they were concerned, there was no going back on their feelings for each other, sex or no sex.

CHAPTER 38

Ahunnaya Anomnachi was the lead scientist for the team. She was all about intellect and scientific results. She taught at Imo State University and was married, with four teenage kids. Her husband was a doctor and a politician. He was Igbo, handsome, and astonishingly brilliant. Ahunnaya was mixed race. Her father was from Nigeria, the Igbo tribe in Imo State, and her mother was from Northern Ireland, under British rule. Her father and mother had met at the University of Liverpool, where both were medical students. Upon graduation, the father wanted to come back to Nigeria to practice medicine. The mother refused to join him. One morning, when the mother went to work, he packed his two kids, Chijioke and Ahunnaya, and left for Nigeria. By that time, Nigeria was changing its currency from pounds and pennies to nairas and kobo. The naira's value to the pound, the dollar, and a bunch of influential international currencies was enormous and encouraging. That was the motivating factor to settle in Nigeria and have a clinic built there. He was also a surgeon. Also, things were relatively cheap in Nigeria then. One could build a two-floor, four-bedroom dwelling in Owerri for under fifteen thousand nairas. Dr. Joseph Anomnachi emptied their bank account of eighty-six thousand pounds and left for Nigeria. He quickly filed for divorce under Nigerian law. He was granted full custody of his children under prejudice, meaning he was presently their sole custodial parent at the time. By international law, the ruling by a Nigerian judge would stand since he was the one who'd filed the divorce lawsuit first.

The two kids thrived in Nigeria. They went to elementary and secondary schools in Owerri, where the family resided. Chijioke Anomnachi went to Government College in Owerri, and Ahunnaya went to Federal Girls' Secondary School in Owerri. Both had distinctions on their WAEC and London GCE examinations. Since they had been born in Britain, they still were entitled to all the glories that came from being British citizens. Both gained admission to Oxford University under British scholarship and grant programs, for which they were more than qualified. Ahunnaya earned a PhD in microbiology, and Chijioke earned an LLD in law and a BSc in medicine. Both returned to Nigeria to practice their professions, despite their mother's pleas and objections. Their mother, Susan, had since married another Nigerian with four kids. She'd married an engineer from Rivers State. She had since frequented Nigeria continuously. Ahunnaya's father married a second wife after his divorce was final. They had an additional three brothers and two sisters. Unlike most Nigerian women, especially from Igbo land, Kath went out of her way to be an exceptional mother to her seven children, and they appreciated her. They called her Mom. That was why they came back to Nigeria after Oxford. They also spoke Igbo fluently and still kept their British accent.

Igbos usually regarded themselves as an endangered species. Wherever Igbos were in a crowd or gathering, they always paired up with their kind. They'd settled on the west coast of Africa some two thousand years ago.

Dr. Oluomolewa heard Dr. Anomnachi's conversation with another scientist in Igbo. He was surprised and interjected his opinion in Igbo. His surprise came from her being of mixed blood and almost passing as a white woman. It was rare for

248

someone with mixed blood born abroad to command a native Nigerian language with such fluency and ease. Her father, though Igbo, also had light skin. Her hard work, her dedication to the course, her Oxford education, and her first and last names persuaded Dr. Oluomolewa to appoint her as the lead scientist for the entire team. It was clear to Dr. Ahunnaya Anomnachi why she got the job. But Professor Oluomolewa could not admit it to himself.

Professor Oluomolewa's mom was an Igbo woman. He had always had a soft heart for the Igbos. He had grown up in Owerri and gone to secondary school there at Holy Ghost College. Although he loved fronting himself as a Yoruba man, he trusted the Igbos to get the job done perfectly. With the exception of one nurse, all his staff, both at LUTH and at his clinics, were all Igbos. His fluency in the Yoruba language had fooled everybody, including Princess Yemisi, to believe he was a true Yoruba loyalist. Princess Yemisi saw Everest and Ahunna together interacting with each other in the Igbo language and thought nothing of it initially. She thought it was routine scientific jargon and appropriate. Princess Yemisi was always included in all the conversations with the lead scientists since they communicated in the English language. Since Dr. Oluomolewa was surprised to find out she spoke Igbo fluently, his conversation with her from then onward was partly in Igbo. He even spoke Igbo with her in the presence of Princess Yemisi. Their conversations moved into high gear, and they started relaying their backgrounds in the Igbo language. That level of familiarity became a fundamental threat to Princess Yemisi. She became jealous, upset, and worried about Ahunnaya's sudden familiarity with her boyfriend, Dr. Oluomolewa.

Charity and Edukoya imposed a muted moral limitation to how much they could have fun together, but with Dr.

Anomnachi, there were no holds bar between the two. "Their level of familiarity, if it goes unchecked, will ultimately lead them into bed," Yemisi said out loud to herself. "Princess Yemisi can't have that." She decided to confront him right away.

For the moment, she went shopping for the twins, Chika's children, and Dr. Oluomolewa's three younger children at the hotel gift shops. She went with a few female scientists who had become her friends. All of a sudden, she noticed Ahunna had not joined them. She brought it up in conversation, and one of the scientists, Dr. Chibuozo Aguro, PhD, who taught at the University of Nigeria, Ilorin, said, "She couldn't join us. She was going through the presentation for tomorrow with Professor Oluomolewa in his suite." The jaw of Princess Yemisi dropped; however, she quickly muted her anger and erased any concern with the group.

She decided to give Dr. Anomnachi and Dr. Oluomolewa plenty of time to finish roasting all their corn. Princess Yemisi came in a little late. The presentation's select team had been waiting for her to go over the details of the presentation. They were in her presidential suite living room, going through the papers. Papers were everywhere. They had been at it for the past four hours. Princess Yemisi had been adequately informed by Dr. Oluomolewa about it. He'd pleaded with her not to go anywhere until the whole assignment was completed. However, with anger and jealous rage fueling her mind, she'd forgotten all about it.

When she entered her suite, one of the scientists was using the bathroom in the living room, and Ahunna was using the bathroom in Dr. Oluomolewa's room. Everest was in his room with two scientists, bringing out some overlooked documents they thought would be of importance to their presentation tomorrow. There were six other scientists in the living room, going over the papers and arranging them in the order of their presentation.

Princess Yemisi looked first for Professor Oluomolewa, and they said he was in his room. Then came Dr. Ahunnaya Anomnachi from his room, rubbing her hands with her carry-on lotion. Princess Yemisi assumed the worst. She muted her anger but walked straight to Everest's bedroom to confront him about what was going on between him and Ahunna. She didn't care anymore about making a fool of herself. She had had it with Everest. As she was walking by, the other scientist was coming out from the living room's bathroom. She went into Everest's room anyway to confront him. She saw two scientists with him, going over the documents. Relief flooded Princess Yemisi's face. The two scientists carried the sorted papers and left the room, closing the door behind them.

Princess Yemisi was all smiles. She sat on his lap in his bed with her hands wrapped around his upper body and head. He asked, "Why all the smiles?"

She promised to give him an explanation later, which he would never get from her. She pecked him a kiss on his lips before going to the living room to deal with the presentation of the select team.

CHAPTER 39

The World Society for the Prevention of Cruelty to Animals filed a lawsuit at the world court in Geneva, asserting there were rare reptiles, snakes and turtles, found on the swampy land stretching along the entire fifty-five-mile section in dispute. It was stated that the rare snakes and turtles were on the brink of extinction and needed urgent protection from the world body. Nigeria regarded the lawsuit as an insult, overreaching domestic interference from a foreign body invading its sovereignty, and felt the world court was recklessly stepping out of its judicial boundary. The world court agreed, ruling that the lawsuit was inappropriately and disrespectfully filed in the world court. Even the limited stretch of the law did not apply here. The ruling concluded that the appropriate place to file the lawsuit was in Nigeria since the Nigerian authority would ultimately have the power to enforce the outcome of the court ruling. The lawsuit was dismissed at the world court.

This protocol caused an unnecessary delay in the settlement. It took one and a half years to settle the WSPCA's lawsuit. WSPCA took their chances and refiled the lawsuit in the Nigerian Supreme Court. The Supreme Court intervened, sending the case back to the lower court to work its way through the chain of command like any other lawsuit. The WSPCA saw it as a delay tactic to allow the land settlement lawsuit to go through. Once the land dispute was settled, there was nothing holding the drilling from going on. WSPCA was frustrated. To show good faith, the Supreme Court elevated the lawsuit to be settled at the appeals court level. It then rested on the lap of Honorable Justice Chukwunanyenwa Onyemerekwe. Being a fair-minded judge, he ordered an investigation to know if the rare snakes and turtles were there in the first place and, if they were, to determine their magnitude of impact on the drilling.

Princess Yemisi was briefed on the outcome of Justice Onyemerekwe's recent ruling during her stay in Geneva to make a case at the world court about the poisoned baby cough syrup sent to developing countries by a powerful Oriental country. It was a big relief when she heard the ruling. She called her husband to detail the good news. Edukoya, being an adept lawyer, advised her not to be excited. He argued that the final ruling of the court had the potential to tilt against the governments and Princess Yemisi's team if there were overwhelming and sufficient evidence to prove the plaintiff's case. He added that the world body was watching the Nigerian court to see if it displayed partiality to favor the defendants, Princess Yemisi's team and the governments. He finally added that the burden of proof was on both sides.

On hearing Edukoya's thoughtful argument, Princess Yemisi sobered up. She then went to Dr. Oluomolewa to detail the news and the sobering conversation she'd had with her husband. She wanted to find out his take on the news.

Dr. Oluomolewa, being a member of Doctors without Borders, saw eye to eye with Edukoya. Princess Yemisi said, "How can someone shoot himself in his foot?" She was referring to Justice Onyemerekwe, a Nigerian and a Nigerian-government-appointed judge. "Judges are supposed to pass judgment independently without bias. It is a conscience-driven leadership where the chip may fall on either side."

It was the morning of the third day of the convention, the day when Dr. Oluomolewa and the teams from all countries affected by the poisonous children's cough syrup would give their presentations to the world body. With videos of babies sick and dying from drinking the poisonous cough syrup and with detailed graphs, charts, and test samples, the audience in the convention and the world body, after ten long hours of listening to the presentations, condemned the Oriental nation for its arrogant display of inhumanity in handling the outbreak. It then set the stage for perpetual lawsuits at the world court by all the countries affected, which were mainly developing countries. However, the Oriental nation quietly settled all the lawsuits through quiet diplomacy without taking any responsibility. The news was further wiped out from the surface of the world.

Princess Yemisi, once happy with the ruling by Justice Onyemerekwe, sobered up with the low expectations and concerned advice from Edukoya and Everest. The potential problematic consequences of the ruling weighed on her mind. They could lose billions of dollars if the final rulings were negative. The jubilation of a perfect presentation by Everest and his team did little to change her mood. She began to think she was a failure. She asserted that her ambition had robbed her of the real essence of life: happiness. Her honest purpose in coming to the convention had been to get away from Edukoya and Felicia and be in the arms of a man she adored, Everest, the man she knew she shouldn't have anything to do with. Her real purpose had been to make passionate love with him repeatedly. The bed was perfectly made for this lustful indulgence with the ultimate disruption of guilt. She imagined how she would have his body inside her body. She imagined how exciting it could be to have his body lying next to her forever. She imagined that it could be the start of their being together forever once he had a taste of this goddess's forbidden fruit.

With those thoughts, her face began to brighten up. Suddenly, she caught herself, telling herself that it was all in her head. It was about six thirty in the evening, and an impromptu miniparty sponsored by WHO was going on in the lobby of WHO's headquarters in Geneva. Nobody knew what the powerful Oriental nation was going to do next. The signs of humble results began to surface as the powerful nation began segmenting the countries by wheeling and dealing. The delegates from the epicenters where the infant deaths had occurred most—Ghana, Haiti, and virtually all developing countries involved—had already been invited to that nation's embassy in Geneva. They accepted the invitation but only agreed to listen. Nigeria and South Africa were the biggest elephants in the room. Although they'd had the potential to suffer the most casualties, they'd been spared the casualties by the defaults of greed and corruption. However, both countries would be duly compensated for emotional damages, which ran into millions of dollars. The Nigerian shipments had entered the Nigerian shore and been delayed, but the South African shipments had been intercepted before they arrived at their shores. If any compensation was due, it would be discussed at the highest level of the three governments. Nigeria and South Africa independently declined the invitation to their embassy in Geneva.

Princess Yemisi was not in the mood to celebrate anything. However, with her cheerful and receptive face, nobody suspected anything out of the ordinary or knew she was disgusted with the whole trip. She could not sleep with her man, no matter how much she tried. One thing or another always foiled it. Professor Oluomolewa knew her well and sensed she was not happy. However, he couldn't pin down her source of unhappiness, and he blamed it on Justice Onyemerekwe's preliminary rulings on the land case. He did not know he was at the center of her issue. Going into the third night with no sex with the man she adored most seemed like a lifetime of disappointment to her.

A bright spot came when a white couple from the University of Chicago, who were both biologists and had been invited to the convention as outside observers, greeted them as a couple. The woman said, "What a lovely couple. How long have you guys been married?" That put a smile on Princess Yemisi's dull face.

After the party, Yemisi and Everest came back to their suite and went to their respective rooms, took showers, and went to bed. This time, Everest made sure the door was not locked. Princess Yemisi got bored and streamed into his room for a chat. The chat led to a little romance in his bed. She signaled she had a lot on her mind and was not in the mood to have sex. She said, "Hold me," and he held her gently from behind. They slept for the first time in bed together, but they did not make love with each other, and this time, it was by her own choice.

CHAPTER 40

The fourth day of the convention was the final day. The team of Professor Everest Oluomolewa had technically won their social and scientific wars against the world's second-largest economic power. They had effectively conveyed their message, and the whole world had taken notice. Usually, at the end of a convention, the winners and the losers got together for a party. The party would be held at 9:00 p.m. in the Dome Hall of the Days Inn International Hotel in Geneva, where the convention had been held and where 80 percent of the convention guests resided. It would go on until about two o'clock the following morning.

For the rest of the day, there was little to do, with the exception of tying up minor loose ends, such as the morning conference with the ambassadors of American and European continents who'd secretly sponsored their trip to the convention. They wanted to highlight the atrocities committed by the powerful Oriental nation's companies and backed by their government.

Their flight back home to Nigeria was at 8:30 a.m. the following morning. The only time to go sightseeing would be if Dr. Oluomolewa shortened the time of their conference with the ambassadors and took Princess Yemisi for a tour of important landmarks in Geneva. Princess Yemisi had done an extensive tour of Europe and had visited 95 percent of Europe's important landmarks and sites. She had been to the Swiss nation several times. She was not interested on a tour of the city. She preferred to stay indoors with Everest and perhaps get in a little bit of romance and sex before departing home for Nigeria the next morning. She was in the mood for affection. She did not convey her lack of interest in the Geneva tour to him, however, lest he might think of her as a spoiler for the rest of the team and as being unappreciative of the importance of their trip and of the progress made at the convention. So she muted her concern.

That third night of the convention, lying in bed with Eva was special. It was a memorable night and the most peaceful night she'd had in a long time. She overslept, thinking Everest was still holding her. Everest, seeing how peaceful she was, did not wake her up. Instead, he went jogging around the hotel's premises without even brushing his teeth. He felt the running tap water would wake her up.

Princess Yemisi got up and wanted sex from Everest badly. Everest was nowhere to be found. She assumed the worst. She assumed maybe he was with Ahunna. The suspicion dwelled on her mind throughout the morning. Ahunna was exceptionally attractive and brilliant, and her skin color generally appealed to most men. But with Everest, her skin color was a turnoff. Everest preferred black-shaded and dark brown women like Princess Yemisi and his wife, Charity. In his mind, those colors stood the test of time and were adorable. He had lived twelve years in America and dated all kinds of women before settling down with Charity. Everest appreciated the white race a great deal, but conjugating with their women was not his thing. Besides, Ahunna was happily married to her husband, Nnadoze, and was not looking to conjugate with another man. Ahunnaya and Everest respected each other on an intellectual level—nothing more and nothing less.

Princess Yemisi could not contain herself that morning. She even forgot to call Edukoya to brief him on the latest itinerary and developments in general about her working vacation in Switzerland. Her contemplations ran wild, until an impromptu visit by Dr. Anomnachi alone without Everest. Ahunna had spent all night fighting to reschedule their meeting with both the European and the American continents' ambassadors at the European embassy, which was originally scheduled for later that evening. Princess Yemisi was expected to attend the meeting. She had been informed by Dr. Oluomolewa last night in his bed. With Everest occupying her mind all the time and her disgruntlement with the entire trip, it was bound to slip her memory. As a matter of fact, in his bed last night, Everest had informed her about Ahunna trying to reschedule the meeting that morning to free her travel time back to Nigeria that night. That was why she had been scarce at the party. Dr. Anomnachi was leaving early for Nigeria that night on a 10:00 p.m. flight. She was participating in presentations by three doctoral students at Imo State University. They were looking forward to earning their PhDs in microbiology that year.

Princess Yemisi invited her in to sit and wait for Dr. Oluomolewa, who'd gone out jogging. It was a big sigh of relief to see Ahunna come in alone without Everest. She went to her room to brush her teeth. She hurried her teeth brushing so she could have some conversation with Ahunnaya before Everest arrived from his exercise. Everest took a little longer because he was enjoying the exercise equipment the hotel provided for guests. He did a workout on most of the machines before he left for his suite.

Meanwhile, Princess Yemisi was engaged in investigating Ahunnaya's background and motive toward Dr. Oluomolewa. Princess Yemisi sounded unusually ordinary for a woman in her position, with enormous wealth and power. Dr. Anomnachi appreciated her personality a great deal. She found Princess Yemisi outgoing and easy to talk to, unlike most princesses and people in royal positions. Princess Yemisi went first and shared her background with Ahunna. In getting the conversation near Everest, the princess highlighted her passion and hinted at her eternal love for one man without mentioning Everest's name. She framed the conversation in such a way that Dr. Anomnachi assumed she was talking about her husband.

Princess Yemisi was a master of interrogation, and she tried successfully to balance the conversation by evoking a little bit about herself. It triggered a response from Ahunna. Ahunnaya, being a highly trained and sophisticated academician, leveled with her by giving her as much information about herself as Princess Yemisi had given about herself. Academic discussions could be boring at times, even to those who were academically minded, so Ahunna stayed away from such topics. Princess Yemisi had hinted at her love for sports, especially basketball, so Ahunnaya took the conversation there. Dr. Anomnachi was a big fan of basketball and still played casually at Imo State University whenever she encountered an interest. When she saw the topic was gaining some traction, she made sure the conversation stayed there. It freed her from Princess Yemisi's getting to know too much about her background, so Princess Yemisi got nothing out of her. She'd met her match again, as with Felicia. Yemisi was no fool, and she thought to herself, *These PhDs, whether they got their degree from Ibadan or from Oxford, tend to act as if they were in the same classroom.* She found Ahunnaya easy to talk to, like Felicia. She was also disappointed and frustrated that she learned no meaningful information she could hold against her.

Everest entered the suite to hear that the meeting with the American and European continents' ambassadors had been rescheduled for 10:00 a.m. that morning and would last for about an hour. It was about seven fifteen, and it did not take Everest a long time to dress. As for the women, that was a different matter altogether. Princess Yemisi and Ahunnaya hadn't dressed up. Princess Yemisi complained he should have woken her up to join him for the exercise. However, Ahunnaya's success in rescheduling the meeting to suit her convenience was appreciated and overshadowed Princess Yemisi's little complaint from missing the exercise with him.

Ahunna departed for her compartment, while Princess Yemisi and Professor Oluomolewa went to their rooms to dress for the occasion. Princess Yemisi told Everest that she'd slept peacefully last night and that it had been her most peaceful rest in a long time. Everest said he'd sensed that, which was why he hadn't wanted to wake her up. She asserted that was thoughtful of him. She demanded he kiss her before going to his room. He told her he had not brushed his teeth, fearing the running water would wake her up. They excused each other and went to their rooms to shower and dress.

Dr. Oluomolewa took a quick shower, dressed, and came into the living room area to go through some of the papers for their presentation to the ambassadors. The European ambassador was sending a chauffeur for them. It was about eight forty-five, and the chauffeur would be arriving at 9:15 a.m., which would give them enough time to swim through the rush-hour Geneva traffic and get to the European embassy on time. The embassy was located a stone's throw from the Holiday Inn hotel complex. Princess Yemisi called Eva to come to her room to help her select appropriate attire for the meeting. He came into her room, and she was putting on her underwear, facing the door. She had no bra on yet, and she was about to put on her panties. On seeing Eva, her panties dropped onto the floor, and she was practically naked. He was about to excuse himself till she at least put on her bra and panties. She said in a swift voice, "Don't go."

At her age, about sixty years old, her breasts were still standing. Her panties half covered her butt, exposing her pubic hair. She had no gray pubic hair at all. Looking at her, Eva thought, *She is the perfect creation, an immaculate goddess, stunningly beautiful.* Her body was so naturally pretty, with a tucked-in, flat tummy and no wrinkles or stretch marks, which was rare for women her age. She was a dazzlingly pretty woman.

The temptation was rapidly building up and raging like wildfire, about to get out of control, and Princess Yemisi rescued him by lavishing him with kisses. She had no bra on yet. On embracing her, he put his hands inside her panties, holding her butt, fondling it gently and romantically pressing it to his fully erect, hard penis. His erection was as hard as a rock, finding an exit window, ready to take action. He then trailed down her breasts to her vagina, sucking them as he went.

The princess and Everest were ready to engage sexually, when the telephone rang. The chauffeur was waiting in the hotel's lobby, and Dr. Anomnachi was already inside the car, waiting for them.

CHAPTER 41

That night was the last night for Princess Yemisi and Dr. Everest Oluomolewa to seal their relationship with conjugation. They were together in the same suite with unrestricted access to each other's body. They had massaged each other's body, applying lotion to each other's back while halfway in their birthday suits. Everest had sucked Princess Yemisi's firm breasts every chance he got when they were engaged in numerous romantic, passionate moments. That night, both would make a decision as to what their relationship was all about and whether to go all the way to have sexual intercourse or stop at their childish kissing game. Princess Yemisi felt she was ready to hear the verdict from him. It was more on Princess Yemisi's part than Everest's. She finally admitted to herself she was consumed with thoughts of having sex with Everest.

Passion twisted with genuine love for him and the excitement that came with lust, and she felt less guilty at the thought of having sex with him. *What if I slept with him while wearing a sexy see-through nightgown with no bra and no panties on, and his penis became erect and as hard as a rock, penetrating my vagina, and I slept through it?* She would have preferred to call it an accident and not actual sexual intercourse. She perceived that would be too much to swallow. She thought about confronting him about her needs; he was the only man on the trip who could fulfill them. However, she felt a direct approach would label her as being too needy. She wouldn't dare surrender.

Whenever she checked, every man's eyes were on her, admiring her nature-gifted body and facial attributes. Princess Yemisi laughed hard when a thirty-six-year-old doctor from Ghana was attracted to her. The young man, Dr. Alexander Soffie, MD, could dance. He had that in common with Princess Yemisi. He was tall and dark and had a remarkably built body. After several dances, Princess Yemisi began to lust for the young man and was tempted to invite him to her suite for more chatting since she found his conversation interesting. Seeing how sex-starved and vulnerable she was, Dr. Soffie seemed interested in getting it on with her that night. She noticed while they were dancing close that his erect penis was trying to break open a window to exit his pants. He pulled her closer, and his erect penis, which was as hard as an iron rod, rubbed on her repeatedly. She feared he would misconstrue platonic touching as an invitation to have sex, which might result in his raping her.

Princess Yemisi knew better than to take such a chance. What if Everest walked in on them? That would be a whole new explanation. Princess Yemisi did not invite him over; instead, she introduced him to one of her female acquaintances she'd met there, and she got the hell out of his sight. Dr. Yolanda Ebboni, PhD, a stem cell expert from the University of Accra, Ghana, her friend, was also from Ghana. Dr. Soffie spoke the same language as Dr. Yolanda Dede, a microbiologist. Yolanda and Dr. Soffie were a match made in heaven.

Meanwhile, Dr. Oluomolewa escorted Dr. Anomnachi to the airport to board her 10:00 p.m. flight to Nigeria. Princess Yemisi had refused to go with them to the airport, fearing she would be the odd person out when their conversation was largely in the Igbo language. Yemisi was right; they found themselves close and spoke the same Igbo language. It turned out the village where Ahunnaya had gotten married, Oratta, was the same village Everest's mom, Nnejiaku, came from. Both knew the most famous faces in the village too, such as retired Justice Evens Amadi. They became like sister and brother.

Princess Yemisi felt lonely at the party. She waited for Dr. Oluomolewa till about midnight before turning in to bed. Ahunnaya's flight was running a little late, and she finally took off at eleven fifteen. Dr. Oluomolewa called Princess Yemisi to inform her about the delay. Throughout their conversation at the airport, they never mentioned Princess Yemisi's name. They talked about their families, and they showed each other the wallet-sized pictures of their families they had with them. Both appeared to be in love with their spouses and their families. When departure time came, they hugged and said goodbye tearfully. Ahunnaya gave Everest a kiss on his cheek, and she wiped her lipstick off his cheek with her head tie.

By the time Everest showed up for the party, the party's population was very thin. He avoided drinks, even soda. Being somewhat like a host of the party, he waited until the last person left. He called the hotel management and handed them the hall. He was tired after a long day but was happy everything had gone well, even more than he had expected.

He stumbled into his suite at about two forty-five. He sat on the couch to watch TV and fell asleep there. The lights and the TV were still on when he dozed off.

Princess Yemisi had stayed awake, awaiting his return from the airport. She waited for him to rest and relax a little bit before inviting herself for a good-night kiss, a little romance, and perhaps some sexual engagements. Who knew? She didn't hear the door close as an indication he had gone to his room. In fact, she did not hear his door open. Princess Yemisi meticulously tailgated Dr. Oluomolewa in every aspect of his life. She displayed borderline possessiveness.

She came out from her room, wearing a sexy see-through white silk nightgown. She walked past the couch and headed straight to his room. She wanted to sleep with him. She'd bought the nightgown there in Geneva, at an upper-class department store. She didn't have on anything underneath the nightgown. When she walked by, she didn't realize the TV and lights were on, because Everest had dimmed the lights and kept the TV sound low. Her attention was so focused on having Eva that night, damn the consequences, that everything else went to a faded memory. She went into his room, and Dr. Oluomolewa was nowhere to be found. She became furious, disappointed, desperate, and, at the same time, very horny. In her anger, she said out loud, "I am so frustrated about this trip!"

As she was coming out from his room and going to her bedroom, she noticed the light and the TV before going to her room. She hardly watched the living room TV. She also saw someone lying on the couch. She approached closer and saw it was Everest. Rather than waking him up, she went to her room and brought out two blankets. She laid one blanket on him and pecked a kiss on his forehead, saying, "Sweet dreams, my darling." She went to the recliner, sat on it, stretched out, put her legs on the extension, laid the other blanket on top of her, and dozed off. The lights and the TV were still on.

At about sixty thirty that morning, a phone call came, saying there had been a mix-up in the flight schedule. Rather than the flight taking off at 8:30 a.m., the actual departure time with Swiss Air would be 10:30 p.m. The call woke up Everest and Princess Yemisi. They made desperate phone calls to their spouses to relay the sudden change in their flight schedule.

Swiss Air, as a matter of policy, liked to land in Nigeria in the morning hours. Edukoya said, "Better late than never."

After their conversations with their spouses, they went back to the living room to continue their badly needed sleep. Princess Yemisi came to the couch, and they cuddled together with their blankets and went back to sleep on the couch. They slept like a typical couple.

The silk nightgown without panties was a dream that came true for Dr. Oluomolewa. His erection was naturally positioned to deliver its desperately needed duty to the princess. Princess Yemisi was soaking wet, and her visibly gushing vaginal fluid accepted his penetration with the utmost ease from behind her. Her nipples were enlarged, and when he gently grabbed and fondled them, it aided the rock-solid longevity of his penis. With that type of erection, his penetration went farther in than usual. She pretended it was all accidental. They had all day to make up for lost time. To the sex-starved Yemisi, nothing could stop them now from having the time of their lives. However, Dr. Oluomolewa's erection slowly became weak inside her vagina when he suddenly remembered his critically ill patients practically on life support at LUTH, awaiting his return from Geneva. They'd had to reschedule their surgeries. He would have a huge job to tackle upon returning to the hospital.

There were a handful of highly trained Nigerian physicians who operated in the field of open-heart surgery. A slight technical mistake could cost a patient's life. Quite a number of those casualties occurred even in the developed countries. Not all hospitals could perform open-heart surgery in Nigeria, even teaching hospitals. They lacked the expertise and the technical equipment to see it through. Professor Everest Oluomolewa was a world-class surgeon. He was paid in foreign currency of his choice to practice at LUTH. He was also paid an untold amount of money to teach at the university. Since he had taken over the critical-care unit at LUTH, the deaths of patients as a result of his surgery had been zero. His talent was badly needed at the hospital, in his two clinics, and in the classroom, where he taught Elements of Critical Surgical Procedures.

As he lay on the couch with Princess Yemisi against him, his mind was on those patients. He was also paying tons of money for two additional cardiologists who temporarily took over his assignments in his two clinics in Lagos. One was located in Yaba, near LUTH, and the other was located in Eko. He wanted to open more clinics to dent the overwhelming demand for heart disease care in Nigeria, but he could not find highly skilled physicians to occupy the positions. He had made it his most pressing duty to turn out as many skilled cardiologists and cardiothoracic surgeons as possible at Nigerian universities.

Yemisi saw that all her efforts to arouse him were fruitless. His mind was five thousand miles away from their presidential suite in Geneva. His erection further went blank as he was pressed with those thoughts.

He tried to get it erect but with zero success. Princess Yemisi tried to give him a massage to arouse his erection. She repeatedly fondled his penis with her left luxurious, soft palm, but it was like beating a dead horse. She lay cuddled with him in her see-through silk nightgown, watching TV, still soaking wet. They took showers separately in their rooms around eleven thirty, late in the morning. They dressed without Princess Yemisi seeking advice from him on fitting attire. At that point, she concluded it was no use for him to come arouse her without any penetration. They went out to eat, did some shopping, and indulged in some sightseeing before departing back home to Nigeria. When they got home, their spouses made sure they made up for lost time.

PART 11

FUN WITH CHIKA

CHAPTER 42

Justice Onyemerekwe received the findings on the endangered reptiles, and it was a shock. It turned out the rare snakes and turtles were foreign to the west coast of Africa. The snakes and the turtles were rare breeds of reptiles used as delicacies for luxury meals in high-class restaurants for the rich and famous. The snakes were from Indonesia, and the turtles were from China. Someone had brought them to the swampy areas to make an environmental point about pollution from fossil fuel. The turtles and snakes were highly domesticated, and their venturing outside their environment could be deadly for them. They were not wild reptiles, especially living in salty water.

They were above average in size compared to reptiles of the same species in the wild. The reptiles had an enormous appetite and were frequently eating. The reptiles had died at a record number; about 98 percent of them had died. The remaining 2 percent of them were weak and near death and suffered from hunger, dehydration, and heat. Researchers collected them and quickly sent them back to their places of origin. The sabotage aimed at stopping the drilling of crude oil did not work. The findings were presented in Justice Chukwu Onyemerekwe's courtroom, and the evidence of foul play was overwhelming. Justice Onyemerekwe threw out the entire lawsuit as an act of sabotage and overreaching. One could see the WSPCA's long face.

Princess Yemisi called for a celebration following Justice Onyemerekwe's final ruling on the case with WSPCA. It was one more hurdle to put behind them. It had caused an unnecessary derailment in the case and a costly one too. With all the excitement and her unsettled, confused relationship with Dr. Everest Oluomolewa, Princess Yemisi fell sick. The illness was triggered by fatigue, and it escalated to a deadly high fever, which, in most cases, could result in fatality. It happened in Lagos, in her villa. Felicia joined her for a two-week stay for a minivacation. Princess Yemisi was to return to Orissa the following morning to be with Edukoya, while Felicia would be vacationing in Lagos, staying at the villa. Chika rushed to Dr. Oluomolewa's house to let him know about Princess Yemisi's high fever and to ask for his assistance.

It was Charity she met. On her way back to the villa, Charity escorted her to the front door, worried. As God would have it, Dr. Oluomolewa was just pulling into their garage. Charity beckoned him to rush to Mama Yemisi's house. Chika and he rushed to the villa, and he saw Princess Yemisi lying on the floor unconscious. He gave her two injections that revived her quickly. He asked Ephram, her live-in chauffeur, to rush the princess to LUTH while he joined them in the car. Felicia, who was with Princess Yemisi when the doctor arrived, was hopelessly traumatized. She called Edukoya and relayed the situation when they left for the hospital. Dr. Oluomolewa held her hands and escorted her to the car.

On getting seated in the backseat of the car, Yemisi rested her head comfortably on Everest's right shoulder as Ephram drove them to the hospital. Everest held her hands and gently massaged her fingers to make her feel better. The confidence she had in his healing went a long way to stabilize her. Princess Yemisi, who was in and out of consciousness, recovered a little bit by the time they got to LUTH. She began to feel better, with the fever slowly diminishing too. Nevertheless, Dr. Oluomolewa insisted on keeping her in the hospital for close observation for a few days. Dr. Oluomolewa spoke to Edukoya about keeping Princess Yemisi for round-the-clock observation in the hospital, and the king agreed with him. He thanked the doctor for his quick response. Dr. Oluomolewa stayed by her side for a few more hours. In the process, he visited some of his critically ill patients, especially the ones he recently had operated on, before calling it a night. Princess Yemisi finally went to sleep after she talked to her husband. He promised to visit her first thing in the morning.

Edukoya's jet touched down at Murtala Mohammed International Airport in Ikeja by six thirty in the morning. His chauffeur was waiting for him at the airport in his Range Rover. He went straight to LUTH, swimming across the traffic. Thank God his driver knew Lagos well. He knew a shortcut to LUTH from the airport. They arrived at LUTH by seven fifteen, and Yemisi was still asleep from all the medications given to her. He told the nurse attending to her not to wake her up. He promised to wait for her as long as it took her to get proper rest. At about nine o'clock, Professor Oluomolewa showed up and reiterated what the king had said about not waking up Princess Yemisi. She woke up at about ten o'clock and asked the nurse where she was.

In her unconscious sleep, she was still conversing with Felicia, who had come to Lagos for a minivacation when she suddenly collapsed. Thus, the first person she asked for was Felicia. The nurse assigned to her rushed straight to call Dr. Oluomolewa's office and alerted him that the princess was awake and hallucinating. Kabiyesi Adekunle III, who was waiting for her in Dr. Oluomolewa's office, tagged along with him to see

Princess Yemisi. Dr. Oluomolewa personally supervised the morning check of her vital signs, and he concluded they were within the normal range, given her age. Princess Yemisi was not an ordinary woman; she was a superwoman.

She was still an unbelievably pretty, attractive, and stunningly beautiful woman who could arouse the utmost sexual needs of men. She complained about serious and continuous irritation in her vagina, thinking Dr. Oluomolewa would examine her. Instead, he assigned the examination to a female gynecologist, Dr. Esther Ngozi Nwafor, MD. Every symptom of sickness was taken seriously at LUTH, where dozens of specialists were trained. Dr. Nwafor was an associate professor of medicine. She taught Early Conception at LUTH too. Dr. Ngozi Nwafor brought her entire class of students with the aim of examining Princess Yemisi's vagina. An alarm went off in Yemisi's head, and she refused to be examined in front of the entire class made up of mostly male students. Two of Dr. Nwafor's male students were just coming off from their teens but were brilliant students.

Princess Yemisi forgot at the moment that she was a trained nurse and that this practical knowledge was essential for the students, regardless of who the patient was. She also forgot she was the matron of Orissa Polytechnic Medical Center, a teaching hospital. Her husband, Edukoya, who was with her in the room when they came in, refused to call her memory to bear; he instead intervened, supporting his wife. It was a high-stakes drama. Dr. Oluomolewa, who had given the assignment to Professor Nwafor, came in and resolved the situation. Dr. Nwafor examined Princess Yemisi alone with Chidiebere, a highly experienced staff nurse. She had a minor yeast infection. Dr. Nwafor added mild antibiotic medication to her drip, and it cleared up the yeast infection. At LUTH and most teaching hospitals, for a reduced fee, about 10 percent, most patients were encouraged to sign away the right to their bodies' privacy in order to educate the physicians of tomorrow. The form was not brought to the attention of Princess Yemisi, and she did not sign it with her permission.

The yeast infection was caused by outside contaminated vaginal fluid, which was a mild, common form of yeast infection, even in teenagers. Princess Yemisi was constantly discharging a bucketful of vaginal fluid whenever she was around her boyfriend, Everest. It could also be caused by pneumonia, another form of bacterial infection. In Princess Yemisi's case, it was pneumonia compounded by cross sexual bodily fluid transfer as a result of multiple sex partners by her and her husband. Her frequent discharge of vaginal fluid added to the mess. Cross-transfer bodily fluid tended to be comfortable with time with most people in multiple sexual relationships. Multiple sexual activities involving different persons could create mild yeast infections due to the different pH levels in different people, until those partners got used to each other; then the pH level would create a state of equilibrium, leveling off. It also occurred in women who kept their vaginas very clean, because their vaginas became less immune to natural mild outside vaginal fluid contamination. There had to be a balance. That type of yeast infection occurred in most women, regardless of their social status. Some women reacted to it quickly, but most women didn't at all.

Minor yeast infection was an early indication that something was going wrong. Normally, bodily fluid cross-transfer caused no harm if all the sexual partners were STD free. However, in a few cases, the relative difference in body temperature due to the difference in pH levels could cause rejection in the cross-transfer chain until all the partners got used to each other with their living arrangement. Felicia and Edukoya were tested extensively for STDs and general yeast infection, and all the results came out negative. Chika was secretly urged by Edukoya to get tested, and her result also came out negative. Even Dr. Oluomolewa secretly tested himself due to his minor sexual brush with the princess in Geneva, and his test came out negative too.

None of them were carriers of any kind of yeast infection or sexually transmitted disease. Pneumonia's bacterial infection and her vaginal fluid contamination had caused the yeast infection. It was caused by her multiple tasks. Some of them were self-imposed, and others were thrust on her. It was compounded by the presence of Dr. Felicia Adekunle. Yemisi was worried about not getting enough romance from Edukoya, her husband. Before Felicia had entered the scene, she could just snap her fingers, and Edukoya would be in their bedroom, making love to her. Now, with the presence of Felicia and Chika, more so Felicia, she seldom saw romance and sexual intercourse. In the absence, she engaged constantly in masturbation, which scarred and increased yeast contamination, which in turn aided the irritation.

Felicia compounded the situation since she had managed to position herself as Edukoya's preferred choice recently. Princess Yemisi's stress had brought weakness to her immune system, thereby causing her pneumonia. Edukoya's open-heart surgery had given him renewed energy and a new lease on life, which was a blessing in a way but not so much a blessing in another way. He had an enormous increased sexual appetite, but the lion's share went to Felicia and Chika, the younger women. Edukoya took Princess Yemisi's age for granted as an excuse not to have frequent sexual intercourse with her, although he still found her an attractive woman. Because she muted her feelings and her desire to have frequent sex with him, Edukoya assumed she did not need it. He was wrong. Unfortunately for most women of that age, no matter how sexually active they were, naturally, society labeled them as nonstarters.

The issue was compounded when younger females lusted over their husbands, and their husbands welcomed it. Thus, the older woman felt neglected and unwanted; hence, she resolved to mechanical means to stimulate her orgasm herself, such as massaging her clitoris and fingering her vulva frequently. All that came with masturbation. Most times, if the sex organs were stimulated often, the friction could produce tenderness and induce mild contamination, which aided yeast infection. If it went untreated, it could become a full-blown yeast infection. Usually, yeast infections were harmless because there was no invitation from foreign bacterial bodies. They usually went away when the immune system got stronger. The constant irritation could be a nuisance. It was an emotional crime for any man not to trigger continuous affections and sexual engagements with his spouse, regardless of her age, especially when there was no intentional sexual withdrawal by his woman.

Most women went through menopause and gave the impression that sex was not their thing. Most women had misplaced social and biological identities, and some might not have been in love with their partners anymore. Some were lesbians still in hiding and caught up in a mixed-up relationship just to please society. As result, their feelings toward romantic engagements with men were purely ordinary. The truth was, self-imposed sexual denial was the worst kind of punishment for oneself. Women needed sex and romance as much men did and sometimes even more so than their male counterparts when they were in the right and comfortable social environment.

Society had trained women to endure and mute such sexual feelings and romantic desires.

Most women wore muted feelings well, and it frequently backfired on them. Their men oftentimes didn't understand what they were going through, especially when such rejection of affections was commonplace and there was zero communication between the two. One could fault bad communication between the two. Such women could be incurring pain from underestimated diseases, such as fibroids, which took time to develop into a full-blown, consequential disease. Each stage of fibroid growth provided the woman with enormous pain during sexual intercourse, and it had the tendency to lead the woman to abstain from sex altogether as the disease grew. The enabler was communication between the spouses. Often, the older woman's sexual and romantic feelings were muted.

If the women had children or had a deep interest in any religion, then morality had the tendency to tame sexual and romantic feelings even more. Women were generally vulnerable when it came to faith, and they had a tendency to be more loyal to their faith because they believed the religion provided them with spiritual and emotional security and comfort missing in their lives. The church loved them due to their unshakable loyalty and commitment to the course. Often, they denied affection to even their husbands when they felt the husbands were not emotionally and spiritually committed to the same course. They shot themselves in their feet. Most women occupied themselves with heavy workloads, from volunteer work to earned-income jobs, so by the time they got home from work or social meetings, they were totally exhausted, and it was time for them to go to bed.

Society called it socially acceptable behavior. In the case of a widow, society was uncomfortable with a man she slept with after the death of her husband. Her choices were limited. Society preferred her to be married before engaging in any kind of sexual activity, especially if she was a young widow with children. It did not work out most of the time. Most times, the intended positive results were limited. Men who wanted to raise children who were not theirs were few in number.

In order to stay with a man, a woman had to wear well sexual and romantic feelings toward him or let him go if she was not up to it for whatever reason. A woman had to make romantic feelings her thing; otherwise, she'd lose the very thing she was trying to preserve: her moral soul. She might as well be single, because her man, if he was not getting it from her, would eventually get it from somewhere else. It was just a matter of time as long as he was still breathing and sexually active.

In the case of Princess Yemisi, the issue was not her lack of being affectionate or romantic. At an age when she needed more affection, she was not getting enough of it due to the bed she'd made for her husband out of love and out of lust for a handsome young physician, Dr. Everest Oluomolewa. Rather than having patience and waiting for Edukoya's erection to come back, she'd presented him with a quick-fix solution that backfired on her. She could also fault hindsight, but that was a loaded excuse typical of a human being. After a few unsuccessful trials with Felicia, Yemisi had concluded that his erectile dysfunction was not going to get any better. She'd thought Felicia would disappear on her own now that her service was not needed. Instead, Princess Yemisi was simultaneously lusting for a young man she shouldn't have, at least at the moment.

Princess Yemisi chose an attractive married man who happened to be a cardiothoracic surgeon and who was in love with his wife. She chose him to play it safe. It would be all fun since he wouldn't give up his wife to demand marriage from her, and she wouldn't give up Edukoya to marry Eva or any man. However, now she couldn't have either of them fully for herself. She had to unconsciously settle for second best and leftovers.

She was a nurse practitioner and knew her infection was a mild irritation caused by pneumonia and exposed vaginal fluid contamination, which was common with most women who were constantly discharging mild vaginal fluid. She knew it would be cured by the antibiotic medication already in the drip.

Edukoya's and Felicia's unnecessary tests all came back negative. Yemisi was also trying to get even with Chika, whom she rightly suspected of having ongoing affairs with her husband. In fact, the real target was Chika, because Yemisi was convinced Chika was having multiple sexual affairs. Her yeast infection provided adequate opportunity to expose Chika for what she thought she was: an opportunist and practically a gold digger. She wanted to be sure her husband was not infected, but she also wanted to prove Felicia was sleeping around with other young men her age, which had the enormous potential consequence of destroying Felicia's marriage with Edukoya for good. In truth, Chika and Felicia were in love with the king, and they would not contemplate shaming the king by indulging in extramarital affairs. People could be wicked, even Princess Yemisi, and she forgot she was the real culprit. She'd made all the beds.

Princess Yemisi was now being treated for pneumonia, a bacterial high-fever infection that could be fatal. Her doctor saved her. She had four physicians in her family. They were not enough for her, because she couldn't take them to bed and make love to them. In the presence of her husband, she wanted to get her boyfriend to make love to her by the mere touch of her clitoris. The examination of her vagina would involve him inserting his finger deep inside her vagina to collect a fresh vaginal fluid sample for testing. In the course, her vagina would have the potential to be stimulated to induce orgasm, especially in having sex with her boyfriend in the presence of her husband. Everest knew better, and she knew better too. The only person in the room who was naive and ignorant was Edukoya. Out of respect for the king, Everest declined her invitation to have sex with her there, at least in the presence of her husband.

She would be okay. She'd get her health back after a few weeks of weakness. She would be as strong and beautiful as always, and she would be fit to resume all her normal activities. She was a superwoman and the crown princess of Orissa Kingdom. She was Princess Yemisi.

CHAPTER 43

His Lordship Kabiyesi Edukoya Adekunle III had enormous responsibilities in Orissa Kingdom to deal with; however, nothing was so important that it could not wait until Princess Yemisi recovered from her ill health. He was in the hospital beside Yemisi, attending to her few minor errands. He stayed in the hospital throughout the four days Princess Yemisi was there until she was discharged. Sometimes he passed out on the recliner chair brought especially for him. It reclined well into a minibed. Princess Yemisi's room had a full private bathroom, so he could take a shower and change his clothes. He frequently helped Yemisi to take a bath. While he helped her wash up, he couldn't help but focus on such a remarkable work of art by nature, the body of Princess Yemisi, regardless of her age. As Princess Yemisi got better, she frequently invited him to take a bath with her. While Edukoya pleaded with her to wait until she was fully recovered, his erection told him another thing, especially when he washed her from the waist down to her breathtaking legs.

Edukoya was in his mideighties. Despite his being an active man full of reborn energy following his open-heart bypass surgery, age was beginning to tell on him a little bit. He still did not use any medical enhancement when engaged in sexual activities. He jogged and engaged in aerobic exercises, and he could pass comfortably for a man in his early seventies. He had scattered gray hairs, but his dark hair overshadowed his few gray hairs. He had full hair. One of his helpers, Olushade, groomed his hair once a week. Kabiyesi Edukoya Adekunle III was about six feet, four inches tall. Age had not diminished his height. He was sexy and unbelievably attractive to women for a man of that age. Edukoya was far from being overweight, with no bulging stomach at all. He was good for his height.

He still played soccer, and with the help of Felicia and Yemisi, Eduks learned how to play basketball. He built a multigame court at his women's insistence. Yemisi had come to America in her late teens and learned skating quickly, and she had been a prominent feature on the ice-skating team at San Jose State University. The court provided her with an avenue to have fun. They played table tennis, long tennis, basketball, American football, softball, and soccer. He, his wives, all their children, and their helpers staged competitive matches from time to time. Being formidable players, Princess Yemisi and Felicia headed their own team. They took the competition seriously. The losing team would wash and fold all the clothes for the entire family, including their helpers, for one day. Kabiyesi's team lost occasionally, and he had fun joining his team in washing and folding the entire family's clothes for one day—and he was good at it.

Watching her in her hospital bed, fragile and weak, he teased her for the next competitive match when she gained her strength back. As he was reminiscing on the past, tears began to drip from his eyes. Princess Yemisi told him she would be all right and asked why he was crying. He said, "I love you so much, my love." She joined him in crying and walked up to his seat.

She sat on the right side of his lap, supporting herself with the armrest of the chair so she wouldn't put too much weight on his leg. She kissed him passionately, and she held him with her right arm across his shoulders and her left fingers massaging both his arms. It was a beautiful scene. Tunde was visiting, and with his camera, which he always carried with him, he took their picture without their realizing it. It was the most-looked-at picture in the mansion and at the villa in Lagos when he displayed it.

She was under general care in the hospital by a team of doctors. LUTH took persistent high fever seriously because it was an indication of a more fatal illness. Occasionally, Dr. Oluomolewa paid her a visit and thanked Kabiyesi for his support. On that occasion, he saw them holding each other and kissing. He felt a little jealousy but soon caught himself, saying to himself, *They are a couple in love, and no matter how much she loves me, nothing could compare to how much she loves him, and that is a good thing.*

Whether Princess Yemisi loved Dr. Everest Oluomolewa as much as she loved her husband, Kabiyesi Edukoya Adekunle III, was a matter of subjective debate and self-judgment. Princess Yemisi loved both very much. As a matter of fact, she had confessed to Everest she was in love with both men. She had slept with both men, though Edukoya had boldly penetrated her body, and rightfully so as her husband, but Everest had not boldly penetrated her body, not that she didn't want him to make love to her. There had been numerous near attempts that failed, and at one point, on the hotel's couch, his erection accidentally had penetrated her vagina from behind, though she'd had fun pretending to sleep through it.

Both men had had oral sex with her and massaged her vagina on numerous instances till she reached orgasm. She had given both men blow jobs till they ejaculated in her mouth. Both men had stimulated her to orgasm multiple times. Everest had engaged her in oral sex, but they hadn't allowed real sex to take place.

As he sat in his office, reminiscing on their awkward moments together and thinking that just two personalities had been holding them back, Edukoya and Charity, he dozed off on the couch in his office.

Princess Yemisi froze when she saw Everest enter her room while she was hugging and kissing her husband passionately. She reinforced her kissing of Edukoya to avoid his noticing her discomfort when she saw Everest. Dr. Tunde Adekunle drove his father to see his new clinics. It was her third day at the hospital, and Charity surprised her husband by coming to visit Mama Yemisi with the kids. Chika and her boys tagged along. They saw Everest sleeping on his office's couch. Meanwhile, Princess Yemisi was on her way to pay Dr. Oluomolewa a visit in his office to explain the odd moment. When she entered his office, a nurse was waiting to escort Charity, Chika, and their kids to see her.

Dr. Charity Oluomolewa was giving her husband a passionate goodbye kiss when Princess Yemisi walked into his office. Charity plastered her lips on his with her tongue completely submerged in his mouth. She wouldn't let go of him, and she didn't care who was watching or being amused. That was unlike Charity, kissing her husband in public and not caring who was watching them. Princess Yemisi wasn't amused, but she did well to cover up her disgust. She knew it was innocent, but she couldn't help being jealous. Charity hugged Everest tightly with both palms on his butt. She expressed gratitude for his quick response to Mama Yemisi's ill health. Charity said they were on their way to see her, with the nurse escorting them to her room. Yemisi claimed she had come to tell him the oncologist would be discharging her tomorrow.

Charity was happy to hear the good news. They followed Princess Yemisi to her room.

Dr. Charity was ecstatic when she saw Princess Yemisi almost her old self again. Her children had brought a Ludo game board and dice to play with Princess Yemisi. Charity had come in her Peugeot 505 station wagon with Chika and her two boys. Princess Yemisi paid for Chika's kids' private elementary school, Saint Gregory Primary School, where Oluomolewa's children attended school as well. Dr. Charity Oluomolewa was the school's principal. Yemisi had also promised to sponsor them through college and through their bachelor's degrees. They were presently at the prestigious King's College federal high school in Eko, in form two. The king had attended that school.

The relationship between Princess Yemisi and Chikanele had started as a friendship when Chika was an assistant floor manager at the Kingsway minisuperstore on Marina Way in Eko. During hard times in the mid-1980s, Kingsway stores had reorganized, as had the entire United Africa Company (UAC). Chika was laid off. With two boys to care for and a recent widow, the enterprising beauty fell on a hard time. She wouldn't dare sell her body to any man in order to put a meal on the table.

Their landlord told them to move out when they were not able to pay their rent. They owed him rent for the past six months. As God would have it, Chika was in the company of a friend who came to visit her uncle in Ikoyi. The uncle was one of the executive directors at Mobile Nigerian. They were having a birthday party for her uncle's wife. Princess Yemisi had been a close friend of Dorothy, Chika's best friend's uncle's wife, at Orissa Girls' Secondary School in the 1960s. Yemisi was invited to the party as well. Chika was a thoroughbred Igbo girl from Imo State. She had come to Lagos when she was two years old and had lived there since then. Her late father, Ndubusi

Kamalu, had worked as a funnel coal filler for Boardpak, a division of UAC. Chika had dropped out of secondary school at the end of form three when her father died. A painful decision was made to collect all the savings of her father, including his pension with UAC, to put her two younger brothers, Ndidi and Okwusa, through school. When the general manager of Boardpak, Mr. Philip Zanza, heard that, out of his own pocket, he sponsored Chika to take a crash course at a private commercial school to learn typing, shorthand, and elementary bookkeeping. A year and six months later, Chika was proficient with the courses. The general manager made an opening for her at Boardpak to be his assistant secretary.

At Boardpak, Chika met her husband, Ernest Oseni, who was an assistant manager at Boardpak. All open positions in all the divisions of UAC were published and advertised for all the employees on the house bulletin boards in all divisions of UAC. A higher position meant a higher paycheck, and it required an examination and interview to be taken to fill in the position. If no one was interested or a special talent and profession was needed, outside help was sorted to fill in the vacancy. A checking cashier position at Kingsway qualified for the undertaking. Chika applied and got the job. She was so good she was promoted to an assistant floor manager at the Marina Kingsway store in Eko. There she met Princess Yemisi, helping her to pick up items. They became tight friends, and Princess Yemisi would send her chauffeur to pick her up to braid her hair Yoruba style. Chika was a self-taught professional hair braider, and she used that profession to catch up on her finances and supplement her income on her off days from Kingsway.

Princess Yemisi knew Chika's husband well and was sorry about his death and about Chika's Kingsway layoff. At first, Princess Yemisi hesitated to make her an offer, but finally, she summoned the courage to make an offer to Chika to work for her as her maid. She called it her executive assistant. Chika could type and take shorthand with immense speed. She also knew elementary bookkeeping. Chika, who had been looking for a job without any luck or end in sight, jumped at the offer. She moved to Yemisi's main villa in Ikoyi with her boys, Dele and Jeje, while the princess built her a three-bedroom, two-bath house at the corner of their lot. Her paycheck was half of what she had been paid as assistant manager at UAC; however, with free food for herself and her children, free lodging, a free car, free tuition for her children, paid continued education for herself, and a generous pension plan, the arrangement quadrupled her paycheck at UAC. In return, Chika gave Princess Yemisi her heart. Chika was the first person Princess Yemisi wanted to pair up with Edukoya to cure his erectile dysfunction. Although Chikanele was an extraordinarily attractive young woman, Yemisi thought Edukoya might only see her as a maid and would not be attracted to her, so she invited Felicia to be the substitute. She was wrong, because Edukoya had been having a sexual relationship with Chika before and after his erectile dysfunction. Edukoya would have had no problem with Chika being his second wife, because Chika was the other woman he was secretly madly in love with.

Not only was Princess Yemisi her boss, but she was also her best friend. Chika was overjoyed when she saw Yemisi stand up on her own two feet. Immediately, she started filing her nails. Their friendship had moved into a higher gear. All the benefits and the king's generous secret support had helped Chika to save more than 225 million nairas. She had put herself through night school at the University of Nigeria, Lagos, and earned her BSc in business administration. She also was sponsoring her two younger siblings throughout their schooling. Ndidi Kamalu, her immediate younger brother, became a lawyer, and Okwusa Kamalu, the youngest, became a building engineer. She had secretly built six flats and a three-floor house in Owerri, and another one was under construction. The king was about to begin construction on a multidwelling place in Owerri for her forty-second birthday present. Chika wasn't just a maid; she was a highly educated maid to be attracted to Edukoya.

Edukoya had been having a sexual, romantic relationship with Chikanele from the get-go. Few men could have resisted her exceptional attractiveness and astonishing beauty. She had height and an enviable-textured light brown skin color. Her figure and facial looks made men come late to their funerals. She was not an easy pick for the king, despite his money and power. It was the man who attracted him to her. Who could have resisted such a remarkable man as Edukoya? Chika and Edukoya were in love with each other, and Princess Yemisi knew it. When Edukoya returned with Tunde, the eyes of Chika and Edukoya caught each other in the moment. They arranged their meeting point without saying a word.

The family's visit was overall comforting to Princess Yemisi, and they said goodbye, leaving Edukoya with Princess Yemisi for one more night at the hospital.

CHAPTER 44

The federal minister of petroleum and natural resources had asked the court to allow them to allocate the land by parcels to the highest bidder so that when the court settled the dispute, drilling would begin in earnest. The court, under Justice Onyemerekwe, denied the request, claiming it would be a gross conflict of interest and unnecessary overreach that amounted to abuse of power. In his ruling, he said, "The seriousness of this matter led to an appeals court status, which ultimately means there is further higher up to go before this case is finally settled, so such division and allocation of the properties would be premature."

The ruling by the court offended the minister of petroleum and natural resources, who was from the Hausa tribe. He assumed without merit the ruling was a personal attack and insult to him, coming from an Igbo judge, Justice Chukwu Onyemerekwe, to a Hausa man in charge of the petroleum department. The minister claimed Justice Onyemerekwe's rulings were born out of anger, jealousy, and age-old tribal hatred between the two tribes. He wanted Justice Onyemerekwe removed from overseeing the case and replaced with a hand-picked Hausa judge who would rule in his favor. The minister personally appealed Justice Onyemerekwe's removal to the federal attorney general who'd appointed the panel of three appeals court judges overseeing the case, who owed him a favor from the past. The attorney general pleaded with him to give him time to review the case and take appropriate action. The

AG pointed out to him that Justice Onyemerekwe's sudden removal from the case without probable cause would ultimately spell the real tribalism, which was the perception they were trying to avoid.

To be fair to Justice Onyemerekwe, the attorney general assembled legal experts to review Justice Onyemerekwe's rulings on the land-allocation case. The legal scholars included an Igbo law professor from Federal University in Owerri; three Hausa law professors from the University of Nigeria campuses in Kano, Ilorin, and Sokoto; and two Yoruba law professors from the University of Nigeria campuses in Ibadan and Ile Ife, with the AG himself presiding. The rulings were reviewed, and the conclusion was unanimously in the favor of Justice Onyemerekwe. The president of Nigeria heard about the situation, and the minister for petroleum was immediately fired. The president was all about the law. He believed in an equal separation of power. He said to the minister in his office that he would have gone through the appeals process, and maybe the Supreme Court would have seen his point. The president said, "That was a classic case of abuse of power on his part and not tribalism on Justice Onyemerekwe's part, as he wrongly indicated." The president urged the minister to apologize to Justice Chukwu Onyemerekwe, which he reluctantly did. Nevertheless, the federal government did not take any chance; Justice Onyemerekwe was given extra security protection.

Princess Yemisi read the rulings, and she was ecstatic. With the AG refusing to take action against Justice Onyemerekwe, the panel judges concluded to set a firm date to begin the hearing. The judges set the date to begin deliberation in six months. Once the deliberation began, it would take approximately three months to conclude. The justices urged both sides to conclude and submit their depositions within three months from the date. In the appeals court process, there would be no jury.

While Princess Yemisi was recuperating from her ill health, Edukoya insisted that Felicia stay with her, while Chika went with him to take care of the twins, who started their preschool.

The plane ride was disciplined. When they got to Orissa, at the palace, it was about seven o'clock in the evening, and Chikanele was shown her room. Chika frequented the king's palace in Orissa, but she mostly went there with Yemisi. In fact, it was only her fourth time visiting the palace without accompanying Princess Yemisi. Chika did not eat past six o'clock, nor did Edukoya. They asked for tea. Chika went to the twins' room to tuck them into their beds. They remembered her favorite story and asked her to tell them the story again.

The story was about a kind king who sacrificed a lot for his people. As she was telling them the story, Edukoya came to kiss and say good night to the kids. On hearing her telling the story to the kids, he didn't want to interrupt her until she finished with her story. The king noticed the intense concentration on the part of the kids, so he waited quietly by the door patiently until she finished. Edukoya knew the story was about him, reinforcing to the children a positive image of their father.

That night, he later came to kiss them good night. He walked away without saying a word, and he was happy with Chikanele. He came into his bedroom to chat with his two wives, whom he'd left in Lagos. He told them the story, and they murmured, "Incredible. She is teaching them to be proud of their father."

He asked Yemisi, "When was the last time Chika had a raise?"

Princess Yemisi told him it had been when she asked her to look after her garden. He told Princess Yemisi that Chika's salary should be increased by 25 percent henceforth. He advised Princess Yemisi to communicate that to her.

Kabiyesi Adekunle III confined himself to his bedroom. Chika, horny as hell, came to his bedroom to say good night, standing by the door. She was hoping the king would beckon her to come to bed with him, and that was exactly what he did. The night started with a story about the incredible landscape in Italy and wound up with kissing, touching, and breathtaking, passionate lovemaking. In all practicality, the king was married to three wives. Lucky him. He was a remarkable man, and women found him appealing. He had also the overwhelming means to maintain them. Each woman was incredibly attractive. Each woman was athletic. Each woman didn't ask for much. Each woman was intelligent, educated, and capable of running two corporate empires. Each woman trusted him and wanted him. Each woman came self-invited. Each woman adored him, loved him, and was in love with him. Each woman let go of her entire body for him and wanted to make love to him till dawn.

Each woman came with her own individual sexual experiences, and he never questioned her sources, even when she introduced new experiences in bed. Chika wanted to make love to Edukoya badly that night. To Chikanele, no man compared to him. He was about forty-two years older than she, but she still found him extremely attractive. Since her husband's death, Edukoya was the only man who had entered into her body. In fact, even during his erectile-dysfunction days, his penis could become erect a little bit when she came around him. His erection remained firm for a long time whenever he went to bed with Chikanele.

Chika wanted to wait for about two years before she remarried after her husband died. Suitors were coming from everywhere because of her incredible looks, but her love for

Ernest Oseni, her husband, betrayed her morality, until she came to live with the Adekunle family. Their generous benefits were astonishing. She was now practically a rich woman. Kabiyesi positioned her as his equal, and so did his wives, especially Princess Yemisi. They ate and drank at the same dining table together with their children. They also slept with the same man, though Chika did so in secret.

For the few weeks she stayed in Orissa Kingdom before returning to Lagos, Chika slept with Edukoya every night. In fact, her bed was never made. She only came into her bedroom to dress after taking a shower or bath with the king. Sleeping with Edukoya was not just for sexual satisfaction but also was emotionally therapeutic. She called him Daddy and was relaxed when she reached orgasm with him, which was frequent. The frequency of her orgasms with the king was unusual for a girl who was circumcised, and she could not wait to have one again and again with him. Most times, poor Edukoya would be dozing off while she was still on top of him, doing her thing. The morning she departed to Lagos, Edukoya said his greatest regret was letting her go. "No woman can do it better than Chikanele," he claimed. Chika was circumcised, so it took her a relatively long time to reach orgasm. She would keep feeling good over the duration of the exercise and wouldn't want the intercourse to stop. She was an extraordinarily attractive woman with intense sexual firepower to match.

Rather than going through the hell of reaching orgasm, most women in that category muted their sexual feelings to cover up their frustration, their disgust, and their distaste for circumcision. Circumcision was a sexual betrayal to women who had it. The injustice was done with no choice of their own. Also, most women who fell into that category conditioned themselves to go without having sex for a long time. To them, such endurance became second nature. They psychologically conditioned themselves to accept the obvious: most men's erections couldn't stand for the duration it took them to reach orgasm. They projected the impression that sex was not their thing. Some found comfort in religion while they were still tasty for sexual intercourse. In reality, sex was even more their thing than for women who were not circumcised. On the contrary, circumcision increased sexual irritation, stimulation, appetite, and feelings, which defeated the purpose of doing it in the first place. These women were also exceptionally jealous, and their jealousy could result in fatality because they were afraid another woman, perhaps not circumcised, would be a better romantic partner in bed with their men and thereby steal good husbands from them. Often, the women sugarcoated the seriousness with foolish pride and arrogance, thereby preventing themselves from getting badly needed psychological and sociological help to deal with the unfortunate error of a lifetime.

Coupled with the women's distant personalities, most men married to circumcised women had enormous problems in bed due to the women's lack of willing romantic interest and responses. The women avoided romance because they believed romance ultimately led to sexual intercourse, which they preferred to abstain from. Sexual intercourse, to most of those women, was done to have babies. When that score was settled, sexual intercourse became a bore, especially with the same man. If they were not educated to a college level, were relatively unexposed, and had a distaste for reading romantic novels on moral or religious grounds, the odds of their acknowledging the deficiency got worse. The women invented and created misunderstandings in bed to excuse and camouflage their self-imposed sexual resentments. Often, the men made all the advances for sex, and the desire to make love was not evenly shared. However, if the women happened to stumble into a man who knew how to get them to reach orgasm, all bets were off, and the cat was let out of the cage, even in the case of married women. Psychotherapy was recommended to the women in modern times.

After Chika had her first boy, she would never go for a long time without having feelings for sexual intercourse, as it was with most women who were circumcised. Natural childbirth, in most cases, tore up the clitoris and enlarged the vulva in most circumcised women, thereby making penetration of the penis relatively easy, increasing irritation, and increasing stimulation. Even their panties had been known to provide stimulation.

Generally, women who had given natural birth tended to have increased vaginal fluid. The more babies came through the vaginal canal, the more frequent the discharge of vaginal fluid, which created more stimulation and easy penetration, especially when a woman was very attracted to a particular man. The clitoris was the sexual stimulant in women that got cut off during circumcision. The mutilation caused the vulva to narrow to the point that the first time genital penetration occurred, it was very painful and could lead to excessive vaginal bleeding. In fact, that was the main reason for women's circumcision. It acted as a deterrence to preserve virginity until marriage. When Chika and most circumcised women were horny, they needed sex so badly they became disoriented, agitated, angry, confused, and forgetful. Oftentimes, innocent persons could become victims of circumstance. Unfortunately, they bottled their feelings inside them, waiting to explode at the slightest trigger point. However, when sex became continuous and frequent, regardless of how much they loved their men, it became a bore because they could not reach orgasm as frequently as the men.

Chika's infrequent engagement in sexual activities with Edukoya was good for her. The sexual scarcity made her profoundly more grateful and unusually hungry for more sexual activities with the king when they were together. Coupled with being in love with him, she reached orgasm sooner than most women in the same shoes. That morning, before she left for Lagos, their duration of intercourse was unusually long because she couldn't get enough of him. She had two grown-up boys, and she realized she had the means to take care of them now. She realized catering to another man as a wife would impose an undue burden on her. Chika, by her nature, took too long to fall in love with a man. With her two grown-up kids, she thought falling in love with a man might take forever. At the same time, she underestimated the power of nature and love. She had already fallen in love with Edukoya, and she was comfortable with their unspoken arrangement in which she was a secret third wife. Even if Princess Yemisi became aware of her affairs with her husband and even if it broke them up, she now had the means to stand on her own two feet. She was now in a position to adequately take good care of her family. However, she preferred to keep her relationship with the king secret, at least for the sake of her friendship with Princess Yemisi. She thought, *Good people never cut off the hands that feed them.*

CHAPTER 45

Dr. Charity Oluomolewa was at home when Princess Yemisi returned from the hospital. Yemisi had lost a lot of weight due to the illness, about sixty-five pounds. Before her illness, she had put on a bit of weight due to her constant travel, lack of rest, and lack of routine exercise. She had lost all the weight she'd gained, plus more, and she weighed about 105 pounds now. She had slimmed down considerably, and she looked gloriously attractive and younger. At the age of sixty-three, she could comfortably pass for an attractive woman in her early forties. When she came in, Charity rushed to the villa with her kids to welcome her home. She came home with Edukoya. Felicia took to the kitchen and prepared vegetable soup for her. She ate a little bit with Edukoya; Felicia; Chikanele and her kids; Charity and her kids; and five of Edukoya's older kids, Bunmi, Tunde, Ephram, Kenmiejo, and Helen joining her at the meal. It was like a small welcome-home party. Chika's children addressed her as Grandma Yemisi, and she loved it. Both kids were good with fine art. They drew a poster featuring Mama Yemisi in the hospital, playing Ludo with them. It was an exact replica of her. Princess Yemisi enlarged the poster and hung it on the wall of her bedroom.

Felicia used cooked sliced yam to eat the vegetable soup. All the items in the meal, with the exception of roasted smoked fish, came from Princess Yemisi's garden, which was cultivated by Chika. She used vegetable leaves, including *ogu*, *oha*, *ottashi*, and a little bit of bitter leaves, to give it a unique flavor and taste.

Chika had taught Princess Yemisi and Felicia how to cook an Igbo-style menu with a little vegetable oil in the soup and plenty of vegetable leaves. It had since become the preferred cooking of choice for the entire family. One reason Kabiyesi Adekunle III visited Imo State was to eat *ofeh-akwokwo*, vegetable soup, prepared fresh by Chika's mother. The vegetable soup was prepared with gigantic roasted snails, sliced breadfruit, ogu leaves, bitter leaves, and plenty of fresh *okoro* fruits hand-picked from her garden. The *fufu* was mashed yam mixed with *gari* and pounded to give it a uniform, blended look. The soup went brilliantly with the unique blend of fufu.

Traditionally, the Yoruba cooked with plenty of vegetable oil in their soup, with few leafy green vegetables. On the contrary, the Igbos cooked with little vegetable oil in their soup, with plenty of green vegetable leaves. Chika was given a lot of praise for the remarkable job she did with the garden.

On one occasion, after Edukoya regained his erection, while watching Chika at work plowing the soil, soaked with sweat all over her body, with her thirty-eight-cup-sized breasts exposed, his erection burst his pants wide open to the point Chika could see it clearly sticking out. She immediately rescued him by stepping up to the plate. She dragged him to her bedroom and let him have it, after which she returned to her gardening.

Princess Yemisi reiterated how hardworking Chika was. She emphasized her credentials; she had a college degree and now was doing her master's at the University of Nigeria, Lagos. Felicia and Edukoya encouraged her to go for her PhD when she got through with her master's in business administration. She didn't respond and kept quiet at the table. She was asked where she got her strength from. She whispered in Princess Yemisi's right ear, sitting adjacent to her, "You gave me all, and in return, I gave you my heart."

Princess Yemisi started crying for joy. "That was why you stayed." The audience mistook the emotion as her being glad to be back home and alive.

Chika was facing Edukoya at the table, and with their eye contact, without saying a word, they arranged that she would follow him to Orissa for the remainder of Felicia's vacation while Felicia stayed with Princess Yemisi to keep her company and do some minor chores at the villa.

After the meal, Charity left with her kids. She got home to find Everest had already returned home from work. Everest said he'd accompanied Edukoya to escort Princess Yemisi to their car. He asked how she was doing. Charity quickly commented on her severe weight loss but quickly said she looked healthier, young, and more attractive with the weight loss. Everest nodded in agreement and said to himself, *The lady who got away.*

He said he would go see her tomorrow evening when he returned from LUTH. He said, "She will need enough time to rest."

Edukoya left in the morning for Orissa Kingdom with Chikanele. The king had important assignments to attend to in Orissa. The president of Nigeria was coming to Ondo State for an official visit. He would be spending a great amount of time with his old friend Kabiyesi Adekunle III. The visit by the president was important, as he would see the fund Orissa directly got from the federal government and make sure every kobo was applied to useful endeavors and accounted for. The new express road leading to Orissa Polytechnic, where the president's motorcade would be passing through, had been paved by that fund. The president would see firsthand the enviable developments in the relatively small Orissa Kingdom.

Orissa Kingdom exported food all over the country and abroad. The main agricultural products were cassavas, yams, and livestock, mainly chickens. They also grew potatoes and assorted kinds of vegetables. He would see how clean central Orissa's open marketplace was, with paved streets, running water, water-system bathrooms, roofs with solar panels, and well-kept, clean restrooms. The president would visit Orissa's man-made freshwater lake with a dam, where the entire community got their water. Exported food items were surcharged to build and maintain the dam. Sixty percent of the water from the lake went to agricultural developments. The president would be awarded an honorary PhD in political science at Orissa Polytechnic Institute. He would be the keynote speaker at the graduation ceremony. He would then eat lunch at the king's palace.

Chika would be substituting for Princess Yemisi and Dr. Felicia Adekunle. Princess Yemisi wanted that exposure for her best friend as a way of getting her to believe in herself, which amounted to a morale boost. How little she knew Chika. Chika had gotten all the morale boost she needed.

Professor Oluomolewa came to the villa at about eight o'clock in the evening with Dr. Charity Oluomolewa, EdD. Princess Yemisi was happy to see him. He checked her vital signs, especially her blood pressure, and inside her mouth. She held his finger and said, "You wouldn't let your old friend die." Charity was happy with those words coming from her. Charity went to the kitchen to aid Felicia in bringing the tea while Felicia made cocoa for Chika's children. While they were in the kitchen, Princess Yemisi took Everest to her bedroom to show him the medications the oncologist had prescribed for her. He wound up rejecting a bunch of them since she had no symptoms of the potential diseases. He was worried about the side effects of those medications. Charity and Felicia returned from the kitchen and joined them in her bedroom; the door was wide open. Since there was a living room sitting arrangement in her bedroom, they sat there and drank the tea.

They later took the teapot with leftovers to the family room, where another big TV sat. They paired up their conversations; Felicia paired up with Charity, and Princess Yemisi paired up with Everest. Felicia took Charity, who was closer to her age, to her bedroom to get more acquainted with her, leaving Eva and Yemisi in the family room downstairs, figuring they had more in common with each other.

Yemisi sat close to Everest, massaging his fingers and murmuring, "You saved my life."

Dr. Oluomolewa downplayed the value of his being there on time to arrest the situation by saying, "Any doctor would have done the same thing."

It was getting late, and the children were fast asleep. Chika's children slept in their old room at the villa while Chika was away with the king in Orissa Kingdom. They shook hands, but Princess Yemisi went further and hugged Everest tightly, calling him, "My hero." They departed for the night.

PART 12

LOVE AND THE
INCREDIBLE SACRIFICE

CHAPTER 46

Dr. Oluomolewa reminisced all night about the new look of Princess Yemisi. She'd added a considerable amount of youth to her age, and she looked young and breathtakingly attractive due to her enormous weight loss in the space of two weeks. A profound athlete, Yemisi had slimmed down drastically and wore the reduced weight remarkably well on her body. Dr. Oluomolewa feared a potential health problem; her kidneys, her liver, or both might have some potential issues. Although her weight loss for now looked good on her, he feared a continuous downhill slide in her weight could spell a bigger potential health problem.

The following morning, a Saturday, he went for his routine jog around the neighborhood. Yemisi saw him coming out of his house, and she hurried and dressed to join him, as usual. Felicia, who was up early in the morning to catch up on her reading for her lectures at Orissa Polytechnic, questioned her wisdom in going jogging when she was still fragile.

When it came to exercise, Princess Yemisi had a mindset. She explained to her she wouldn't let her good looks slip away from her this time. Felicia joined her to catch her if she fell. Felicia persuaded her to take a walk in her fragility, until she built up her strength over time. She reminded her she had eaten little food yesterday. Yemisi said she was just going to jog around the neighborhood, but she saw eye to eye with Felicia that walking might be the best exercise now. The princess agreed to walk because Everest was nowhere in sight. By the time they finished with their dialogue, Dr. Oluomolewa had jogged past out of sight. Princess Yemisi was not happy but muted her concern. She hoped for better luck next time, when she would be alone and wouldn't have Felicia pestering her. Her intention for jogging was to be in the company of Everest.

They walked about two blocks, and Yemisi opted to sit down on the bus stop bench. She was exhausted and having shortness of breath. She said, "Felicia, you were right."

As luck had it, Dr. Oluomolewa was jogging past them. He was worried about her coming out to jog so soon after her near-fatal ill health. She said, "I'm bored and tired of sitting in one place, doing nothing." He, knowing she was an active lady, suggested she walk on their huge compound. He then suggested coming to her villa to discuss an important issue he was worried about later that afternoon. Yemisi feared the worst; maybe the incident at the hospital, with her kissing her husband passionately, bothered him enough to break off their relationship. She did well to contain her fear in the presence of Felicia. Professor Oluomolewa asked Charity to tag along with him so she could pair up with Felicia, as the discussion would be a private matter. Charity saw eye to eye with him and was in agreement.

During Everest's visit, Edukoya called to check up on them, which he routinely did about four times a day. Yemisi was relieved to see Charity accompany Eva, as the notion of his breaking up with her eased. He wouldn't dare rant about their romantic affair in public. When Charity paired up with Felicia, Dr. Oluomolewa took Princess Yemisi to her bedroom to discuss the matter privately. Dr. Oluomolewa expressed his concern for her drastic weight loss in about two weeks of ill health as an indication of a bigger health issue. He said it might be potential liver or kidney issues. He also suggested it might be normal weight loss caused by near-fatal ill health. He suggested running some tests at LUTH, which would include a blood test, a urinary test, and insertion of a camera into her body to see the extent of the damage, if any. He said they'd better discuss it with her husband before running any tests. Edukoya agreed, and he spoke to Dr. Oluomolewa, suggesting thorough tests should be conducted and saying, "I love that woman." Dr. Oluomolewa got on the phone and arranged the tests with the hospital for the following Monday morning.

On Monday morning, Yemisi did not eat anything, and her chauffeur drove her and Felicia to LUTH. Dr. Oluomolewa, knowing how serious it was, left early in the morning to go wait for their arrival. They took eight blood samples, collected a cup of urine, and inserted a camera through her mouth, her urethra, and her anus under general anesthesia. Yemisi and Felicia left for home at about five thirty after eating the meal they'd brought from home at Dr. Oluomolewa's office. For the first time after her ill health, she ate a sizable meal.

After a week, the oncologists invited them to explain the results. The doctors said the result was inconclusive. They suggested that more tests should be done, and if the testing proved inconclusive again, they would know for sure the result was negative. But as of now, they were leaning toward a negative result. One of the oncologists said, "At most Western medical centers, especially in America, they have better equipment but not better expertise to have conclusive results at the first trial."

Kabiyesi Adekunle III, on hearing about the recommendation, started making arrangements for Princess Yemisi to go to an American medical center, preferably UC Davis or Stanford University Medical Center to conduct the test. They chose UC Davis Medical Center to conduct the test. UC Davis Medical Center was near Yuba City, where Mama Akudo still resided. Mama Akudo was on vacation in Nigeria. Since John's death, she had been frequenting Nigeria. However, she sent the keys to her villa and the keys to her brand-new Mercedes-Benz S550 through a local carrier to Edukoya. Kabiyesies, in general, did not travel on a moment's notice unless it was a matter of life and death. Since it was a test, her company with a physician would be more practical. Liver and kidney diseases could take an enormous time before coming to their fatal conclusion. If it was such a disease, she would return to Nigeria anyway to wait for her demise. Tunde was busy with his three new clinics just opened. Bunmi, whom she was close to, was expecting Princess Yemisi's third grandchild and was about ready to deliver at a moment's notice. Edukoya pleaded with Dr. Oluomolewa to be her company, to which he agreed.

Although he was volunteering to accompany her and not required to be paid for his service when the king offered it, nevertheless, the king made adequate financial arrangements to compensate him for the loss of his time as a physician, a lecturer, and the proprietor of his clinics for cardiac patients. They went on first-class tickets on United Airlines. They wanted to take Kabiyesi's jet, but that would have put his enormous traveling activities on hold for two weeks. Princess Yemisi had leased her jet for three months to WHO, and she couldn't renege on the contract. To compound the issue further, Morocco delayed her air space passing due to a late request. Edukoya, Felicia and the twins, Chika and her boys, Charity and her kids, and Tunde and his family bade them goodbye. Princess Yemisi was consumed by thoughts of potential liver and kidney diseases, and the thoughts followed her to America. The only comfort was in the company of her boyfriend, Everest. The company of either her husband or Everest would suffice, the two men she was madly in love with. As the nonstop flight to Houston stabilized in midair, she gave Dr. Oluomolewa a passionate kiss, rested comfortably on his shoulder, and went to sleep.

CHAPTER 47

On their way to Houston, they experienced harsh, turbulent weather conditions in the middle of the Atlantic Ocean. The pilot came on the intercom and announced there was severe turbulence over the Atlantic. He urged the passengers to remain calm and have their seat belts on. Princess Yemisi woke up from her sleep; her seat belt was already on. She leaned over to Everest and gave him a passionate kiss with her lips firmly plastered on his lips and her tongue completely submerged in his mouth. They stayed in that position for about thirty seconds. Princess Yemisi hugged Everest tightly and said, "If I die now, I'll die a very happy woman because I am with the man I truly love."

Those words stunned Dr. Oluomolewa deeply. He wondered, *What about her husband, Edukoya? What about me? Is she the woman I truly love? What will make a man give up on all his responsibilities—his wife, children, lectures, patients, surgeries, and medical clinics—to follow a woman to God knows where?*

For the first time, it dawned on him that this was no longer lust for her affection but a lust for her soul. It might have started with selfish intent and attraction to an attractive woman; however, it had wound up as a till-death path. *She is truly the only woman I'm in love with.*

The turbulence eased considerably. Princess Yemisi was still hugging him and still kissing him at close intervals. That was why Princess Yemisi had specifically requested corner seats at the back of first class—to avoid people looking at them when she was romantically engaged with Everest. Although having sex with him was not in the cards for now, if it happened, she wouldn't be worried at all about it. As a matter of fact, she would welcome it wholeheartedly.

The announcement came for the preparation for landing when they were about three hundred nautical miles away from Houston. Before eating her breakfast, she went to the toilet, used it, and brushed her teeth. When she came back, Dr. Oluomolewa told her he had ordered breakfast for the two. He then excused himself to the toilet. An old lady was taking too long, so Everest went to the executive-class toilet. He used it and brushed his teeth. When he came back, he noticed the old lady was still there, and the same people were waiting in line. He became concerned and alerted one of the flight stewards. The steward banged on the door, and it turned out the old lady did not know how to open the door of the toilet. The steward brought a safety key and unlocked the door from the outside for her. The woman's son, Keodili Obidike, a young millionaire from Arochukwu, Abia State, who owned a chain of lollipop stands in Houston, thanked Dr. Oluomolewa for his observation. They became friends and chatted in the Igbo language.

The breakfast was a blessing for both Yemisi and Everest. They had not eaten any food since yesterday at about three o'clock in the afternoon Nigerian time. The plane had left Murtala Mohammed International Airport at 10:30 p.m. Because they'd had lunch at about three, they had been full and hadn't needed to eat anything on the plane until breakfast. Yemisi ate two toasted slices of bread with an all-natural mango jam, half a bowl of wheat cereal, an egg, a small bowl of mixed fruit, and a cup of tea. Dr. Oluomolewa ate two pancakes, one biscuit, a small bowl of mixed vegetable salad, and a cup of tea.

The steward noticed they didn't drink anything except water and tea for the entire eight-thousand-mile journey, so she gave each a pack of assorted drinks, mainly wine, champagne, wine cooler, and liquors. Each pack contained eighteen four-ounce bottles of liquid beverages.

All through their journey, Dr. Oluomolewa avoided discussing their mission for coming to America. Whenever she brought it up for discussion, he would railroad her into romance, her favorite interest with him. Princess Yemisi knew he didn't want to raise her anxiety, so she intentionally brought up the matter persistently, knowing it would trigger his voluntary romantic advancements, with more romance, more kisses, and more feeling of each other's body. She wondered if it might be a way of getting him to make love to her on the trip after they landed. The plane touched down at George Bush International Airport at nine thirty Houston time. United Airlines took them to their first-class and executive-class lounge. When it came to the international port of entry in the United States, all passengers had to be checked out completely and reboard domestic or international flights to their final destinations. The process could cause huge delays and some mistakes. Some missed their flights due to luggage-claim problems and other protocols. Now technically on US soil, passengers were free to walk out of the airport as free people.

They were free to reside in the United States and go anywhere in the country with zero questions asked. The issue had been raised in the US Congress because it encouraged illegal migration. Princess Yemisi was carrying six big check-in pieces of luggage and two small carry-ons, while Dr. Oluomolewa carried one big suitcase and one carry-on. The customs agents asked them to identify their luggage because an agent's dog had indicated an illegal substance might be contained inside the luggage. It turned out the luggage was not theirs. When the customs agents demanded Princess Yemisi open the luggage, Princess Yemisi's key wouldn't fit. Someone had switched the important luggage of Princess Yemisi with luggage that looked almost identical. An APB was immediately issued, and it halted all traffic in and out of the airport, while Dr. Oluomolewa and Princess Yemisi were detained for interrogation. Within thirty minutes, they found the luggage.

The culprit had switched the tag on similar luggage when it became clear the antidrug agents were watching him. Princess Yemisi was asked to use her key now in the hands of the antidrug agents to open the luggage found. The key matched perfectly. It turned out the culprit's luggage was carrying cocaine with a street value of $2 million. The culprit was watching her, ready to intercept his luggage when it was successfully checked out, which might have resulted in fatality if the princess had hesitated. Luckily, nothing was missing in Princess Yemisi's luggage. The drug enforcement agents delicately searched all their luggage and found nothing of suspicion, and they apologized before setting them free.

It cost them their flight to SFX. They were put on another flight to San Francisco International. The drug agents made the arrangements with another United Airlines flight. Meanwhile, Kayode, Princess Yemisi's nephew, Iyabo's third child, was waiting patiently for them to take them to Yuba City, near Sacramento, where they would be residing. Most airlines offered free limousine service to their first-class passengers. United Airlines offered it too. The limo chauffeur was patiently waiting for their arrival, as he had been informed of the delay. The limousine took them to Yuba City, and Kayode tagged along in his own car. The limousine was supposed to go within a one-hundred-mile radius from the airport. Yuba City was about

140 miles from the airport. The limo driver called his boss. They contacted the airline, and the drug enforcement agents finally covered the difference. All the discussions were quietly made absent from Princess Yemisi's and Dr. Oluomolewa's ears.

Kayode and the limo driver brought in the luggage. Dr. Oluomolewa wanted to help, but Kayode flatly refused his help. Iyabo, now in her late seventies, was the eldest child of Renmi Lawrence Adeniji. With the exception of Iyabo's eldest son, Patrick, all her children had been born and raised in America. However, the Yoruban traditional, cultural, disciplinary, and respectful attitude never for a moment left them. Her sons still bowed their heads when greeting an elderly person, and her daughters knelt briefly before greeting their elders, so it was no surprise to Princess Yemisi that her nephew extended such respect to Dr. Everest Oluomolewa. It surprised Everest how fluent Kayode, his siblings, and Iyabo's oldest grandchildren, all born and raised in California, were in the Yoruban language and Yoruban culture and traditions. Kayode had gone to Nigeria and married a Yoruban girl. He'd insisted on performing the whole nine yards of the traditional wedding ceremony first before the church wedding ceremony. Kayode had gone to UC Berkeley for his undergraduate in mechanical engineering and earned his PhD in industrial history at Stanford University. He also had a law degree from Golden Gate University. He worked with Silicon Valley firms to write their history. He also taught World Industrial Revolution History part-time at San Francisco State University.

By that time, it was about eleven o'clock at night. Dr. Oluomolewa flatly refused Kayode to leave for the Bay Area late that night. All three went grocery shopping at the nearby Save Mart store. The store closed at midnight. For the first time, Dr. Oluomolewa witnessed Princess Yemisi driving a car. She drove Mama Akudo's Benz to the store.

The following morning, Dr. Adeniji, PhD, finished eating breakfast with them and took off for work in the Bay Area. Princess Yemisi still had her California driver's license, which was current. She continuously renewed her license. She drove them to UC Davis Medical Center in Sacramento, where they booked an appointment to start testing first thing Monday morning. Akudo had bought a brand-new Mercedes-Benz S550. She offered it for Yemisi's use during her stay.

CHAPTER 48

Princess Yemisi and Dr. Everest Oluomolewa told the clinic they came from Nigeria and were working on a tight timetable. Dr. Oluomolewa did something he rarely did: he introduced himself as a physician. He also told them he taught medicine at the University of Nigeria, Lagos, and was a cardiothoracic surgeon, with patients on life support awaiting his soon arrival. As for Princess Yemisi, Professor Oluomolewa introduced her as the crown princess of Orissa Kingdom, who had an ND and managed a progressive empire. All the credentials were relayed to the hospital to let them know that they were managing tight ships and that time was not on their side. It worked, and UC Davis promised to finish the whole exercise in two weeks' time if they found a surgeon on time who would insert the camera if it was deemed necessary. Instead of three cameras being inserted, they would insert one sophisticated three-dimensional camera from her mouth, which would view all the organs from all sides, especially the kidney and the liver, the reason they'd come there.

The first tests would be blood and urinary samples. There would be four blood samples drawn and a cup of her urine. The test results would determine a more complex and sophisticated test that included the insertion of a camera. The hospital scheduled her blood draw for Thursday. The hospital gave them the option to go to the local blood bank center in Yuba City; that way, they could come to the hospital once to obtain the result. UC Davis Medical Center was located in

Sacramento, which was a distance away from Yuba City, where they were residing. The blood and urine samples would be collected there and sent to the hospital for analysis. Princess Yemisi and Dr. Oluomolewa agreed. Seeing Princess Yemisi and Dr. Oluomolewa together, one would have concluded they were a match made in heaven and were married to the wrong persons. Her pains were his pains. They were without a doubt in love with each other.

Iyabo was waiting for them at John Okorocha's villa when they got home from Sacramento. They were parked at the gate for a brief moment before the gardener, on the introduction of Iyabo as Princess Yemisi's elder sister, opened the gate for them. Iyabo and her eldest daughter, Iyadele, came to visit Yemisi. Iyadele, forty-one, was the fourth child of Iyabo. She was well Americanized, though she still greeted elders with the common respectful greetings of the Yoruba tribe and spoke the Yoruban language fluently. To show how Americanized she was, she interjected her opinions in discussions uninvited by her elders. Secondly, when Dr. Oluomolewa was bringing in their groceries from the car, she felt unconcerned until her mother pinched her to help bring in the groceries. Thirdly, she was the one to question the absence of the king when his wife was in dire need of help. As she said, "Giving a goat a fresh yam to keep."

Dr. Oluomolewa was outside bringing in the groceries and didn't hear her. Princess Yemisi went into the kitchen to get a cup of water for her elder sister to take her medications. She overheard something Iyadele murmured, but she could not make out what she said exactly. When Princess Yemisi asked what she was saying, she answered in a typical arrogant American way, "Nothing." It came after her mother gave her an ugly look. Iyabo had plenty of health issues. She was in a motorized wheelchair and used an oxygen tank. Iyabo had complications from emphysema and liver health issues, just as her husband had. She and her husband had depended on each other, and Iyabo's husband's death four years ago had brought enormous health issues on her. When she'd lost him, she'd fallen apart, because he was her life.

Iyabo's husband, Frederick Adeniji, had been sick for a long time. He underwent numerous surgeries. His final wish was to be buried in Nigeria, at his compound in Okitipupa, Ondo State, where he hadn't lived for sixty-four years. His extended nephews resided there now. He lived in America for sixty-four years and died at the age of eighty-nine. Frederick worked for the City and County of San Francisco until he retired. He met Iyabo, a young, attractive, pretty girl, at a mutual friend's get-to-know-other-Nigerians party. He instantly fell in love with her. He proposed to her on the spot, and Iyabo, being a girl who knew where she was going, said, "Why not?" rather casually. Iyabo thought Frederick was joking as a means of getting her in bed for a quick and disgusting one-night stand.

It was the summer of 1964. The breathtaking Iyabo had just arrived in America. She was in a graduate program at the University of San Francisco (USF), where she later obtained her PhD in industrial management. Iyabo taught at Santa Clara University and later at UC Berkeley and was an industrial management consultant until she retired due to her ill health. Every Nigerian man in the Bay Area, especially from the Yoruba tribe, single or married, wanted to sleep with Iyabo Adeniji. She fooled men, as she was termed loose, flexible, and stunningly attractive. The men wined and dined her, and quite a few paid her rent for months. The men were only after one thing, but she was willing to give that to only one man, the luckiest man on earth, who became her husband. The precious cargo hidden under her panties was locked up with her self-made key.

Frederick immediately realized that Iyabo lumped him in with other guys, so he backed off. Meanwhile, he was going through a bitter divorce with his soon-to-be ex-wife, Alice Adeniji, a white American woman. They had two boys. He was on the verge of losing his alien immigrant status during the divorce because his wife claimed he'd married her to obtain his green card. The judge, Judge Spoon, threw the case out of court because they had repeatedly consummated their marriage, by her own admission, as evidenced by their two boys. Judge Spoon gave technical custody to the mother with no child or spousal support exchanging hands. When a judge issued technical custody, that meant the day-to-day minor decisions about the child's welfare rested on the custodial parent; however, in significant instances, such as a school field trip or relocation, the other party must be consulted and approve before the final decision was made. The judge granted them fifty-fifty custodial rights, even on holidays. Because the spouses were gainfully employed with equal measurable income and the children's custody was evenly shared, there would be no child or spousal support issued.

Frederick sat down in the corner of the living room, where they were having the party, upset by her answer. A guilty conscience got the better part of Iyabo, and when the next music came on, Iyabo boldly walked across the room with all eyes on her stunning beauty and asked Frederick for a dance. He accepted it. They danced all night throughout the remainder of the party. Frederick offered to give her a ride to her hostel at the University of San Francisco. She hesitated a little bit but finally agreed to the offer. It was the first time they'd met each other, and she wanted to know if his proposal was serious or if he was just trying to get her in bed with him.

He reiterated his seriousness; however, when she heard he was legally married, she said, "When you're through with whatever you are doing with her, then you can come back to me, and if I am still available, I might consider it." Frederick took it as a no. In his mind, she was too attractive for men to miss the chance to get with her.

Frederick's wife argued for the court to give them one year and six months more to work things out because she was still in love with him and said, "I love this man." Judge Spoon sided with her and granted her request. It was almost four and a half years before Frederick met Iyabo again.

In the summer of 1967, civil war broke out in Nigeria, and America was in the heat of war with North Vietnam. In Nigeria, the Igbo people and the entire eastern region, on May 31, 1967, separated from the union with the creation of a new nation called Biafra. The federal government of Nigeria declared war on the eastern region and launched a massive offensive attack to halt the secession. The separation came as a result of the federal government of Nigeria's lack of action when genocide took place in the mid-1960s in the northern portion of the country. The Hausa tribe slaughtered thousands of Igbo people who lived in the northern region of the country, which was the Hausa tribe's homeland. To compound the situation, the Nigerian rich crude oil reserves were in the southeast. That fueled the appetite for both sides to engage in the war. By the winter of 1970, after two and a half years, the conflict ended. The southeast, mainly the Igbo people, had suffered untold casualties estimated to the tune of three million people and counting.

The civil conflict in Nigeria was carried over to America. The Bay Area wing of the Nigerian Foreign Student Association, which was chaired by John Okorocha, held a series of meetings to address the problem. At one such meeting, John Okorocha, who was fluent in the Yoruba, Igbo, Hausa, and Efik languages, spoke eloquently in the languages for calm and unity and aimed at uniting Nigerians as one in the Bay Area, even while the easterners' separation was, at that moment, successful. He spoke about his dearest friend, Edukoya Adekunle, a Yoruba man. He spoke about all his male and female friends in all parts of Nigeria. He added humor in his speech when he asked, "Do you know how I came to speak the key tribal languages in my country?"

Iyabo, who was in the meeting, shouted, "How?"

He said, "Women," and everybody burst into laughter. He added, "Nigeria is rich in everything, including our fine girls."

At that moment, all eyes were on Iyabo Adeniji. The people murmured, "What an attractive girl."

He said, "This understanding prompted me to understand the languages these fine girls spoke. How can you go to your in-laws' house without knowing their language? It will make you the odd man out. When you speak her language, your potential in-laws associate you as one of their own. And you become one whole family. We Nigerians are one whole family, and I can't forget my dearest friend, Edukoya, who happened to be of a different tribe from me." He spoke for calmness and to wait and see how things would turn out.

After John's speech, Iyabo, now a PhD holder, was taken by his physical attributes and eloquence. She walked up to him to introduce herself and ask for his phone number. She was attracted to him. Frederick Adeniji, who was one of the organizers of the meeting, walked up to her and reintroduced himself again to her. Iyabo, who was brilliant, never forgot a face and murmured, "Come see this Manoo come to put sand in my gari," speaking in broken English. John Okorocha, sensing their previous acquaintance, excused himself from the scene. She said, "Look what you've done now."

Frederick said, "He is a married man."

She said, "So? I only want him to be the father of my baby." They burst into laughter. That sense of humor made her fall in love with him instantly.

They were married in the fall of 1968, shortly after her sister Yemisi Adeniji and her son, Patrick Adeniji, arrived in America. Yemisi was a roommate with her elder sister, Iyabo, in San Francisco. Shortly after Iyabo's wedding, Yemisi moved to San Jose, where she attended San Jose State University with a major in nursing. The closeness of the two remaining sisters of Lawrence Adeniji prompted Princess Yemisi to pay for all her elder sister's medical bills to date.

CHAPTER 49

Three was a crowd, but how about four and the entire family of Iyabo Adeniji? Iyabo's children and the eldest grandchildren took turns helping out Princess Yemisi and Dr. Everest Oluomolewa. They waited on them hand and foot. Kayode's eldest daughter, Funmilayo, and her cousin Mary volunteered to live with them throughout the duration of their stay in America. John Okorocha's villa had ten large bedrooms and four sitting areas. The beautiful villa could accommodate all of them with enormous space leftover. Princess Yemisi did not appreciate their offer but saw the wisdom in it and cheerfully muted her disappointment. She didn't say no; instead, she pretended to persuade them to stay when they made the offer. Any hint to the family that Yemisi and Everest were lusting for each other would have been a moral stain that could not be washed out. It would have confirmed what Iyadele said. The whole family of Iyabo was there when the girls made the offer. Dr. Oluomolewa said, "That is very thoughtful of them," and he showed his appreciation by showing them their rooms.

It ruined all Princess Yemisi's plans to be affectionate with Everest. She had hoped this time there would be no more excuses, and to get his body inside hers was her ultimate dying wish because she loved him extraordinarily. Her thoughts and imagination ran wild. Soon she would be like cooked vegetables, gasping for the last breath of her life, if the test returned positive. She feared that no man would want her, especially the two lovers in her life: her husband, Edukoya, and her challenging boyfriend and the real love of her life, Everest. She would die in self-pity, and Everest, especially, would feel so sorry for her that only his comfort would be the best he was willing to offer her.

At that vegetable stage, she dreaded that his making love to her boldly would be gone forever. She reminisced all through the night, and she started to cry. Everest's room was adjacent to hers, and he heard her crying. He came over to console her. Her two nieces heard her cry, and they came over to console her too. They met Everest at the door. They all went into her room together and circled around her. She reached out to Everest with both arms and said, "Hold me." He held her, putting his right arm across her shoulders, and she held him with her arms wrapped around his waist and burst into tears that gushed down her cheeks.

He consoled her by telling her he was not going anywhere. Everest promised her that he, the king, and all the members of her family would be there to see her through this. He added, "Forever."

That was the word she wanted to hear. "Forever," she said. "You promise?"

He answered, "Unquestionably yes."

She was calm. Funmi and Mary witnessed a classic case of romance, and they loved it without thinking out of the ordinary. The two girls talked about his method of healing and conciliation and termed it "a doctor's touch." They felt that was why her doctor followed her in case of her falls.

Princess Yemisi thanked them for their concern and praised them. She said, "Kayode and Wale's children are very concerned and respectful children. All of Sister Iyabo's children are very respectful."

Dr. Oluomolewa nodded in agreement. When the kids wanted to go to their rooms, she insisted they should stay for a while. Princess Yemisi thought Dr. Oluomolewa would leave with them too. But when he assured her he would stay for a while until she went to sleep, she wished them sweet dreams in a hurry. The girls went to bed, happy about their great-aunt's considerate physician.

Princess Yemisi told Everest to take the girls to the rooms available down the hallway, the rooms farthest from her and Dr. Oluomolewa's rooms. She did it on purpose so the girls would not hear any romantic noises or the noise of the bed squeaking when they were making love. Still, one had to carry the ark of God with two hands. The young kids opted to help them clean up, and they deserved a little respect. With their presence, the villa was kept immaculately spotless. They cooked, washed the dishes, vacuumed the carpet, mopped the kitchen floor, mopped the marble hallway, cleaned the bathrooms, and dusted the windows. They even washed their clothes, folded them, and ironed them. They had the villa in better shape than when Princess Yemisi had moved in. When Okorocha's children came to check up on Princess Yemisi, they were stunned to see the villa sparkling. They relayed their astonishing observations to their mother, Mama Akudo, who was vacationing in Mbaise, Nigeria. They said to her she had been wasting money with her present maid, who was on vacation for the duration of Mama Akudo's vacation in Mbaise.

Funmilayo and Mary were not just cousins; they were best friends. They helped each other in all ways. They were the same age, born a day apart in the same hospital, UC San Francisco Medical Center. They looked like twins born by different mothers. They'd gained admission to Stanford University that fall and were majoring in premedicine. They looked like their grandma Iyabo at that age, breathtakingly attractive. Iyabo was still a stunning beauty if one closely looked at her face and physique. Unlike with Princess Yemisi, her beauty had been severely compromised by her excessive weight gain and health issues. Frederick had smoked heavily and suffered from respiratory problems for twenty-five years.

Iyabo had joined Frederick and smoked to control her weight gain. When she'd stopped smoking due to her doctor's advice, her weight gain had become excessive due to the gain in her appetite. Also, unlike Princess Yemisi, Iyabo ate for the taste of food and not for the nutritional value. Iyabo could put away fried chicken, hamburgers, hot dogs, and a host of fast-food meals as if they were going out of business. She rarely exercised. Though Funmi and Mary loved their grandma, they modeled their lives after their Auntie Yemisi. Still, at sixty-three, she was enviably attractive, slim, and fit. They wanted to be like her. They didn't indulge in poor lifestyle habits. They watched what they ate and did regular exercise. They didn't take their beauty for granted. They also were smart and were not lacking.

When the girls left for their rooms, Dr. Oluomolewa tried to find out what really was making her cry. She said, "If this disease is proven positive, you won't be able to do this with me." She pulled her lips to his and gave him a persistent kiss. "And you won't do this to me at all." She took his hand and placed it on her vagina.

As she placed his hand on her vagina, his penis became erect quickly, ready to penetrate her vagina, but he murmured, "Respect for the kids." He covered her vagina with her nightgown.

They slept together for about four hours, wrapping themselves up in the oversize beddings, before Eva went to his room around five thirty. The girls were still fast asleep.

The blood bank had Yemisi's blood sample drawn in Yuba City. They were now waiting for the results on the following Wednesday, when they would see the UC Davis oncologist. The samples were put on an emergency fast track. On Friday, Iyabo came to spend the weekend with her baby sister to catch up on old times. Kayode brought her again. He took Dr. Oluomolewa to a friend's house in Marysville, Yuba City's twin city, for a cocktail drink. Kayode left the following morning and would come back again to pick up his mother the following Monday afternoon.

CHAPTER 50

Iyabo and Yemisi talked all night on Sunday. They went to bed at three thirty Monday morning. Iyabo was leaving later that Monday evening. Usually, Edukoya waited till 5:00 p.m. Nigerian time to call his wife to find out the updates and latest developments on her health and the tests. Everest called his wife, Charity, by 10:00 p.m. California time to see how the family was doing. That day, Everest and Princess Yemisi discussed Iyabo's visit and her children's relentless help. The king and Charity were grateful and thankful for their help. The king said, "Yes, Iyabo instilled some home commonsense values in all her children, and the result is a respectful display such as this. Even most home kids don't behave like this." Charity insisted on thanking Mama Iyabo, as she called her.

The phone was handed over to Mama Iyabo, thereby briefly interrupting Charity's conversation with Princess Yemisi. Iyabo, thinking Charity was a Yoruba woman, responded to her greetings in the Yoruba language: *"Adukwe Uomo e mi"* (You're welcome, my child). Though Charity did not speak Yoruba, she understood every bit of Yoruba's language, including their idioms. In fact, Charity could write and read in Yoruba fluently. Some of her husband's relatives said she had Igbo pride and arrogance. She understood and wrote the Yoruba language perfectly, but she wouldn't speak it. Her justification came in the form of a joke but well meant. She said to most of her husband's relatives, "You can understand Igbo—why don't you speak it?"

The king invited Iyabo for an official visit to his palace in Orissa. Iyabo joked, telling the king she had visited her sister's place several times, and what would be the difference this time? The king replied, "You came as your baby sister's guest, but this time, you'll be coming as Kabiyesi of Orissa's guest."

She responded, "Amen, if life permits me."

Little did she know that visit would be her last visit with her baby sister, Yemisi. Iyabo died just after Yemisi and Dr. Oluomolewa left for Nigeria a month later. She died in her sleep with no struggle, just a peaceful rest.

In Okorocha's villa, Dr. Oluomolewa pulled Yemisi aside and told her to spend as much time as possible with her only sister, as he was afraid this would be her last time together with her. He said he was talking as a physician after checking all her vital signs. Princess Yemisi said, "Since we're on this topic, what about my vital signs?"

Dr. Oluomolewa jokingly asked her, "As your physician or as your boyfriend?"

It was the first time Princess Yemisi had heard him say *boyfriend*. She was overjoyed to hear him associate her as his girlfriend. She gave him a romantic kiss with a hug, and tears of joy dripped down from her eyes. She said, "Both."

Dr. Oluomolewa said in broken English, "You *dey kamkwe*."

In the evening, with daylight savings, the night came at about eight forty-five. It was Saturday, the second day of Iyabo's visit to the villa. All the family of Frederick Adeniji were at the villa. Iyabo knew her baby sister was an active woman; however, she didn't know how active her younger sister was at the age of sixty-three, a little shy of hitting sixty-four. "Amazing," she kept saying. They staged a basketball competition, with Dr. Oluomolewa and Princess Yemisi leading their teams. Kayode stood still and watched her aunt dribble like a twenty-year-old professional basketball player. Yemisi was a fierce competitor when it came to competitive games. Dr. Oluomolewa loved her for that reason. She did not act her age when it came to anything she did.

In her tight-fitting sportswear, with sweat gushing down her pretty body, well soaked, one could see the trails of wetness on her butt, and the sweat-soaked lining of her light blue shorts highlighted her private parts. Her breathtaking beauty prompted one of Wale's guests, a middle-aged white man, to shout, "You are beautiful! Marry me!" Princess Yemisi, in all categories of life, was desirable and stunning.

Dr. Oluomolewa could not keep his eyes away from her. He responded to Wale's friend's request and shouted, "She is taken!" He immediately added, "By a king." His response spared the embarrassment of assumed ownership of her, but it didn't erase Iyadele's suspicion.

Iyadele played ball, though not well and not much. She watched Everest's and Yemisi's body contact and saw he was the only one to lift her up from her falls. She concluded something was fishy with their relationship. She told her mother she suspected Princess Yemisi and Dr. Everest Oluomolewa were lovers. However, it erased almost all her suspicion when her mother told her the amount of money Dr. Oluomolewa was getting paid for his caretaking of Princess Yemisi. Kabiyesi Adekunle III paid Dr. Oluomolewa about sixty-five million nairas, approximately $190,000, to care for his wife. Iyadele said, "That will do it. I will wipe her butt for that amount of money."

After the game was over, Iyabo told Princess Yemisi there was nothing wrong with her. She was impressed by her baby sister's performance. Funmi and Mary had told the family how active she was, as they played every evening with her; however, the rest of the family still had underestimated their aunt. And it was amazing how Dr. Oluomolewa, at the age of fifty-three, a doctor practicing in Nigeria, was so active. His belly was flat, and so were the bellies of Charity, Yemisi, Edukoya, Felicia, and Chika. In fact, all the immediate members of Princess Yemisi's family on her husband's side had flat stomachs and full hair. They were disciplined, indulging in sports activities a lot, and they lived a healthy, active lifestyle as a whole. They ate small portions of food, and they ate food based largely on nutritional value. They could afford luxuries, but they chose to remain self-tamed.

When it came to food, Iyabo's family was not as disciplined as Yemisi's family. Iyadele was a pretty woman, but with time, her weight gain had taken an upper hand on her. It had begun to show the signs, but she'd never admit it. She often looked at herself in the mirror and admired how thin she was. Iyabo's eldest son, Patrick, fifty-nine years old, born out of wedlock in Nigeria, was all belly, but his wife was slim, fit, and pretty. She joined Dr. Oluomolewa's team and played well. They had two children, both girls. The kids were grown, had finished college, and were married. They had three kids each, all boys. Patrick had been diagnosed with lung cancer and kidney failure. He was presently on dialysis because of his kidney failure. Still, he would not quit smoking cigarettes. Iyabo's grandchildren refused to take after their parents and their grandparents. They, on their own, had cultivated strict discipline when it came to food. Unlike their parents and grandparents, they didn't smoke and seldom indulged in alcoholic beverages. Wale and Kayode's older sons were positioning themselves to join major-league teams in basketball and football, respectively.

With every member of Iyabo's family there, there was no point for Princess Yemisi and Dr. Oluomolewa to visit them one by one. Seeing their aunt Princess Yemisi, for the first time for most of them, especially Iyabo's younger grandchildren and great-grandchildren, they saw for the first time what royalty was all about. They heard the governor of California had called her to pay his respects to the crown princess, and they understood why their aunt Princess Yemisi, as pretty as could be, was an adorable goddess.

By ten o'clock that Saturday night, all the members of the family were gone, except Funmilayo, Mary, and Iyabo. The family cleaned up their mess and left the premises immaculate. Afterward, Princess Yemisi went to take a shower. Dr. Oluomolewa and the girls retired to their rooms to take showers too, and they went to bed. Before the girls retired to their rooms, Princess Yemisi gave good-night kisses and said, "Sweet dreams." Iyabo had long slept with medication. Iyabo had emphysema, and she walked slowly with a cane and used a motorized wheelchair to get around. Princess Yemisi's good-night kisses to the girls were to prevent them from having any reason to disturb her romantic engagement with Eva. Everest usually left his door unlocked, unless he was dressing, out of respect for the girls and Iyabo, who had come for the weekend. Since it was night and the girls had gone to bed, he assumed there would be no disturbances, so he left the door unlocked for a quick emergency response for the two women.

Princess Yemisi walked into his room without knocking, and for the first time during the trip, she found Everest naked, walking to the bathroom to take a badly needed shower. Princess Yemisi quickly undressed, locked the door, and followed him to the bathroom. She said, "I might as well take my shower here."

As the warm water dropped on them, Funmilayo knocked on Dr. Oluomolewa's door with intense force. She said that when they went to say good night to Grandma, she was lifeless and didn't respond. Princess Yemisi was quiet in Dr. Oluomolewa's bathroom, naked, with the warm water dripping all over her remarkable skin. Everest came to the door. He put on his robe and carried his first-aid kit. As soon as they left for Iyabo's room, Princess Yemisi ran to her room, put on her nightgown, and followed them.

It happened that the tube connected to Iyabo's oxygen tank had come loose, so she wasn't getting sufficient oxygen to breathe. Dr. Oluomolewa fixed it within seconds, and she could breathe again.

It was another close call. If Funmi had found out they were lovers, she would have lost all respect for her dearly beloved auntie forever. It was then that the respect of the two girls became meaningful to Princess Yemisi. By God's grace, Funmi had chosen to knock on Everest's door first.

After Everest stabilized Iyabo, everybody went to bed. Eva and Yemisi continued with their shower together. They talked all night and finally went to bed together in Everest's room, cuddling together but without making love, out of respect for Iyabo, Funmi, and Mary, though Princess Yemisi, the sex-starved goddess, tried in vain to persuade Dr. Oluomolewa to make love to her.

CHAPTER 51

Princess Yemisi, cuddling in bed with Everest, felt as if heaven had sent him for her ultimate comfort. She couldn't have relaxed and rested as much as she would have liked without sleeping next to him. Iyabo's near death consumed her thoughts throughout the night. If Dr. Oluomolewa hadn't been there, Princess Yemisi would have been talking about her only living sister's funeral arrangements. Dr. Oluomolewa, the on-time doctor, had done it again. Princess Yemisi reflected on her near-death experience and how the good doctor had saved her. An ambulance, as quick as they were, would not have saved Iyabo. It would have been the death of the only sister she had in the world. Iyabo could have died as a result of a loose oxygen tube. It was as simple as that.

Yemisi was used to Eva snoring; after all, it was not the first time they'd slept together. In fact, she embraced it to see her man got his needed rest. She woke him up around three o'clock that Sunday morning to air her deep-felt thoughts. Dr. Oluomolewa was quickly on his feet, thinking it was another close call. Princess Yemisi turned, facing him, and said, "Listen to me carefully. I love you. I love you with all my heart. Stack Edukoya next to you, and whom will I choose? As much as it is a tough choice to make, there is no contest. I will choose you. I mean it."

As she said those difficult words, tears gushed from her eyes to her cheeks and onto the bedding, because it was an emotional betrayal that was unconscionable. She continued. "I have never loved anyone as much as I love you, including my parents, my children, my husband, and my siblings. I love Edukoya as my husband, who has done everything in his power to make me the happiest woman on earth. Edukoya makes me very proud of myself, and I will forever owe him enormous gratitude. I'm very grateful for his kindness to me. Edukoya has done everything in his power to make sure I remain happy, and I appreciate all his kindness to me. But I hate my heart right now because my heart is telling me that the man I really love is you."

The tears gushed down more but eased considerably when Everest took her fingers and kissed them. She responded with a kiss on his lips. She scissor-crossed her legs against his legs and said to him, "Make love to me now."

Everest didn't know what to say. The thoughts had given him a huge concern and a weak erection. He was consumed with Princess Yemisi's confession. *Choosing me over the king!* he said to himself. *I feel the same way toward her, but I dare not say it to another ear, even Yemisi's, because it will be the utmost betrayal of my love for Charity and my children. Her trust and her commitment as my wife and the mother of my children. Charity trusts me, and she has given me every comfort to make me very happy. Though she is most of the time late to romance, she has made up for this shortfall in many ways. Even in times of bitter disputes, she never says no to my sexual advances. Charity loves me.*

The more he thought about Charity, the more his erection weakened. Yemisi held his penis in both hands and tried in vain with a blow job and massage to give him an erection. His penis occasionally got erect but then fell back to a crawl. At the intervals of his erections, Princess Yemisi would insert his penis inside her vagina, but it soon got weak and came out. She was soaking wet and horny. She tried in vain to have his penis hold steady in her vagina till she reached orgasm, but his weak penis exited her vagina quickly. Finally, she gave up and murmured, "Men."

Everest heard it but decided not to respond, to avoid encouraging more sexual activities, because he was not in the mood. Yemisi was angry with him. She knew he was thinking about the trust he had for his wife, and that trust had ruined every act of romance between them for that moment. She said to herself the comfort was that she at least could force his penis into her body when it was not totally weak. She concluded that half a loaf of bread was better than none. Unfortunately, it was not a full erection, and he did not penetrate into her body but let her do it. At best, it was a shallow penetration with the aid of the soaking vaginal fluid coming from her. It also was a nonstarter for sexual intercourse. He tried to convince himself that sexual intercourse had not taken place just now, but Yemisi reached partial orgasm anyway with his weak erection submerged totally inside her vagina.

Princess Yemisi didn't verbally abuse him; she let her silence do the talking for her. It was about four thirty in the morning, and she excused herself from his bed and went back to her room. She did not sleep for the rest of the morning. She hated Eva for that moment.

Dr. Oluomolewa did not sleep either for the rest of the morning. He too hated himself for not saying how he truly felt about this stunning, pretty, and amazing woman. Maybe an honest understanding would have cured his temporary erectile dysfunction. As he had these thoughts, his penis stood up, but it was of no use now; her ship had sailed.

Princess Yemisi's eyes were wide open for the rest of the morning as she thought about her hope and her future. She thought about everything under the sun. With her wildest imagination, she thought the king might have been having a secret romantic affair with Chika, but she quickly brushed the thought aside. The king was now in Lagos, having left Felicia in Orissa. His excuse was that Felicia was preoccupied with her lectures at Orissa Polytechnic. Yemisi had begged the king to keep his eyes on things going on in Lagos while she was away, so the king came on Friday mornings and left on Saturday evenings and would do so until Princess Yemisi came back. She returned her suspicion back to Chika. Chika was stunningly attractive, and any man in his right mind would want to go to bed with her and keep her there forever, she thought. Chika was smart, athletic, and educated. Chika was an Igbo woman with enormous common sense. Chika was romantic, and the king liked her a lot. Chika was young and full of energy and never aged. Chika had never had a man or boyfriend come over to visit her, other than her polite and respectful relatives. She finally decided Chika was respectful and could not betray her friendship and her trust. She would never ask her about her ridiculous assumption about her having sexual affairs with her husband, and she dared not ask the king about it, as it would have amounted to an insult. She just had to catch them in the act.

She said, "I hate men. I have thrown myself to this stupid man with no response." She meant Everest. If Edukoya was having romantic affairs with Chika, then he technically had three wives. At Edukoya's age, with three attractive women chasing after him who were educated and full of energy, it was bound to wear him down soon. She began to feel sorry for him. She returned to thinking of Chika and asked herself, "Why not?" She said to herself if that was to be the case, she would encourage her just to see how Felicia felt about it. She then dismissed the whole idea altogether again, saying, "Chikanele is too smart to do that to me." Her thoughts went to

Felicia. She asked herself, "Why do women, single or married, like married men a lot?" She answered the question herself: "Maybe the forbidden fruit, safety, and security, especially with an attractive, rich, and considerate king, such as my husband." She then added, "These are too-easy answers." She then concluded that money had nothing to do with it at all, especially when the women were highly educated and extremely attractive. They could have gotten rich single men of their choice. She concluded, "It is the moral make of the man, the self-sense of giving, the self-sense of inclusion, and the self-sense of consideration. Those are the qualities that attract these women to married men or unmarried men, and my husband possesses these three qualities in abundance."

She went on. "Men who possess these qualities are very few in number, and they can be trusted. Women are attracted to them, married or unmarried." She thought of an example: her niece Iyadele, her niece-in-law Susan, Patrick's wife, and even her grandnieces, Funmilayo and Mary, now of age, were all attracted to Dr. Oluomolewa, even though they knew he was a happily married man. The reason the kids volunteered to help them was because of Everest. They were useful to impress him. Unfortunately, men with those exceptional qualities were few in number, and most were taken. As a result, the married women had to share their quality husbands with the women looking for those qualities in men. Yemisi said to herself, "These qualities are hidden, nicely tucked into the moral well-being of the man. Marriage exposes them, acting as a displayed billboard to show these qualities in the man who has them." She concluded, "Selfish and self-centered men are saved bets for women intending to have their husbands exclusively."

Everest was in his bed with his eyes wide open, looking at the ceiling, imagining what it would be like to give the wonderful

Princess Yemisi 100 percent of his attention. He wondered why he couldn't have sex with her and damn the consequences. He considered that Yemisi had all grown children, so they did not need anyone to set social, ethical, and moral standards for them. The king had two wives, and judging from the way he made constant eye contact with Chika, he probably had three wives. That gave Princess Yemisi reason to stray from her marriage with the king. But he had to worry about Charity, a woman who gave him plenty to come back home to. Charity had not denied his affection. She had never denied him sex, even in the heat of a serious dispute. She always was excited and cheerful to see him back home. She was always dragging him to bed to have sex with a genuine effort to participate fully in the act, even though she experienced shortfalls when the sexual act got heated.

Charity had never questioned his manhood and never doubted his love, respect, commitment, loyalty, and devotion to her. She trusted him. Whenever she had a reason to doubt him, she always approached him directly and thoughtfully. His explanation was always sufficient for her. There was no yelling or foul language. The children never heard a word about their disputes when they occurred. Charity would never make a fool of herself by invading her suspicions on another woman. She was too educated to indulge in such nonsense. She muted her jealousy and accepted his explanation. He had never cheated on her. Charity was always considerate, going out of her way to do good deeds for others. She positioned him as the center of her universe and with pride.

Charity was extremely considerate and was a pretty and desirable woman. Charity was intelligent, with a doctorate degree in education. Princess Yemisi had been entrusted into his care by the king and, most importantly, by Charity, who called her Mama Yemisi. Going to bed with Mama Yemisi was like going to bed with Charity's biological mother, and that was a nonstarter for him. Besides, a dog did not chew the bone that hung on its neck; it was the bone to keep.

It was about seven o'clock Sunday morning. The girls had made breakfast for the family. Princess Yemisi and Everest took their showers separately in their rooms and got ready for church. Iyabo was doing well, and she got ready for church service too. She thanked Dr. Oluomolewa for saving her life. Yemisi couldn't hold her anger any longer because she loved him so much. She took him to her room to have a chat with him, and in the process, they kissed passionately and made up.

PART 13

DEAR SISTER IYA IYABO

CHAPTER 52

Princess Yemisi could not think enough about her only living sister, Iyabo. Seeing her in almost a vegetative state triggered endless tears and memories. Iyabo was the first of five children of Lawrence Renmi Adeniji. Their father was an area manager with the old United Africa Company (UAC), and their mother sewed dresses for a living. Iyabo was about fifteen years older than Princess Yemisi. She went to Orissa Girls' Secondary School and got her bachelor's from the University of Nigeria, Ibadan, with first-class honors in industrial management, a feat rarely seen in those days, especially from female students. When her father encountered death due to uncontrollable high blood pressure, Iyabo's accumulated scholarship funds came in handy for the family, as they were able to subsidize greatly the funds from her mother's sewing and the little money coming from her late daddy's pension fund from UAC to pay for Isaac's secondary school fees. Isaac was a year and three months younger than Iyabo.

After Isaac's birth, Comfort encountered acute bleeding. It took five years for her to conceive another child, but her pregnancies from then onward went smoothly as long as she took at least three years before she conceived again. After her graduation from UNIBADAN, Iyabo went to work for Liver Brothers Nigerian as a manager, through which she helped raise her three younger remaining siblings and her son, Patrick. Iyabo raised Yemisi and Isake, the last-born of her mother, as her own children. Iyabo stopped Yemisi from calling her Iya (Mom), and now she addressed her as Sister Iyabo; however, Isake, her baby brother, continued to address Iyabo as Mommy. Iyabo put all her siblings through secondary school and university. She was the architect of Yemisi's acquiring federal scholarship funds to study in the United States. She sent for her and for her son, Patrick, to live with her in San Francisco.

Yemisi, Isake, and Patrick lived with Iyabo right after she got housing accommodations in a government-reserved area in Apapa, Lagos, working for Liver Brothers. Liver Brothers subsidized her three-bedroom flat with a single-carriage garage. Yemisi was eight years old when Iyabo took her. Neighbors used to associate Yemisi and the two boys as Iyabo's children. Iyabo wouldn't let any harm happen to them. She bathed them one after the other, hand-washed their clothes, and ironed their clothes. She paid for a babysitter to watch over them when she was at work. She dressed them up, braided Yemisi's hair frequently, and took the boys periodically to the barbershop. She even tied their shoes. By then, the national stadium had not been built in Surulere. The land was an imitation park; nevertheless, it provided families with a recreational park where they could go to play. On weekends, Iyabo took the children to the park and bay beach on Victoria Island to play in the pure white sand. Yemisi remembered the numerous hide-and-seek games they played there with Iya Iyabo. Iyabo put Yemisi and the boys through an expensive private primary school in Lagos.

Comfort Adaniji, their mom, taught all her kids, including her grandson, Patrick, how to sew clothes. Iyabo's sewing machine helped Yemisi and her siblings a great deal in learning how to sew clothes. Yemisi remembered the first shirts she sewed for Isake and Patrick. She forgot the necks. Yemisi called it "American style." She was eleven years old then.

Comfort, their mom, was pretty, with shaded light brown skin. Yemisi's father, Lawrence Adeniji, was tall and redeemably built. He was handsome. After graduating from Orissa Boys' Secondary School, at his first interview, UAC hired him. After six months on the job as a clerical clerk dealing with the cost of raw materials, finished products, and retail goods, UAC split up into divisions, and a new division, A. J. Steward, which made household products, was acquired. A. J. Steward featured him in commercials for their new skincare products, Nku Gold Cream and Nku Gold Soap. UAC had a guilty conscience, as the new products were the talk of the country, and they sold untold tons of the products. The company rewarded him by sending him to management training courses. He bypassed supervisory and assistant management positions and was promoted to full management at the age of twenty-three. It was unheard of, given UAC's culture and tradition.

He returned home with a brand-new Opel car to impress his parents. The senior Adeniji, Felix Adeniji, and his mother, Elizabeth Adeniji, insisted on their son getting married before his vacation was over. They assumed hot-flying Lagos girls would derail their son. He was the only son and only child of his mother and the first son and child of Felix Adeniji. Senior Adeniji married a second wife in the search for children. The woman, Ashakpo, gave him an additional seven children, five boys and two girls. Yemisi's father, Lawrence Adeniji, didn't have to look any further for his wife, because his mother handpicked Comfort Ashiolu for him to marry. She was a lightning rod. She was the envy of men. Comfort Ashiolu was astonishingly pretty. She was an unqualified beauty in all categories of beauty, and she passed her good looks on to her children, especially the girls.

Their first-sight meeting spelled marriage instantly. To ensure no man would come near and extend an invitation to marry her, Lawrence Adeniji slept on a floor mat in his potential in-laws' home for four days until she agreed to marry him. A quick traditional wedding ceremony was performed, and the Anglican pastor in charge of Epele parish performed an impromptu church wedding ceremony after the dismissal of the congregation that Sunday. Senior Adeniji was a key ranking member of Saint John's Anglican Church parish committee in Epele, Orissa Kingdom. The pastor went out of his way to do the impromptu wedding as a favor to the church elder gentleman.

Yemisi was two years older than the last boy. Isake Konyide Adeniji was the second son and the last-born of Lawrence Adeniji. Yemisi was the fourth child of her parents and the third of the girls. Yemisi lost her immediate older sister, Funmilayo, to high fever. The older people of Epele said she was the most beautiful girl on Earth. Isake was a month old when their father, Lawrence Adeniji, died, leaving Comfort the load of the family to carry. Comfort Adeniji was about thirty-three years old when her husband died, and she did not remarry after her husband's death. She was later involved with Ojowule Adeniji, the third son of Felix Adeniji's second wife, purely for pleasure and comfort. She had no children for him. Ojowule was already married, with five children: three boys and two girls. It was deliciously tempting for the sexually active beauty to seek outsiders to satisfy her sexual needs. Technically, Ojowule absorbed her as his second wife.

Comfort Ashiolu married Lawrence Adeniji at the age of sixteen. On her wedding day, she turned sixteen. She had just finished form three at Orissa Girls' Secondary School. She had to drop out of school to follow her husband to Lagos. She later went to a local fashion and design school in Lagos to learn how to sew clothes. After she miscarried her first child, she returned to Epele to heal. She couldn't stay in Lagos with her husband; she wanted to avoid the temptation of another pregnancy when she was not healed properly physically and, more importantly, emotionally. She was just sixteen years old. She stayed with her mother-in-law, Elizabeth. Lawrence Adeniji was a smart young man. He took a 2,500-pound loan from UAC to build a two-floor house with indoor plumbing, an indoor kitchen, indoor water-system toilets, and indoor marble bathrooms in his village of Epele, Orissa. The house was big, with twenty bedrooms and four bathrooms. Ten bedrooms were located on each floor. The house accommodated his parents, his stepmother, and her seven children. Later on, he built his stepmother a three-bedroom house at the corner of the compound, but her boys remained in the big house, with each boy occupying one bedroom. Lawrence helped put all his siblings through secondary school. Most of them gained scholarships to attend college in Nigeria and abroad.

Konyide was a month old when their father, Lawrence Adeniji, died. Iyabo had delayed her entering the University of Nigeria, Ibadan, due to her out-of-wedlock pregnancy. She was almost twenty years old when she reentered the university. She sacrificed a lot by sharing the balance of her scholarship funds with her family. The funds eased the financial burden on her poor mother. She got scholarship funds from three sources: a federal fund, the Anglican diocese of Orissa, and an Orissa community scholarship fund established by the late Kabiyesi Lawansin Adekunle II. Therefore, paying the school fees for her siblings was not too much of a burden for Comfort Adeniji. After she graduated from the University of Ibadan with first-class honors, Liver Brothers bribed her to work for them in a full managerial capacity. She was soon promoted to senior operation manager, a senior executive position; hence, the company subsidized her three-bedroom flat in Apapa's GRA. She took Yemisi, Isake, and Patrick, her son, with her to Lagos. Yemisi remembered Iya Iyabo braiding her hair.

When Yemisi was in form two, attending the prestigious Queen's College in Lagos, a company-sponsored fellowship scholarship fund came through for Iyabo to attend the prestigious University of San Francisco to do her doctorate in industrial management for four years. Yemisi, thirteen years old then, all grown up, with remarkable beauty that wet a man's underwear, went back to live with her mother, along with Isake and Patrick, in Epele. Princess Yemisi finished secondary school at Orissa Girls' Secondary School. She gained admission to the University of Nigeria, Ile Ife, from which she got her scholarship with the help of Iyabo to attend San Jose State University.

As Yemisi reminisced on her past history and watched her once impeccably beautiful sister now in a vegetative state due to largely self-inflicted ill health, tears began to drip from her eyes little by little, until she saw Everest, when she burst into tears. It was so huge a cry that Funmi, Mary, and Iyabo came to see what was going on. The moment Yemisi saw Iyabo, she cried even louder, and she asked Iyabo to hug her as tightly as she could. Yemisi said to her, "I love you so much, Iya Iyabo." It was the first time the girls and Dr. Oluomolewa had heard her address Iyabo as Iya Iyabo. It sounded natural coming from her.

CHAPTER 53

Iyabo's eldest son, Patrick, was born out of wedlock when she was seventeen years and eight months old, just shy of her eighteenth birthday. Iyabo finished secondary school at the age of seventeen, and she was one month pregnant when she graduated from secondary school. She carried her pregnancy and sat for her London GCE, which she passed with distinction, scoring six aggregates. She was an easy pick for the University of Nigeria, Ibadan. She was five months pregnant before her father's death. Lawrence Renmi Adeniji was sick and weak, which prompted Comfort to hide Iyabo's pregnancy from everybody, especially her own father. She was sent to live with her grandmother during the course of her pregnancy.

Iyabo was outgoing, brilliant, and the prettiest girl both in Orissa Kingdom and at Orissa Girls' Secondary School. Every man wanted to marry her, and every boy around her age wanted to date her. She was cheerful and polite to everybody. Iyabo credited her extravagant beauty as something nature made that happened to belong to her. She would, in a crowd of disco dancers, pick the ugliest man to dance with. She never looked down on those with less beauty. Iyabo had unique things to admire about everybody, which inadvertently overshadowed the person's shortcomings in her eyes. She was the smartest student in her school and perhaps in the western region. She earned distinction on her London GCE with a clear six aggregates.

Iyabo finished secondary school at the age of seventeen and was admitted to the University of Nigeria, Ibadan, at the first pick. She was already three months pregnant. An emergency meeting was held at the university on her behalf by her mother; her uncle Ojowule, who was the headmaster of Saint John's Primary School in Epele; the dean of the faculty of business and management; and the vice-chancellor of the university to discuss reserving Iyabo's seat until she had her baby. Iyabo had already been seated at the university when her belly started to show off her pregnancy. The four promised to keep the situation under wraps out of respect for her dying father. The request was granted because her entrance examination, her admission interview, her GCE results, and her first-semester academic performance were highly impressive. "This university must have this type of academic brain," said the dean of the faculty of business and management.

Who had gotten Iyabo pregnant? Roni Akintola was a senior at the University of Ibadan. He was light-skinned and mixed race. His father had studied at Oxford, where he'd met his mother, a white English woman. Roni's father practiced law, and he was a high-court judge. Regardless of the color of his skin, Roni was handsome and intelligent. He was finishing up his degree in law that year. He was one of the brightest students conducting the preliminary interview for the upcoming freshman students for the following year. He and Iyabo fell in love instantly after a series of meetings. Iyabo was among the cream of the pie admitted to the freshman class of 1951. She had to wait for her GCE results to be fully admitted to the university.

Meanwhile, Roni and Iyabo were dating. Also, Iyabo had a close platonic friendship in her hometown with a boy named Adebayo. They were so close that some people thought they were siblings, and their secondary schoolmates thought they were lovers. Adebayo and Iyabo paired together at almost every village function, and they were the smartest kids in their various schools. Ade was attending Orissa Boys' Secondary School, Agbala, and Iyabo was attending Orissa Girls' Secondary School in Epele. They took turns sleeping at each other's house. Iyabo was his sister's best friend, and Ade was Iyabo's younger brother's best friend. Roni proposed marriage to Iyabo after three months of dating. After thinking things through and with a thorough consultation with her family and her best friend, Adebayo, and with Roni's promise to wait until she graduated from college, Iyabo accepted his proposal.

Her father was near death, and a quick preliminary dating ceremony was scheduled. The official introduction of both families was made while Renmi was still alive. In Yoruba tradition and culture, there were three key stages of traditional marriage ceremonies to be attended before the all-out, big fourth-stage traditional wedding took place. At the event, the bride hid among her peers in the same uniform clothing, and their faces were masked. The groom had to pick out his bride among them, and then the couple were officially married. At the first introductory ceremony, the potential bride usually followed the potential groom to his home for a few days' stay with his family before returning to her home about two days later. They were not supposed to conjugate with each other at their first meeting. However, at that first family introductory meeting, she got carried away by Roni's reassuring sweet talk, and she let Roni steal her virginity. That was the night she became pregnant with Patrick.

When she came back from Ondo City, where Roni and his parents resided, Iyabo went to tell her best platonic friend the good news. She thought Adebayo would be happy for the good things happening for her in spite of her father's serious poor-health condition. Adebayo was extremely angry to hear she had gone to bed with Roni, her fiancé, and had sex with him. It was even more painful to him to hear that Roni had stolen her virginity. However, he did well to conceal his anger and his pain. Iyabo slept at his house that night with Adukpe, his sister, her best friend. She usually shared Adukpe's room and her bed whenever she passed the night at Ade's house. That night, Ade arranged with his sister to keep the door of her room unlocked so he could surprise Iyabo with a gift she would never forget when she was not expecting it. At about twelve thirty in the morning, Ade quietly came into his sister's room. His hand held a wrapped object his sister assumed was a gift. He woke up his sister calmly and begged her to stay out of her room for a while so he could be alone with Iyabo and surprise her with the gift.

His sister naively thought it was kind of her brother to surprise his best friend, Iyabo, with a gift. Immediately, Adukpe left the room, and he locked the door. Ade took off his pants, pulled up Iyabo's dress, and climbed on top of her body to rape her. He gently struggled to pull down her tight shorts panties she'd used in playing sports earlier that evening, with his penis hard and fully erect, ready to penetrate her vagina. Iyabo suddenly woke up, pushed him off her, and screamed at the top of her voice. She sprang up to see the utmost betrayal of friendship and trust by a person she would have given up one of her kidneys to. Iyabo was not only beautiful and smart but also athletic and strong. She fought off his advances and bit his fingers as he tried to close her mouth. She shouted at the top of her voice louder and more. A struggle ensued to prevent him from raping her. His penis was as hard as stone, but her vagina was as dry as the Sahara Desert.

Adebayo's parents, Adukpe, and the entire family rushed to Iyabo's aid. Her dress had been torn during the struggle, and Ade had sustained injuries. He was bleeding a little bit from his finger bite by Iyabo. That night, his parents sent him to their neighbors' house to spend the rest of the night there after they gave him a thorough beating. Iyabo couldn't stay in the same house with him that night. Iyabo left for her home early that morning and told her mom what had happened to her. Comfort promised her she'd quietly discuss the incident with Ade's parents and would keep it between them since no rape had actually occurred. Comfort also promised Iyabo she wouldn't tell her dying father and her brother, for fear of escalating the fight between the two families. Iyabo interjected that his parents had already taken steps to show their remorse. They later replaced her dress, which she reluctantly accepted.

It didn't end there. Roni surprised her with a visit, and he spent the night in their home. Roni was not told about the attempted rape by Adebayo. Adebayo was also admitted to the same university to study medicine. He also earned distinction on his London GCE with a clear six aggregates. Roni knew Ade well because he and Iyabo were together during their interviews at the campus. When Iyabo was serving Roni breakfast in their guest room, romance ensued between them, and they made love again. The next month, she could not see her period. Obviously, the natural person to be held as the culprit was the man who'd penetrated her vagina with his penis and ejaculated there. Also the man with whom she was madly in love. Roni owned up to the pregnancy initially, until a rumor surfaced that Iyabo had slept with Adebayo voluntarily and not faced an attempted rape by him.

Adebayo's cousin Bello, the village idiot, started the rumor. In the process of showmanship to his peers, Adebayo owned up to the pregnancy. He asserted that when Iyabo slept over at their house, he had sex with her all the time. To impress his peers further, Ade asserted he was the one who'd stolen her virginity. Iyabo was not circumcised, and for most girls who were not circumcised, the initial penetration of the penis did not tear the vulva, so they did not bleed during their initial sexual encounter as long as there was gentle penetration. There was no rush with Roni, who was a perfect gentleman. She didn't bleed during her first or second time with him. Thus, there was no way to tell if her virginity had been stolen by Roni or by Adebayo, especially when Roni's penetrations were done with the utmost gentleness. Adebayo's claim that they had ongoing voluntary sexual encounters between them compounded the lie and made the rumor more believable.

Adebayo was bragging to hurt her for being in a romantic relationship with Roni, a stranger she'd just met, instead of him, her old-time buddy. He was jealous of Roni. The news reached Roni and his parents. Roni was disappointed with Iyabo, and he and his parents denied the pregnancy and called off the wedding.

Six months into her pregnancy, Iyabo's father died. By then, her stomach was showing off her pregnancy. Iyabo was a pretty, slim girl. It took five months for her stomach to really show off her pregnancy at the University of Ibadan. Her father never got to see his first grandson.

Iyabo had the baby by natural birth. She incurred zero stretch marks on her body, and her breasts didn't appear like those of one who was breastfeeding her baby. When she was pregnant, she practically starved herself, eating mostly vegetables, and did an enormous amount of exercise and aerobics. After she had the baby, she continued with her routine, regimented lifestyle to avoid gaining excessive weight, which she feared would make her look like a madam on the university campus. Comfort raised Patrick as her last-born. Patrick called Comfort

Mama instead of Grandma. Patrick looked exactly like Roni, his biological father.

When Roni heard that Iyabo had delivered a handsome baby boy and that the child was his carbon copy, out of guilt, curiosity, and love, he came nine months after the baby's birth to see the baby. He was surprised the child looked like his twin from a different mother. Meanwhile, Iyabo went back to the University of Nigeria, Ibadan, and she was doing well. Roni knelt down in front of her and her family and wept and apologized. He asked Iyabo for forgiveness and for them to continue where'd they left off. Iyabo reminded him he and his parents had called her an *ashawo*. She told him that visit would be his last. She walked away, got into a girlfriend's car, and went back to school at the university.

CHAPTER 54

Princess Yemisi pressed on her sister Iya Iyabo to stay till Wednesday, when she would get her test results. Iyabo thought about it momentarily and agreed. From the look of things, she perhaps was seeing Yemisi for the last time. Yemisi gave her the spiritual and emotional current to live through those days. Yemisi told her sister she had a damaging and serious confession to make to her. She asked Iyabo to promise never to tell a soul about it for the remainder of her life on earth. Iyabo wholeheartedly agreed. Yemisi said to her she would label her as dirty, ungrateful, stupid, and a cheat, but she had more problems in containing her disappointment than the shortcoming she might associate her with. Yemisi told her she was not a crazy woman and knew exactly what she was doing. She said the situation she was about to communicate to her made her happy. Yemisi added that she'd thought about the consequences, and she had no regrets; the situation was of her own initiation and her own doing.

Iyabo listened patiently. Iyabo's mind went everywhere; however, her suspicions didn't include Yemisi's affair with Dr. Oluomolewa. Though Yemisi was still breathtakingly attractive, she was more than eleven years older than Everest, and their age difference was apparent. Dr. Oluomolewa was younger than Patrick, Iyabo's first child. He should have called Princess Yemisi Auntie or—as his wife, Charity, did—Mama Yemisi. The idea of Princess Yemisi falling in love with this child, as she thought of him, a mere doctor, was absurd. Iyabo refused to contemplate the thought. Iyabo felt the confession must have been a financial deal she'd made in the absence of the king's knowledge, which was unlike something Yemisi would do. Iyabo thought another man in the picture would have had to be of equal heavy weight for her to damn the consequences. There was a brief pause, and Iyabo said, "I'm listening."

When it was time for Yemisi to resume her conversation with Iyabo, the king saved her day. He called from Nigeria to find out where the situation now stood. Yemisi purposely kept the king in their conversation for quite a while, until Funmi further saved her by escorting her grandma to the bathroom. Yemisi caught herself quickly: she had been about to make herself undesirable to her elder sister. Her confession would have meant losing Iyabo's trust and respect forever. She asserted the best-kept secret was the secret you kept to yourself. Besides, how would her second party, Everest, have felt about her grapevine gossip? He would have thought she was completely out of her mind. Yemisi was not God and could not determine how long Iyabo would be around.

What if she confided the secret to someone else—maybe her first daughter, Iyadele? Being the type of woman Iyadele was, with all her Americanization, she would hold that against her for as long as she lived. Iyadele might even demand money for her silence or, at worst, demand affection from Dr. Oluomolewa to buy her silence. Iyadele was divorced and single, with two teenage boys gearing up for college, and she was horny as hell. She couldn't be trusted to keep a secret of that nature, no matter the gravity of her promise. She might even demand both money from Yemisi and affection from Everest forever to buy her silence, thereby pushing Yemisi toward the unthinkable in order to silence her for good. One could push a person only so far, especially when the stakes were so high.

Princess Yemisi was not naive, and she sensed Iyadele correctly suspected her relationship with Dr. Oluomolewa was more than a patient-doctor relationship. She had better not hear it confirmed. *Let her assume all she wants.* It did not faze her one bit, because she was happy and comfortable with having Everest in her life. Princess Yemisi never brought up her secret again, and Iyabo, being the older sister, wise and smart, never asked about her confession again until her death. Yemisi retired to her room, awaiting tomorrow to see Dr. Jefferson, the oncologist at UC Davis Medical Center in Sacramento. The governor of California called her again to wish her better luck tomorrow and invited her for a dinner with his family, which she gladly accepted.

The dinner was set for Thursday because Princess Yemisi was pressed with time to get back to work in Nigeria. She accepted the dinner on one condition: the governor's upcoming visit to Africa should include a visit to her palace in Orissa Kingdom. The governor was honored, and he accepted. CHP officers in unmarked squad cars would lead them to the governor's mansion. The dinner was set at 4:30 p.m. to accommodate Princess Yemisi's on-time last-meal schedule for the day. They would leave John Okorocha's ranch by about one thirty, giving themselves enough time to run through the I-5 corridor and get there in time to deal with a few protocols, such as a formal introduction to the family and few invited guests and toned-down speeches before dinner was served. She would go to the dinner with Everest, Funmi, and Mary.

Dr. Everest Oluomolewa finished his exercise at John Okorocha's in-house gym. As he was walking along the hallway to settle down in his room, Princess Yemisi met him by his door and suggested he escort her to the gym if it was not too much of a burden on him. He gladly accepted the offer—any chance to be with his lover alone. She suggested they check Iyabo's vital signs when they came back from the gym. Dr. Oluomolewa thought now would be a good time to check, before he forgot. Yemisi asked him to check hers too before her exercise engagement. He brought his first-aid kit from his room and checked both of them. Princess Yemisi looked at him after he checked Iyabo's vital signs, and his eye contact told her he would discuss it with her later. Iyabo wanted to know about her health condition, but Yemisi saved him by bringing up the governor of California's invitation for dinner on Thursday at 4:30 p.m. Yemisi intentionally let the details of her potential meeting with the governor last a little longer to overshadow Dr. Oluomolewa's potential explanation.

While they were walking to the gym, Dr. Oluomolewa started discussing his findings of Iyabo's deteriorating health. Funmi and Mary accompanied them to the gym. Out of reflex, Princess Yemisi drew closer to him with her arm wrapped around his waist and her head leaning on his shoulder. She started to cry. Dr. Oluomolewa put his right arm across her shoulders. It was another classic love scene encountered by the girls. Funmi and Mary thought, *What a kind doctor*, without making anything out of their consoling romance. They correctly assumed the pain of watching their grandma in such deteriorating health was too much for their grand-aunt to bear, and that was why she leaned on her doctor's trusted, consoling shoulder. For the first time, the girls heard from a doctor's mouth how sick their grandma was.

After a short exercise on the treadmill, the girls, with tears, retired to their rooms for the night. Yemisi and Everest said good night to them before they left for their rooms.

When the girls were out of sight, Princess Yemisi asked him about her vital signs. She'd wanted to be alone with him before she could ask the question, wondering what his response would be.

He teased, "As your doctor or as your boyfriend?"

That was the most effective medicine Dr. Oluomolewa prescribed for her poor soul in order to cure her deep sadness. She laughed out loud, and with her deep dimples still showing at her age, she gladly said, "Both."

Dr. Oluomolewa said, "You *dey Kamkwe*," in broken English. He said, "It is your sister I'm worried about."

Meanwhile, Iyabo was sedated on medication, mostly painkiller medicine. She was deeply asleep. Dr. Oluomolewa and Yemisi came to her room to see how she was feeling. He checked her oxygen tank to make sure the tube was fitted properly. He also checked her heartbeat. He looked at Yemisi and shook his head in disappointment. They left her room and retired to his room for the night. Princess Yemisi was too afraid and shaken to sleep alone by herself. Both damned the consequences; they took a shower together and went to sleep in the same bed together.

All through the night, Princess Yemisi told Dr. Oluomolewa about her childhood and growing up with her big sister Iyabo. It was four thirty in the morning when Yemisi realized she was now talking to herself; Everest had dozed off. She slipped into her room quietly without waking up Everest. She slept without him for the remainder of the morning.

PART 14

HOPE AND OPTIMISM

CHAPTER 55

Out of respect for his fellow physician and for the crown princess of Orissa Kingdom, Dr. Jefferson, onetime associate dean of the School of Medicine, saw them in his office rather than the common doctor-patient reception room. Professor Jefferson could not hide his smile when telling them the good, unexpected news. He told them there was no trace of any liver or kidney damage found. He jokingly added, "You are as healthy as a horse." He then said, "Running a maximum invasive test, like inserting a camera in your abdomen, was absolutely unwarranted and unnecessary." He jokingly added, well meaning, "We can be sued for such an invasion."

Princess Yemisi asked, "Can I make a quick phone call to my husband?"

Dr. Jefferson was a joker, and he asked, "To Nigeria?"

Princess Yemisi was caught off guard; she didn't realize he was joking. UC Davis Medical Center allowed such a phone call anywhere in the world. She offered to pay for the cost of the call, and Dr. Jefferson said, "I'm joking! It is on the house."

Kabiyesi Edukoya Adekunle III was in Lagos, waiting for Princess Yemisi's phone call to know the outcome of the test results. He couldn't sleep that night. Chika tried everything romantic to get his mind off Princess Yemisi for a while at least, including food and lovemaking, but she had little luck. He drank just a cup of tea. When the call came in about seven thirty in the evening Nigerian time, Kabiyesi Adekunle III, in spite of all his power, chickened out on answering the call. He was afraid to answer and hear bad news. After six rings, Chika grabbed the phone with a slap in mild anger and calmly said, "Hello?"

Princess Yemisi identified herself. "It's me. Yemisi."

Yemisi's voice sounded enthusiastic and full of energy. Meanwhile, Dr. Oluomolewa was reading the test results, nodding in agreement, full of smiles. Princess Yemisi asked Chika about Edukoya, who was sitting on the corner of the couch, shivering with a handkerchief soaking wet with the tears from his eyes. He'd been staying in Lagos since Monday evening and made about a dozen phone calls a day to Princess Yemisi. He frequently asked if she had enough food for dinner and if her hair was braided impeccably to look sharp at the hospital. Princess Yemisi wasn't offended by the barrage of phone calls or his questions. In fact, she welcomed them and fed the discussions because she realized that meant he still cared deeply for her.

The thought of losing Yemisi brought back memories of Bola. Bola had died on January 15, 1970, due to complications from miscarriage, but her memories still lived on in his heart. He nearly hadn't married her. He remembered the year he'd met Bola and how she had come between him and his best friend, John Okorocha. When Bola had a series of heated arguments with him while they were dating, she kept mentioning the sacrifice she'd made for him. On further probe, he came to find out he and John were the two rivals chasing after this breathtaking, adorable beauty called Bola. John Okorocha was the smartest kid at King's College, Lagos. He was light-skinned; tall, about six feet seven, like his father; and breathtakingly handsome. His height qualified him to play on the men's basketball team at Stanford University in the early to mid-1950s.

Nature had accorded him the gift of a pointed nose, and he comfortably passed as mixed race. When Queen's College was invited to King's College and vice versa, the most exceptionally pretty and outgoing girls at Queen's wanted to pose with the two most adorable and attractive boys at King's College, John and Edukoya. Among the outgoing girls at Queen's College was the young Bola. Bola was the most all-around attractive girl at Queen's. She was five feet eight, slim, fit, pretty, brilliant, and athletic too. She, like John Okorocha, had earned distinction with six aggregates on her London GCE. Edukoya also had earned distinction on his London GCE, with eight aggregates.

Edukoya demanded Bola tell him the sacrifice she'd made on his behalf. Bola didn't waste any time in pumping out the garbage from her mouth, as Edukoya put it, saying she'd chosen him instead of John because he was a Yoruba boy. Bola knew they were friends, but she wasn't aware of their type of friendship. They were practically brothers from different moms. Edukoya then gave up Bola. Bola went to plead with John for Edukoya's forgiveness and a second chance at marrying her. Their friendship did not stop because of that; instead, the bond between them grew stronger. John delayed for three weeks his departure to America to attend Stanford University in California on a full scholarship just to be the best man at Edukoya's wedding with Bola. John was lucky another merchant ship was leaving for Oakland, California, the week after the wedding.

The best thing Bola did for Edukoya was to kneel down before John Okorocha and apologize for her narrow-mindedness in using tribalism in her decision to be with Edukoya. It happened moments before John left for the United States. Bola surprised everybody by doing that of her own accord. Seeing that it was a heartfelt apology, John forgave her. Bola and Edukoya were among many who saw John Okorocha off to America at Apapa Wharf on June 16, 1950. That apology saved their marriage; Edukoya never threw it in her face again. Two months after John's departure, Edukoya departed for the London School of Economics in England to study law, while Bola continued her studies at the University of Ibadan. Edukoya was also John's best man at his wedding with Akudo.

Edukoya reluctantly took the phone from Chika, who was sitting on the couch next to him. He said to Princess Yemisi, "What is the bad news?" Then he immediately caught himself and said, "Give me the verdict."

Princess Yemisi came to realize he was even more stressed out than she had been to hear the outcome of the news, so she went straight to the good news: "I have no liver or kidney diseases." The king was quiet, and Yemisi assumed he hadn't heard her, so she said, "Hello? I have no liver and kidney diseases."

Edukoya could not contain his joy. He said, "I miss you so much, my love. Thank God."

Yemisi said, "I miss you more, my love."

Dr. Oluomolewa was quiet, listening to their conversation. He came to realize he had always been a substitute to her, regardless of her spirit-of-the-moment confession that she would choose him over the king. He realized her behavior was not an act of making the king jealous. It was not resentment or an act of getting even with the king for marrying Felicia and dating Chikanele. It was an act of feeling desperately lonely. Princess Yemisi was anchoring herself with a friendly dog she knew wouldn't bite her, and Everest provided the anchor adequately.

Kabiyesi wanted to talk to the oncologist. Dr. Jefferson started by praising the LUTH doctors, who gave them a lot of foundations to work with. In the end, Dr. Jefferson predicted that Princess Yemisi would live to be well over ninety. Dr. Oluomolewa reiterated Dr. Jefferson's assertion to the king. Dr. Oluomolewa gave the phone back to Princess Yemisi, who said good night to the king. When she hung up the phone, Dr. Jefferson wanted to know the time in Nigeria now. Dr. Oluomolewa told him it was about eight thirty. He nodded in surprise.

The king wanted to know about their itinerary for the remainder of their stay in America, but she told him it would be discussed at a later time, and she hung up the phone. They drove to the park near the Capitol. Princess Yemisi drove the car after struggling to make Everest drive. Everest refused to drive Mama Akudo's brand-new Mercedes-Benz S550. They walked around the park, most times holding each other's hand. At times, they stood still, hugging and kissing. At times, she hugged him from behind and vice versa. At times, she held him with her arms wrapped around his waist as he held her by her shoulder. They walked slowly and stopped to kiss several times. They sat on a park bench, reminiscing about how their friendship had started and the different numerous experiences they'd had together. At times, they hugged and kissed persistently with their lips plastered on each other and their tongues totally submerged in each other's mouth. They took turns submerging their tongues into the other's mouth.

They talked about what was keeping them from really making love with each other. They poked fun at various times she'd forced his weak erections into her vagina in desperation. They were taking showers and sleeping in the same bed together practically every night, so why the delay in their having full-blown sexual intercourse? They concluded that a higher power must have been preventing them from making the biggest mistake of their lives. They laughed and said together, "Nah."

It was a hot day in the city of Sacramento. They bought ice cream with multiple flavors from an ice cream stand in the park. They sat on a bench and licked it. Princess Yemisi licked half her cone, and Dr. Oluomolewa licked three-quarters of his cone. They licked from each other's cone and sometimes licked the excess from each other's lips with their tongues. In those instances, they plastered each other with kisses. It was like a scene from a high school dating game. They threw the remainder of the ice cream cones into a garbage container in the park.

Before they departed for Yuba City, Princess Yemisi asked Everest to give her one more kiss because it might be the last they would kiss that day. They hugged and kissed again before departing for Yuba City.

On their getting there, Iyadele, who'd volunteered to pick up her mom, Iyabo, was waiting to say goodbye to her aunt and Dr. Everest Oluomolewa. She had come to pick up her mom in part to glance for the last time at the forbidden fruit she would never get the chance to eat: Professor Oluomolewa.

The good news brightened everyone's face for the day. Iyabo gave Princess Yemisi and Dr. Oluomolewa hugs. She gave Everest a peck on his lips, and they departed. It was the last time they would see each other; Iyabo died a month later.

CHAPTER 56

Princess Yemisi had promised Dr. Oluomolewa sightseeing in San Francisco during their visit to see Iyabo. She promised to take him there on Sunday, when there would be less traffic on Highway 80 and also smaller crowds at Fisherman's Wharf, Golden Gate Park, and Lombard Street. Thursday would have been a better day to go, because there was slack in traffic on the freeways on Thursdays. She wanted to show him how busy the financial capital of the West really was on weekdays; however, the dinner invitation with the governor erased that plan. One couldn't rush San Francisco's sightseeing. It took on a life of its own.

Plans usually never went as planned in a tour of the city. They were still planning to go to Market Street on Sunday to take some pictures of the shining marble on the street. They planned to shop at Macy's and use their parking-ticket validation from the store to park their car for free and then go sightseeing around the beautiful city. They were to dress casually to fit in with the unofficial dress code on the city bus ride, the cable car ride, and the BART ride. They wouldn't say the estimated time to return to Yuba City, which was about 110 miles from San Francisco. Iyabo's visit would determine their return time to Yuba City. Funmi and Mary would be tagging along.

When Iya Iyabo departed to Daly City, where she now lived in a hillside enclave facing the Pacific Ocean, they asked the girls if they could take them out to dinner. The girls jumped for joy at the excitement of eating out. Princess Yemisi and Dr. Everest Oluomolewa didn't particularly like to eat outside, especially in restaurants, if they could avoid it. However, they would indulge on special occasions and wanted to show their appreciation to the girls, their caretakers. The girls had been sweating in the kitchen, cooking all their meals. They cleaned the house, waited on them hand and foot, did their laundry, folded and ironed their clothes, and kept John Okorocha's villa immaculate. The least they could do was take them out for a treat. Dr. Oluomolewa was the first to suggest it. Princess Yemisi, jubilant at her good news, welcomed the suggestion with open arms. The girls chose the Hometown Buffet. Princess Yemisi laughed, but Dr. Oluomolewa interjected, granting them their wish, and it would save them money. He added, "It is a win-win situation."

They took their table, and the girls wanted to have some fun. They frequented the menu tables as often as they could. They took a little bit of the foods on each table. Hometown Buffet was a middle-class all-you-can-eat restaurant that also offered steaks and specially prepared meal courses for an additional cost. Soda, water, iced tea, dairy beverages, and ice cream were included in the package. It was largely a self-service restaurant. The specially prepared meals were served by waiters. The girls did not eat much; they just wanted to have some fun, so they feasted on the all-you-can-eat choices.

Princess Yemisi decided to join the girls and pig out. They didn't order any special dish. Hometown Buffet's food menu had fried chicken, a mixed salad bar, fruits and vegetables, bread, rice, beans, soup, assorted varieties of cakes, mashed potatoes and gravy, and more. They had many full-course meals to choose from on the table. Customers could pig out on a fixed moderately priced meal under twenty dollars per person.

However, they were not allowed to take home any food, with the exception of the remains of the specially ordered food.

For a moment, Dr. Oluomolewa played it cool, and later, he decided to join them in pigging out. "That is the whole excitement of eating at Hometown Buffet—to pig out," Funmi said.

"You do it once and don't do it again for a very long time," Mary added.

In Princess Yemisi's and Everest's minds, there would be a whole lot of treadmill running that night to burn off the extra calories. It turned out the girls were right: they had a good time at Hometown Buffet. Seeing all of them together having fun, some asked if they were new to America—a silly question that went unanswered. Some also wrongly assumed they were the parents of the girls.

Two white couples with their children asked if they could join them. They made allowance for them. The white couples brought their cameras and said they belonged to a picture-taking club. The couples took multiple breathtaking pictures of them, individually, as a couple, and as a group. They also took multiple pictures with them together with their families. The couples asked for their address in Nigeria and promised to send copies of the pictures to them there. As a matter of fact, they made good on their promise. They did send the pictures to them in Nigeria. A huge DHL package full of pictures arrived.

On further introduction with the couples, Princess Yemisi and Dr. Oluomolewa told them about their doctor-patient relationship and why they visited America. When sending the pictures, they included two copies of each picture and sent two packages in one big parcel envelope, one for Yemisi and one for Everest, which they shared on the arrival of the pictures. The couples also sent a package of the pictures each to Funmilayo and Mary since they were residing in the United States. Dr. Oluomolewa, Princess Yemisi, and the girls individually wrote back to the couples, thanking them for their thoughtful, unexpected gifts; kindness; and surprise.

Their visit to Hometown Buffet took much longer than they had anticipated. They spent about four hours altogether inside and outside around the restaurant. Half their time was spent taking pictures. Mark Ducken, one of the persons taking pictures, fell for Princess Yemisi. He went on taking her picture over and over. At one point, his pants bulged out with his penis fully erect. Funmi noticed it first and alerted Mary. When he took pictures together with Princess Yemisi, which he often did, it bulged out more in search of an exit window. It was obvious. His wife, Jane, looked the other way when she saw it. The girls murmured quiet laughter and said, "Nothing!" when Princess Yemisi asked them about their amusement. Then Dr. Oluomolewa whispered in her ear what they were laughing at. When Yemisi looked down at his pants and saw it, it was even more obvious, but she contained her laughter until they got into the car. She invited his wife to join them for the final photo op, and she avoided his putting his arm on her shoulders by bringing his wife and Everest in the middle to pose with them. Princess Yemisi noticed his erection became firmer and longer when his arm was around her shoulders. She stood near Dr. Oluomolewa, with his arm firmly crossing her shoulders. She even held his fingers tightly with her right fingers.

Yemisi, Everest, Funmi, and Mary had all dressed casually for the dinner at Hometown Buffet. All the women had put on leggings with simple blouses to match. Dr. Oluomolewa wore regular pants and a blue T-shirt to match. He wore regular black shoes. The girls showed off their expensive Jordan athletic footwear Princess Yemisi had bought for them. The footwear cost about $164 per pair. Princess Yemisi had bought two pairs of Jordan footwear and wore one pair. They were comfortable athletic shoes for a change.

Everest had complained that Nike footwear was not suitable for his feet after trying a dozen pairs. With a fellow customer's recommendation, he'd settled for inexpensive New Balance footwear, which was a blessing on his feet. The customer took two pairs of New Balance and murmured, "Nike is just a waste of money. I wonder why people buy these shoes. Maybe it's their stupid brand name." The New Balance shoes were so comfortable on his feet that he bought four pairs to wear in Nigeria. He tried all four pairs, and they all fit perfectly with zero pain on his feet. Dr. Oluomolewa's feet were flat like those of most older gentlemen, and that was why he had zero luck with Nike footwear.

The leggings on Princess Yemisi fit perfectly, wrapping her butt like that of a displayed mannequin. She looked like a twenty-one-year-old girl from behind from a near distance. To compound her beauty, on Tuesday, the girls showed off their hair-braiding handiwork on their beloved auntie Princess Yemisi's hair. Funmi and Mary were self-taught in professional hair-braiding. They did it for fun part-time, mainly on Saturdays and after church service on Sundays, to supplement their pocket money. The kids were so industrious that people came from as far away as Los Angeles to have them braid their hair. They braided different types of hairstyles for approximately $120 per head, plus tips.

Most of the time, the tips could top $200 or be as little as two dollars. The girls were always cheerful and grateful and simply said, "Thank you," no matter how small or big the tip was. They asked no one to tip them. They were so fast that it took them an average of two and a half hours to braid one head, depending on the features added. The girls got to work on Princess Yemisi's hair by eight thirty on that Tuesday morning after they broke their fast, and by eleven o'clock, before lunchtime, they were done, and the vicinity was immaculately cleaned up, with not a hair on the floor. Princess Yemisi saw herself in the mirror and beckoned Iyabo and Dr. Oluomolewa to see a genuine work of art.

Dr. Jefferson looked at Princess Yemisi's hairstyle in admiration and marveled at the perfect work of art. He said, "Whoever braided Princess Yemisi's head is invited to braid my wife's hair." They all laughed. Princess Yemisi gave the girls $300 each, plus an additional $100 each from Everest, for their handiwork. They refused to accept the offers. The girls said they were having fun practicing the latest style they had learned. Iyabo had taught Iyadele and all her granddaughters how to braid hair from their preteenage years. Yemisi knew well how to braid hair. Bunmi and her siblings were her practice since she had no biological daughter of her own. They'd learned from Comfort, their mother, who did sewing for a living too.

Most Yoruba girls knew how to hand-braid hair from their childhood. Igbo women used thread to braid their hair, and Yoruba women used their hair as the thread to braid their hair. Both hair-braiding techniques, which had become common with all women, especially in the Western Hemisphere, were age-old traditions handed over from generation to generation in both tribes. Most black women now used hair attachments to elongate their hair. Attachments on hair looked gorgeous when done with taste. The story was told of a madman at Ogbaette Market in Enugu ejaculating in public and wetting his pants with his sperm when he looked steadily at an attractive woman who braided her hair.

With her leggings, simple blouse, and impeccable, stylish braided hair, Princess Yemisi looked stunning. She could have comfortably passed as a twenty-one-year-old girl. Dr. Oluomolewa had his eyes fixed on her physique and nodded in approval. He said to himself, *Tonight will be the night.*

When they came back from Hometown Buffet, they played a basketball game with the girls for about an hour and fifteen minutes to burn off the excess calories. When it became really dark at about ten o'clock, they quit playing. Dr. Oluomolewa went to say good night to the girls, and Princess Yemisi joined him. They retired to Dr. Oluomolewa's room and took a shower together with lots of touching and kissing.

They retired to his bed, with Princess Yemisi wearing an impeccable see-through silk nightgown with no panties on. The king called again to know their itinerary. She went to her room to detail it for him, and in the process, she dozed off on the phone while she was talking to him. Edukoya heard his wife snoring and quietly hung up the phone on his end.

Chika was in bed with the king at the villa in Ikoyi at the time of his call. He would be waiting for them in Lagos on Tuesday when they arrived in Ikeja. The king went back the next morning, Thursday, to Agbala to attend some important meetings.

Meanwhile, Everest waited in vain for Princess Yemisi to come back to his bed, when he heard her snoring. He too called it a night and went to sleep alone.

CHAPTER 57

On Friday night, Princess Yemisi had had it with Dr. Everest Oluomolewa about his true feelings and loyalty to their relationship, his true gut feelings, and his perspective on where their relationship was heading. Princess Yemisi was tired of the obstacles—the ones that happened naturally, the ones they invented, and the ones they created, including the interrupting phone calls from the king and Charity, the invented excuse of "Let's give the girls some respect," and the created excuses that had happened countless times in Geneva, where they'd used WHO as a defense mechanism preventing them from making love. The question that kept disturbing her was "What does it take to get this man to make love to me and damn the consequences?"

After twelve years, still, no sex had occurred between them. It had taken John Okorocha to brokerage sex between her and Edukoya. She was an exceptionally attractive woman, yet men she was in love with found it difficult to have sex with her for the first time, especially when she was horny as hell. However, this particular relationship had taken too long to engage in sexual activities. She had begun to doubt Dr. Everest Oluomolewa was really in love with her. She wrongly assumed it was all in his head, an illusion, a fantasy to be flanked by a woman so astonishingly pretty and desirable that countless attractive men in their early thirties had no problem soliciting her for dates, even given her age of nearly sixty-four. Yemisi, by all accounts, was pretty, with makeup or no makeup. There were no wrinkles visible for the naked eye to see at a glance, and she'd had no plastic surgery. She was a genuine article.

That Friday night was not an exception to their rules. They had been sleeping together and taking showers together, and no sexual engagements had occurred between them. She said, "Why can't we make love now in this bathroom? For one thing, making love in the shower has a bundle of advantages with zero side effects. You don't have to clean up after yourself. This bathtub is oversize, which means there is enough space to take any position making love. Why can't we do it here right now?"

Everest kept quiet and pointed in the direction of the girls' rooms.

He hurried up his shower and jumped out of the bathtub. As he was reaching for a towel, Princess Yemisi sprinkled water and soap foam all over him. "Look what you've done now. I'm going to have to rinse all over again," Everest said.

While he was rinsing, Yemisi jumped out of the shower and said in a mean, loud voice, "I've had it with you." She stumbled out of the bathroom into his bedroom without padding her body with a towel. She grabbed one towel and wrapped it around her body with her shoulders exposed. She quickly hurried to her bedroom. Luckily for Dr. Oluomolewa, there were several towels on the rack. He used one of them to wipe his body. He then brushed his teeth and went to bed.

Princess Yemisi brushed her teeth too and went to her bed. Before she retired to sleep, she called her husband to tell him the final itinerary. The king had gone back to Orissa, where he was presiding over a number of local board meetings. Kabiyesi Adekunle III promised to be at the airport to welcome her home. When he mentioned bringing Felicia along with him, he could sense a little withdrawal in Princess Yemisi's voice, so he quickly erased that idea. They said good night to each other, and he added that he would personally thank the girls for their usefulness tomorrow.

Meanwhile, Dr. Oluomolewa called Charity to see how she and their kids were doing and to reinforce their final itinerary to her. Saturday and Sunday would be busy for them, so he knew he had better call her now. He, Yemisi, and the girls would be going for their final shopping on Saturday to pick up a few personal items and gifts. Sunday would be spent in San Francisco. He emphasized the sightseeing sites, and Charity reminded him to take lots of pictures to show them when he came back home. Charity expressed how much she missed him, and they kissed on the phone and said good night.

After waiting for a while, with the girls deeply asleep, around one thirty Saturday morning, Princess Yemisi entered Everest's room and crawled into his bed, facing away from him with her butt pressing against his penis. All seven and a half inches of it, about three inches in diameter, firmed up upon touching her almost naked butt. She had no panties on under her see-through silk nightgown. After a few minutes, she turned toward his face. Her turning partially woke up Dr. Oluomolewa, who had been snoring heavily, having an intense romantic encounter in a dream with Charity, his wife. He was deeply asleep, completely submerged in his dream, making passionate love with Charity. When Princess Yemisi gently massaged his chest hair, it slowly halfway woke him up, and his dreams turned into a temporary reality. He grabbed Yemisi close and kissed and hugged her tightly. He placed her on top of him, spreading her legs between his legs. With his full erection as hard as stone, the amusement caused her to be in a full sexual mood instantly.

When Princess Yemisi started crying, he was quiet, lying down in the bed close to her as she sat at the edge of the bed.

He faced her back, with his penis touching her naked butt, slowly weakening. His semen was still dripping down, wetting the bedding. He quickly put his penis in between his lap to avoid the embarrassment from the girls when they washed the bedding. He'd loved every bit of his little sexual experience with the princess. He thought, *It is why the king is spending a lot of money to see that she lives, because this lady, Yemisi, has no duplicate. She is like an addiction. Once you've had it with her, you are hooked for life. You want to have it with her all the time. She's his wife. I am a damn fool.* Dr. Oluomolewa was now completely awake, and he realized the forbidden fruit, whether he had been dreaming or not, had now been eaten.

He also thought, *When will she get over her tears and continue where we left off?* The best way to deal with the situation was to employ what he'd learned partially growing up in Igbo land, where his mother came from. He realized that no matter how small the ark of God was, it must be carried with two hands. He would accord her much-needed respect, empathy, and time to deal with the situation. He had to show her he was genuinely concerned about her feelings. He would wait until he was invited and then say, "I understand. It'll be all right."

Princess Yemisi was badly hurt. Dr. Oluomolewa claimed he was in love with her, and it should have been her he was having sex with in his dream, not his wife, Charity.

He shifted closer to her, and by then, his erection had gotten weak. He began gently massaging her back while she sat at the edge of the bed. At first, she politely said, "Don't touch me." He slowly removed his hand halfway, guessing her seriousness. After a few moments had passed, he put his left arm on her back again. This time, she didn't say anything. She seemed to like the touching and the massage. In fact, she directed his hands where they would give her the greatest pleasure. Then she said, "How long have we known each other?"

Dr. Oluomolewa didn't know how to answer the question, lest he insult her in her state of fragility, so he politely responded with a question of his own: "You mean?"

Yemisi rescued him. "How long have we confessed we are in love with each other?"

He had to get the correct answer this time.

Women kept track of most of their relationships with men they deeply cared for, romantically or platonically. Men generally lost track of whether they cared for women or not. To measure men with the same standard as women regarding capacity to remember the details of a relationship was overreaching. He dared not say that to her; otherwise, she would get up and leave the room. But he wanted her to stay there in his bed, making love with him. His erection became firmer and longer again. With great pain, he put it in between his lap and shifted down, allowing only his belly to rest on her butt, in order to avoid his erect penis touching her butt. Any verbal or body language that might signal lack of concern for her feelings was dealt with. He answered, "Roughly four years."

She shouted, "Has it been that long, and we haven't had sex? You must be kidding me. This is absolutely unacceptable."

When she said that, he thought they were getting closer to continuing their lovemaking. However, she proceeded with her lecture. She said to him, "Actually, for more than ten years, when you count when we started kissing and touching each other's body. You are not in love with me; you are in love with your wife, Charity, and that is how it is supposed to be. I respect you for that." His erection went dead at that instant. She proceeded. "That is the reason you are creating and inventing excuses to avoid making love to me. In Geneva, common phone

389

calls from people I don't give a damn about prevented us from having sex. In my bedroom in Lagos, your mother's arrival prevented you from making love to me. My husband, the king, who has multiple wives, also prevented you from making love to me. They can wait, for crying out loud. The latest excuse is Iyabo, my sister, a woman who is sedated by medication and can't tell her left from her right. Now you are pointing your finger in the direction of the girls' rooms, which are quite a distance away. You are making love to your wife in your dreams, and I bet you have been making love to your wife in your dreams while sleeping with me."

His erection practically went dead. He thought to himself, *All she is saying is the truth.* He went speechless and remained quiet. All of a sudden, his hand stopped moving, and the massage stopped too. Yemisi had to remind him of his volunteered duty on her back. After Yemisi finished talking, she gave him a chance to say his piece. Dr. Oluomolewa said, "I understand. It will be all right going from here." But he asked a crucial question: "Where does this relationship lead us?"

Princess Yemisi answered, "I honestly do not know. However, I won't ask you to leave your wife and your family for me, and I'm sure you won't demand that from me either.

"Look, Edukoya has his hands full. He is practically married to three wives. Chikanele is the unofficial wife of the king, which makes three. I just want to have some fun while I am still alive. I just want to have some fun with this man I'm in love with, and if not for Edukoya and, especially, Charity, I would have dragged us to the altar and stayed there till we said, 'I do.' I don't know what it is about you, but I love you with all my heart extraordinarily. If not for Charity and your children, I would have been open about our relationship and damned the consequences. Charity calls me Mama Yemisi, and your children know me as Grandma. It means a lot to me, and I won't betray such trust by coming out in the open with our relationship. That is where I draw the line. I understand your loyalty to Charity and the kids. When I'm invited, that is when I will come in. And where you tell me to stay, that is where I will stay. I don't want you to ever stop loving me or cut me off completely from your life."

When she said those last words, his erection came back in a big way. He drew her face gently to his, and this time, he initiated the kissing and most of the romance. He gently took off her nightgown, which left her wearing her birthday suit. She gently removed his clothes too. She worked her way from his tongue to his chest and down to his penis. There was no rush this time. She gently inserted his penis into her mouth. They turned in opposite directions, both having the time of their life licking each other's genitals.

Then a phone call came in. This time, it was from Felicia, who muted her crying while talking to Princess Yemisi.

The princess would have said, "I'll call you back later," as she and Eva were beginning to break the ice for the first time, but on second thought, she knew the call must have been important. Felicia never called her to chat with her unless it was an important issue. Princess Yemisi gently pushed aside Eva, who was still lying on top of her with his fully erect penis completely inside her vagina. She remained calm, waiting for Felicia to finish talking. Felicia finally went out of control, bursting into tears, and said, "Kabiyesi just had a massive stroke, and I don't think he will make it this time."

It was the most awkward moment in Princess Yemisi's life. She was in bed in a faraway land, making passionate love with her boyfriend, and just as the love affair heated up, in came news about a potentially fatal incident with her other lover, her husband of almost forty-five years.

Her romance with Everest came to an abrupt halt. By the time Felicia called, his fully erect penis was totally submerged inside her vagina, with his penetration racing to the never-ending bottom of her ocean. When the news sank into her head in seconds, she suddenly cried out, saying repeatedly, "Oh my God! Oh my God!" Enormous guilt riddled her for a sickness that was clearly not her fault. There she was, in an intense romantic affair with another man who was not her husband, and her husband was clinging to his last breath. The guilt became intense. In her mind, regardless of what Edukoya had done by marrying three wives, it was no match for hurting him by engaging in a serious romantic affair with another man.

Though Edukoya did not know of the romantic affair between her and Dr. Oluomolewa, she blamed herself for partially contributing to his stroke. Princess Yemisi felt that Edukoya was not a fool and was not stupid. She felt that the trust he had for her prompted him to wait until she came clean with her affair. She also felt she could never hurt Everest, the man she was deeply in love with from the bottom of her heart. If Everest stopped loving her, she'd take poison and die, because life wasn't worth living without him. Princess Yemisi would never say a word about her affair with Dr. Oluomolewa to anyone. She felt Edukoya's assumption was correct, and she was not ashamed of it either. It might have eaten him inside and caused him to have the stroke. However, Edukoya remained blinded by her love affair with Everest till his death.

In spite of his enormous appetite to have sex with a variety of women, Edukoya still loved her. Dr. Oluomolewa kept quiet and allowed her to sort things out in her mind on her own. Her vaginal fluid slowly dried up, with her dried fluid partially cementing the hole. Eva's erection shrank and crawled back into its shell with dripping semen wetting his lap. He used tissue to cap it. They had an immediate change of plan. There were two first-class seats left on a United Airlines flight departing at 1:30 p.m. to Houston on Saturday afternoon. The girls woke up by four o'clock Saturday morning to clean up the house. Princess Yemisi and Everest joined them, to the girls' disappointment. At one point, when the girls were cleaning Princess Yemisi's and Dr. Oluomolewa's bathrooms, Princess Yemisi put a $5,000 cashier's check in each of their handbags. Dr. Oluomolewa followed suit, inserting $200 in each. Iyabo's family saw them off at the airport, with Kayode leading the way. They departed at exactly 1:30 p.m. for Houston that afternoon.

PART 15

THE DEATH OF A KING

CHAPTER 58

The death of His Lordship Kabiyesi Edukoya Adekunle III stunned Orissa Kingdom, Ondo State of Nigeria, the Yoruba community, and the nation. It was felt as far away as Mbaise in Imo State, Nigeria. The people of Ife in Mbaise wept. They even sent a delegation of four to Orissa to find out if what they were hearing was the truth. It crushed Princess Yemisi. She called him "My strength." Felicia was devastated. Chika cried like a baby, which confirmed that Edukoya had seen her as his wife and treated her accordingly. Edukoya had bought Chika a brand-new Mercedes-Benz G500 SUV. He'd furnished her live-in house at his villa in Ikoyi. He'd built a two-floor house at her father's obi in Imo State. He'd taken over the sponsorship of her boys, now in college.

Edukoya anticipated his death; thus, he provided adequately for Chika in his absence. He built an apartment complex in Owerri for her, which he gave to Chika on her forty-second birthday. The apartments were rented out, with Chika collecting the lease money while the king was still alive. Kabiyesi Adekunle III visited Imo State six times on the whole and slept with her at her house in her village of Amaraku in Isiala LGA. Edukoya was truly in love with Chikanele. His death was perturbing to her because she was madly in love with him too. Chika, who took a needed time-out to visit her kids at UNILAG, was temporarily confused and disoriented upon hearing of the king's death. People saw her as crazy. It took about a year for her to get her faculties in order. The reading of the king's will was delayed because of it.

Edukoya advised his family he wanted to be treated at Orissa Polytechnic Medical Center following his recent massive stroke. The hospital, though in a remote area of the country, had adequate medical facilities that rivaled those of any hospital in the world. All forms of surgical procedures were done there. Kabiyesi Adekunle III and his family made annual contributions of tens of millions of dollars to the hospital so it could meet the challenges facing it. The hospital provided him with the highest medical and nursing care. He was assigned two nurses, and doctors frequented his hospital room around the clock. Upon Princess Yemisi's arrival from the United States, she joined Felicia in taking turns staying with him at the hospital.

Chika insisted on joining them to look after him, but Felicia adamantly refused to allow her. Although they suspected she was in a serious romantic relationship with him, they wouldn't confront her about it. Princess Yemisi was reluctant to intervene on Chika's behalf. Princess Yemisi, whom Chika believed to be her dearest friend and, at the same time, a silent archenemy of Felicia, came to the middle ground, offering what she gave as the solution to the situation. She agreed to frequently take Chika to visit him. Princess Yemisi was not happy with Chika, who, as her maid, had no business sharing their husband with them. Yemisi's compromise, Chika later found out, did not hold water. Princess Yemisi had no intention of allowing Chika to see Kabiyesi in any condition. She kept giving excuses for why they would not go together to see the king, though the king repeatedly asked about her. He began to wonder about her lack of empathy in his present condition after she'd repeatedly said she was madly in love with him. His Highness, sensing Felicia hated Chika because of her tribe, refused to be stereotypical in labeling it as a tribal divide, though he didn't see any wrong Chika did to her and was also influenced by his brotherly friendship with the late Dr. John Okorocha. Felicia, who was a tribalistic Yoruba woman, didn't want Chika to visit the king because she wanted to leave the impression at the end of his life that Chika was a gold digger, an Igbo woman. She thought that an apple did not fall far from its tree and that Igbo people could not be trusted. That stereotypical notion was not reality. People were people in the king's and Princess Yemisi's eyes. They'd raised their children to have an open mind and not be prejudiced.

Princess Yemisi found what she thought was a way out of preventing Chika from visiting the king at the hospital. She sent Chika on complicated, meaningless errands when she was about to leave Lagos for the week's stay with the king at the hospital. Chika raised her hopes high and packed her few needs, thinking she was going to finally visit the king at his hospital bed, only to have her hopes shattered when Princess Yemisi left without her. Princess Yemisi's excuse she gave to Edukoya was "She went on a very important errand."

Chika realized her game, so she took off on her own to visit the king. She traveled on a first-class ticket, which was the only seat available on the lone plane to Akure Metro Airport that Tuesday morning. From the airport, she took a local taxi to Orissa Polytechnic Medical Center to visit the king. On her arrival, she met an Igbo medical doctor doing his internship there. He escorted her to the king's private quarters. Princess Yemisi was in Lagos, taking care of some business, taking care of a few legal loose ends, and also spending time with her boyfriend, Dr. Oluomolewa, who was now in a full-blown romantic relationship with her. However, out of respect and empathy for the king's condition, they had delayed engaging in sexual intercourse until the king got better. Felicia resumed her lectures at the polytechnic school as a way of easing her frustration.

Kabiyesi was with the two nurses assigned to him when Chika got there. One of them was sitting down reading a novel, and the other nurse was trimming his toenails and fingernails. Chika walked into his hospital room nervously, hoping to receive a warm reception from the king. She stood and leaned on the doorframe. She had come all the way from Lagos uninvited to see the king of Orissa Kingdom. Princess Yemisi, without saying a word to her, so she couldn't get quoted, had signaled to her that the king would prefer only close blood- and marriage-related family members see him in his present condition. He would prefer to see her and the other maids when his condition improved. It was the first time Princess Yemisi had addressed Chika as her maid and not her executive assistant. Chika, hurt by the words of insult, felt disappointment in the person who was supposed to be her best friend. To compound the issue further, Chika and Princess Yemisi addressed each other by their first names at Princess Yemisi's request.

It made her realize Princess Yemisi was playing games and toying with her emotions. She realized Princess Yemisi accurately suspected her ongoing affair with her husband and pretended things were normal, only waiting for her to come clean about the affair. Deep down in Princess Yemisi's heart, she felt betrayed by Chika, the one person she trusted, who was supposed to watch her back and catch her in her falls. After Chikanele thought about it a lot, she came to the conclusion she was doing right by venturing out on her own to see the king in his hospital bed. Chika realized she had accumulated enough wealth to see her through for the rest of her life should Princess

Yemisi disengage their relationship because she'd disobeyed her command by venturing out on her own to see the king.

Immediately when the king saw her, he lifted up on his own to greet her. Edukoya was so overwhelmed with joy to see her that he started talking clearly again and walked toward the door, stretching his arms to hug her. He used both his arms to hold Chika. The nurses witnessed a miracle. They wanted to give him support, but he politely told them to stay back. It was unbelievable to see the king, who'd been paralyzed from the shoulder down, stand up on his own after two and a half months, walk up to Chika, grab her warmly, and kiss her without minding who was watching them. All his movements were restored at the instant. The nurses telephoned the doctors to come witness a miracle. The team of doctors rushed in and saw Chika sitting on his right leg. The king wrapped both his arms around her slim, fit waist. Kabiyesi Edukoya Adekunle III introduced Chika to the doctors and the two nurses as his third wife, joking that she'd been hiding from him.

The doctors were an eye specialist, a psychiatrist, an oncologist, and a cardiologist. They believed something dramatic had occurred to him. Why the sudden change in his physical and mental condition? They invaded to find out what had happened. They asked the nurses if they'd suddenly woken him up after he'd been in deep sleep all day and paralyzed from the neck down. The nurses said no but relayed the event they had seen unfold before their eyes. While they were debating their assumptions, hypotheses, and analyses, the king excused them from his room to give him a moment with Chika. They left the room, and he asked that they close the door and the drapes and not allow anyone to enter the room, even Princess Yemisi and Felicia.

Princess Yemisi jumped onto a plane the following morning and headed to Orissa to see the miracle for herself. It was an awkward moment when Princess Yemisi arrived at the hospital to see Chika lying in bed with her husband. Edukoya lay on his belly, while Chika sat on his butt with her legs spread on either side, giving him a massage. She wore no underwear, having the pleasure of rubbing her vagina on his butt. The garment the hospital staff had given to Chika was white and semitransparent. One could clearly see her nakedness when looking closely. She was massaging the king's back. Her underwear and clothes she'd worn yesterday hung on the bathroom rack after she'd washed them. Chika was a neat woman. She hadn't planned to stay overnight, so she hadn't brought any clothes or panties to change into. Chika was wearing a borrowed hospital gown designed for patients when Princess Yemisi arrived at the king's room.

Princess Yemisi was battling why Chika had disobeyed her by going to Orissa without her permission after she was told not to go there alone, as Kabiyesi preferred to see his helpers after his condition improved. Chika had come on the first flight in the morning to Akure, and Princess Yemisi had assumed she would come back on a late flight that evening. She had been surprised when Felicia called her and told her Chika would be staying put. She'd told her about the miracle and how Chika's surprise visit had cured their husband.

Princess Yemisi was calm and polite. She did not want to trigger a relapse of another stroke. Chika had already claimed Princess Yemisi had persuaded her to come and bought the first-class ticket for her. The king, knowing Chika lied to protect her, thanked Princess Yemisi for her thoughtfulness and for doing nothing to stop Chikanele from coming to visit him. Felicia said, "Chika, welcome to the family of Edukoya

Adekunle III," in an overtuned voice. Yemisi sincerely thanked Chika for disobeying her in this instance and going with her gut feeling.

Chika relocated partially to Agbala to stay with the king for five years and eleven months, until his death. Princess Yemisi actually welcomed the move, as it freed up her time to spend with her boyfriend, Dr. Oluomolewa. They now engaged in a full-blown romantic relationship, short of engaging in actual sexual intercourse, out of respect for the king. Yemisi wouldn't engage in sexual intercourse to shame the king while he was still alive and in a questionable health condition.

Princess Yemisi and Dr. Oluomolewa found countless excuses to be together and asserted if their love was strong enough, it would wait until the king's death or until his health improved dramatically. Because Yemisi loved Edukoya so much, she wouldn't put a time limit on how long she was willing to wait, though she was horny as hell whenever she was around Everest. It would have to run its course. Charity and the king blinded themselves to the obvious and chose not to ask.

The eighty-nine-year-old king was fragile emotionally, but he was physically strong. He would live for another six years before his death. The woman he was still engaged in sexual activities with was Chika. Yemisi and Felicia seldom had sex with him. However, when they did, they did all the work, and most times, his penis was responsive to them. They got tired of beating a dead horse, inadvertently punishing him to prevent Chika from having all the fun. With Chika, he didn't need any medical or creative intervention to get his penis erect. For some reason, he always had an erection when he engaged in sexual activities with Chikanele without any medical enhancement. It stood as tall as a pine tree, ready for Chika to sink all of it inside her soaking-wet, palatable body.

Before Chikanele left for Lagos, Edukoya told her he had included her and her two boys in his will. He showed her a copy of the final testament of his will and gave her copies to keep for the future should the need arise, because he'd left her a substantial amount of his assets. He advised her not to alter it should there be a legal challenge to his will in a court of law. He also told her the name of the law chamber handling his will.

A week later, after Chika came to Lagos to spend quality time with her boys, who were in their second and third years as students studying at the University of Nigeria, Lagos, His Lordship Kabiyesi Edukoya Adekunle III passed away in his sleep. The last words Princess Yemisi heard him say were "John, wait for me. I'm coming." He reminisced about his best friend, John Okorocha, even with his last breath. What a friendship. Princess Yemisi was lying in bed next to him at the final moment of his life. His death was peaceful.

CHAPTER 59

Twenty bishops from different denominations would be in attendance at the funeral. Retired Anglican archbishop of Lagos Reverend Samuel Archibo would be in attendance. He would read a personal eulogy in a tribute to the king. The Reverend Samuel Archibo, Edukoya, and John Okorocha had been best friends at King's College, Lagos. He was now ninety-four years old and going strong. He'd led the procession at John Okorocha's burial, after which he'd retired, but he still resided at the parsonage. He was now a widower. The governor of Ondo State would personally supervise the king's funeral and clear the main entrance to Agbala, where the procession would be taking place. Edukoya Adekunle III had touched the lives of millions of people worldwide. The governor of California, his personal friend, sent his closest delegates. An ex-governor of Georgia would be attending the funeral. He and the US ambassador to Nigeria would lead the official US delegates. An ex–prime minister of Britain would be attending the king's funeral. The best thing the living could do for the dead was to bury them. After all, Jesus Christ had been buried on the same day. Invitations were issued in a hurry, and the burial was set for Friday, a day short of three weeks. The president of Nigeria would be in attendance, and twenty governors whose lives he'd impacted would also be in attendance.

Twelve African heads of state would be attending his funeral. Ife in Mbaise sent a delegation led by Dr. Nkemjika Okorocha, MD, John Okorocha's first son, to Orissa Kingdom.

Mama Akudo returned from the United States to support Princess Yemisi. She stayed at the palace for four weeks. Dr. Oluomolewa was a darling. He took off from work for a week to support his girlfriend, Princess Yemisi. Dr. Oluomolewa's support gave her enormous strength, and as a result, she did not collapse. Charity, her kids, and her maid would be staying for days in Orissa. They would be housed with Dr. Oluomolewa in the main mansion. The main palace villa had thirty-two large bedrooms, six sitting areas, and three gourmet kitchens. Princess Yemisi had rebuilt the entire palace from the ground up, giving it state-of-the-art architectural facelifts with up-to-date, modern amenities.

Orissa Kingdom needed to have a king when there was an important occasion, such as the funeral of their king, so an emergency meeting of the elders and the chiefs was held to crown Dr. Tunde Edukoya Adekunle IV, Edukoya's first son and the first son of Princess Yemisi, the king of Orissa Kingdom. That was a little bit of light at the end of the tunnel for Princess Yemisi. A twist came via a 150-year-old constitutional agreement. A curious doctoral history candidate at Orissa Polytechnic, working on her PhD, read the handwritten agreement. With poor English and grammatical errors, it stipulated that the reigning king's hand-picked crown prince or princess would be crowned the king or queen of Orissa Kingdom upon his death. It was the only sentence in the 150-year-old constitutional document that was correct. Kabiyesi Lawansin Adekunle I had personally handwritten the constitutional amendment to ensure the smooth transfer of power upon his death.

That meant Princess Yemisi Adekunle would now be crowned Queen Yemisi Adekunle I of Orissa Kingdom. The constitutional document had been drafted by Oyo Durenmi, who'd led the revolution that installed Kabiyesi Lawansin Adekunle I as king of Orissa Kingdom. The document had been preserved intact and was displayed in the main lobby of Orissa Polytechnic's library. The grammar was good, given that Oyo had attended only standard six in elementary school. When Kabiyesi Adekunle I had seen the document, he'd left the grammatical errors and wrong spellings as they were for the sake of history. A graduate of the Cambridge University campus in Ibadan, he had been the vice principal of King's College, Lagos, before ascending the throne.

Most of the signees of the historical document had used their tombs. The document was of historical importance. It was the first known constitutional agreement by a people in Nigerian history. It limited the power of the king and the chiefs and installed the king and the chieftaincy titles by vote, which was certified by the elders and chiefs. It stipulated clearly the veto power of the king and the overriding of his veto power by the chiefs by a vote of at least 60 percent. It clearly stipulated the functions of the king and the chiefs. It allowed for the overthrow of the king by an 80 percent majority vote and the overthrow of the chiefs by a simple majority of the people's vote, thereby bringing fairness to the rule of law, leadership, accountability, and order. It stipulated the functions of a chief as a regional leader elected by his own people, certified by the elders of his own village, and installed by the kabiyesi of Orissa for life. That meant there would be only one chief in a village.

It also called for equal justice under the law for all, and a sitting king or chief could be tried by the elders for wrongdoing and, if found guilty, removed by a simple majority vote of the people. If the king or a chief was caught or suspected of stealing anything or committed a gross abuse of power, such as being involved in the illegal killing of an Orissa person, that would automatically call for his removal by the people's simple majority vote after he had been tried by the committee of chiefs and elders and found guilty. The document stipulated also accountability. Any money assigned for a project had to be accounted for to the last penny. It called for the immediate removal of the king or a chief if he was found guilty of stealing money by the court of elders and chiefs. All the rules had been tested before, with the exception of one: the crowning of a woman to be the queen of Orissa Kingdom when the son of the kabiyesi groomed to take his place was still alive. To compound the situation, the crown princess was his wife, not his biological daughter.

A question arose: What if the woman was from a different community order than Orissa or, worse, from a different tribe, country, or race? It prompted a serious discussion to amend the document for future generations. However, any change was too late for now, and Princess Yemisi was the crown princess of Orissa. She would become the queen of Orissa Kingdom. It was the first time a woman had been crowned the queen with executive power in Yoruba land. It would be the second time a person not related by blood was crowned kabiyesi of Orissa Kingdom. Some members of the Orissa community did not like it and called for the overthrow of the new queen if she was installed.

However, most members of the community welcomed the change with open arms. The committee of elders and chiefs unanimously voted for a historic change. They voted for Crown Princess Yemisi Funmilayo Adekunle to be installed as the new queen of Orissa Kingdom. History was made as the daughter of Lawrence Renmi Adeniji, who used to be a relatively unknown commoner, was installed the reigning queen in Yoruba land.

Her father, her mother, and Iya Iyabo hadn't lived to see this history made. When Dr. Oluomolewa came to greet her as the new queen of Orissa Kingdom, she hugged him tightly, crying, and said, "Iya Iyabo didn't live to see this."

The responsibilities of kingship were familiar to her. After all, she already had been performing those duties as the crown princess of Orissa Kingdom but giving the credit to her husband. She was now in a position to do more good deeds for her people she loved so much. The first executive order she exercised was to install her son Dr. Tunde Lawansin Edukoya Adekunle IV as the new crown prince of Orissa Kingdom. She did it with the sole aim to neutralize any idea to amend the historic constitutional document, and it worked. She regarded the amendment as an overreach of the community's power and felt it would prevent her from doing her job with precise authority as the new queen of Orissa Kingdom. Although she didn't publicly call it an insult, she confided to her boyfriend, Dr. Oluomolewa, just that notion. To her, equal right was equal right, whether the installed kabiyesi was man or woman, by bloodline, or by marriage.

The second call of duty was to give Edukoya an outstanding send-off. Charity, her maid, and her children would stay at the palace for four days for the funeral. Chika was confined to the king's bedroom because she was acting crazy. Two psychologists treating her recommended the treatment to ease the pain of her huge loss. In that bedroom, when she remembered the countless romantic love affairs they'd had there, she would cry a lot more, and gradually, she would ease her loss and pain, and that would bring her back to normalcy. The treatment worked. By the time the funeral came, Chikanele was able to attend the funeral service and the burial site. She was flanked by her two sons, Felicia, and Dr. Oluomolewa. Chika was hopelessly devastated by the king's death. She'd loved him so much.

He was buried at his palace, next to his beloved father and grandfather. The funeral procession was excellent. The president of Nigeria, who had been his junior at King's College and a close friend, was the keynote speaker. He wrote the eulogy by himself. He spoke for twenty-five minutes about his childhood friend in Lagos, whom they used to call Eduks. He spoke about Eduks, John Okorocha, and Reverend Sam Archibo, who had been among the friends and family members who saw him off to England on June 30, 1948, when he departed to attend the Royal Military Academy at Sandhurst. He spoke about Eduks's unselfishness. The president paralleled the late king to Jesus Christ. His beautiful kingdom had been built out of his own compassion and kindheartedness. He'd taken no penny from the community, not even a day's pay. Instead, the king had given to his last penny from his pocket.

He remembered playing with Edukoya and John Okorocha on the school's soccer team. John pointed at a girl he thought was a match for him. It turned out he later married that pretty girl still waiting for him when he returned home from England. It didn't matter to John Okorocha that the pretty girl was from his own tribe. In his conclusion, he turned to the open casket, walked up to it, bent down, and kissed Edukoya's forehead. He said, "Goodbye, my friend. Goodbye, Eduks," and he burst into tears. The whole congregation stood up and wept along with him. The tears from the audience could have filled a dozen fifty-five-gallon barrels.

Edukoya was buried on that Friday. The law chamber summoned a hearing to read his will one month after the king's departure. Chika was in no condition to attend the hearing. The hearing was postponed for six months to allow Chika to fully recover from her psychological impairment since she was already making enormous progress. Because Chika was featured prominently in the will, a delay to read the will was appropriate until she was fully recovered, to avoid unnecessary contesting of the will and testament. If she didn't recover in six months' time, a court hearing, which had already been filed by the law chamber, would have to read the king's will.

After the funeral, Dr. Oluomolewa sent Charity and the whole family back to Lagos. He stayed for an additional three days at the tearful request of Queen Yemisi Adekunle I. At the queen's request, Mama Akudo stayed for an extra three weeks before she left for Ife, Mbaise, in Imo State. Yemisi said, "Mama Akudo, you're now my biological mother." Felicia contained herself with unexpected flawless, stable emotions. She had been confronted with the death of a much-loved husband before.

Given Edukoya's age of almost ninety-four years and Felicia's diverse knowledge, Felicia handled the absence of her lover remarkably well, better than Yemisi and Chika. Chika, though the king had left her with enormous, unbelievable wealth, wished they could make love one more time. When she remembered the last sexual encounter they'd had and how full of life he'd been, constantly wanting more from her, she wished she had not traveled to Lagos. Chika felt the king's seeing her there with him would have been his last breath of clinging on to hope to live.

Although she was staying for only two weeks with the boys, she'd forgotten to leave a firm, unconditional promise and commitment that she would be coming back in two weeks. That lack of firm promise and commitment, Chika assumed, might have left a vacuum on his mind, and that was why he'd sorted for his closest friend, John Okorocha. It was obvious

Chikanele was his most loved wife at the end of his life on earth. In the end, nothing mattered to him more than the love and comfort he got by having endless love affairs with Chika. To Chika, it was a moral call to duty, and she let him have it extravagantly with no reservation. They didn't use any medical enhancement to make love.

PART 16

THE KING'S WILL

CHAPTER 60

Chika reminisced about her time with the late Kabiyesi Edukoya Adekunle III of Orissa Kingdom. She remembered writing him a letter. The letter was found by Felicia in the cabinet drawer where the late king saved special and important documents, such as his vast business holdings and all the romantic letters from the queen and himself from the time they'd met till his death. Felicia confronted Chika, who was standing by the door, watching with disgust and surprise as Felicia ransacked the documents. Only the queen was to go there. Kabiyesi had given a spare key to Chika but instructed her never to open the cabinet unless she was instructed to do so. Without showing her what it was, Felicia called it "the damaging evidence" about her past, and she advised her to pack her bags and leave the mansion before she exposed her dirty laundry. Chika agonized but was sure she had no disturbing past that could set ears ablaze.

After Chika's husband died, the only man she'd slept with was the king. Chika's husband had died seventeen years ago, when her boys were under five years of age. In the course of jogging her memory, she remembered the letter she'd written and hand-delivered to the king. In the letter, Chika had outlined the damage the letter would cause her if it fell into the wrong hands. She was both physically and mentally ready to deal with the letter's fallout. Felicia was jealous of the king's attention to Chikanele and addressed her as a maid. She made a heartbreaking, dangerous, and unsubstantiated accusation

415

that in the king's state of vulnerability, Chika had caused him to leave her an unbelievable, substantial amount of wealth. She claimed the king had been brainwashed in his final days of vulnerability by Chika, and that was the reason he'd stopped having sex with the queen and Felicia and been only with Chika. Felicia found that odd, because she was younger than Chika, though not more beautiful, and because Chika was what she called "just a maid."

Even after his stroke, he'd repeatedly had sex with Chika when he recovered. They'd had sexual intercourse every morning, every night, and sometimes in between. Felicia claimed that overwhelming exhaustion from the repeated sexual encounters with Chika had compounded the stroke and his open-heart surgery nineteen years ago. All together, it had led to what she called his "untimely death." Felicia claimed, without seeing the date when the will was written, that the final testament had been amended to give Chika and her boys a chunk of the king's wealth. The letter was her proof that something had happened behind closed doors, and being an Igbo woman, she couldn't put anything past her. Felicia urged the family to unite and contest the will whenever it was read.

Chika, with her lawyer, who was her younger brother she'd put through his academic career, including law school at an American university, petitioned the court to allow for an additional three months to enable Chikanele to fully recover before the will was read. The court granted her an additional six months.

The letter was what Felicia, in her twisted mind, could possibly hold against her. Chika had kept a copy of the letter. In the presence of Edukoya's family, Tunde, now the crown prince of Orissa Kingdom, pressured Felicia to show the evidence of her accusation to the entire family. The evidence was the only letter Chika had written to the king. Tunde took the letter from Felicia and, with Chika's permission, read it to the entire family.

Dear Kabiyesi Edukoya,

My heart today is filled with overflowing joy to communicate with you in this letter. I am so happy to see your speed in recovering from your stroke. Everybody is giving me credit for your recovery; however, I place the recovery totally in God's hands. I had absolutely nothing to do with it. I am so happy the Lord heard our prayers. You're so mighty and very much a big man; it is very difficult for me to stand before His Lordship and to speak before you. I can't find my feet to stand on, let alone the words to express myself. Ever since you gently grabbed me in the corridor of the hotel in Canada and kissed me, my life has never been the same. Maybe it is my fantasy, maybe my imagination is carrying me too far, and maybe I'm living in a utopic world to have you kiss me. That kiss, with all the passion you put into it, was more than a brush of a kiss. It was a kiss meant for someone you wanted to stay permanently in your life. Me too. I loved that kiss.

That was why the first time you beckoned me and expressed your desire to make love with me, I did not hesitate, and I did not struggle. I reached out to you and let you have all of me without setting any physical or emotional limit, because I wholeheartedly wanted you, and I wholeheartedly needed your love. You read my mind. I just wanted to make love to you because I wanted you very much. I was not afraid of anything and was ready to damn the consequences. As long as I am with you, nothing is more important. Nothing can't wait till I am done pleasing you and myself. Satisfying you has always been my ultimate objective in your household. I am not ashamed of what I'm doing, and I hope you are not ashamed of what we are doing. As it is now, a life without you is no life at all to me, and I might as well be dead. If you don't mind me calling you Edukoya for now, Edukoya, I love you so much. You don't have to return my love. I just want you to believe it, because I'm telling you the truth.

I'm risking everything I have worked for by writing you this letter to express how I really feel about you. A letter is documentary property. The words written are documentary property. It can be shown as evidence in a dispute or disagreement. Words in writing are very powerful tools you can hold against a person. A letter can also serve as a perfect tool to destroy a person, because it cannot lie, and it can always get into the wrong hands. I am risking the welfare of my children; I'm risking my friendship with Princess Yemisi; and above all, you might see me as pressuring you to pay more attention to me. That notion will make you give up our relationship altogether. It may cost me my friendship with Sister Yemisi, and it may cause me to lose you forever. However, I don't care.

I'm not asking you to give up Princess Yemisi and Felicia to be with me. I'm not asking you to marry me either. In fact, I don't even think I want to be married again. I have sown my seeds in this world. I am not mentally prepared to babysit a child anymore, unless my boys grow up, get married, and have children and, of course, your lovely twins too. God, I love those kids. All I want from you is to keep me somewhere in the corner of your heart. I won't bite you, and I will never make noise. Just keeping me there in that corner of your heart will suffice forever for me, all because I love you so much. You may think your handsome looks, wealth, and power are the most attractive features you have. I'm saying to you, stand by the mirror and look very hard at the man, and you will see what a remarkable man you are. Believe me, I don't care about your wealth. I care about your substance and about your making me and my children feel at home and welcomed. I care about my children calling you Grandpa and calling Princess Yemisi Grandma, and I care about both of you accepting them as if they were really your biological grandsons.

When I spank the boys, I beg them to keep the noise very quiet because you will be mad at me when you hear their cries. You play soccer and basketball with them. You taught them how to play your favorite game, chess. You taught them how to play Ludo and cards. You spend quality time with them both in Lagos and in Orissa. You can't wait to have them spend their holidays with you in Orissa. You have given my children love, stability, and a sense of purpose. What only a father can do you've done for them a thousand times, and I thank you from the bottom of my heart. The boys love you dearly. The only person I am concerned about here is Princess Yemisi. I believe if she knows about us, she will feel I betrayed her. Believe me, I didn't mean to do that. It's all about the love and about the feelings I have for you. Feelings for this remarkable family who accepted me. You have also accepted my friendship without any reservation. You have shown it in kind and in the flesh. Thank you.

When you introduced me to the nurses and the doctors in your hospital room as your third wife, though it came off as a joke, deep down in your heart, I know you meant it; otherwise, how could you be that nice to me and to my children? There has to be something about it. Yes, I wholeheartedly accept marriage to you. Whenever you're ready, I will be ready too to permanently join your family. I will never remind you about this conversation, and I will never rush you to make it official. It will be our little secret. Thank you for asking. The words meant the world to me. I would like to emphasize this again if you'll indulge me: the attractive feature has always been the man, Edukoya, not the king of Orissa and definitely not your wealth. You have done so much for me without my asking for it. To ask for more would amount to stealing, which is born out of greed. In fact, I will use the term *highway robbery* to describe it. I love you so much. The boys are grown now, and they thank you and Princess Yemisi for helping them live well. I'm going to visit them at the university. I wish you'd come with me to see your handiwork. The kids are really amazing. I will be staying for a few weeks, and I'll come back to you. Thank you so much again. I love you.

My love,
Chika

The first daughter, Kenmiejo, spoke on behalf of all her siblings after Tunde finished reading the letter. She spoke of the unqualified love and respect Chika had always accorded her father and the family when he was alive. The entire family remained quiet. One could have heard a pin drop. She addressed Princess Yemisi by her first name. In fact, the queen had insisted early on that the first four daughters of Edukoya address her by her first name. Kenmiejo was only three years younger than Yemisi. She was a gynecologist and the first doctor in the family. As a young intern at San Francisco General Hospital, she had escorted Queen Yemisi I to the hospital, where her five boys had been delivered. She had been studying in the United States then.

Kenmiejo remarked, "Let he who has no sin cast the first stone." That statement became personal to Yemisi and Felicia. Felicia thought she was referring to her affairs with Kenmiejo's father before their marriage, which had brought about the twins. Yemisi thought that she knew about her affair with Dr. Oluomolewa and that out of respect for her and as a woman who had romantic needs, she understood and didn't question her about the affair. With the three women chasing after her father, there had been little of him to go around. They remained quiet. Felicia and Chika addressed her as Mama Kenmiejo.

Kenmiejo continued. "There is nothing in this letter that means harm to anybody. And there is nothing in this letter that says she even remotely caused the death of my father." She caused laughter when she added jokingly, "I wish my husband would write me this type of passionate letter. Where is he?" She continued after the laughter died down. "Leave my daughter alone to grieve. It is harder on her because she has lost someone she saw as her dad, her lover, and, most importantly, her best friend. And I'm not a party to contesting the will of my father. We all have to move on." Her statement was brief, and the audience loved it, especially Queen Yemisi I and Chikanele.

Queen Yemisi I opened her arms, and with tears running down her cheeks, she hugged Chika warmly and said, "Welcome to the family. You are here to stay. Because of you, our husband and our father had a few more years to stay with us. You never disobeyed me before. You have been a loyal administrative assistant from day one. What made you disobey me must be something I cannot explain. I don't believe you knew in a million years that your visit would have such a positive effect on him. I must confess he was constantly asking about you and when you'd visit him in the hospital, but when I thought about what seemed like a betrayal, my anger and jealousy got the better part of me. I just didn't want you to see him in any condition. Thank God. *Omashe Olowun, Ekwushe Oluwa.*" She repeated those words several times in the Yoruba language.

"And because of you, my husband planned his funeral while he was still alive. He was able to arrange and put things in order before he departed. Chika, you were my friend before you came to live with me. I hope we can put all this nonsense behind us and go on being best friends again. If not for you, I would have been dead before Edukoya. You thought fast and called Dr. Oluomolewa, and he saved my life. What a team. Thank you for coming into this palace. Although Edukoya didn't officially marry you, he instructed me to treat you as if you were his wife, and I will honor his request. I will not contest his will."

The entire family decided not to contest his will. Felicia, feeling she would have been the odd man out, joined the rest of the family.

CHAPTER 61

It had been one year since Kabiyesi Edukoya Adekunle III died. All the members of his family were anxiously waiting for his will to be read. Meanwhile, Justice Chukwu Onyemerekwe gave his final ruling on the land case. Two justices were in favor of the ruling, but one justice, Justice Anthony Ashade, dissented, siding with the plaintiffs who got the weaker compensation. Justice Anthony Ashade had a natural legal mind. He saw justice in the abstract; hence, he had a tendency to uncover the overlooked. In his dissent, he wrote, "This ruling has the tendency to invade our morality and dignity and is capable of destroying consequentially our overall well-being and integrity. Therefore, I could not possibly support this latitudinal, unconstitutional moral invasion of an individual's first right to claim the ownership of his or her property, be it land or any other property. It also sets a very dangerous precedent that government can have the power, authority, and capacity, short on morality, to grab your property at will for its own benefit. Regardless of how much you paid for the property, regardless of the future worth of the property, and regardless of the future benefit to the larger society, such property belongs to you only. This judgment, in my opinion, is not inclusive, is not conscientious, has a serious moral flaw, and is arrogant."

Justice Chukwu Onyemerekwe wrote for the majority. He wrote, "The system of land ownership gives the government outright right to usurp landed properties at will for the benefit of the larger society. The constitution provides for adequate compensation based on the present market value of the property. The constitution does not allow the court to exercise emotional and moral consideration. The constitution allows the court to exercise only two legal options, and they are equity and fairness. Therefore, this land, from this moment, will revert back to the original owner, the government." Justice Chukwunanyenwa Onyemerekwe said he would stay the order of the court till the plaintiffs were duly compensated to the last kobo either by the full amount or by stipulated installment agreement, and then the drilling would begin. He advised that the court would reconvene at a later date to determine if the compensation due to the plaintiffs had been fully exercised. Also, the court would issue the order regarding when the drilling would begin. Justice Onymerekwe said, "This is the appeals court," and he advised his rulings to be appealed in a higher court.

The late drilling angered the federal minister of petroleum and natural resources. Lagos State's compensation and the delay in drilling angered Lagos State's commissioner for natural resources. It also angered Lagos State's governor. The federal and state governments wasted no time in appealing the rulings to the Supreme Court of Nigeria. They called it "a tribal war." Unfounded rumor had it that Justice Onyemerekwe was trying to get even for the federal government's takeover of oil fields in the southeast with little or no compensation to the landowners. Justice Onyemerekwe gave 25 percent of the oil proceeds to the landowners. He gave 4 percent to the state government and the bulk, 71 percent, of the oil proceeds to the federal government. The federal government was to pay all the attorneys' fees, filing fees, and drilling fees. The plaintiffs were dumbfounded. They waited for the Supreme Court rulings on the federal and state governments' appeals to determine their options.

However, the Supreme Court of Nigeria refused to hear the case, and Justice Onyemerekwe's rulings stood. The federal government reluctantly accepted his rulings. Not to incur a further delay in drilling, both houses of Congress quietly approved massive compensations of an untold amount of money to be paid to the plaintiffs, and the president of Nigeria signed the agreement. To avoid national alarm, the compensation amount of money was sealed by the court. The court imposed a gag order, which stipulated that no soul other than the eyewitnesses at the midnight court forum would know the amount of money paid. However, according to leaks, the total was estimated at $1.5 billion. Queen Yemisi I was in the court that midnight with Dr. Oluomolewa to receive the final settlement checks. Sixty-five percent of the amount was due to Adekunle's family, who owned the lion's share of the wetland. Fifteen percent was due to Eleyenmi's descendants because his 5 percent portion of the land parcel had the greatest oil reserve. Twenty percent would be shared, in proportion to size, among twenty-five landowners who owned relatively small portions of the land parcels on the outskirts of the main oil reserve. Seventy percent of the late Kabiyesi Adekunle I's descendants' share was due to Edukoya's family.

Charity, her children, and her maid were vacationing in Northern Ireland, visiting her elder brother. It was the first time after a long nine months Queen Yemisi I visited Lagos. Queen Yemisi I was busy mastering her leadership role on the throne. She was to depart for Akure the next morning to get ready for the will reading, which would occur that Friday. Chika was already at the palace with her boys; the doctors had declared her fit.

Dr. Oluomolewa escorted the queen to the court. When they returned, they went straight to Dr. Oluomolewa's house

and spent the night together there. They didn't wait for the
door to close before they started to invade each other's body. In
their rush to make long-awaited love, Dr. Oluomolewa forgot
to bolt the lock. He remembered it after their second round of
sex was over. They went for four rounds, and then exhaustion
carried them to sleep. She slept adjacent to him, anchoring
herself to his chest. It didn't matter, because the door's lock
was good enough.

He carried Queen Yemisi, with little effort, to the bedroom
and dumped her into the bed, and her blouse almost detached
from her body. They never stopped kissing. When they finally
wore their birthday suits, their dream of making love, a dream
for almost fifteen years, could not come soon enough. At the
age of fifty-eight, Dr. Oluomolewa's body seemed made of an
enviable, expensive marble, with few gray hairs. Yemisi had
always been remarkable and adorable. At the age of almost
sixty-nine, her body miraculously looked like that of a twenty-
five-year-old woman. Their enviable slim, fit, and tight bodies
were the result of constant exercise and a fairly strict diet that
paid off handsomely in their later years. Dr. Oluomolewa and
Queen Yemisi I never drank alcoholic beverages, and they never
indulged in smoking of any kind. They ate small portions of
food with a strict dietary regimen. They never ate past five
o'clock. Yemisi's body, regardless of her age, was a joy to lie
next to.

Dr. Oluomolewa said, "There is something nice about
making love to a queen."

Yemisi burst into laughter and asked, "Was it worth the
wait?"

He replied rhetorically, "Tell me!"

Both smiled and nodded in agreement.

CHAPTER 62

Dr. Oluomolewa came Thursday evening to the palace in Agbala, Orissa Kingdom, to support Yemisi. He was also included in the will. He slept in one of the guest rooms. Yemisi passively went there to chat with him and wound up making breathtaking, passionate love with him before she returned to her bedroom and went to sleep. First thing in the morning, she returned to the guest room to say good morning to him. The door was closed but unlocked. As a toddler, Everest had cultivated the habit of leaving his bedroom door unlocked because he had too many frightening nightmares. He'd believed he wouldn't have a nightmare if his bedroom door was unlocked. Children's belief worked, and he'd had no more nightmares.

Dr. Oluomolewa's bed was empty when Yemisi walked into his room. He was taking a bath. Yemisi safely locked the door before joining him in the bathtub. They started with their usual kissing and touching and wound up making out-of-this-world love. The bathwater aided the penetration—not that the queen needed the water, because even at her age, her vaginal fluids gushed out like a waterfall whenever she was around Everest. They did it multiple times in various positions and various styles, including dog style, multiple times.

Before the will was read, the lawyers said to Chikanele, "I believe you have a copy of this will."

Everyone pinched each other when Chikanele said, "Yes." Besides the lawyers, only Chikanele had a copy of Kabiyesi Edukoya Adekunle III's will.

Kenmiejo interjected. "He must have loved you extraordinarily, and you kept quiet and said nothing all this time."

Felicia also interjected, murmuring quietly, speaking mainly to herself. "*Omo* Igbo. She was waiting to take us to court."

The lawyers proceeded by asking Chika to verify their copy's authenticity. After comparing it to her copy, she nodded in agreement. Chika then gave her copy to them. They looked it over, and the lawyers came to the same conclusion: nothing had been altered. They gave her copy back to her and proceeded.

One lawyer said, "Kabiyesi Adekunle III called us and said he had given a copy of his will to Chika. I asked him why. He said it was to protect her interest. I asked him, 'Did she ask you for it?' He said no. Before I read this will, does anyone want to say something?"

Their anxiousness to hear what the will said kept all of them on the edge of their seats. Her Lordship Queen Yemisi I stood up and spoke. "I have a copy of the checks for the final settlement of the land portion where crude oil was found. The original checks have been deposited and cashed at the three banks Edukoya did business with: First Bank of Nigeria, Union Bank of Nigeria, and United Bank of Africa Nigerian. The checks are made out in equal amounts. Because it was sealed by the court and a gag order was imposed by Justice Chukwu Onyemerekwe, I cannot say the amount out loud in the open. By the order of the court, this amount is to remain sealed in perpetuity. The attorneys will pass the checks around for you to see them as the parties involved. Even Eva, who was kind enough to escort me to the midnight court forum, didn't see them. The money was added back to his assets."

She went on. "As Edukoya promised the four local government areas in Orissa Kingdom, as you remember, thirty percent of Edukoya's proceeds from all his assets, as always, will be given to them in death or in life, and that includes thirty percent from the land settlement."

She sat down, and the lawyers proceeded with the reading of the will. The king was a generous man even in death. He made sure everybody in his household got something when he departed. He even included his immediate kindred and his helpers in his will. Right off the top, the four communities that made up Orissa Kingdom got 30 percent of the proceeds from his assets. Overall, Chika and her boys got 5.5 percent of his assets, worth hundreds of millions of dollars. Chika got 2.5 percent, and her boys, whom Kabiyesi Edukoya Adekunle III had secretly adopted toward the end of his life, received 1.5 percent of his assets each.

It was revealed by the attorneys during the reading of his will that Kabiyesi Edukoya Adekunle III had secretly adopted Chika's boys. Chika was not aware of the arrangement. In the final testament of his will, he asked the attorneys to draw up the articles of adoption for the two boys. Chika was to know about it at the final signing of the adoption papers when she returned from Lagos. Edukoya had feared if it was discussed with Chika in advance, she would turn it down, so it was a surprise. Queen Yemisi, Kenmiejo, and Tunde were aware of the arrangement, and they'd promised the king they would keep his secret. It was to be a huge surprise to Chika when she returned from Lagos after visiting with her kids. Whether the king was alive or dead, when Chika signed the papers of adoption, the boys would be fully adopted by the king. In anticipation of his death, he had signed the documents before his death. Chika signed the adoption papers in the presence of the Adekunle family and the lawyers after a few moments of consultation with her boys and her brother, who was acting as her lawyer. They were present at the reading of Kabiyesi Edukoya Adekunle III's will. Both sons were under eighteen years old. They were in their second and third years at UNILAG, studying medicine.

Felicia got 2 percent of his assets. Dr. Oluomolewa got 0.5 percent. All his fourteen biological children got 2.5 percent each. His immediate relatives got 3 percent of the proceeds from all his assets. There were forty-four of them living. His helpers got 1 percent to be shared among them. The queen got 20 percent, and she would reside at the palace till her death. In fact, all his wives, including Chika, would reside at his palace till they died or remarried. All his villas around the world and his palace were made available to all his wives, including Chika, and all his children, including Chika's boys, till their deaths. His palace was declared a homestead, which meant it could never be sold at any price. The other villas were not homesteaded. With the exception of his villas in Ikoyi and Abuja, the queen made adequate arrangements for all his villas around the world to be sold, and their proceeds would be added back to his assets. She was to settle all the lawyers' fees. Two and a half percent of the proceeds from his assets was set aside for emergency interventions and for periodic contributions to his foundation.

Chikanele was the topic of the day, particularly how she had taken the heart of the king lock, stock, and barrel. Everybody got wealthy in the millions of dollars. Even his helpers, including his chauffeurs, got about $200,000 each. They were to share 1 percent of the proceeds from his assets. At his death, he had about two dozen helpers. All his assets were tied to his vast investment holdings. All the will recipients would receive their monies disbursed as paychecks monthly, including interest. That meant they would receive paychecks from the will forever. The bank loved that arrangement because a huge amount of money stayed with them and provided the three banks with enormous lending cushions, and in return, the banks paid higher interest rates to the recipients of the late king's will.

With the exception of Professor Ephram Adekunle, all recipients of the will were entitled to do whatever they wanted with their shares of the will, short of withdrawing the share in its entirety. They could will it, donate it to charity, sell it, or keep it as an income base. It was up to them. The financial management of the will was handled by First Bank Trust, Union Bank Financial House, and UBA Financial Management Trust. All recipients of the will were allowed to choose among the three financial management institutions to receive their money monthly. For that reason, the banks offered a uniform payment plan. The assets had been allocated and were already managed by the financial institutions. All the recipients of the will were expected to pay all the taxes and fees involved. Chika's yearly proceeds topped $22 million and would be paid in full in thirty years.

The monthly payments had been arranged by the late Kabiyesi Edukoya Adekunle III because of Professor Ephram Adekunle, his second son and Queen Yemisi I's second son. Although he was educated, had a PhD in mathematics from Harvard University, and was a Harvard mathematics professor, Ephram drank too much and spent money like a drunken sailor. He was always broke, which had led to his divorce from his white American wife, Dr. Lois Adekunle, MD, who kept her wedding name after the divorce. They had four children, a girl and three boys. The king had feared Ephram might wind up a homeless person living on the streets of Cambridge, Massachusetts, soon after he was gone. Per the will, he would receive checks every month in addition to his $300,000 annual salary from the university. Ephram was allowed to will his share to only his children at the time of his death.

After the king's will was read, everybody in the meeting burst into tears and hugged each other. Barrister Konyide, the lead lawyer, whispered to his team to join the family to show their empathy of sadness, and they all did. Dr. Oluomolewa was at the queen's side all the time to support the emotionally fragile queen. By then, their secret love affair was fairly known to all the members of the Adekunle family. Even Charity was beginning to suspect their relationship was more than a mere close platonic friendship. She had gone to Ireland to get away and rethink her priorities and options. She had confronted Eva about it, and he had admitted the affair, though he'd said he was not having a real sexual relationship with her at the time, due to circumstances. He had not elaborated on the circumstances. Charity had accepted his denial of sexual intercourse out of respect for the queen and Edukoya. She hadn't followed up on his answer with questions.

Now that the king was gone, Dr. Oluomolewa and Queen Yemisi had sex every chance they got, even in Charity's bedroom when she was not there. They continued to exercise together. They were now in a heavy romantic relationship, and they didn't care who found out, even Charity. However, nobody dared ask her about it, even Tunde and Bunmi. The family struggled to accept their romantic relationship as long as he made the queen happy. Yemisi promised Everest that Charity would come around, and if she didn't, she would marry him in a heartbeat. Queen Yemisi said she would be in Eva's life till her dying day and told him, "I'm not going anywhere, even if it means giving up my queenship. I'm in love with you."

Meanwhile, Tunde was beginning to romantically eye Chikanele. His feelings were compounded by his weak relationship with his wife. They had gone six months without having any sexual contact with each other. Tunde spent most of his nights at the villa in Ikoyi. He had gotten Chika's interest. They had kissed and touched each other's body frequently, but there hadn't been any sexual intercourse yet, even when they repeatedly slept together during countless naps. Chika was a desirable woman and pretty. Her long legs and firm, shining skin made men ejaculate before seeing her vagina. She was close to Tunde's age. At the age of forty-four, she could best most women in their midtwenties. Feeling her lips glued to Tunde's lips justified to him why his father had loved her best. Tunde ejaculated without penetrating his penis into her vagina whenever he engaged in a romantic encounter with Chika.

Chika was eager to have sex with Tunde; however, she wouldn't dare consider it until his divorce was final. She had repeatedly swallowed his sperm during blow jobs she gave him. She had also repeatedly used his penis to massage her clitoris for a climax that induced her to reach orgasm multiple times. Most times, she inserted his penis cap to incur further stimulation. She had not told him what was holding her back from allowing actual penetration of his penis all the way into her vagina, for fear Tunde would assume she was pressuring him to get a divorce and marry her. Chika was a wealthy woman and an adorable lady. At that time in her life, with two grown sons, she did not want a husband yet. She just wanted to have some fun, and Tunde had always been nice to her. He treated her with love and respect, always protecting her and her interests. Because Tunde was a younger man, the fear of conception was also on her mind. She wouldn't have minded being pregnant by Tunde as his wife but not as his side chick, a mere girlfriend. Chika wouldn't use condoms when having sexual intercourse with his father, and certainly wouldn't use one with Tunde.

Tunde had yet to file for divorce. For one thing, the divorce would be complicated, given the enormous wealth involved on both sides. The second issue involved religious and moral grounds. For the crown prince of Orissa Kingdom, a divorce wouldn't look good on his résumé. On religious grounds, the Adekunle family were devout Christians. Tunde was one of the deacons at Saint Mathew's Cathedral in Agbala. There had to be an overwhelming and compelling reason for divorce, such as adultery, murder, or theft. Also, he and his wife had five children, two girls and three boys. Two of them were off at college, and the remaining three were teenagers in high school. The children badly needed them to stay in their marriage. Victoria, his wife, was gorgeous. She didn't look as if she'd had a baby. Queen Yemisi I loved her and would not allow her first son's home to break apart.

Ephram's divorce had been a shock to the family. It had happened in America and still haunted Kabiyesi Yemisi I to that day.

Chika had fallen hopelessly in love with Tunde. However, Tunde did not realize how deeply in love she had fallen. He had also fallen deeply in love with Chika, and that complicated the situation further. Tunde wanted to be with Chika. He was a good-looking man, a carbon copy of his mother, Yemisi.

Felicia was secretly dating one of her students, a thirty-two-year-old biological sciences doctoral candidate at Orissa Polytechnic Institute. They had kissed and had sexual intercourse repeatedly.

Everyone had determined his or her road map.

ABOUT THE AUTHOR

Ijeoma Ononuju was born in Nigeria, from the Igbo tribe. He was raised there. He attended several primary schools because his guardian, his elder brother, Martin, was relocating quite often because of his job. Martin was single, extremely handsome, and extremely intelligent. So, his company, British American Insurance Co. Nigerian Ltd, found him an easy asset to the top jobs. His secondary school education was stable. He went to Ife Grammar school and Obube High School. He repeated high school. High school was not all a struggle for him. He made quite impressive grades during the course of his schooling in secondary school, but when it came to the general examination, WAEC, he had a disappointing result. When he came to university, he found what was the problem. He schooled all his children to be aware of this pitfall, and he is glad they have avoided such a costly mistake. His first son is an associate professor at North Arizona State University, Prof. Ijeoma Ononuju.

He came to America forty years ago, on January 29th, 1980. First, he attended New College of Calfornia for one semester and then moved on to San Francisco State University, where he got his bachelor's degree in Business Administration. He took his master's in business at Golden Gate University. He found a love in entrepreneurship, and he has been self-employed since then. Simultaneously, he engages in day trading stocks and several monetary instruments. It freed his time to concentrate on his passion, "Writing." He has developed two super cleaning detergents which he named "Forgive and Mr. Shoe." Both products occupy his weekends. He goes to the Flea Markets to sell them.

Ijeoma is now a proud citizen of the United States of America. He is a married man with eight children, Ijeoma, Ogochukwu, Adaihu, Chidimma, Chiwendu, Nkemjika, Chinyere, and my last born, Chioma. His wife, Regina, is the glue of the family. Family is very important to him. Though he may not show his feelings as often as he should, owing to his difficult upbringing, growing up as a child, however, his love is invested in all his children, and more importantly, in his wife, Regina. He loves people, especially young people, and several of them call him daddy. He remembered when he used to be in their shoes, and he can't help his heart going for them.

He has been helped by strangers he does not know growing up as a kid, which prompted him to assert that, "On our way to that beautiful city, up there in the mountain, we got a lot of help." Simply put, there is no such thing as a self-made person. He also owes his gratitude to Batha Johnson. She said to him, "Just call me Mom." Mrs, Florence Enebunwa, "I am one of your big sisters..." Bola Oseni, "Children don't owe their parents anything..." George White, "Gene, you can be trusted..." Ken and Emeka Nwadike, and his surrogate dad, Chief Nathaniel Nwafor, "You're my son, of course..." He also values greatly his nephew/son, Ahamefula, for constantly persuading him to write a book and tell his story.

Lightning Source UK Ltd.
Milton Keynes UK
UKHW021850120922
408771UK00003B/90

9 781982 273811